Appetizers

Geonn Cannon

Supposed Crimes LLC • Matthews, North Carolina

This book is a work of fiction. Names, characters, places, and incidents are products of the author's imagination or are used fictitiously. Any resemblance to actual events or locales or persons, living or dead, is entirely coincidental.

All Rights Reserved
Copyright © 2018 Geonn Cannon

Published in the United States.

ISBN: 978-1-944591-44-1

www.supposedcrimes.com

This book is typeset in Goudy Old Style.

TABLE OF CONTENTS

Backroads & Boneyards, 5
Kathleen's parents tried to calm their wild child with religion and a
Bible college, but the end result is nothing like what they hoped for.

Curvy Privateers & Scurvy Sea Dogs, 21
Two employees at a theme park use their characters to overcome
their nerves.

Celestine & the Gypsy: A Radiation Canary prequel, 37
1979. Metairie, Louisiana. Debra Kent and Celeste Lafitte begin a
friendship that will take them through their final year of school and
into a life neither of them ever anticipated.

Clothes Maketh the Man, 66
Hannah is captivated by a beautiful man she meets at a coworker's
party, but fails to get any contact information from him. When she
finally does track him down, she discovers she's made one very big
assumption about her crush, and following through on her
attraction may require more than she's willing to give.

Common Tongue, 82
Two women in a foreign country form a powerful and special bond
despite the lack of a common language.

Even Money, 120
Marlin Kensleigh is a bookie, and her outwardly geeky appearance
tends to make people think they can push her around. But Marlin is
no pushover, a fact tattooed mechanic Sidney Gracen is about to
find out for herself

Every Savage Can Dance, 134
Inspired by Jane Austen, who never let her female characters have
any fun together. A very proper young lady sees her friend in an
unexpected light after a torrential downpour. (Requested and
Graciously Shared by Michelle Rinehart)

Open Sesame, 147
A retelling of 'Ali Baba and the Forty Thieves'. A poor urchin in a
crime-ridden city takes an opportunity to rob from thieves so she
and her lover can have a better life.

Knockout Stage, 158
Goalie Steph "Dagger" Thomas' soccer team made it to the
Olympics, but their dreams of gold were shattered by a single goal.
Back home, Steph sinks into a depression that threatens her love of
the game until a chance encounter gives her something else to fight
for.

A Perfect Stranger, 174
Sofia Kennedy's first time with a woman is a magical and anonymous encounter during college. (Sofia Kennedy also appears in my novel 'Breaking Anchor')
Sexiled, 184
A girl blocked from her dorm by an amorous roommate finds a kindred spirit to share the night.
Storm Sirens, 193
A girl seeking shelter from the storm witnesses an intimate moment and makes a drastic, criminal decision to create a happy ending.
Those Who Consort with Beasts, 202
A classical *canidae* story, set in the Underdogs universe. A wolf and her daughter living on the outskirts of Salem in the 1690s must decide what she's willing to risk when the woman she loves is arrested as a witch.
Unscripted, 216
Penelope and Caroline are a typical California couple who work in "the industry" as actresses. Their stage names are Wanda Lust and Evie Archer, and you won't find their movies on Netflix anytime soon...
Without Him, 229
A drunken escapade between friends leads one of them to unexpected revelations.

BACKROADS & BONEYARDS

(Author's Note: inspired by Josh Ritter's music, specifically the songs "Getting Ready to Get Down" and "Where the Night Goes")

FAMILY PICTURES on the wall of their den charted the evolution - or devolution - of the Lawrence family's daughter. When Kathleen was ten, she was the ideal Girl Next Door. Pink gingham shirt, huge smile, and a bow in her long brown hair. Her parents were standing on either side of their ideal daughter. Her mother's hand was on her right shoulder and her father's hand was on her left. It was a catalogue shot, and no one could blame the Lawrences for wanting to recapture the image a year later. At eleven, Kathleen's smile spread a little less wide. When she was fourteen, her parents were standing together with Kathleen off to the right. She wasn't smiling at all anymore, but at least her expression wasn't actively hostile.

At sixteen, when she was forced to attend the portrait session, she chose to wear a black T-shirt and a dog collar she'd bought specifically for the occasion. Her hair had been chopped off in the closest thing to a buzz cut the town barber was willing to attempt. Her parents forced her to take off the collar, but there was nothing they could do about the hair. Their faces were full of resignation while Kathleen had a look of smug success.

The final portrait was taken when Kathleen was nineteen, but she wasn't in the picture. She was four hundred miles south at the

Pelican Bible College in the southern part of the state. It was a last-ditch effort to "save" her from the dark path she'd been stumbling down. She was rude and disrespectful. She disregarded curfew, she smoked and drank. She didn't do drugs, but some thought that was only because the town of Royal City didn't have a thriving drug trade. She had played baseball sophomore and junior years, she even made varsity, but she didn't even try out for her last year of high school.

A secret meeting between her parents and their pastor led to the decision it was their only chance to get their daughter back. Kathleen came home not long after graduation and found her things packed and waiting by the front door. She begged, she pleaded, she promised to straighten out, but the decision had been made. She was on the bus that night and arrived at the campus the following day. She was going to spend the summer with her aunt who lived close enough to the school to keep an eye on her. Aunt Taylor had a farm, and her summers were to be spent working off her room and board.

Between school, working on the farm, and her petty anger at being banished, it was four years before she went back home.

Kathleen still remembered the outskirts of Royal City like the back of her hand. The bus was empty enough that she moved to a seat next to the window so she could watch as the familiar territory unfolded next to the road. Royal City was the middle of nowhere, three quadrants of a square surrounded by foothills and miles of scrub. When she left town, her head had been shaved on both sides with locks of purple and red hair falling from the tuft on top of her head. Her hair now was a conservative length, but now it was purple and black. Everything she owned was in a bag tucked overhead or the other one stowed underneath in the cargo department.

She was excited about seeing her parents. She looked forward to seeing the old hometown, the streets she remembered, the people who had grown into near mythic stature in her mind, but there was one person in particular weighing on her mind. She didn't know what to expect from their reunion. In four years there hadn't been a single email in either direction. No contact, not even a whisper of keeping in touch. It might mean nothing. It might mean everything.

Kathleen bit her thumbnail and watched as Mr. Amos' field rolled into view. He had alpacas, and Kathleen smiled as she thought about Vicky's insistence that they were just funny-looking horses. "He got them from Chernobyl," she declared, "and that's why they look that way. They're radioactive." Vicky was always making up stories and telling them so matter-of-factly that she almost dared anyone to contradict her. Kathleen was the only one who ever fought back. She wondered who had been challenging Vicky's stories over the past four years.

The world was flat enough that she could see Royal City well before they broke the town limits. It was barely afternoon, but she could only think of it at night. The sky, blue-purple fading to black so they could see the stars, with the town shining underneath. They could see Second Street lit up like a runway until ten o'clock when half the lights snapped off one after another. Kathleen had seen that curfew darkness more than once during her wild days.

Her smile faltered when she remembered how she was before she left. Disrespectful, angry at everything, lashing out at anyone who tried to help her... School helped her immensely. Once she stopped digging in her heels and actually listened, she discovered there was more to it than "religious stuff." Aunt Taylor was the true godsend, though. The day Kathleen showed up on her doorstep, her aunt laid down the rules.

"No brats. You start to look like a brat to me, I'll throw you out. I love my sister, but I don't know you. I won't lose any sleep dropping you back at the bus station. You may want to be top of the food chain, but that ends right here. I'm in charge. You try to knock me down a peg and take over as alpha, I'll put you on your ass. Then it's right back to the bus station. You disrespect me, my home, or my friends, and you're gone."

Kathleen had said, "You want me to be a Kewpie Doll, too?"

"I don't want games. I don't want stupid posturing. I know you're a teenager, stupid posturing is like ninety percent of your personality. But out here it isn't worth shit. Just be whoever you are, and we'll get along fine."

"What... what if I don't know who that is?"

Taylor swept an arm out to indicate the farm. "Then this is a great place to find out."

Kathleen said, "Are you going to help me with my bags?"

"No one here works for you, Kathleen."

"No one calls me Kathleen."

Taylor turned to go back into the house. "Your mother said. Kitty, Kate, Lean... you've had a different name for every semester of school, seems like. Until you figure out what you want to be called long-term, I'm sticking with Kathleen."

She left Kathleen alone there in front of the house until, finally, Kathleen picked up her bags and followed her aunt into the house.

In the end she stuck with the name she was given. They were almost to the feed store, which was the real start of civilization as far as Royal City was concerned. She sat up straighter and smoothed her hands on the thighs of her pants. They were brand-new jeans, and her blouse was also new. She and Taylor went shopping the weekend before her triumphant return so she could make a good impression. She was surprised she *wanted* to make a good impression. Her parents had spent a lot of money to banish her, but now she could see it was exactly what she needed. She could also accept just how far she'd pushed them. They wouldn't have made such a drastic decision lightly. They loved her. They'd been worried about her. They did what they thought was in her best interests, and she loved them for it.

The bus station was on the northern side of town, which meant they had to drive through the whole of Royal City to reach it. She watched the window as intently as a movie screen, eyes skipping over the familiar and unfamiliar. The bank had a new sign, one that lit up with actual video instead of lights scrolling along a single bar. Jacqui's Fine Dining had a new paint job, and her mouth watered when she thought of their Rough and Rugged Burgers. She hoped their fries were the same.

She found herself tearing up when they passed the high school. She was home. After four years and a few weeks, after being sent away to save her from herself, she was back. What if the new version of her was unacceptable to everyone else? What if they still looked at her and just saw hair color and a stud in her nose? What if they rejected her even after all the hard work she'd done to find out who she was?

Kathleen wiped at her eyes. The bus pulled up to the station with a lurch and a squeal of brakes. She took a deep breath and swept her hair out of her face before she stood up and gathered her bag. She remembered what Taylor said before hugging her goodbye. "Your parents didn't send you here to fix you," she said. "They sent you here to shut out the noise and the bullshit. They just wanted you to find yourself without the distractions. You did a great job, Kathleen. I'm proud of you. And if they do throw a hissy, you just get back on that bus and come on back here."

Knowing she had somewhere to fall gave her the courage to walk down the aisle and out into the sunshine. She didn't even have to look around once she reached the pavement; her parents were directly across from her in the parking lot. They looked exactly the same until she got up close. A bit more aged, a bit grayer at the edges, and more real. She hadn't seen her parents in so long that she could see them as actual people rather than just "Mom" and "Dad." Her father looked prepared for the worst, his eyes locked on the hue of her hair, and her mother's eyes were wide with hope.

Kathleen put down her bags and embraced them both. "Hi, Mom. Hi, Dad."

"Hello, Kathleen," her mother said. "We've missed you so much."

"I've missed you, too." She stepped back so they could see her face. "I'm sorry. For~"

Her father cut her off with a wave of his hand. "You don't have to list anything, Kathleen." His voice was rough but tempered with emotion. Hearing it again made her breath catch in her chest. He looked down at her hands so he didn't have to lock her in the eye. "Sorry is enough. Sorry... is good. For what it's worth, we're sorry, too."

"Do two sorrys make forgiveness?" Kathleen asked.

He smiled a little. "Yeah, probably works out that way." He bent down and picked up her bags. "Come on. Let's get you home so you can rest."

"Actually, there's someone I have to go see. I wanted to take care of that first and then we could have the night together. We could talk over dinner. If that's okay."

Her parents looked at each other and communicated silently before her mother nodded. "I think that would be fine."

"Okay." She hugged her mother and kissed her father on the cheek. "I won't be out too late, I promise. And if I am, I'll call."

Her mother looked shocked. "We would appreciate that, Kathleen."

"And thank you for coming to pick me up. It was so great to see you."

"Sure." Her father gestured with her bags. "We'll take these home and leave them in your room."

"Thank you, Daddy."

He nodded and left them to put the bags in the car. Her mother looked at Kathleen's hair and chuckled softly.

"I guess, um, some things don't change."

Kathleen matched her chuckle, surprised that she'd never noticed how much their laughs sounded alike. "Yeah. So, um. I'll see you in a while."

"Do you want a ride?"

"No, I want to walk." She looked around and smiled. "Little town's really changed a lot in the past four years. I want to take it slow and see everything."

Her mother nodded. "Okay. We'll see you at home, then."

She stepped back and watched her parents get into the car. She waved as they pulled out of the parking lot, then she stuck her hands in her pockets and took a deep breath. Home again. With so much changed, there was one thing she hoped was still the same. She wet her lips, summoned her courage, and started walking west.

Romero McGiven was out in front of the gas station, cowboy hat tilted back at just the right angle to block the sun while still allowing him to see the street. He glanced toward her as she approached and she saw the angle of his shoulders change when he realized who she was. Her hair color was probably a dead giveaway. She smiled broadly and waved hello to him. His hand came up a bit off his thigh, not quite a wave but not shunning her, either. He was probably too shocked to see that she was back to think about judging her.

A block later she turned onto Second Street. The main drag was flanked by rows of furniture shops and antique shops, a five and dime, some boutiques, and a variety of storefronts that served as revolving doors for restaurants and bars. She wondered how many had cycled through while she was gone. Burgers and tacos and Indian food, Italian subs, it had all been served on Second Street when she was in high school. Now there was a Mexican restaurant and something that smelled like barbeque.

At the end of the block, Imogene North and Delia Child were standing outside the antique shop. They were mid-gossip when Imogene glanced over and froze. Delia followed her gaze and just barely stopped herself from covering her mouth in shock. Kathleen felt bad for them. They were fine, church-going ladies, and as such they'd been big targets for the teenage hellion she'd once been. She mooned them once, shouted horrible things when she drove past them on their way to church, and made holidays hellish by rearranging the Nativity display into obscene positions. They huddled close to the building as she approached as if trying to blend into the brickwork.

Kathleen slowed and smiled. "Miss North. Mrs. Child." She wanted to apologize for everything she'd done in the past, but it didn't seem like the right time or place. "I hope you have a lovely afternoon. It's great seeing you."

Imogene stumbled over her words but finally said, "He-hello, Kathleen."

"Have a great day."

She didn't look back once she was past them, but she knew they would spread the word about her return far and wide by that evening. She didn't care. Let people talk. Let people remember what a horrible beast she'd been. It would only make it that much more impressive when they saw how much she had changed. The Bible College didn't force her to become a Jesus freak. It didn't try converting her into a Bible-thumping evangelist. It just showed her how to be a good person. It taught her to think about others and act accordingly. But Aunt Taylor had been a much bigger educator than anyone at the school.

One night, the exile and abandonment had pushed Kathleen to the breaking point. She ended up in the barn, sobbing, when Taylor found her.

"Do you know why your parents sent you here?"

"Because they hate me."

"Wrong. Because you're still trying to figure out who you are. And you're fighting everyone who might have a problem with it at the same time. You're on the offensive every minute of the day because you're worried about what people will think. Just take some time, figure out what skin you're comfortable wearing, and settle on the real Kathleen. Whoever she might be."

Kathleen had sniffled. "What if they hate that?"

"Then who gives a damn? They don't have to live in your skin. They don't have to be you, or experience your life. Why the fuck should they get a choice in how you turn out?" She patted Kathleen's arm and squeezed her shoulder. "If who you are is an asexual purple-haired feminist, then be that. Don't lash out at people who might not find that aesthetically pleasing."

"What if I want to be a gay rancher out in the middle of nowhere?"

Taylor grinned. "It's a lonely life, kid. But I like it just fine." She rubbed the top of Kathleen's head and walked away from her. "Dinner's on the stove in the kitchen. I don't become your serving girl just because you cried a little bit."

Kathleen had laughed and, when she felt like her eyes weren't puffy anymore, had gone in to make herself dinner.

"Well, sugar honey iced tea! It really is you!"

Kathleen stopped and smiled. Only one person used that phrase, and even after her long absence there was no doubt in her mind about who was crossing the street behind her. She turned and smiled as Brenda Lee Miller hurried to catch up to her. Brenda Lee had been everything in high school; class president, cheerleader, valedictorian, and literal cover girl for the senior yearbook. She also liked to smoke and drink, which was how she and the wild child became acquaintances. The main change to Brenda Lee was that now her expensive blouse had a name tag pinned to the breast and the amount of jewelry hanging from her wrists.

"Look at you!" Brenda Lee said. "Nice to see a few years away didn't make you boring."

"Never boring. Maybe a bit mellower." She wanted to catch up with Brenda Lee, wanted to know what life after high school was like for the prom queen, but most of all she didn't want to be rude. "I don't want to try catching up with everything right here on the street. Why don't we have dinner some night? I have dinner with my parents tonight, but I should be free this weekend sometime?"

"That sounds great! Let me get your number."

They exchanged numbers, and Kathleen allowed herself to feel proud. In the past she would have focused entirely on her goal, her mission, what *she* wanted. It was a small victory, but it was progress nonetheless. As Brenda Lee was saying goodbye, Kathleen realized she had the opportunity to further her own goals after all.

"Vicky is still living here in town, right?"

"Vicky? Oh! Victoria Tanner? She goes by Tori now. But yes, she's still here. This time of day, she's working the counter at Lillian's." An unusual expression crossed her face. "So is that your first stop? Before you see anyone else, you're going to see her?"

Kathleen nodded. "Unless for some reason you think that wouldn't be a good idea."

"No, no, no reason. I'll let you go. But I can't wait to catch up!"

"Me neither. Good to see you."

They parted ways and Kathleen continued on. She was grateful she'd run into Brenda Lee; her intention had been to try Vicky... no, Tori... at home where she'd lived in high school. If she hadn't been home, or worse if she'd moved, she had no idea what her next step would have been. Now she had a destination in mind.

Lillian's was an old-style diner fashioned to look like a train car. It was close enough to the exit to be seen from the freeway, so they were a favorite of long-term truckers looking for a quick meal. It was also near the high school and a favorite hangout after three o'clock, which meant they were always busy no matter what time of day it was. Sure enough, as she approached, the parking lot was full of mud-encrusted trucks with a trio of big rigs parked in the empty lot next door.

Kathleen's hands trembled as she closed the distance to the diner. Four years and four hundred miles had shrunk down to a few minutes and the length of a football field. Windows stretched all the way across the front of the diner, but the sun was shining at an angle that turned them into mirrors. She could see herself, tall and purple-haired, the sharp edges of her reflection turned fluid by distortions in the glass.

She was almost to the parking lot when the door opened and a girl came outside. She looked as if she had started to run, but caught herself just as she crossed the threshold. It made her look like she was tripping. She wore bright blue jeans and an orange polo shirt - the Lillian uniform since time began - and there was a white apron tied around her waist. Her hair, once so long it whipped in the wind, was cut short to show off the long slender line of her throat. Kathleen stopped where she was and stared, and the other girl put a hand over her mouth as she walked forward.

"You're back," Tori said.

"Hi," Kathleen murmured. "I didn't know if you'd want to see me."

Everything depended on what happened next. The weight of their last night together had been crushing down on this moment, waiting for the punchline, for the payoff. Kathleen's eyes were wide and unblinking; she didn't want to miss any subtle clues that she was about to be told off or slapped or asked politely to walk away.

Tori let out a sob and took two steps forward, wrapping her arms around Kathleen just as the tears started to flow. Kathleen put her hands on Tori's back and closed her eyes in relief and bliss.

"You're back," Tori said again.

"I had to come back," Kathleen whispered. "You still have my jacket."

Tori laughed and buried her face in Kathleen's hair.

Tori left the bar well before last call, even though Adam and Paul both insisted she stay to judge the karaoke contest. She claimed exhaustion but promised the next time she would stick around until the cows came home. When she left, Peter had just gotten onstage to torture "Life on Mars?" She counted her blessings that she was escaping in the nick of time. It was easy to ignore the passage of time with the drinks flowing and everyone yelling to be heard over the music, but once she was outside the stillness of the night left no doubt in her mind about how late it was.

Another long day at Lillian's. Another night trying to unwind enough to sleep so she would be well-rested for the next long day. She'd worked there for almost three years and, while it was better than anything else the town had to offer, she still wanted more. She felt like she was on hold, waiting until she earned enough money or acquired enough life experience to move on to the next thing. She couldn't imagine still working that counter in five years.

Tori sighed. Then again, nothing would change if she didn't change it. She didn't even know where to start.

She sang under her breath as she walked, and she arrived at her door before she started a fourth song. Her laptop sat untouched on the table, but her phone would have informed her if there were any emails waiting. Nothing again today. Everyone she knew was at the bar or had seen her at the diner. Why would they have to send anything electronically? They knew where to find her. She was predictable. Boring. Dull.

She took a shower and put on a pair of shorts and a T-shirt before going into her bedroom. The letter jacket was draped over the back of her armchair and she smiled when she saw it. The body was dark crimson wool, and the sleeves were white leather. A large white R was branded on the left breast. It certainly wasn't new, but it still looked sharp enough to wear in public. Not that she ever did, of course. No, that would be too difficult to explain.

Tori picked up the jacket and slid her arms into the heavy sleeves. It was still big enough that the hem stretched just past the bottom of her T-shirt. When she buttoned it up, it looked like she wasn't wearing anything under it. She smoothed her hands across the material and leaned forward to see how her legs looked sticking out from the elastic waistband.

She got the jacket on the greatest and most tragic night of her life. English class taught her that the difference between comedy and tragedy was how it ended, so there was no doubt in her mind that it was tragic. Graduation was still recent enough that parents weren't yet pushing their kids out the front door or asking about future plans. The world seemed to open up without school, and all they had were opportunities. Not long after dinner Kathleen Lawrence came by to abduct her. Tori's parents hated Kathleen. They said she was a bad influence and a delinquent, she smoked and drank and skipped school.

All of that was true, but she was also the most exciting person in Royal City. So when she heard the rumble of Kathleen's truck engine on the next street, Tori turned her radio up and slipped out the window to meet up with her. She climbed into the passenger side of the truck and Kathleen started driving before her door was completely closed. The inside of the truck reeked of cigarette smoke, and Tori remembered that she always had to stifle a cough when she got in.

On those nights it didn't matter where they went. Sometimes they would park behind the old supermarket and listen to music. Other times they would circumnavigate the outskirts of town. Once they took a walk through the town cemetery to look at all the headstones, trying to find the oldest person who had ever lived in Royal City. Eventually the groundskeeper sent them away and, on their way back to the truck, Kathleen had very softly said, "I'm not going to end up here. I know I have to die someday, but I'm not getting put in this ground."

Tori sat on her bed and brushed her hands over the material of Kathleen's jacket. She didn't remember if she'd made the same vow, but it was looking less and less likely she would be able to keep it if she did. She dreamed of getting out. But where would she go? What good was an escape if she didn't have any kind of destination in mind? Did she really want to rip up her entire life just to go be a waitress in a different town? What was the point?

She finally took off the jacket and draped it over the back of the chair. She turned off the light, slipped her feet under the blankets, and rested her hands on her stomach as she stared up at the ceiling.

Kathleen was like an invisible friend. The jacket helped remind her that her crazy, wild friend had really existed. It also reminded her that everything that happened their last night together really did happen the way she remembered.

They'd been parked on a backroad, lying in the back of the truck. There was a four-pack of Lost Continent Double IPA between them, three of the bottles emptied and stacked near the cab. The last one was being held on Kathleen's stomach. Her shirt was pushed up so the curved bottom was touching skin, and Tori found her eye constantly drawn to that strip of usually-unseen flesh. They didn't talk about the future. There was no epic conversation because they didn't know it would be their last. But something did happen that would've made that moment live on in her memory even if Kathleen had stayed in Royal City.

She remembered rolling onto her side to watch Kathleen's profile. Kathleen was focused on the stars. Earlier she had taken off her jacket and draped it over Tori because the night was unseasonably cold. Kathleen was always doing things like that. She never spared a thought for anyone else, but she could tell when Tori was a bit cold and did what she could to fix it.

"Kathleen..."

"Mm?"

She let the silence linger. Kathleen pushed her bottom lip out, eyes half-lidded either from exhaustion or the alcohol. When Tori went a full minute without speaking, she turned her head and focused on Tori. She would have blamed it on the beer, except she'd barely had a full bottle, and she would have said it was a meaningless peck between friends if Kathleen had been around to be offended by it. But at the moment all she could think about was that shine of alcohol on Kathleen's bottom lip and how much she wanted to smudge it away.

She put her hand on Kathleen's cheek. Kathleen didn't pull away as Tori leaned forward. Their lips met and remained closed while their eyes stayed open. It was something she had wanted to do since junior year but she'd never had the guts. The longer Kathleen didn't pull away, the more Tori wanted to do more. She'd fantasized about this very moment, but she was always more determined and confident in those dreams. She had seen herself getting on top of Kathleen. She had watched herself undo her buttons and peel off T-shirts, and she had heard her voice saying, "Tell me if you want me to stop."

Instead, she had been a coward. She could still hear the smack when their mouths came apart, the finality of it sounding like a vault door being slammed shut.

"I'm so drunk," Kathleen said. There was a smudged red line under her eyes, spreading slowly down her cheeks.

"Yeah. Me too." It seemed like the safest thing to say.

Kathleen put her hand over Tori's face. Tori closed her eyes and smiled, resisting the urge to kiss Kathleen's palm.

"We... should probably head back in..."

Tori wanted to refuse. "Okay."

They sat up and sat together. For the longest time neither of them spoke. Tori hugged Kathleen's jacket to her chest, worried that when she gave it back it would signal the end of their friendship. School was over. It made sense they would drift apart. The kiss had just sealed the deal.

"You never made me seem weird."

Tori looked at her. "What?"

"It didn't matter what color I dyed my hair or what name I wanted to be called or what I wore. You just accepted it. You accepted me. You don't know what that means to me, Vicky."

"Sure."

Kathleen grimaced. "Don't. Don't just say 'sure,' okay? Because it's fucking important to me. All those nights when I accidentally fell asleep on your bedroom floor? It's because I felt safe there. I felt like no one was judging me. I can relax around you, Vicky. I don't have that with anyone else. You don't know how much I needed it sometimes."

"You're welcome."

"Better."

Kathleen put her hand on top of Tori's and brushed the fingers. "We're both really drunk, okay? What happened just now, we don't have to say anything about it. Okay?"

Tori blinked back tears, grateful for the escape. "Okay."

Kathleen hopped down. "Come on. I may not give a shit about my curfew, but I know you do. Let's get you home." Tori started to hand back the jacket. "Keep it. It's still cold. I'll get it in the morning."

But by morning, Kathleen was gone. Tori's parents considered it a miracle, an answer to their prayers. They tried telling her she was better off losing that "bad influence." They told her to look at it as an opportunity to find out who she really was without toxic people trying to push her one way or the other. She took their advice to heart. She used her savings to get an apartment and clerked at the food co-op until she got hired at Lillian's.

Since then she hadn't done a hell of a lot. She went to work. She hung out with her friends. She watched TV and surfed the internet. She couldn't date because she wasn't out. There weren't enough gay women in Royal City to make it worth her while and, frankly, the few she knew about or suspected weren't her type. She dated online a little and once even made the two hundred mile journey for a weekend in Boise in the hopes she could get laid for her trouble. She did meet a woman, they went back to her hotel room, and Tori awkwardly lost her virginity to a woman twice her age. It was far from fantastic, but it was more than what she'd had before, so she treasured the memory.

At some point her reminiscing had led to sleep. She opened her eyes and saw the sun streaming in past the curtains. She stretched and looked at the clock. Three hours until she had to be at work. She would fill it with food and television and maybe a trip to the library to get something new to read. It was her routine. It was good. It was fine. It was a life. She pushed the blankets out of the way and got her routine underway.

Breakfast was oatmeal with bits of banana cut up in it.

The mail came as she finished eating, and she sorted it into urgent, unnecessary, and junk before she got back into the house.

A few emails, an RSVP to an anniversary party, her boss at Lillian's asking about a shift change, and a message from someone she'd met on a dating site.

She went out and paid a bill, stopped by the library and checked out one of the new releases, and went to the diner. She had an eight hour shift to figure out what to do with her evening.

Tori had been at work for three of those hours when the Greyhound bus rumbled past on its way out of town. Sometimes the driver would stop so passengers could eat, and she dreaded the flood of people trying to get their order in before the bus got back under way. Eight or nine to-go orders, all rush, all needing to be done within ten minutes or the customer risked losing their ride. She didn't feel bad about watching it go past without stopping.

A man sitting at the counter had turned at the sound of its approach. He was around her father's age, his graying hair covered by a red trucker's cap. She had seen him around hundreds of times - the curse of small-town life, but she wasn't sure of his name. He shook his head and hooked a finger over his shoulder at the fast-disappearing bus.

"You'll never guess who I heard was coming in on that."

"Who?" Tori asked.

"My buddy Dave's daughter. Dave Lawrence? Girl was a damned hellion. She was the one who had purple or red or blue hair all the time."

Tori had stopped moving, stopped blinking, and only breathed because she had to. "Oh. I remember her." She looked toward the windows. "You said she's coming in on that bus?"

"That's what Dave said. Ask me, she can just stay away. Royal City don't need that kind around here. Save that for the city."

"Uh-huh," Tori said. "Are you about done here? Can I get you a refill?"

He refused the refill, so she took it as permission to move off to another customer. Her mind was racing. Kathleen was back? Was she here to stay or just passing through? Would she have time to see Tori before she left? Would she even want to? Would she stay away because she thought that's what Tori would want?

Anne passed by her on the way to the kitchen and Tori stopped her. "Hey. I need the rest of the afternoon off. Do you think you could get Mary to cover for me?"

"Everything okay, sweetie?"

"Yeah, fine, everything's... fine, I think. I j-just, there's something I need to do." She was distracted by movement outside the restaurant. She turned toward it as if she'd known who she would see.

Kathleen Lawrence. Purple hair, still strutting down the sidewalk like she owned it. Tori moved away from Anne without turning away from the sight of her prodigal friend.

"I have to go, Anne. Please get Mary to cover for me. Or... or I don't know, fire me."

She left the diner without waiting to hear what Anne's response was. If she had heard it, she doubted she would have processed the words. She was too focused on Kathleen's imminent return. She was breathing hard, hands shaking, smiling like a goon as she crossed the parking lot. Kathleen smiled when she saw who was coming out to greet her. She stopped and let Tori close the distance.

"You're back," Tori said.

"Hi. I didn't know if you'd want to see me."

Tori's eyes were burning with tears. They broke free with a shrill sob as she lunged forward and embraced Kathleen as hard as she could. Kathleen had always been tougher than her, so Tori knew she could take it. She felt Kathleen's hands on her back, Kathleen's breath on her neck, and they sagged against one another. Tori didn't know if she was holding Kathleen up or vice versa; they both seemed in danger of collapsing.

"You're back," Tori said against Kathleen's neck, saying the words into her skin as if that would make it more real.

"I had to come back." There were tears in Kathleen's voice. "You still have my jacket."

Tori laughed and stepped back. She cupped Kathleen's face in her hands and, without waiting for a signal or giving any warning, she kissed her. Kathleen returned the kiss with passion, moving one hand up into Tori's hair. They both seemed to be trying to convince the other it was more than just a friendly hello, and they both met with great success. When the kiss ended, Tori pecked Kathleen's bottom lip and then the corners of her mouth.

"Sorry," Kathleen whispered.

"What for?"

"For making you wait so long for a real kiss."

Tori grinned and gripped Kathleen's collar with both hands. "I have a feeling we're about to make up for it."

Kathleen smiled, and Tori was blown away by how much she had changed. She looked comfortable in her skin. The terror barely-disguised as anger was gone, and it left her eyes looking so, so blue. She had grown up so much. She was so beautiful.

"Do you have to go to work?"

"No. Maybe. I don't care. They'll cover for me or we'll figure something out. I've waited long enough for you to be back. I'm not waiting another five hours. Do you still have your truck?"

"It's at my parents' house. Want to go get lost?"

Tori took Kathleen's hand. "Let's see where the night goes."

Kathleen grinned and squeezed Tori's fingers before pulling her close. Tori leaned against Kathleen's side and let herself be led back down the street. It didn't matter where they ended up. Now she understood why she had stayed in Royal City for so long. It was the same reason she'd kept Kathleen's jacket all these years. She was just waiting for her friend to come back. Now she was here, and whatever the night had in store, she knew her routine was out the window. Whatever she and Kathleen came up with to replace it, she was sure it wouldn't be boring.

CURVY PRIVATEERS & SCURVY SEA DOGS

JENNA TENSED as the first group of the day came surging toward her. Parents with little kids, teenagers intent on mocking everything they saw, and retirees who wanted to power-walk somewhere other than the mall for a change. They moved en masse through the front gates with shoes thudding on the wooden boardwalk. Jenna straightened her posture and tried to put some peppiness into her voice. She'd been cited by Craig for coming across as "sullen" or "grouchy." Another demerit and she'd be put on trash duty until her demeanor improved.

"Welcome to Shallow Cove," she said as soon as the guests were within earshot. "We hope you'll have a swashbuckling time."

Most people ignored her. Others gave her a perfunctory smile or nodded as they passed by her station. She was dressed in a striped shirt under a black vest, with a red sash tied around her waist. A black bandana kept her spiky strawberry blonde hair - an "era violation" according to management - out of sight. Her right eye was covered by a patch and she was armed with a rubber cutlass which she was required to use if any children challenged her to a swordfight. She admitted that the first couple of swordfights were fun. It got boring after about a dozen. By the fortieth, she started wishing she could actually inflict some damage on her opponents. Not the kids, of course. The high school football jerks who considered it flirting to charge at her with their souvenir swords drawn.

But that was the cost of working at Shallow Cove, the state's biggest and most successful theme park. Four hundred miles from the ocean and someone had the brilliant idea of a park dedicated to pirates. The owner found a large lake in the foothills of the Lost River Range and created an "authentic recreation" of the port towns in the Caribbean which were once home to pirates when they weren't plundering the high seas. A huge galleon sat in the lake, looming over the rides. There was a cannon show every day at five o'clock and, if the staff didn't wear earplugs, they risked permanent tinnitus from the constant explosions.

Jenna hated it. Despised it. She hated the hours and the people, she hated standing in the sun and she hated shivering in the cold. The smell of the concessions - grilled chicken and corn dogs and gooey caramel odors - blended into a nauseating mélange that seemed to congeal in her pores by the end of every day. But it was better than smelling like garbage.

Of course, on trash duty, she could at least listen to her own music instead of the chanties being constantly piped through speakers every twenty yards. Maybe it would be worth it.

"Welcome to Shallow Cove," she said without thinking as another group moved past her. "We hope you'll have a swashbuckling time."

"That doesn't work, you know."

Jenna turned toward the person who had spoken, forcing her brain back into the here and now. It was another park employee, one she didn't remember ever seeing before. She was wearing a man's shirt (baggy, distressed, and unbuttoned enough to show the lacy top of her slip) and a burgundy-and-black dress which reached the ground. Her blonde hair was done up in ringlets. It was the costume of someone who worked in the saloon, a family-friendly term for "whorehouse" (couldn't offend mom and pop!). The illusion was ruined by the loop of earbud cord hanging from the pocket of her shirt.

"What doesn't work?" Jenna asked.

"Have a swashbuckling time. Swashbuckling is a verb, not an adjective. You could wish for them to swash some buckles, I guess, but that sounds weird."

Jenna shrugged and faced forward again. "I guess. Tell the boss. I just chirp what they tell me to chirp."

The other woman rested her shoulder against a wooden post. "So is that your job? Stand there and say things that don't make sense?"

"Greet the customers, point them in the right direction if they ask, generally add flavor to the park."

"It's a shame they have you dressed up like Smee. They could at least let you look like a badass pirate. You'd look pretty sexy in the right gear." She pushed away from the beam and started to walk away. "I'm Caroline," she said with an almost dismissive tone, as if she was saying that instead of 'see you around.'

Jenna said, "I'm Jenna."

"I know," Caroline said without turning around. "I asked a couple of people."

Jenna furrowed her brow. Asked some people? About her? Why? She faced forward as the next group wandered near her. "Welcome to Shallow Cove. Have a sw— a swell time." Once the group had passed, she looked in the direction Caroline had vanished. Maybe she would have to ask a few questions of her own.

There was a hierarchy to the employees of Shallow Cove. Buccaneers were the performers who actually got to play pirate. They spent an hour every day running through the little town, shouting and acting rowdy until they reached the galleon. Sometimes they fought their way up the ramp, other days they carried loot as townspeople chased them down. It all depended on the script they got that day. Privateers worked concessions and also got to play a part. Bartenders and wait staff dressed in period clothing and pretended to be astonished by the sight of a guest's smartphone were called Corsairs.

Then there was the general staff, like Jenna. They were the Sea Dogs, and it was just as glamorous as it implied.

At the end of the day, exhausted from standing and strolling around all day, Jenna went home and took a long bath to soak her feet and not worry about being upright for a while. She lit a cigarette, put on Paramore, and relaxed. An ex once admitted he'd only asked Jenna out because she looked like Paramore's lead singer. She was flattered at first until she realized it meant he wasn't interested in *her*. He just wanted the fantasy of being with a famous rock star. She was nothing more than a masturbatory fantasy for him. But at least he'd introduced her to a band she loved. So it wasn't a total loss.

She thought about other things that ex had said about her. One of the things he hated about her was that she was "always so angry, about everything." Absolutely false. She wasn't always angry. Sometimes she was annoyed or tired or frustrated. People irritated her, the world at large was a trash pile, and she hated her job. She couldn't be bothered to add nuance to every emotion that passed through her at any given moment.

So fine. Cut it down to the lowest common denominator, she was angry. She was an angry person. That was a label she could deal with.

Jenna placed the cigarette on the soap dish and lifted her feet onto the side of the tub. She slid down and let the water cover her breasts, then her shoulders, up to her jawline. Her mind was clear, but telling herself not to think about Caroline meant that Caroline was all she could think of. She moved her hands under the water and let her fingers brush her hips. There were enough instances in her past where she'd had feelings for women that she considered herself bisexual, but she never acted on it. She could accept who she was without making it a statement.

But for some reason, being flirted with had thrown her for a loop. Maybe she never acted because she thought the burden of making the first move would be on her. Now all she had to do was respond. Acknowledge a shared interest. She let herself slip further down until her face was underwater. She held her breath and moved her hands over her belly. She slipped one hand down and the other up, spreading the fingers of both hands for the exploration.

Trapped air escaped from her nose, one wobbling bubble at a time. She used two fingers between her legs and massaged one breast, moving her body under the water without breaking the surface. She felt the familiar tightness in her throat but kept her head down. She might one day admit she was bisexual but she doubted she would ever tell anyone about this particular practice. She didn't want to freak anyone out, and she certainly didn't want anyone who might be *too* into the idea of cutting off her air during sex.

It meant she had to get off quickly. There was no time for teasing or wasting time. It forced her to confront her fantasies and the things that turned her on. This time it was Caroline, specifically the shirt she'd been wearing. The shoulders mostly exposed, unbuttoned enough to give a hint of cleavage. She wanted to brush the hair away from her neck and kiss the skin as she pulled the shirt completely down. She wanted to cup the breasts with both hands as Caroline pushed her against the wall.

Jenna broke the surface and sucked in air as she came, her whole body tensed and her feet pressed against the curve of the tub.

She let herself float in the aftermath, limbs drifting until they bumped against each other or the side of the tub. She pushed her hair out of her face and decided if Caroline gave her another opportunity, she wasn't going to squander it. She wouldn't waste time pining, fantasizing, wondering 'what if.' She had done the endlessly pining thing before and wasn't interested in doing it again.

When she recovered after her orgasm, she climbed out of the tub and toweled off on her way to bed. By this time tomorrow, she expected she would either have made her move or Caroline's flirting would be a distant memory.

Every morning started with a team pep talk in the break room. It was a cafeteria attached to the locker rooms, so no one could avoid showing up. Jenna sat among the other performers: hungover pirates and wenches in era-appropriate garb checking email and social media on their phones. Jenna sat in the far corner next to the vending machines. Sometimes the motors hummed loud enough to drown out their manager's droning.

"--and we're going to want to keep an eye on, mm, uh, unauthorized photos by the guests," Chad said, eyes locked on his tablet computer to read his notes. "A few selfies are okay, but there are authorized, ah, photo, ah, opportunities where visitors can pay for, for official... official... pictures with costumed employees. So we'll, um, naturally, be wanting them to go to... those areas."

Caroline came out of the lockers in her costume. Jenna had seen her arrive in a faded T-shirt and leggings with a tear across the knee. It was a little shocking to see her in normal clothing, and now seeing her dressed like a bartender from the eighteenth century seemed normal. There were plenty of open spaces at the folding tables, but Caroline sat on the same bench as Jenna. She folded her arms in front of her and watched Chad for a moment, then let her gaze drift lazily around the room. She stopped when she landed on Jenna and the corners of her lips curled up in a smile.

"Morning," she said softly.

Jenna flipped her fingers in a lazy greeting. 'Hey."

Chad poked his screen. "And, um, if there's no pressing

business anyone wants to bring up--"

Caroline raised her hand.

He was surprised. Normally people just wanted to leave as quickly as possible so no one ever prolonged the meeting by asking questions. "Uh, yes. Sorry, uh... you're new, right?"

"Right. Caroline Gilbert. I was wondering why some of us have really authentic costumes and others look like cartoon pirates."

There were a few scattered laughs. Chad cleared his throat. "Well, uh, I think that's a question which could be better addressed by, uh, by the owners, but there's the, the high turnover of employees in those lower positions and, and, and the requirements to create more period-accurate outfits. I think it's, um, easier to, um, just make them generic. One-size-fits-all."

"Oh. Okay. I just thought it would hurt the whole reality of the situation they were going for. But whatever."

There were a few more snickers at that, but Chad ignored them. "Well, if nobody has anything else to say, I think we can get the day started. Get out there and swash some buckles!"

"Oh! About that," Caroline said, but Chad was already halfway through the door.

Jenna brushed by Caroline as she left. "It was a nice try. But don't try to change the phrasing. It's part of the brand. They have that in the damn TV and radio ads. It would take an act of Congress to change it at this point."

"I'm just trying to make life easier on you, matey."

They left the cafeteria at the same time and ended up walking in the same direction past the empty rope mazes where guests would soon queue up to ride the Roulette (a hurricane ride in which riders sit in hanging baskets which spin in faster and faster circles around a central spire which is designed to look like a roulette wheel) and the Buccaneer Bumper Cars.

Caroline said, "I don't mean to imply you look bad or anything."

"Huh?"

"The outfit. You look fine. I didn't want you to think I was insulting you."

Jenna shrugged. "Didn't cross my mind."

"Good." They were almost to Jenna's station. "And I like your hair. I didn't get to see it yesterday, but it looks cool."

"Thanks." She glanced sideways at her. "What's with you?"

Caroline shrugged. "What do you mean?"

"You're all... friendly."

"I'm..." Her shoulders sagged. "I thought yesterday I might have come across the wrong way. Bitchy. People tell me I can come off as bitchy to people who don't know me. This is a new job and I don't want to alienate people my first day. Especially not people who might end up being... you know. Cool."

Jenna laughed. "Well, you don't have to worry about that. First, I'm not cool. At all. And second, if anything, I preferred the way you acted yesterday. At least it was honest. It was you. I get that 'bitchy' thing all the time. It's just a bullshit word that means you aren't living up to someone else's expectation."

"Right on." Caroline held up her hand.

"I'm not doing that."

Caroline dropped her hand. "Fair enough. So... a long day of standing around saying the same grammatically-wrong thing...?"

"Yep. You?"

"Serving beer to guys who try to look down my shirt."

Jenna said, "The ladies don't try to look down your shirt, too?"

Caroline grinned. "Some. But I don't mind them as much."

"I'll keep that in mind."

"You should come by for your lunch break."

Was that an invitation to ogle her...? The timing seemed suspect, but maybe she was just making the offer since they were about to part company.

"Sure. Better than just grabbing a corn dog from one of the vendors."

"I'll watch for you."

Jenna nodded and assumed her station. It was still a few minutes until the official opening, so the wide streets of the fake island town seemed abandoned and spooky. The early morning sun was aimed right down the main drag, glinting golden off windows and the chrome parts of rides. Caroline walked toward the saloon in the midst of this glow, letting it shine across her shoulders and through her hair like threads of...

"What the fuck," Jenna said, snapping her head around and squeezing her eyes shut. She didn't need to be thinking things like that. People who made a huge deal about Valentine's Day and two-month-iversaries thought like that, and only about people they'd been dating for a while. She wasn't the sentimental kind. She didn't get dopey if she liked someone. She took the bandana out of her pocket and wrapped it around her head, tying it tight in the back.

When the first group arrived, she growled, "Welcome to Shallow Cove. We hope you'll have a swashbuckling time!"

Jenna went to have lunch at the saloon. Caroline served her, but the interaction was professional. No flirtation, no prying. Jenna read her book and ate her food. The only thing that went beyond the ordinary social parameters of waitress-patron relationship was that Caroline waved goodbye when Jenna was on her way to the door. Jenna nodded to acknowledge the wave and continued back to her station.

The next day was similar, and they settled into a routine for the rest of the week. Smalltalk on their way out of the morning meeting and lunch. Caroline wasn't pushy like some people. If Jenna was hungover and didn't feel like talking, Caroline didn't push. And the conversation wasn't dumb, banal stuff that some of the other staff liked to torture her with. No celebrity gossip. No recaps of the previous night's reality garbage. Definitely no politics. Caroline just talked about her life and what she hoped her job at Shallow Cove might turn into.

Caroline kept her ideas vague until the first Monday of their friendship, when they met in the parking lot and walked inside together Maybe it was the fact it was slightly earlier than usual and she was still mostly asleep, but she was suddenly very forthcoming.

"You might be shocked, but I don't plan to retire as a Corsair wench. I want to open my own place. I've been saving up since I got out of high school."

"What kind of place?"

"You're going to think it's lame."

Jenna said, "Yeah, probably."

Caroline swung her foot out and kicked the back of Jenna's boot. "Bitch." She took a deep breath and let it out before she answered. "I want to open a comic book store. When I was growing up, there was a place on the corner by Circle K. I grew up with two older brothers and a single dad. If I wanted a strong female role model, I had to find her myself. Wonder Woman, Supergirl, Jean Grey, Storm. These women were just so amazing. But there were always these asshole guys hanging around who told me girls didn't belong in 'their' store. Comics were their territory, and I wasn't allowed."

Jenna grunted. "For people who have free reign of the entire world, they sure are defensive about keeping every square inch of it to themselves."

"Right. Well. I'm going to change that. I'll sell to guys, obviously, but then I'm going to have Ladies Nights. Tuesday and Thursday from, like, eight until ten. Only women and girls allowed in the store. That way they can discover the heroes I loved without worrying about some guy telling them they don't belong. They can ask questions without being afraid some pimply-faced punk is going to make her feel stupid."

"That's not lame. If I had any money whatsoever, I'd want to invest."

"You don't have to do that. Just promise when I open, you'll come and hang out so I can keep seeing you every day."

Jenna didn't know how to respond to that. It was so touching that her knee-jerk reaction was sarcasm and deflection, but she didn't want to minimize the sentiment. So she just nodded and followed Caroline into the locker rooms. She almost ran into Caroline's back because she had stopped short just across the threshold.

"What's all this?"

Jenna stepped to the side so she could see. Six of the lockers, including Jenna's, had dry-cleaner bags hanging from their doors.

Torri, a Buccaneer, was standing near the sinks already in costume. She turned with a grin. "Wait until you see them. I guess Chad mentioned your comment about the Sea Dogs costumes breaking the reality of the park. Someone in the office apparently thought it was worth the expense, so now there are new costumes. They're still not tailored or anything, but they look damn good. Nice job, new girl."

Jenna went to her locker and unzipped the bag. Inside was a linen shirt which had been distressed to look like it was old and in need of mending. It was basically the same as what she usually wore - pants, vest, sash, bandana - but every element had gone from Disney to *Black Sails* in terms of realism. She looked up and saw Caroline watching her, looking smug.

"Nice job, new girl," she echoed.

Caroline grinned and went to her own locker, and Jenna took down the bag so she could begin getting ready for her shift.

Toward the end of summer, the park began closing earlier in the evening due to the new school year. By mid-August, it was only open until six o'clock. The gates were closed at five, and the crowd slowly filtered out as the sun fell low behind the pirate ship. Jenna had no reason to remain at her station after the last few crowds passed through, so the end of the day usually found her wandering to see where else she might be needed.

When she got to the saloon, she was surprised to see Caroline alone behind the bar. She was gathering the last few dirty mugs left behind by the guests. She hadn't looked up yet, so Jenna paused in the doorway to watch her for a moment. They were friends now, on the verge of losing the thing that held them together. When the park closed for winter, nothing would be forcing them to see each other every day. That meant they would soon have to hang out on purpose, make plans, exchange information. And that, in Jenna's mind, created a problem.

Caroline finally looked up. "Oh hey. You scared me... I thought I had a customer."

"Sorry." She came inside and let the door swing shut. "Slow day?"

"Yeah. Mostly families these days, and they want to leave early to have a proper dinner at Red Lobster. It's been kind of a ghost town in here."

Jenna walked to the bar and took a stool. "So... this place is closing down soon."

"Mm-hmm. You got a winter job lined up?"

"Yeah. Rosauers is always looking to replace summer kids who have to go back to school. I usually get in there. You?"

Caroline said, "I'm not sure yet. I might just coast a little until Wal-Mart needs seasonal help around Black Friday. Dig into my savings."

"You can't do that. What about the comic book shop?"

"I'm a long way from that."

Jenna said, "Even farther if you keep digging into your savings."

"Yeah..."

Jenna rested her arms on the bar. "So. Once this place closes, I guess we'll have to go out of our way to see each other."

"Guess so." She looked up, her hair covering one eye. "I want to keep in touch, if that's what you're asking."

"Yeah. Me too. That's part of why I came here. I've been meaning to bring it up."

"Okay." She reached under the bar for her phone. "Let me give you my stuff..."

Jenna said, "Wait. Before you do that, there's something I should confess. I don't want to make things weird. But if we actually become... you know... *friends*, and then it comes out later, it'll be even more awkward, so it's better to just get it out of the way now."

Caroline straightened. "Oh, God. You killed my parents."

"What? No. Your parents are dead?"

"No. But I can't think of anything else that would require that kind of drama." She pushed her hair out of her face. "I'm intrigued." She leaned on the bar across from Jenna. "Spill the beans."

Jenna was afraid she was blushing. She used her right hand to worry the cuticles of her left fingers. "All right. Well, when we first met, you were kind of... flirtatious. At least that's how it came across. And I thought, whatever. She's pretty. Sure. What if? You know? So... yeah, a couple of times after we met, there were times, uh... you know... where I'd... you'd come up when I..."

Caroline's face spread into a huge smile. "You jerked off to me?"

"Gross. Don't say it like that."

"Fine. You *fan-ta-si-i-ized* about me?" She laughed and ran her hands down the edge of the bar. "Wow. I've never had someone just come out and tell me something like that before. I think I feel honored. So what did you think about me doing?"

"Oh, no. No, I'm not going to actually tell you *details...*"

Caroline pouted. "Oh, come on. Please? I mean, you cast me in this role. The least you can do is keep me in the loop. Was I aggressive? Were you the one who came on to me?"

Jenna slid off the stool. "You know what, I'm sorry I brought it up." She started for the door. "It's a small town. I'll probably see you around."

"Oh, don't be mad. I'm sorry. I was just teasing. Jenna. Jenna!" She had reached the door. "Hey, sailor. Ship ain't leaving just yet. Why don't you pull up a chair and sit a spell?"

Jenna stopped with her hand on the door. She didn't turn around. She could just slip out, could pretend she hadn't heard that sincere plea in Caroline's voice before it transformed into some strange but unaccented affectation. She knew what Caroline was doing. She was playing a part. The setting sun cast the galleon's shadow across this whole section of the park. It was easy to ignore the mountains and believe they were on some island in the Caribbean. She rested her hand on the door. It would also be easy to just leave.

"I never said how much I liked your new outfit. You look real authentic-like. I'm sure your crew is showing you the proper respect now."

Jenna said, "You'd be surprised." She turned. "You sure I'm not too late for a drink?"

Caroline had come out from behind the bar. "Always got time to pour one for my favorite Sea Dog. C'mon. Sit a spell. At least 'til you get your land legs back."

"Sounds kind of nice." She walked back to the bar and took her seat again. "So what's on tap?"

"I got some new stuff for you to try. Just got a shipment today. I'll give you a discount."

Jenna looked toward the door as Caroline poured her a drink. "So you get many sailors like me in here?"

"Sailors, yep. Like you? Not enough."

"Careful, barkeep. Lady might get the wrong idea with all this sweet-talk."

Caroline put down a full mug. "Or the right one."

Jenna hesitated before meeting Caroline's eye again.

"Thing is, sometimes I'll throw a flirt out there, see if I can hook the fish I want. If she doesn't bite, no biggie. Move on to the next one. But sometimes if I miss, it bugs me. It bugs me a lot. Because I was really interested in that fish—"

"Can we move on from the fish metaphor?" Jenna said under her breath. "I feel like you're comparing me to a salmon here."

"Oh. I just meant—"

"I know, I picked up the meaning. I just..."

Caroline nodded, voice still low. "Right. I just meant that sometimes I'll test the waters with someone I like to see if there's any interest. And if it doesn't look like there is, I move on. I didn't do that with you because you seemed cool. You seemed like someone I might want to know even if you weren't interested in me romantically. But now you're telling me you *did* take the bait, I'm just disappointed I didn't get to..."

"Enjoy the fruits of your fishing."

Caroline looked into Jenna's eyes. "Exactly."

Jenna moved her hand closer to the middle of the bar. Caroline moved her hand as well, their fingers almost touching. Caroline looked at their hands but Jenna kept her eyes on Caroline's face.

"If we're being totally honest with one another," Caroline said, "I'd be lying if I claimed my thoughts about you were always totally pure friendship."

"Really?"

"Especially after you got this new costume. I've had some really, really unfriendly thoughts about this costume."

Jenna said, "Well, your costume isn't too bad, either."

Caroline said, "Come around the bar for a second."

"Why?"

"Just..."

Jenna got up and moved to the other side of the bar. Caroline stepped in front of her, hands on the bar on either side of Jenna's waist to pin her in place. Their hips pressed against each other. Caroline was close enough that Jenna could smell the sweat of a long day on her skin and the faint traces of whatever perfume she'd put on that morning. It was easy to see the fine details of her face from this distance. Jenna held her breath so she wouldn't exhale into Caroline's wide eyes.

"When you thought about me," Caroline whispered, "were you in bed?"

"The bath."

Caroline nodded slowly. "Just your fingers?"

"Yeah."

"Good." She leaned even closer and craned her neck. Jenna tensed but didn't pull away. Caroline moved one hand from the bar to Jenna's waist, holding her as she nuzzled her neck. "I love your short hair. You have such a great neck. And every time I see you, I've just wanted to..." She began to kiss it. Jenna's eyes rolled back and she curled her hands into fists to keep from responding vocally.

"My neck is... sensitive..."

"Do you want me to stop?"

"Did I say stop...?"

Caroline pressed harder against her. Jenna wrapped her arms around Caroline's waist and moved her feet apart, giving Caroline a space to step into. After a few seconds exploring Jenna's neck, Caroline straightened and touched her cheek.

"C'mere..."

Jenna parted her lips to say something but it turned into a kiss. Caroline's tongue pressed against her mouth and retreated before Jenna could meet it with her own. She pursued, grabbing handfuls of Caroline's dress knowing it was futile to try lifting it far enough to reach bare skin but willing to try. She shifted her weight and used her chest to shove Caroline backward. She pinned her against the row of bottles behind the bar and broke the kiss.

"Oof. Aggressive."

"You expected a wallflower?"

"Never." Caroline reached up, yanked the bandana from Jenna's head, and ruffled her hair. "God, it's a crime they make you cover up this hair." She grabbed a handful of it and pulled Jenna's head back, holding her there as she kissed her again. Jenna growled into Caroline's mouth but didn't try to pull away. "I'm so glad you took the first step. I'm such a coward. I was just going to let you walk away."

Jenna said, "That would've been dumb."

"So dumb," Caroline agreed. She slipped away and grabbed Jenna's hand. "Come with me."

"What about the saloon? Someone could come in."

"I think it would be better if they see an empty room than walking in on what I'm about to start."

Jenna shivered in anticipation and let herself be led to a small room under the stairs. A bare bulb shined down onto them and onto shelves filled with extra napkins, condiments, and extra mugs. Everything cast a long shadow as Caroline reached past Jenna to pull the door shut behind her. They were chest to chest, eyes locked on each other as they caught their breath and let their minds catch up to the moment. Jenna licked her lips and Caroline took it as an invitation to kiss her again. Jenna put her hands on Caroline's shoulders and let them drop until she was cupping her breasts through the blouse.

Caroline aimed lower, untying the sash around Jenna's hips. When it fell, she grabbed the button of her pants and got it open. Jenna rolled her hips from side to side and let the pants fall until they were caught on her boots. Caroline angled herself back and looked down.

"That underwear is not era-appropriate."

"Take them off, then."

Caroline pushed them down. Jenna moved back and sank onto a box, guiding Caroline to her. Caroline lifted her dress, spread her legs, and sank down onto Jenna's lap. She pulled down her shirt enough to expose her strapless bra, which Jenna helped her remove and toss aside. Caroline took a breath and then rolled her head back as Jenna kissed, licked, and nuzzled her breasts. Caroline hunched her shoulders and leaned back.

"God, that's nice." She bit her lip and squirmed, one hand on the back of Jenna's head as she moved the other between their bodies. "You know, I thought about you, too."

"Yeah? Details."

Caroline said, "I used toys. In bed. A vibrator." She panted, brow furrowed. "A couple of times, actually."

Jenna brushed her cheek against Caroline's breast, feeling its warmth, her eyes closed. "Tell me what you wear to bed..."

"Sometimes panties... s-sometimes little shorts and a T-shirt. Some nights nude. Lying under the blankets. Thinking about you."

Jenna slipped her hand down alongside Caroline's. She lifted her hips off the box and gasped. Caroline looked down. Their eyes locked.

"We kind of abandoned the whole roleplay we had going."

"Uh-huh," Caroline mumbled, eyes unfocused and bottom lip trembling.

"I liked it," Jenna said.

Caroline nodded. "Yeah."

Jenna moved her head to the side. "Kiss my neck again..."

Caroline immediately complied, rocking her hips against Jenna's hand. Caroline's tongue against her neck made her feel like a string was being tightened around a coil inside of her. Her entire body tensed when she felt the scrape of teeth against her neck and she uttered a quick and involuntary sound. Her fingers were slick against Caroline and she pushed two of them upward. Caroline choked off her cry of surprise and pleasure against Jenna's neck and shuddered through her climax. Her lower body jerked and thrust in the aftershocks.

"You okay?" Jenna asked, turning her head to kiss Caroline's chest.

Caroline nodded. "Mm-hmm. Are you? Did you...?"

"No, but I'm—"

Caroline began moving. "Let me go down on you..."

"Wait, wait, wait," Jenna said, holding Caroline on her lap. "Not right this second. I don't want to come just yet." Caroline settled again, and Jenna kissed her chest some more. Caroline stroked her hair. The string was still wrapped around the coil inside of her. Taut, but not close to breaking. She felt like she could feel the tension trembling through her fingers and all the way down to her toes. She liked the feeling. It was better than most of her actual orgasms, and she wanted to hold onto it as much as possible.

"Are you sure you're okay?" Caroline whispered.

"Mm-hmm." She waited another few seconds before she said, "Okay. Okay, please..."

Caroline lifted up and dropped to her knees. Jenna grabbed the shelf and held her breath, but she immediately released both when Caroline's mouth found her. Her foot smacked the ground and she rose up off the box before sitting again. She made a noise halfway between a grunt and a growl as her whole body trembled and twitched involuntarily. And then it seemed like there was no way for her to sit up straight, like all the vertical had been erased from her body. She slumped back against the shelf and watched as Caroline kissed her thighs, lips shining in the dim light of the storage room.

Jenna coughed. Caroline looked up. They both smiled awkwardly at each other.

"So I guess we're going to keep seeing each other after the park closes for the season, huh?"

Caroline put her head down on Jenna's lap. "Yeah, I think that's a pretty safe bet, matey."

Jenna smiled dreamily, eyes closed, and played with Caroline's hair. She was content to stay in that position until her body was capable of movement again. She wasn't particularly concerned with how long it might take; she was perfectly comfortable right where she was.

CELESTINE AND THE GYPSY

1

THE SKELETON of every city looked the same. The main streets that people saw from the highway or passed through on their way somewhere else or filmed for television, those were all different. That was where the city showed its personality. But beyond that were the suburbs and the gas stations. There were schools and churches and mechanics and furniture shops. Once on those streets it would be difficult to tell one state from another. The main thing that made Metairie different from any other city in America was the heat. Louisiana was where all the heat on Earth lived, and it settled into the diagonal slices of the town's streets every summer.

Debra Kent was sitting on the driveway behind her father's car, legs crossed in front of her, squinting in the summer sunlight. Everyone else had big plans for the next few weeks. Vacations to take, jobs to start, cars to learn how to drive. Her brother and his friends were on a summer trip to London, so she couldn't even count on him to keep her company. She was seventeen and completely terrified of the future. In the fall she would start her final year of high school. What came after that? It would be the eighties, a whole new decade. And there'd be no college for her, not with the expense of David's trip and her father working less and less, so maybe getting a job of her own? What could she possibly do? Work the counter at McDonalds?

Only one car had gone by in the past hour. She was thinking about going inside when a black girl on a bicycle zipped into her line of sight. She wasn't riding like a kid but as if the pedals were growing out of her feet. She stood on them, ass in the air and arms bent above the handlebars with the elbows straight out. She was wearing a purple tank top over a pink T-shirt and her jeans were bedazzled with intricate designs Debra couldn't quite identify from a distance and given how fast she was pedaling.

The girl turned her head toward Debra and skidded to a stop. Her back tire effortlessly fishtailed and she planted one bare foot on the pavement. She ended up facing Debra, who sat up straighter in anticipation, of what she didn't know. Getting beaten up? Getting made fun of?

"Show me how to get to Lake Pontchartrain."

Her voice lilted up at the end, turning the order into a question with the last syllable.

The lake was less than a mile north; all she had to do was keep going the same direction she'd been going and it would be impossible to miss. Debra could have just lifted her arm and pointed but something made her stand up and brush off the seat of her pants. She approached the bike.

"Okay."

"You can stand on the pegs and hold onto my shoulders."

"Is that safe?"

The girl lifted one shoulder. "Safe as anything else. I'm Celestine Lafitte."

Debra blinked. "That's not really your name."

She grinned. "Yep, sure is. You can call me Celeste."

Debra carefully got on the pegs, her feet curling around them as she leaned forward so as not to put all her weight on the tiny pieces of metal.

"I'm Debra."

"Okay, Debra. Hold on."

Debra yelped as Celeste started pedaling. Her fingers dug into the hot skin just above the collar of Celeste's T-shirt. It took her a moment to figure out her center of gravity and adjust her hands so she wouldn't tear out a chunk of flesh if she fell off. Celeste was actually a very good pilot. She went fast but not so fast that Debra ever felt she was in danger. They rode through neighborhoods and down the Esplanade, with Debra occasionally stretching her arm out in front of Celeste to point where she should turn. Every time she did, she smelled Celeste's shampoo and sweat.

When they reached their destination, Debra stepped off onto the grass and bent her knees to get acclimated to solid ground again. Celeste straddled the bike and looked at the water.

"This is it? No beach?"

"Not really," Debra said. "It's just a lake..."

Celeste twisted her lips into an expression of distaste. Debra felt as if the failure was hers and started trying to come up with a solution.

"Um... I think maybe if we go—"

"No, it's fine." Celeste swung her leg over the bike and walked it forward. "Come on."

Debra followed. It wasn't like she was going to just turn around and walk home, though now she was wondering how long she would be out. Her parents might worry if she just vanished from the driveway. Seventeen was still young enough to get abducted. She stuck her hands in the back pockets of her jeans and trailed Celeste over the grass. They found a place where they could sit down and Celeste let the bike fall before she dropped down. She folded her legs the way Debra had been sitting when they met. Debra sat down next to her with a good amount of polite space between them.

"So how do you live in Metairie without knowing where the lake is?"

"We just moved here. Literally still have more boxes than furniture. But I just had to get out. It was either this or the Mississippi, and I thought this had a better chance of having a beach."

Debra said, "But if you'd gone to the river, you wouldn't have met me."

Celeste grinned. "That's true."

They settled in, Celeste leaning back on her elbows while Debra rested her elbows on her knees. There were boats out on the water for them to watch, and occasionally Debra pointed out one of the multitude of birds that swooped and swept across the water.

"Where'd you live before here?"

"Atlanta. Brother got a scholarship to Tulane. So my parents decided it was better to uproot us all and move close by for him, and screw Celeste's senior year of high school."

Debra winced. "That sucks."

"Nah. Most people have to wait until college to reinvent themselves. I get a whole year head start on deciding what the new me is going to be."

Debra brushed her hair back behind her ears. "That would be cool. You're lucky."

"There's no rule that says you have to wait, just because you've lived here longer. If you want to change who you are, just do it."

"I don't think it's that easy."

"No need to make it hard. Like what was keeping you from coming to the lake yourself? The Earth didn't have to move underneath you, you just had to get up off your butt and move yourself. Other people see you the wrong way? Fix it. Make them see you right."

Debra considered that advice, still not quite convinced it would be that easy. But why shouldn't it be? Why should she let other people's opinion dictate how she acted? That was just dumb. She and Celeste fell into another comfortable silence that was occasionally broken with biographical questions going one way or the other. It wasn't long before they independently decided it was time to head home. Celeste helped Debra up and walked her bike back to the road before she climbed onboard. Debra got back on the pegs, much more relaxed this time, and held on tight as Celeste pushed off with her foot.

"So what else is there to do in this town?"

Debra had always been a homebody, content to do her homework and get to bed early. But just a few hours spent killing time with her new friend had shown her that maybe she'd been missing out. Maybe she should spend her last year of high school exploring all the possibilities the world had to offer.

"I don't really know," she said. "Let's find out together."

Celeste laughed. "That's a deal."

After Celeste dropped her off, Debra went into the house and spent the rest of the afternoon trying to convince herself it really happened. It all seemed surreal once she was back in familiar territory. Maybe she'd passed out from heat stroke and imagined everything. A cool new friend named Celestine Lafitte definitely felt like a hallucination. But that night before dinner the phone rang. She reached it before either of her parents could, knowing deep down who was on the other end.

"He~"

"We need a nickname for you."

"Uh. Huh?"

"Debra Kent doesn't have a lot of possibilities. It's so bland.

Celeste and Debra sounds lopsided, you know? So you need a nickname."

"I can't think of anything..."

"Well duh. You don't come up with your own nickname. That's lame. But I'm working on it, don't worry. So I rode around town after I dumped you off and I found some places we can go this weekend. If you're up for it, I mean..."

She was up for it. Saturday afternoon, Celeste showed up on her bike again and Debra climbed on the back pegs without hesitation.

"Where are we going?"

"The bowling alley. They've got an arcade. You ever play *Space Invaders?*"

"No."

"You're gonna learn!"

By the end of the afternoon, Debra was trouncing Celeste and anyone else who stepped up to try beating her score. Celeste dominated at air hockey; none of their new friends could touch her. Debra watched the other kids laughing with Celeste and just assumed they would overtake her position, that Celeste would go off with them and forget her new friend. But when the game ended, Celeste exchanged phone numbers with a couple of the kids and broke away from the ground to lean against the machine Debra was playing.

"Dang, girl. We should've been playing people for money. Where do you wanna go next?"

They had dinner at a drive-in, sitting at a plastic table while carhops zipped around them on roller skates. They got burgers and milkshakes and detailed their arcade victories to each other. On the way home they took a detour along Lake Pontchartrain and saw an informal concert had popped up on one of the docks. A crowd had formed around a group of sweaty scarecrow men playing steel guitars, trumpets, and saxophones. The drum set was a cluster of upturned buckets. Celeste and Debra joined the crowd just as they started playing a Cher song, giving the tune a slick zydeco flair.

"Ah's born in da wagon o' a travelin' show, ma mere used tah dance for de money dey t'row..."

Debra whooped and threw her arms up. "I love this song!"

Celeste said, "It doesn't make any sense, though. You know what's south of Mobile? Water!"

"Who cares?" Debra laughed and sang along with the chorus at the top of her lungs. By the time the chorus came around again, Celeste was singing along with her. The crowd was small enough and they were making a big enough spectacle of themselves that the band noticed and spurred them on. When the song ended the band thanked them for their help and the girls ran back to Celeste's bike.

"I think I got a nickname for you," Celeste said.

"Uh-oh."

"Gypsy."

Debra threw her head back and laughed. "Okay. Out of that song, that's probably the best one, right? I think I can live with it."

Celeste weaved the bicycle from one side of the road to the other and started singing it again. Debra held on tight and sang with her.

2

The rest of the summer was full of adventures with Celeste. Sleepovers, movies, excursions over the city limits to New Orleans with fake IDs. Celeste told her it wasn't that big of a deal since they were only a few months shy of eighteen and that was basically twenty, and what was one more year to twenty-one? Debra didn't follow the logic, but she agreed because it was better than being left behind. Celeste made it clear that if Debra didn't want to drink, they could do something else, but she wanted to experience life the way Celeste did: no cares, no worries, no fear. She didn't like drinking or being drunk enough to worry about it becoming a problem, so she went along.

At one point they found themselves walking down the street just after dusk when Celeste stopped, hooked her arm around Debra's, and pulled her forward.

"Don't do that," Celeste said.

"Do what?"

"Lag behind. Let me lead. You don't have to do that. We don't always have to do what I wanna do." She squeezed Debra's arm. "You and me. Not me and my shadow. We're a team."

Debra said, "Okay."

"Good. Keep that in mind, Gypsy."

When school started up again, Celeste and Debra discovered they shared an English teacher but no actual classes. After a brief debate about changing their schedule they decided being separated was probably for the best. They both found new friends but always gravitated back to each other at the end of the day. Debra's parents gave her a used car as a senior present. It was barely able to make the trip to school and back every day, but it was enough for Celeste to be demoted to passenger status.

The Gypsy nickname not only stuck, everyone at school picked up on it with astounding speed. Soon even her oldest friends were using it almost exclusively. Debra was only annoyed because she thought it would just be a special thing between her and Celeste, but she actually liked it too much to complain. She also couldn't complain about how relaxed she felt around other people. There was no anxiety, no sense that she didn't belong. She'd been accepted by the coolest person she'd ever known, so it didn't matter if a bunch of punk kids rejected her.

Though they spent most of the day apart, they reunited every day after school in the parking lot. Debra would drive them home and they'd do homework in Debra's room. Celeste revealed her weakness was math, so Debra helped tutor her in exchange for Celeste's help with Biology.

Celeste glared down at her notebook, then shifted her irritation to Debra's nearly-full page. "I don't know how you can do science with your arms tied behind your back, but math gives you fits."

"Math is dull. Just numbers not doing anything. Science makes the numbers do stuff."

"Whatever, weirdo," Debra said.

With their mutual tutoring, they both did well in school for their first shared semester. After Christmas, they were allowed to switch electives. Celeste went to Art, Debra went to Music, and it was there that she met Wayne McSwan. He was the shy kid, the one who kept his eyes on the ground when he moved from class to class because the jocks would notice if he didn't. They picked on him from time to time, but mostly he seemed content to be a nonentity. Except in Music. He would later confide in Debra that he'd been taking classes all his life, that reading sheet music came as easily to him as reading comic books came to other kids. He was a virtuoso.

Just as Celeste had freed Debra from her shell, she saw Wayne as her chance to pay the effort forward. She felt stronger, cooler, and more confident because Celeste gave her the opportunity to be herself. So why couldn't she do the same thing for someone else? She sat next to him, listened to him ramble about "the beauty of the notes," and invited him out to lunch - he was forced to the backseat so Celeste could ride shotgun; some things were sacred. When the

Valentine's Day dance arrived, she tried not to laugh at how his voice trembled when he asked her to go with him.

"I'll only go if Celeste has a date. You got a friend you can hook her up with?"

Wayne looked up at her. "Celeste? I thought... nothing. Never mind."

Later that night, Debra called to see if anyone had asked Celeste.

"No one I'm interested in."

"You're being too picky. It's just one dance. You don't have to marry the guy."

Celeste chuckled on the other end of the line, then sighed out a "Yeah."

"Don't make me go alone!"

"You'll be going with your music man."

Debra rolled her eyes. "You know what I mean. Come on, Celeste. Please? Pretty please?"

"You go. I'll find my own fun, don't you worry."

Debra reluctantly agreed, then called Wayne and forced enthusiasm so he wouldn't feel it was a pity date. He was handsome and she really did enjoy spending time with him. She just wished she could share the night with her best friend as well. It would only be half as fun without Celeste to provide commentary on everyone's dresses and dance moves. She quashed her disappointment by focusing on how great the night would be, how awesome she would look in her dress, and how everyone would think she and Wayne were the coolest couple in school.

She stopped by Celeste's house on her way to pick up Wayne. She wanted to show off her dress and make one last appeal to get her best friend to come with them. It didn't matter that it was far too late for her to get a ticket. They could hang out in the parking lot all night for all she cared. She parked behind the strange car in Celeste's driveway and headed around to the always-unlocked back door. She didn't think very hard about why the car was there or whose it was. Subconsciously, she assumed Celeste's parents had friends who came over and then they all went out together in the Lafitte family sedan.

Celeste's bedroom faced the backyard. The window was open against the night's humidity, curtains apparently breathing as Debra approached. She could hear Tom Petty singing "Louisiana Rain" as she reached the window and pushed the curtains out of the way.

"Hey, loser~"

A woman was sitting on the bed, her blouse unbuttoned to reveal her bra. Her pants tangled on the mattress behind her like a twisted ribbon. Her legs were spread wide but Debra's view of anything obscene was blocked by the back of Celeste's head. Celeste wasn't wearing a shirt. She was sitting on her feet, the soles of which were pointed toward the window. The woman looked up and, despite her hair being down and her features being twisted in shock and fear, Debra recognized her as Miss Touhey, Celeste's History teacher.

"Gypsy..." Celeste said.

"I'm sorry so sorry I'm leaving."

Debra retreated from the window and ran around the house. She had just gotten to her car when the front door opened and Celeste came out. She was still tugging on a lilac shirt with a big blue butterfly on the chest as she ran barefoot across the lawn. Debra felt her ears burning as she fumbled with her keys. Celeste grabbed her arm and she dropped the keys.

"I didn't see..."

"Please don't tell anyone..."

"...anything I won't..."

"...we'd get in so much trouble and my parents..."

"...say anything I'm just gonna go..."

"...and she'd get fired and look at me please..."

She couldn't look at Celeste, couldn't risk a flashback to what she'd just witnessed. "You were... y-you were..."

"Please don't hate me."

Debra looked at her and saw tears in her eyes. "Why would I hate you?"

"Because that's what happened in Georgia when people found out." The tears rolled down her cheeks. "I didn't have any friends when we left. No one would even look at me in the halls. But I didn't have anyone like you back there. I'll never do it again, just don't hate me, Debra."

Debra stepped in and wrapped Celeste in a hug. "My name is Gypsy."

Celeste sobbed against her shoulder.

Debra didn't want to go to the dance after the revelation, but Celeste convinced her it wouldn't be fair to stand Wayne up. She promised to spill all the details another day and they separated with another lingering hug. Debra watched Celeste go back into the house and tried not to think very hard about what was happening inside. A teacher, an adult, a woman. She didn't know which one was worse. She pushed her hands against her face and tried to push all that aside to focus on the dance. Wayne noticed she was distracted but he was too nervous and sweaty-palmed to blame her.

The next morning, she drove to Celeste's house at six-thirty. Celeste was waiting for her on the porch, almost as if she was as eager to confess as Debra was to hear it. They drove to Lake Pontchartrain and found a secluded spot where they could talk without being overheard.

"I wrote a paper about Jean and Pierre Lafitte at the beginning of the year. My family isn't related to them, but it's a cool connection. Pirates are cool, you now? She really liked it. She thinks I have talent as a writer. I told her I had some short stories but I'd never let anyone read them."

Debra tried not to feel betrayed. "I didn't know."

"You wouldn't have. They're all... I mean, I work out a lot of stuff through 'em. Stuff about... girls. I don't know how the hell I got the guts to hand them over to her, knowing she might have thought I was sick or a pervert. But she just asked if I was okay. If I had anyone I could trust or talk to." She was crying now. "I thought about you, Gypsy, but I saw the way you were looking when you caught us. You thought it was gross."

"I would've thought the same thing if you'd been with a guy."

"Really? Exactly the same?"

Debra blushed. "I don't know."

"Yeah." She took a Starburst out of her pocket and unwrapped it without looking. "She told me she felt the same way. It was all me, though. I'm the one who kissed her. I'm the one who asked her to touch me. I had to beg. You know what's sick about it? I was glad she could get in trouble. She could lose her job and be run out of town. Shit, I'm underage, so she could go to jail. But she was willing to risk all that just to be with me. That made me feel real special."

Debra looked out over the water. She tried to imagine how she would have felt in that situation. Alone. Terrified of someone finding out. She remembered dancing with Wayne the night before and how she was starting to Feel Things for him. If she wanted to hold his hand in the hall, she could. If she wanted to kiss him between classes... hell, there were enough couples playing tonsil hockey that no one would notice another one.

But if Celeste kissed Miss Touhey... if she even sent a

Valentine card to a girl, she would be mocked. She would be called names and people would tell jokes behind her back.

Debra reached out and took Celeste's hand. "You don't think I'm gross."

"Aw, Celestine," Debra said. "You put ketchup on your scrambled eggs. Of course you're gross."

Celeste laughed and curled up with her head on Debra's lap. Debra stroked her friend's hair. She didn't think she was quite okay with the new information, but she knew she would have time to process it. She wasn't going to risk losing a friend over something as ridiculous as who she was attracted to. It would be like if Celeste shunned her for liking Wayne instead of some meathead jock. People liked who they liked and it was stupid to judge them for that.

The next time Debra saw Miss Touhey in the hall, the teacher froze and stared at her as if she'd pulled out a gun. Debra had just smiled kindly and nodded as she walked past.

"Hello, Miss Touhey."

"Miss Kent."

A few weeks later, Debra and Wayne "went all the way." It was her eighteenth birthday and she wanted to do something special to mark the occasion. At first they were just going to do things with their hands, but it quickly became apparent neither of them would be satisfied with that. So she suggested the backseat. Wayne was an adorable combination of eager and nervous, so she kept whispering to him that everything was going to be okay.

She didn't start sweating until it was over, like her body was so unprepared that it couldn't catch up. Wayne lay on top of her and caught his breath. He whispered that it was amazing, but she was just sore and felt gross under her dress. But she kissed him and told him it was great. Eventually she used her mouth on him, just to see what it was like, and she enjoyed it more than she thought she would. He did the same to her and she liked that a *lot*, though she did once flash to what she'd seen through Celeste's window and almost killed the mood.

When she broke the news to Celeste, she got a high-five and a big hug. "He didn't push you into anything, did he?"

"No, no. It was my idea. I had to tell him it was okay about ninety times."

Celeste said, "Okay, then. Then it's great." She slung an arm across Debra's shoulders. "I'm proud of you, kid."

They did it more. She got better at it, and started to really enjoy it. Things really took an upswing after Wayne lost some of his anxiety and became an actual partner.

"You can still ask me if I'm liking it," Debra whispered into his ear one night after they finished.

"Yeah?"

"Yeah." She grinned. "I like that part where you're talking."

As they got better, they also got dumber. They were almost caught by Debra's parents on a few occasions, and she was forced to have a conversation with her father while pants-less and wrapped in her blanket hoping he didn't ask her to come to the living room for anything. Neither of them were comfortable going into a convenience store to buy condoms, so they used whatever Debra could snag from her older brother's desk drawer without him noticing. And when they ran out, she didn't think it was that big of a deal.

Three weeks before graduation, she called Celeste. She had waited until everyone was out of the house and tried to keep her breathing steady so she wouldn't cry.

"Do you ever... like... just sk-skip one of your periods?"

"What? No. How would you even do that?"

She started crying silently, but Celeste could hear her sniffling.

"Oh, shit, Gypsy."

"I'm scared."

"Don't be scared. I'm on my way over."

They went to the lake. Debra stared at the water and Celeste rubbed a hand up and down her back. Neither of them spoke about the options; they both knew there was no good or easy way out of the situation. Debra stared at her hands, watched the fingers trembling, and pressed them hard against her face. Celeste bent down and kissed her shoulder.

"Whatever you want to do, I'm your sidekick. Doesn't matter if I disagree with your choice, don't matter if it's against my religion. If you decide it's the right thing to do, I'm right there. You need cash, you need a ride somewhere, you know who to call."

Debra snorted. "I don't think I'd fit on the pegs of your bike if I have a huge belly."

"So you can ride on my shoulders."

Debra laughed and wiped her face. "Ask me how I could be so stupid."

Celeste clucked her tongue against her teeth. "You made a mistake. It's~"

"No, I'm serious. I need you to do it before my parents do."

Celeste took a deep breath. "You are a smart girl, Debra. What the hell were you thinking? Having sex is one thing. Sure, experiment, whatever. But no condom? That is the dumbest thing I've ever heard, and now you're stuck between a rock and a hard place." Debra was crying. "Gypsy, I didn't–"

"It's fine. Thank you." She sniffled. "They're going to murder me."

"Then I'll come in and kill them right back. No one hurts my girl, not even the people who made her."

Debra put her head down on Celeste's shoulder. "I love you."

"I love you, too." She kissed Debra's forehead and sighed heavily. "If you were just gay and dating me, this whole thing would be impossible."

Debra laughed and shoved Celeste before pulling her close for a tight hug.

3

Debra waited two weeks before she told her parents. She wanted to be absolutely sure she'd missed the period and that it wasn't just late. She looked up information about abortion clinics, but no part of her ever felt like that would be a viable option. She lay in bed at night with her hands folded over her stomach trying to imagine a life growing there. She thought back over the years to things she'd experienced with her parents and tried to reverse their roles. Suddenly she was the one saying no to candy and toys. She was the one soothing bruises and scrapes and bumps. She was the one making room in her bed for a little thing frightened by a nightmare.

She told Wayne and watched the blood drain out of his face. She felt like she'd pressured him to have sex and now that the worst-case scenario actually happened, she was coming back to close the trap. She'd told Celeste as much and got a loving swat upside the head.

"You force that boy into the backseat? He say you should wait when you didn't have a condom?"

"Well..."

"Nope. No, you may have wanted it as much as he did, but he wasn't innocent in it. He knew the consequences and he can damn well live with them."

She thought about how much he loved music. He was going to

get a scholarship and go to college. He was going to make something out of himself. Debra watched him and saw every hope and dream he ever had slipping away. He saw the future that had been laid out in front of him crumbling. Her future had been empty. Her plans had been nonexistent. She couldn't believe she was going to be one of those girls who let the boy off the hook; he'd been instrumental in what happened so he should bear the responsibility.

"You ever think about the right thing?"

"Huh?" He sounded out of breath.

Debra said, "The right thing. You know the right thing would be us getting married and having this baby and making a family."

He inhaled and nodded, eyes locked on the ground.

"But what kind of marriage would that be? What shitty life would that be?" She pushed her hair out of her face. "It would be a mistake we'd have to fix, but we'd be doing it years down the road. Starting all over with the baggage of a divorce and everything behind us. The right thing and the smart thing are two different choices right now. I want you to do the smart thing."

His eyes were watering. "I can't leave you by yourself."

Debra smiled sadly. "You would eventually. You'd be miserable. You'd resent me and the baby. You'd cheat on me, I'd catch you, I'd cut your balls off, it would be a whole thing."

He apparently didn't know if he should laugh, so he exhaled sharply and rubbed his forehead.

"I want you to want to do the right thing."

"I do. And the right thing, I think, would be... to help you... but not to force anything we-we're not ready for." He looked cautiously at her from the corner of his eye. "Right?"

Debra leaned in and kissed him. "I think that's the right thing and the smart thing."

"But you'd be alone!"

"No," Debra said, putting her hands over her stomach. "I'm never alone. Not anymore."

Telling her parents went much, much worse. Once the news was out, her father simply stared at the wall as her mother began making a list. Her car was now a thing of the past, as was her life outside of school and home. They were going to the doctor as soon as she could make an appointment to confirm the situation was dire as they feared. "Even if you're wrong," her mother said, "all these punishments stand. Having sex at your age? What were you thinking, Debra?"

She just stared at her shoes and answered with monosyllables. "Okay. No. Wayne. No. I don't know. Yes." Sometimes she broke the trend: "A couple of times" and "I'm sorry."

The inquisition finally ended. "Go to your room. Get comfortable there, because you aren't going to see much else."

She went down the hall and lay face-down on her bed. She dozed just enough to lose track of time, but the sun had gotten closer to the horizon when she heard a soft knock on her door. Her mother's voice was so quiet it almost sounded like a different person.

"Are you okay?"

"Yes, ma'am."

"I love you."

Debra pressed her face against the pillow. "I love you too, Mom."

"I made you a plate in the kitchen. You're going to need to change your diet."

"Okay."

She heard her mother's retreat down the hall and wiped her face before she went to retrieve her dinner. She noticed that her hand already moved to her stomach of its own accord, resting on the spot that would one day soon begin to swell and grow with her child. It still seemed unreal but, now that everyone knew, she couldn't imagine an alternative where her life continued without the baby.

"You're stuck with me, kiddo."

Rumors swirled over the last few days of school. Celeste tried to deflect some of the gossip, but by graduation everyone seemed to have figured out Debra was pregnant. When she walked across the stage to accept her diploma, she heard someone in the crowd cover the word "slut" with a cough. She ignored it, smiled at the principal and shook his hand, then went back to her seat. Kent and Lafitte were close enough alphabetically for their small school, but Alice Knox was placed between them. Debra leaned back to look past Alice, and Celeste leaned back as well to give her a wink. That was all Debra needed to forget the losers and focus on her accomplishment.

And then it was summer. The first summer that wasn't just a hiatus between classes, but the starting line for the rest of her life. She thought it was appropriate that her stomach grew larger with every passing day. She had stopped being a student and a child; the time for being an adult was at hand. There were kids in her class who wouldn't get that memo for years.

She read about everything she needed to do. She changed her diet. She took supplements and vitamins. She went to the doctor as often as she could. Her parents supported her to the point where she thought they understood. She thought that up until the night she started talking about names over dinner. Her father looked at her mother like he expected gunfire, and she carefully twisted her fork in her hands before she spoke.

"Honey... I don't think you'll get to name it."

Debra tilted her head. "Who else would?"

"Whoever ends up adopting it."

"He."

"Debra..."

"Not it. And I'm not giving him up for adoption. I'm keeping it."

Her mother put down her fork. "Honey, we haven't talked about this because I thought we all agreed it would be for the best if you gave it to someone who is better equipped to handle a child."

Debra's eyes filled with tears. "I'm not giving him away."

"We can't support that decision, sweetheart."

She took a deep breath and closed her eyes, well aware that she was suddenly at a major turning point in her life. In one, she was simply inconvenienced for nine months before life got back to normal. All it would cost was a child she would always wonder about, who would always wonder about her. On the other path, she saw hardship and solitude and struggle. Her hands were shaking. She was terrified, but she had already accepted the child as part of who she was, and of who she was going to be.

"Fine. Can I go to my room now?"

"Of course."

She pushed her chair back. "I'll be out of the house by the end of the month."

Her father finally spoke. "Debra, that's not necessary."

"You either support me or you don't," she said as she walked out of the room.

She didn't start crying until she was back in her room. She didn't speak to anyone until two mornings later when she met Celeste outside her house. Celeste was seated on the concrete front porch, legs splayed out in front of them in a wide V, wearing her purple-and-gray uniform from Cheryl's Shack. The brim of her cap was pulled low over her eyes as she listened to the play-by-play. When it was over she pushed out her bottom lip and leaned forward with her arms across her knees. She squinted across the street and then nodded.

"Okay."

"What do you mean?" Debra's eyes had started watering as she retold the story. She wiped the moisture away with the back of her wrist.

"I'll do it. I mean, I'd like to have a little more in savings, but you have some saved, right? I mean, I know a lot of that is going toward the baby. But you can pay for groceries sometimes. Or buy me dinner. I'll let you use the discount at Cheryl's."

"What are you talking about?"

Celeste said, "Your share of the rent. Of the apartment we're going to get." She slung an arm across Debra's shoulders. "You're not going to do this alone, Gypsy."

Debra buried her face against her friend's shoulder. "You don't have to do this."

"You're just pushing up my schedule a little. Hell, without a shove, I might have never have had the balls. So yeah. Sounds good. I'll even help you think of a name."

"Oh?"

"Mm-hmm. Just for the record? Celestine Kent is an awful name. I won't be offended if you choose something else."

Debra laughed and wrapped her arms around Celeste's waist.

"If we're moving out on our own anyway," Debra said, 'maybe we should think about going all the way. Choose a whole new city instead of just skipping down the street. I mean, I know you just got here and all..."

Celeste said, "Eh, I'm not in love with it. I got what I needed from Metairie." She rubbed Debra's arm. "Where you thinking about going?"

"I don't know."

"This is Loo-se-yan. We could just get in the car and drive north until we find something nice."

Debra shook her head. "No. We can't do that. We're choosing the place my baby is going to grow up. It's going to affect her entire life, consciously and unconsciously. We have to pick the right place so she grows up right."

Celeste said, "She?"

"Hm?"

"You've been calling the baby 'he' since you found out about it. Something change?"

Debra shrugged. "I don't know. It just happened." She tucked her hair behind her ears. "I don't want anywhere like New York. Everyone wants to be New York. I want my baby to be something unique. And not Los Angeles. Too hot. Too much fakeness."

Celeste pursed her lips and thought. "If you choose somewhere like Wyoming or Nebraska she could be a cowgirl."

"Yeah..."

"You don't have to decide right now."

Debra said, "I better figure it out soon, though. Once I hit the third trimester, I can't fly. And you won't want to be in a car with someone who has to pee every twenty minutes."

"Just relax your mind and it'll come."

"You think?"

"I think everyone has a little bit of psychic in 'em. Not, like, helping the cops find a missing kid like on *Starsky & Hutch*. But little things we don't even know are psychic. Flashes when we know everything is going to be okay or everything is going to go to shit. A lot of people never talk about it because they think it's intuition or something normal like that."

Debra said, "So just wait for my brain to give me a psychic flash about where to go."

"Yep."

"Okay. Sounds good."

She spent the next few days looking over atlases at the library. Sometimes she checked them out so she could go through them with Celeste on her lunchbreak. They were seated together in the back booth with a big book open in front of them. Celeste reached to turn the page, but Debra stopped her.

"It's gorgeous."

Celeste looked at the picture Debra was pointing at. The city was beautiful and green, a slice of nature curving around a beautiful blue harbor. Mountains were visible in the distance like a wall protecting the city from the rest of the world, and amid the downtown buildings was a single beautiful spire stretching toward the sky. Debra dragged her fingers over the picture, eyes wide with a smile spreading across her face.

"Seattle," she whispered.

"Seattle," Celeste said. "I think I could do Seattle."

Debra slumped against Celeste and smiled down at the picture.

It was a huge step, something monumental that was dwarfed only by the fact she was creating a life, but with Celeste by her side, she had faith it would all work out for the best.

4

Not everything went right. Not everything that could go wrong did. There were fights with both sets of parents. There were plane tickets to buy and transportation to arrange. Despite insisting that they wouldn't continue supporting her, Debra's parents continued paying for all of her doctor appointments. They didn't say anything, they simply sent the checks in and told the doctor to refuse any payment she tried to offer. She wanted to defy them out of spite, but money was far too precious for pride.

She was three and a half months pregnant when she and Celeste boarded the plane for their new lives. They'd known each other for fifteen months by that point, but neither of them had any doubts about what they were doing or throwing their lot in with each other. They held hands over the middle of America and Celeste reassured Debra everything would be okay at least seven times before they reached the Rockies.

When they came in for a landing, Celeste squeezed Debra's hand. "You ready, Gypsy? 'Cause once we step off this plane, everything moves in high speed."

Debra took a deep breath. She exhaled and nodded slowly. They walked off the plane together, Celeste carrying both bags so Debra didn't have to ("You're already carrying a person," she said as she tugged the bag from the overhead compartment) and they walked into the crisp, surprisingly cold Seattle winter air.

Celeste proved to be right. As soon as they left the airport, everything seemed to explode around them. They found the apartment that Debra's brother's friend's parents knew about. They unpacked and began setting up their home. A week later, Celeste started her new job at Safeway. A week after that, Debra was hired as a "placement specialist" at a temp agency. Wayne sent checks at semi-regular intervals along with short notes about what he was up to.

Celeste scanned one. "Let's see, not paying for doctors, not carrying around a goddamn baby, not cutting all ties with her parents in order to keep his child. But he did have a little bit of a flu last week. Poor baby."

Debra said, "If I wanted him here, he'd be here. It wouldn't be fair to any of us to force him to stick around."

Celeste shrugged and tossed the note onto the coffee table. "At least he's sending money. For now, anyway. Guess that's something."

On another night when they were having their elegant dinner of mac-and-cheese, Debra sheepishly said, "Do you want to go to bed with me?"

Celeste coughed on her milk. "Say what?"

Debra shrugged and avoided eye contact. "You uprooted your whole life for me. Came here to help me. I just thought... I don't know... it's stupid. I thought since you were gay, maybe you... wanted to. And if you did, I mean..."

"I don't want to sleep with you, Debra. I'm doing all of this because you needed help. You're my friend and I love you."

"Okay. I just... everything you've done for me... I don't know how I could repay it."

Celeste pushed her plate toward the middle of the table. "Start with doing the dishes and we'll go from there."

At seven months, Celeste met Jenny at the bus stop. Jenny was older - it seemed to be a theme with Celeste's choices - and worked as a receptionist at a law firm. They started dating and soon Celeste was hardly ever at home. Debra was torn between feeling abandoned and wishing her friend well in her new relationship. She didn't want to jinx it or ruin things by complaining, so she just stayed home after work and watched TV by herself, ate dinner in a silent apartment, and went to bed without knowing if Celeste would come home that night or not.

The closer it got to her due date, the more present Celeste became. Her relationship with Jenny no longer required constant contact so she was able to take a few nights off to take care of her friend. She was there when Debra decided the cramps she'd been feeling were more than just indigestion and hustled her to the car they shared.

"We still don't know her name," Debra said between breathing exercises.

Celeste said, "We can think about that after."

"I want her to have a name when she's born. She needs to come into this world with a name."

"Okay. I get that. Uh... Sarah Kent. Michelle Kent. Barbara."

"No..." She closed her eyes. "I could really use one of those psychic flashes right about now."

Celeste waited until they were at a red light to reach over and squeeze Debra's hand. "Catherine. Elizabeth. Lindsey."

"Those names are too long," Debra said. "I want something short. Simple."

"Um... uh... shit, why can't I think of any short names! Leigh?"

Debra grunted. "Leigh is good. Leigh Kent... Lisa Kent..."

"Lana Kent..."

"Lana." Debra reached out and squeezed Celeste's leg. "Lana. Yes. Lana Kent."

Celeste grinned. "Did I just name your baby?"

Debra laughed breathlessly. "I think you did." She repeated the name again under her breath. "Lana Kent. Lana Kent. This is my daughter... Lana Kent."

Eight hours later, the squealing infant was placed in her arms. The nurse let Celeste come in and see, and Debra looked at her with eyes swollen shut by tears.

"All the clichés, huh?"

Debra nodded. "Every damn one of 'em." She bent down and kissed the baby's forehead. "I promise," she whispered, unsure of how she would finish the thought. "I promise. I promise."

Celeste kissed Debra's hair and laughed. "Me too."

The baby seemed to realize crying wasn't going to get it anything. She closed her mouth and opened her eyes, big black eyes that focused first on Debra and then on Celeste. She sucked her bottom lip into her mouth and made a quiet, helpless whimper that made Debra hold her tighter. They'd come out to Seattle to start a new life for this little baby. They had taken six months to build the foundation. Now it was time to get to living.

Everything in her life was suddenly about Lana. Sleep schedules, feeding schedules, when she would go out or stay inside. The apartment had to be baby-proofed. Money was more of an abstract concept than a real thing she could touch. She was barely aware of time passing because the days flowed into each other. An hour walking the baby around the living room in the middle of the night, going to bed at dawn, waking up only a half hour later because the baby was crying again. Celeste started spending the night at Jenny's and Debra didn't blame her.

Time seemed to inch forward until suddenly it was Lana's first birthday. Celeste's gift was to babysit for the entire afternoon so Debra could nap and go see a movie. She spent the entire time worrying about how the baby was. She ran the entire way home, uphill, and cried when Lana was placed in her arms.

"I appreciate the gift," she said, "but next time maybe not the whole afternoon."

Celeste laughed and brushed Debra's hair out of her face. "Deal."

Lana continued to grow. Debra went back to work and Celeste continued to see Jenny. The second birthday arrived, seemingly only a few weeks after the first. Celeste got promoted to shift manager. Debra stayed at her job, putting other people into temporary positions at companies all over Seattle. She managed to put away a little money, aware that eventually she would lose her roommate when Celeste moved in with her girlfriend.

She talked to Wayne on the phone. She sent him pictures of Lana. The interval between checks began to grow, but not to a degree where she felt comfortable complaining. Any money was a help, and maybe he wasn't doing very well. She understood there would be times when he couldn't afford to send anything. Those were the same months she ate whatever cereal Lana didn't finish and called it dinner.

Lana was walking and talking, a whole person taking up space in Debra's apartment. She tried to remember that just five years earlier she'd been a child herself. Wondering where life would take her. Wondering what her life would look like. Somehow she didn't imagine anything close to this tiny apartment with a demanding toddler taking up all of her energy.

"Where Daddy?"

They were in the park, Lana was three, and she was watching a boy playing with his father.

"Daddy's in Boston. He's going to school there."

"Why?"

"Because that's what I wanted. I chose this life, but he would have seen it as a trap. So I told him he didn't have to come. And he didn't. So..." She smoothed down a flyaway feather of hair from the top of Lana's head. "So I get you all to myself."

A few months later, Wayne called. He'd met someone. It was serious. It would be hard to explain why he was sending so much of his paycheck to Seattle.

"Hard to explain," Debra said, standing in front of the kitchen window, staring at her shoes that desperately needed to be replaced. "Really."

"I've been a good guy," Wayne insisted. "I've helped."

"Yeah. Almost four whole years. You're a prince."

Wayne said, "You said you didn't want me involved."

"No, I..." She closed her eyes. Maybe she had. Maybe she'd only thought she was setting him free to make the choice to do the right thing. Maybe it didn't matter. "So four years is all you're willing to give your daughter."

"A daughter I've never even met."

"Well, it's not like I can afford a plane ticket to Boston."

"You think I can fly out to Seattle whenever I want? I have responsibilities here, you know."

Debra squeezed her eyes shut. "You want to be done with her? Fine. You're done."

She hung up on him and pressed her forehead against the glass.

Lana turned four. Celeste finally moved in with Jenny, but she was still around enough that it didn't feel like she was gone. They still went to the park where Celeste taught Lana games Debra had never heard of. Debra sat on the bench, one leg crossed over the other, and watched the two most important people in her life playing in the grass.

When "Auntie Celeste" begged for a break, Lana took a dump truck out of Debra's backpack and started rolling it across the pavement. Celeste sighed as she sat next to Debra.

"That little girl is using up all her energy for her whole life today."

"Today and every day," Debra said, but she smiled as she watched Lana scoot the toy in a wide circle. "She's got an endless supply."

Celeste sighed. "So... listen..."

Debra tensed. "Something bad is coming, isn't it?"

"Yeah." She rubbed her palms over her slacks. "Jenny decided to go to law school. She got the acceptance letter last week."

"That's great news!"

"Yeah. In Chicago."

Debra stared at Lana. "Oh."

"Yeah."

"So how are you going to break up with her?"

Celeste looked at her. "I—"

"I'm kidding, Celestine." Debra hugged her tightly. "Of course you have to go. You two are practically married. I mean, if you could…”

“Yeah. But what about you?”

“I have to fly solo eventually. There’s no way I’m letting you stall your life just because of me. You’ve already given up way too much as it is.”

Celeste cupped the back of Debra’s head. “What are you talking about, giving up? Gypsy, when I met you, I was the mistake. I was the accidental child who got dragged along when my brother got into college. You looked at me and you saw *me*. You have any idea how big that was for me? I flew under all the radars when I was growing up.”

“No one ever paid attention to me, either,” Debra said. “You’re the one who made me believe I was worth looking at. Worthy of… you know, being listened to.”

Celeste said, “We’ve come a long way from you riding on the pegs of my bike, huh?”

“We made it together.”

Lana came back with her truck and Debra helped her choose a new toy to play with. “When do you leave?”

“A month or two. Jenny’s going first and she’s going to find the apartment, get everything set up. Then I’ll go out and join her.”

Debra twisted on the bench and hugged her. “I’m going to miss you.”

“All you’ve gotta do is call me, and I’ll fly, drive, crawl, ride my bike…”

Debra laughed. “Deal. Same goes for you.”

Celeste said, “I feel like I’m abandoning you.”

“You’re living your own life. No one’s going to fault you for that. I’ll never be able to repay you for everything you’ve done for me. Even the nights when you brought take-out so I wouldn’t have to cook. You were a lifesaver.” She looked at Lana and started to cry. “Without you, I’d have given her up. Thank you so much.”

“You’re welcome, Debra.”

They held each other on the bench while Lana, oblivious to the emotions playing out behind her, taught a plastic T-Rex how to fly.

Epilogue

Debra opened her eyes and stared at the ceiling over her bed. She had been sleeping all day, but the effort of keeping her eyes open was almost too much for her. There was no one else in the room so she gave in. The diagnosis had come as unexpectedly as everything else in her life. Cancer. Malignant. Very little to be done. She'd gone to the doctor expecting bad news, but that had been the absolute worst case scenario. It wasn't just bad news; it was life-ending. She was going to die at thirty-three, unless she lasted another month in which case she could claim thirty-four.

When she opened her eyes again, Lana had appeared in the corner chair. Lana, her beautiful fifteen-year-old daughter. Her hair was so long it touched the middle of her back. Currently one wave of it was covering her face. Her feet were up in the chair, legs bent out to either side like a grasshopper. She had her Walkman in her hands but the headphones were around her neck.

"Hey, little girl."

Lana's head snapped up. "Mama. Hey." She unfolded her limbs and moved closer to the bed. "I wanted to let you sleep."

"You should be asleep."

"It's the afternoon."

"Then you should be in school."

Lana shook her head. "Not a chance."

Debra smiled and cupped Lana's cheek. "School." Lana's face wrinkled and she put her head down on Debra's chest. Debra moved her hand into Lana's hair. "I know, sweetie. But you have to, okay? No reason for this to take both of us out."

"Okay."

"Okay," Debra repeated. "I'm proud of you, kid."

Lana sniffled.

"I am. You're so strong. I was lucky to get to know you."

"I was lucky. You're my mom."

Debra smiled. "Good girl." She bent down and kissed Lana's hair. "Come on, sit up. Is today when Auntie Celeste comes in?"

Lana sat up. "Yeah. I'm picking her up after school and we'll come right here."

Debra smiled. She couldn't wait to see her friend again. It had been far too long. Celeste came out when Debra was diagnosed, and she helped find ways for Lana to stay in school and make ends meet by herself. Celeste and Jennifer were having problems of their own, and Debra was grateful for any time Celeste could spare to come out and lend a hand.

"Lana... one thing before you go. Life is tough. Don't try to take it on alone. Find a friend, find someone who will go to the mat for you. You might not recognize who it is at first, but when you do get that, don't let it go. Not for anything."

"I got it, mama."

Debra nodded. "Good. Wake me up when you get back with Celeste. I don't want a minute to go to waste."

"Okay." She stretched up and kissed Debra's smooth head, the chemo having taken all her hair. "Sweet dreams, mama."

"Be good. Learn a lot of stuff."

Lana let her hand slip out of Debra's. Debra watched her go, but she was asleep before the door closed behind her.

Falling asleep was different, now that she knew there was a chance she might not wake up. The darkness no longer seemed relaxing. It was vast and endless. She tried to notice as the details slipped away but it snuck up on her every time. This time she found herself instantly in what she assumed was a dream. She was still in her hospital gown, still bald and thin, but she was standing in a hallway. The far end of the hallway was bathed in blue and yellow lights. A crowd was cheering as music played. Debra moved toward the noise.

It was a nightclub. Either very small or seemingly small because of how many people were crammed into the space in front of the stage. Debra stayed against the back wall rather than try to move closer. She could see the band clearly from where she was. Four girls: blonde with a violin, black woman on keyboard, Indian on drums. The guitarist was white, her back to the crowd, but Debra knew who it was even without seeing her face. Debra's brother had given Lana a guitar when she was a little girl and from that moment on, it became her fifth appendage.

Lana turned and approached the microphone. Debra couldn't believe how beautiful her daughter was, how perfectly confident she was standing behind the microphone. She clapped a hand over her mouth and let her tears fall.

"Quiet, you ruffians!" Lana shouted.

That only made the crowd cheer louder. Lana grinned and stuck her tongue between her teeth. She played a chord and then grabbed the microphone.

"Seriously, shush. I want to talk about something before we play this next song." The crowd demurred slightly. "This next song is a cover of an oldie... some of you might know it. But it has special meaning for me. Today would have been my mother's birthday."

The audience applauded for her and Lana paused to take it in.

"My mother was a... god, she was so strong. I look back on how we lived and what she had to do, and I have no idea how she pulled it off. She sacrificed so much for me. And she always found time for me. We would have dance parties in the kitchen while she was cooking dinner. She taught me how to drive when I was fourteen because we lived in Seattle where the streets are vertical and she assumed I could use all the practice I could get."

There was another laugh.

"Our song 'Holding My Breath' was written about her and it's about all those moments in life when you're just beaten down and beaten up and everything is coming at you. The bills are due, the engine won't turn over, your favorite pair of glasses break, dinner's burnt. Mom taught me that you can get through those moments if you just don't give up. She would say just look around at all the good things you have to fight for, and the fight for them.

"My mother had a nickname. And it came from her favorite song, which she always used to sing to me. Now... don't ask why my mama was singing this song to a five-year-old. I didn't know what it meant. I just knew it made my mother dance and laugh and sing. And it sounded like a fun circus song. So in honor of my mom, and everything she did for me, I want to play that song tonight. I hope you like it. Happy birthday, Gypsy."

She stepped back and nodded to the pianist, who played the opening note of "Gypsies, Tramps, and Thieves." Lana joined in and enough of the crowd recognized the tune that they cheered again.

"I was born in the wagon of a travelin' show," Lana sang, "mama used to dance for the money they'd throw..."

Debra watched with awe as her daughter commanded the entire room with her strong, sure voice. The guitar hummed under her fingers. The lights reflected off the sweat on her bare arms, her face. The rest of the band sang with her on the chorus and Debra could feel the drum of the music in her chest. Four women singing out in harmony, turning words like "gypsy" and "tramp" into badges of honor.

When they reached the chorus, Lana kicked away from the microphone and spun around to face the other girls. The violin screeched and the drum pounded. The keys whistled through the interlude, and Debra watched as Lana faced each of the three girls in turn, sharing a moment with all three of them before she returned to her position at the front of the stage to finish the song.

The song eventually ended and the crowd roared. Lana stepped back and bowed her head, turning away to surreptitiously wipe her hand across her cheeks before she spoke again.

"Thank you. Thanks. That was for my mama. Debra Churchwell Kent. Love you, Mama. Mama."

She opened her eyes, the sound of the music still ringing in her ears as she looked up at a suddenly younger version of the woman she'd just seen dominating a room. Her heart swelled with pride and she gripped Lana's hand.

"You're so talented, baby."

Lana smiled, confused but welcoming the compliment. "Thanks, Mama. Hey. Look who's here."

She moved to one side so Debra could see Celeste without sitting up. "Celestine."

"Hey, Gypsy," Celeste said, coming closer to the bed.

Lana backed up. "I'm going to go down to the cafeteria. Give you some time."

"You don't have to go," Celeste said.

"I should eat. And you need some time to catch up. So... I'll be back soon."

Celeste sat on the edge of the bed, sandwiching one of Debra's hands between both of hers. "How you holding up?"

"As well as I can," Debra said. "But you know there's no good news waiting here, so let's focus on you. What's going on in Chicago?"

"It's all going well. Jennifer wishes she could've come, but she has court. She sent her love."

"Thank her for letting me borrow you for a little while."

Celeste patted Debra's hand. Neither of them knew what to say to fill the silence, to build what was most likely going to be their final conversation.

"That girl of yours is something else."

Debra smiled brightly. "She's amazing. Beautiful and talented. Make her sing for you before you leave. Her voice is just so... so wonderful."

"She said she was going to be a dancer."

"She dances, she plays guitar, she sings. Whatever she does, she's going to end up in the spotlight. I guarantee you that."

Celeste said, "Oh, you guarantee it, huh?"

"I do. You remember what you once said about... psychic flashes? How we all get these little visions we think are dreams or whatever." Celeste nodded. "I think I had one about Lana."

"Oh?"

"I think she's going to be okay."

Celeste nodded. "Well, that's good to hear."

Debra cleared her throat and grimaced at the tremors of pain that washed through her chest. "Tell me more," she said. "Tell me about where you and Jennifer live. I want to know everything."

There was enough room for Celeste to stretch out next to Debra, so she did. They faced each other and Celeste began telling Debra about their apartment building, the neighbors, the squirrel who lived in their courtyard. At some point during the story, Lana came back in and sat quietly in the chair so she wouldn't interrupt, chewing on a sandwich and smiling at the funny parts of Celeste's story. Debra began to drift off in the middle of the story and Celeste stopped.

"Don't stop now," Debra whispered. "I'm still listening."

"You sure?"

"Mm-hmm."

Celeste went on. Debra would never have planned her life the way it ended up. But she loved Seattle, and she adored the baby who had grown up into one of the most amazing daughters anyone could have hoped for, and she was spending her final hours with the best friend she'd ever had. It wasn't a life she would have scripted but it was also a life she would never trade for anything. She might have changed the ending if she had that ability. She would want to see Lana grow up, be there for her in times of hardship, but no one got everything they wanted. Everyone had to deal with disappointment, and leaving early was the only thing she could really complain about.

She drifted off to the sound of Celeste's voice and her daughter's laughter, knowing she wouldn't have traded the treasures she'd been given for anything.

CLOTHES MAKETH THE MAN

HANNAH DIDN'T even want to go to the party, almost left the invitation on the fridge and stayed in to treat herself to her own version of Netflix and chill: DVDs and ice cream. But after she dressed in her trusty sweats, she caught a glimpse of herself in the closet mirror. She was a young, successful woman with plenty to offer a partner, and she was about to get into bed at six-thirty on a Saturday with a pint of Ben & Jerry? She refused to give in to that when she actually did have somewhere to be. She changed into something flashy, did her hair and makeup, and still had time to wait for an Uber without being late.

The party was being thrown by a friend from work. An acquaintance, really. A woman she'd only barely shared three words with, to be completely honest, but it was a chance to get out of her apartment and socialize. When she arrived at the building, she smoothed a hand over her dress and checked the time as she rode up in the elevator. She was actually on time. She didn't know if that was a faux pas; was she supposed to be fashionably late? The lobby had seemed abandoned, so maybe everyone else was waiting ten or fifteen minutes.

On the fifth floor, she saw that the door to apartment 502 was standing open. She could hear music and conversation and let her anxiety go. The hostess, Debra, greeted her enthusiastically and accidentally let it slip that she really didn't think she would come. "Everyone is going to be so thrilled to see you," she said. "Let me show you where the refreshments are."

She got a beer and positioned herself where the music wasn't too loud and there wasn't much foot traffic. It was a place where she could interact and be seen as approachable without forcing herself into any conversations. She danced with herself to the music and tried not to mentally calculate how quickly she could leave without seeming rude. Forty-five minutes was the bare minimum, and two hours seemed like too much.

Hannah was still trying to work out the time frame when she spotted him. Tall and slender, but with wide shoulders. He was wearing a blazer over a white V-neck shirt that was cut just right to reveal the hint of a tattoo on the curve of his shoulder and creeping up onto his neck. She loved his hair, dark black and shaved on the sides with a lank wing dropping down over his right eye. He was absolutely gorgeous.

She couldn't take her eyes off of him as he made his way through the crowd, pausing now and then to talk to other guests. Hannah thought back to the vision at her apartment, the sweats and the ice cream, and forced herself out of the comfortable corner and moved on an intercept path. She met up with him at the same time he finished talking to someone. He was smiling at whatever the other guest had said and turned to lock his gaze on her.

"Hello," he said.

"Hannah Nygaard." She realized an introduction required a handshake, so she extended her arm. "I'm... sorry, I'm Hannah Nygaard. I work with Debra."

He smiled and took her hand. Nice grip, and the way he moved... rolling his shoulders and dipping his head just a little as if he was trying to sneak in a bow. "Hey. Regan Patterson."

"Regan. That's an interesting name. Isn't there a soccer— er, football player named Regan Poole?"

"Yeah, that's right," he said.

"I think he's Welsh."

"So am I. Well, on my grandparents' side. You like football?"

Hannah tried not to sound over-eager. "I do. I call it soccer a lot just because... you know, born and bred American. Habits are hard to break. Besides, we have a football. So it's confusing." She was talking too fast. She cleared her throat and stopped to breathe. "But yes, yes, I... I like football a lot. The European kind. American, not so much."

"All right, all right. Cool. Most people I meet are all about the American sport."

"That's what we get for hanging out with Americans."

"Guess so." He bobbed his head agreeably. His chin was pointed and he had perfect cheekbones. He looked like a damn model. And those eyes... blue or green, it was hard to tell in the apartment light. He put his hands in his pockets and swayed a bit to stand on the balls of his feet. "So are you enjoying yourself, Hannah?"

"At the party?"

"Or in general," Regan said.

Hannah smiled and shrugged. "Can't complain about either."

He returned her smile. "That's great. Uh, listen," he touched her shoulder and moved to one side, moving her out of the way as gently and politely as possible. "I just need to get through here real quick. I hope I'm not being rude."

"Oh, no! No, not at all. I'm the one who ambushed you. I'm sorry."

"Don't be sorry," he said. "All you did was give me the chance to meet a beautiful woman. Nothing to apologize for."

Hannah felt herself blush and hoped he couldn't see. "Maybe we can catch up later."

"I hope so," he said, already on the move. "Excuse me, though..."

She watched him go, trying not to stare too openly at his ass. Low-hanging jeans that, if it wasn't for his damn blazer, would have shown off his underwear. She might have whimpered, but thankfully the music was too loud for anyone to have heard it if she did. Regan disappeared into a back room that made her believe he was either a roommate or Debra's boyfriend. Probably a boyfriend. Men that gorgeous were usually off the market by the time they crossed her path.

Her bravery used up for the night, Hannah moved back to her corner after refreshing her drink. She decided she could wait twenty or thirty extra minutes before making an escape. She didn't admit to herself why she was willing to linger, but she did keep an eye out in case Regan reappeared. Eventually she spoke to people. She enjoyed herself to the point where she wasn't keeping an eagle-eye on the door where Regan had disappeared. She realized she had probably missed his exit, but it was a small price to pay for actually enjoying the party.

When guests began filtering out, she realized she could go home with a clean conscience. She took Uber again since she'd been drinking, and she spent the entire ride staring out the window fantasizing about Regan. By the time she got home, she was certain she'd fudged some of the reality in favor for her fantasy. She changed into a T-shirt and climbed into bed, but she couldn't shut off her brain. She kept imagining his eyes, that awkward smile that started on the right side of his mouth and spread slowly to the other side.

Eyes closed, Hannah moved her hands under the blankets. She moved her legs apart and pressed the fingers of her right hand against the crotch of her underwear. She kept her hand stiff and moved her hips, rising and falling slowly as she imagined the possibilities of the party. Standing in front of Regan, the center of his attention for however briefly, she could have said anything at all to him. If she had been braver or less inhibited, she could have gotten him to take care of this itch.

"I want you to fuck me," she would have said. She could imagine his stunned expression, the widening of those gorgeous eyes as she stepped forward and kissed him. He could have had a girlfriend. He could have been gay. But no, this was a fantasy. And in this fantasy, he was a red-blooded straight man who hadn't been laid in months, so he was ready and willing to be taken. And since it was a fantasy, Hannah didn't have to worry about her inhibitions getting in the way.

"Right here," she whispered into the still air of her bedroom. "Right now."

She imagined Regan turning her around and pressing against her from behind. Everyone at the party would have turned to look, but she didn't mind. She put her hands flat on the table and leaned forward, arching her back as he pressed against her. She could feel the length of his cock through his pants and the thin material of her dress. In bed, she was breathing heavily as she pushed her underwear aside and began rubbing herself, biting her lip as she felt how wet she was.

"Fuck her," she imagined people at the party saying. They were all as eager as she was, as eager as Regan felt, and her breath shook as she heard the rasp of his zipper. She really could almost hear it. And then he would lift her dress up. She remembered his hands, an artist's hands, thin and fine-boned with such long fingers. She imagined them gathering her dress and lifting it up over her ass.

"Yes, yes," she whispered, rocking from side to side on the mattress. She pushed two fingers inside herself and imagined it was him. "Yes, Regan, fuck me... I need it..."

She came with the image of his hands on her hips, squeezing her fingers and imagining it was his cock. She whimpered his name as she thrust against her hand. In the aftermath she wrapped her fingers in the hem of her shirt and brought her other hand to her mouth, kissing the fingers and imagining it was Regan's lips. She hummed as her lower body twitched with aftershocks, then chuckled at herself and rearranged the blankets.

The reality was probably that Regan was gay or taken or both. The reality was probably that he was a smug asshole who knew just how sexy he was, and that would be a huge turnoff. It was better to keep him in the realm of fantasy. She plumped up her pillow and settled on her side to get some sleep.

It would have been better to keep him in the realm of fantasy, but as it turned out, it was nearly impossible. She found herself thinking about him at odd times during the day. She kept stopping herself from tracking down Debra and asking for any information she had on him. By the weekend, she realized she was operating on a memory that had been, at best, partially alcohol induced. He couldn't be as beautiful as she remembered. She knew if she actually saw him in the light of day, while sober, the mystery would be shattered.

On Saturday she found herself near Debra's apartment and decided to get it over with. The fact she could barely remember the apartment number supported her theory that Regan was nowhere near the dream guy who had colonized her brain. She knocked and tried to come up with a reasonable excuse to be there. She didn't want Debra to know how desperate she was. She didn't want that reputation in the office. But she couldn't think of a way to obliquely ask about Regan's contact information without giving away her intent.

The door opened and revealed a woman who was not Debra. Her hair was unwashed and hanging limp, and she was wearing a white dress shirt under a pair of overalls.

"Oh. Hi. Sorry, is this Debra Harmon's apartment?"

"Yeah, it is. Can I help you?"

Relief flooded her mind. She didn't have to reveal her desperation to Debra! "Uh, maybe. I was at the party here last week..."

"Yeah, I remember you."

"Oh! Okay. Well, I met someone, and I didn't get his contact information, and I was thinking... if maybe you or Debra knew him, maybe you could arrange... I mean, I don't want you to give me his number without permission or anything. Maybe I could give you *my* number, and if he's interested you could give it to him..."

The woman laughed and nodded. "Yeah, okay. Who was the guy?"

"Regan... uh, Regan... something. Not Regan Poole. That's a footballer."

"Oh. Regan?" Something strange passed over the woman's face. "The guy you're interested in is... Regan Patterson?"

Hannah smiled. "Yes! That was it. Oh. Is he dating someone. He's not your boyfriend, is he? God, I'm so sorry if I..."

"No, he's not my boyfriend. Uh, do you wanna come in?" She stepped back and let Hannah into the apartment. "I'll see if I have his number or, or email address around here somewhere."

"Thank you." She went into the apartment, still curious about the other woman's reaction. "I don't usually hunt guys down like this. It's not... not really my nature."

The woman walked past her to a rolltop desk between two windows. "It's fine. It's kind of romantic. I know I'd be honored if someone came hunting me down." She sat in the chair and began aimlessly looking through address books. "So Regan must've made quite an impression, huh?"

Hannah chuckled. "Well, you've seen him. He's gorgeous. He likes football. We really didn't talk much. But he seemed kind. Funny. I've spent this whole week wondering what might have happened if I'd been brave for once in my life and asked him out. So this is really just an attempt at a do-over."

The woman stood up and offered her a slip of paper. "Here's Regan's email address. It'll be fine. Just tell him you got it from Debra's roommate."

"I will. Thank you so much."

"Sure."

"I won't keep you. I'm sure you have stuff you'd rather be doing."

The woman laughed and shrugged. "I'm always willing to take a break in the interest of a good love story."

Hannah blushed. "I don't know about *love*."

"Well. It's only at the beginning. Too soon to tell."

Hannah was so thrilled that she'd actually managed to get the email address that she was back on the street before she realized she'd never gotten the roommate's name.

Her first email was embarrassingly trite and overly apologetic, but she sent it before she could rethink the entire thing. She put the laptop aside and prepared herself to focus on housework so she wouldn't constantly refresh the inbox. As she was standing, the computer beeped to let her know she had a new message. "Damn it, Mom, if~" but she stopped when she saw the screen. A reply! From Regan P. She sat down and put the computer back on her lap before she clicked.

"I do remember you," he started. "You were gorgeous. I'm glad you came looking for me. You're a beautiful woman, and I was sorry we didn't have more time together at the party. I almost said goodbye on my way out, but you seemed engrossed in conversation with someone else. Now I regret not doing it. But I have to confess I may not be exactly what you're looking for. I don't want to go into it over email, but if you wanted to get together for a drink, I could explain in person. Let me know. I look forward to hearing from you again." In a post-script, he added, "Even if you decide not to pursue anything romantic, I've been dying to find someone to watch football games with. I hope you'd consider that, at least."

Hannah couldn't quite make sense of the email. Was he trying to let her down easy? If so, what was with the invite? She hated the term 'friend-zone,' but it seemed like she was getting that treatment from him. If he wasn't attracted to her, then... well, could she just be friends with someone she was attracted to? It was worth investigating, at the very least.

She opened a reply and sent back the address of a bar that was between her apartment and Debra's. "Is tonight at seven too early?" He agreed to the time and place and promised he would be there. Hannah grinned and high-fived herself, grateful there was no one to see her doing something so dorky, and then went to find something to wear. She didn't care about his overly-defensive email. Unless his excuse was something extremely dealbreaking, she couldn't see herself walking away from a man like that.

Since Regan didn't seem overly interested in dating her, she kept her outfit understated but classy. She didn't bother changing her hair, but she did touch up her lipstick. Once she determined it was a nice, middle of the road approach, she headed out. She arrived just before the time they'd agreed upon, so she got a table by the window so she could see him approaching. She was facing the window when someone lightly touched her shoulder.

"Hannah?"

She twisted and looked up at Debra's roommate. "Oh, it's you! Hello. We weren't properly introduced earlier. I'm Hannah."

"Uh, yeah. I-I know." She took Hannah's hand. "I'm Regan."

Hannah's smile wavered. "Oh. That's... that's, uh..." She repositioned herself to look at the other woman straight-on. Her hair was styled differently and disguised the fact it was shaved on the sides, but the shape of her chin, the jawline, those magnificent eyes... And the real telling trait was the tattoo that was one again visible on her throat, black flames licking up from the open collar of her blouse. It was Regan, without a doubt, but for a moment Hannah couldn't make her mind connect the two realities.

"You're a woman."

"Yes, I am." Regan carefully settled across from Hannah, as if expecting to be dismissed at any second. "I'm sorry. I didn't realize you didn't realize when we met. I should have said something when you came looking for me this afternoon, but to be honest I didn't want to dash your hopes. It really was romantic. And I guess I was flattered. I didn't want to just dump the truth on you." She furrowed her brow. "I don't know why I thought it would be better this way."

Hannah said, "I don't know which way would be better, so I can't really blame you for the one you chose." She was trying not to stare, but it was like one of those optical illusions. She'd met this person twice, and both times she saw a different gender. Now that she knew the truth, she could see both at the same time. Regan was handsome and beautiful, somewhere right in the middle of the traditional measure for either. If she wore something a bit less androgynous in either direction, she would tip over into that gender.

"You're staring."

"I know. I'm sorry. I just can't get over the fact. You're definitely a woman. But... at the party, I would have sworn you were a man."

Regan smiled. "I was feeling masculine that night. I was going to a concert. So I dressed the part. This afternoon I was just hanging out at home, so... I wanted to be girly."

"You just go back and forth?"

"No," Regan said. "I just dress appropriately for the situation, just like anyone else. Like you did when you got ready to come out. I don't decide I'm going to look like a boy or a girl. I just wear what I want. It's other people who make the assumptions."

Hannah nodded slowly. "Okay. Well, now I understand what you meant when you said you might not be what I'm looking for."

Regan smiled. "I didn't think so. But hey... no hard feelings. Like I said, you like football, so we do have that in common. I'd love to catch a game with you. Just as friends, if you'd be willing."

"Well... wait..."

Regan said, "Oh. I was under the impression you were straight."

"I am. I mean... I think I am." She scratched her eyebrow and tilted her head to the side. "I've never really thought about it because I've always just focused on meeting men. Whenever I'm looking to start a relationship, I just went for men by default. And men have never exactly been hard to find. But I can appreciate a beautiful woman. And the way I reacted to you... to your looks... that didn't have anything to do with gender."

"So you're saying..."

"I'm saying maybe I never realized I was ambidextrous because I've never seriously tried writing with my left hand." She wet her lips and focused on Regan. "I still think you're beautiful. And something about you is just so appealing that I don't want to walk away. I'd be really pissed off at myself if I was the one who said no just because you happened to have the wrong parts. And if someone like you is actually interested in me, then I'd be a fool to say no for any reason at all."

Regan said, "If it affects your decision, I am interested. You're gorgeous and you like football."

"I don't really like football all that much."

"You knew Regan Poole."

Hannah shrugged. "Yeah... so what are we talking about here?"

"Dinner and drinks. Getting to know one another beyond the two minutes we spent chatting at the party. And with no deceptions. Everyone's gender on the table, no whiff of anything like deception, intentional or accidental."

"There's an Italian place nearby that I love."

"I'm not a big fan of Italian."

Hannah smiled as she slipped off the stool. "See? We're getting to know each other already. Let's see what else we can learn before the night is out."

They had a great time together having decided on Korean barbeque, something neither of them had ever tried before and both agreed was a miss. But they were able to get to know one another and confirmed they had enough in common to secure a second date. No, meet-up. Hangout. Were they too old to call it hanging out? Hannah didn't know. All she knew was that she really enjoyed spending time with Regan. It didn't matter how she dressed or what she looked like. She was just a spectacular person to be around. Funny and willing to try anything once. She liked Elvis Costello and drank great beer. She seemed to enjoy Hannah's personality as well; laughed at her jokes and enjoyed her cooking.

They'd been "whatevering" for about three weeks, a time span that covered eight nights and four afternoons spent in each other's company, when Regan invited Hannah over to watch football on the satellite. Debra was spending the night at her boyfriend's, so they'd have the entire apartment to themselves. "You can scream and yell and get as hooligan as you like."

"I do not go hooligan."

"Of course you do. And it's adorable because you're so tiny."

"Dynamite is tiny, too. Better watch your mouth, sister."

Regan was butch that night, wearing a Seattle Reign jersey over a baggy pair of black shorts. Hannah found herself staring when Regan's attention was on the game, or when she went into the kitchen to get another drink. They were seated together on the couch. Regan had her long arms draped over the back and sat with her legs apart. Hannah couldn't see her as a man anymore, but she also couldn't think of her as entirely female, either.

"Regan? I want you to be honest with me."

Regan looked at her. "Sure."

"If I had been hitting on you that first night. Would you have been interested?"

Regan looked back at the TV. She sucked her bottom lip into her mouth. "I'm not sure what you want me to say here."

"The truth." She scooted closer, their thighs touching. "Because the more I've gotten to know you, the more I've realized that my first instinct was probably right."

"Then yeah. If you had asked me for a drink that night, I might have blown off the concert. But that doesn't mean I expect you to... or that I'm..."

She stopped speaking when Hannah leaned in and kissed her

cheek. She turned to look at her, their faces inches apart. Hannah reached up and gently touched the stubble above Regan's ear.

"There have been times recently when I look at you and I don't even notice if you're dressed masculine or feminine. All I see is you. And I keep waiting to be less attracted to you now that I know the truth, and it's only getting worse. All the time I've spent with you... I've been trying not to call them dates, because if I did, I'd have to admit they're the best dates I've ever been on. And I've been trying not to kiss you because I'm worried it'll be too good to stop."

Regan said, "Okay."

"So if I kiss you... and I don't stop..."

"That would be fine by me, Hannah."

"Okay." Hannah tilted her head to the side and moved her neck, pressing her lips softly against Regan's. Her lips were plumper than Hannah originally thought. She shifted on the cushion, pulled one leg up underneath her, and put both hands on the back of Regan's head. Regan had one hand on Hannah's thigh, rhythmically massaging the muscle through her jeans before she moved it to her hip. She pulled and Hannah found herself being moved even closer. She lifted her leg and settled on top of Regan, suddenly straddling her. She gasped in surprise and found her mouth invaded, an eager tongue moving against hers as Regan moved to cup her breast.

"Wait, wait," she said, squirming back and away.

"Sorry. I'm so sorry." Regan was breathless, her cheeks pink.

Hannah said, "Don't be sorry. I'm sorry. It was just a little fast for me." She guided Regan's hand back to her breast and moved closer to her, settling more comfortably on her lap. "This is all new to me, remember."

Regan nodded. "If you'd be more comfortable with it, I do have a strap-on in the bedroom."

Hannah felt herself redden. She shook her head. "No. I know exactly what I'd do if you had a cock. I want to find out what I'd do to someone without one. But... another time."

"Yeah."

They kissed again, the sounds of the football game echoing through the apartment as they explored. Regan whispered against Hannah's mouth every time she wanted to move. "Can I touch you here, Hannah? Can I put my hand here?" Hannah initially felt as if she should find it annoying, but hearing Regan's throaty voice asking permission to touch her in increasingly intimate ways was too much for her. She nodded or breathlessly said, "Yes," or "please, Regan," and then moaned when Regan followed through.

"I want to take you into the bedroom," Regan said.

Hannah nodded and lifted off of Regan's lap. They went down the hall with the TV still playing behind them. Regan turned on the lights and twisted as they entered her bedroom. She cupped Hannah's face and kissed her again, and Hannah kicked the door shut as they shuffled toward the bed. Regan stopped her by the nightstand.

"It's in there. Bottom drawer. If you change your mind."

Hannah said, "What if I want to wear it?"

Regan gave her the lopsided smile again, the slow spread of it crossing her face. "Dealer's choice." She slid her hands down Hannah's body, cupped her ass, and lifted her up onto the bed. Hannah laughed as she fell backward, instantly covered by Regan. More kissing, more hands exploring. Regan's powerful legs squeezed Hannah's hips, and Hannah worked her hands under the shirt to feel her stomach and the dimples above the waistband of her shorts. Regan moved her head down and began kissing and licking Hannah's neck, each pass of her tongue making Hannah gasp and twitch underneath her.

"Talk to me," Hannah whispered.

Regan stretched out on top of her, fitted perfectly against the curve of her hip and the line of her torso, and pressed her mouth to Hannah's ear.

"I'm going to undress you, take all your clothes off and kiss everything I see." She nipped at Hannah's earlobe. "Then I'm going to spread your legs... and I'm going to show you how a woman can fuck you."

Hannah grunted and closed her eyes. "Then get on with it, dude."

Regan laughed and began tugging at Hannah's clothes. She sat up and Hannah looked at her, this powerful and lanky woman, this masculine lady, and felt a surge of arousal and attraction. She lifted her arms to help Regan get her shirt off, then unhooked her own bra to speed up the process. Regan took the opportunity to cross her arms and peel the jersey off, leaving her topless except for a sports bra. Her full tattoo was exposed for the first time, a complex series of flames and spheres that spanned from her shoulder to her collarbone. Hannah sat up and pressed her face to Regan's chest, skimming her fingers up over Regan's ribs and peeling the bra up and off. Regan's breasts were small enough that someone might still mistake her for a man, but Hannah could tell the difference. She kissed one pink nipple and closed her lips around it.

Regan raked her fingers through Hannah's hair and arched her back. "You're good at that."

Hannah smiled and moved to the other breast, pinching it and closing her mouth around the erect nipple. Regan put her hand on the other breast and Hannah used her fingers to keep it hard, teasing and pinching it based on Regan's responses. Regan pushed her back and Hannah fell onto the mattress again, gasping as Regan moved down her body. She watched as her pants were unbuttoned and tugged down her legs. The pants were briefly tangled on her shoes, but Regan pulled them off without bothering to untie them and then Hannah was practically naked. She tried to steady her breathing as Regan ran her hands up the inside of her legs, easing them apart.

"What are you going to do," Hannah whispered.

"I'm going down on you." Regan kept her hands on Hannah's thighs as she dipped her head down. She kissed the crotch of Hannah's underwear and dragged her bottom lip over the smooth material, lifting her eyes to watch Hannah's reaction. Hannah nodded, not that Regan needed the encouragement. When Regan kissed her again, Hannah closed her eyes and collapsed on the mattress. She brought her feet up and rested her heels on the edge of the mattress, toes curled, and spread her hands out to either side. She held her breath and then let it out in an explosive gasp when Regan pushed her underwear out of the way and kissed her center.

The flat of her tongue moved over her folds, then became a point and teased her clit. Hannah gripped the blankets with both fists and focused on the texture of the ceiling, the small brown water spot near the wall, the way the shadows formed a diamond in the corner of the room. She breathed deeply and smelled Regan's scent - spicy, woody, aquatic - on everything around her. And that was Regan's tongue inside of her, Regan's lips spreading her open, Regan's fingers~

"Oh!"

She could feel Regan's smile through the tremors of her orgasm, her body trying to escape and go rigid at the same time. Her feet dropped off the mattress and made hard contact with part of Regan's body.

"Sorry..."

"No, no," Regan said. "It's okay. Are you okay?"

Hannah said, "No. I'm good. I'm great. I'm..." She moved a hand between her legs and covered herself, laughing breathlessly. "Fuck!"

Regan slid up her body and kissed her lips. Hannah caught the tip of Regan's tongue and tasted herself, causing another post-orgasmic shudder. She ran her hands over Regan's chest and around to her back. She pulled Regan down onto her.

"I just fucked a woman," she whispered.

"You just let a woman fuck you," Regan said. "I think there's a difference. But... if you want to be accurate..." She reached out and dragged her fingernails over Hannah's palm. Hannah's fingers twitched in response. Regan kept her eyes on Hannah's face for cues to stop, but Hannah was focused on the way her hand was being manipulated. Regan brought her hand up and used her bottom lip to lift the first two fingers. She took them into her mouth, never taking her eyes off Hannah's as she sucked them. Hannah was struggling to keep her breathing steady when Regan let the fingers out of her mouth and moved her hand down.

Hannah's hand was moved down Regan's body, to the waistband of her shorts. Hannah held her breath and pushed under the elastic without Regan's help. She rubbed the folds with the back of her fingers, then turned her wrist around.

"Don't let me hurt you..."

"You won't hurt me," Regan whispered. "Do you feel how wet I am?"

Hannah's breath caught. "Yeah."

Regan gasped softly, her hand still on Hannah's arm. "Just like you do to yourself. Do you touch yourself, Hannah?"

Hannah laughed weakly. "Yeah. I've been thinking about you when I do it."

"Good. I've been thinking about you, too." She pressed her lips to Hannah's cheek. "So just do it to me. Make me come."

"I... it's... m-my hand..."

Regan said, "Here." She repositioned herself and twisted until she was lying on her side in front of Hannah. She pushed her shorts and underwear down; Hannah noticed absently that she was wearing boxer briefs and felt her arousal spike. "Spoon me, sweetheart. Give me your hand..."

Hannah did as she was told, pressing tight against Regan's back and cupping her mound. This was a position she was comfortable with, and now she had the added ability to kiss Regan's neck. She parted her lips and ran her tongue over the lines of Regan's tattoo. Regan went stiff and pressed her face into the mattress to expose more of her neck. Hannah kissed, sucked, and licked as much of the ink as she could, pecking along the black and red design as she teased with two fingers. Her other arm slid between Regan and the mattress and she spread her fingers wide across Regan's stomach. She hooked her leg over Regan's and moved her lips up to her ear.

"I want to make you come every way possible..."

"I'd be... very open to that endeavor..."

Hannah moaned against the curve of Regan's neck.

"But you have to get the first out of the way." She covered Hannah's hand with her own. "C'mon, babe. I'm close." She twisted and Hannah lifted her head so they could kiss. She felt the quake in Regan's lips when she came and the small vibration in the tip of her tongue that preceded the "Oh..." that signaled her orgasm. She bit Regan's bottom lip ever so gently, and then moved her lips up to her hair. Regan burrowed her face into the curve of Hannah's neck and sobbed, just once, quietly, and then went limp against her.

"That..." she said.

Hannah grinned and clung to Regan. "Yes. That."

Regan flipped over and kissed Hannah's throat, the underside of her chin, and then her lips. Hannah gave herself over to the kiss, thrusting her tongue into Regan's mouth. There was nothing hesitant or exploratory about it this time. She didn't care that she was kissing a woman. She was kissing Regan. She had made Regan Patterson orgasm, and that was something that passed beyond gender or sexuality.

"Regan," she whispered, testing the way it sounded. It wasn't her friend's name anymore; it was the name of her lover. When she pulled bac she saw that Regan's hair had fallen over one side of her face. She swept it up and back, revealing the arched eyebrows and both brilliantly blue eyes. The beauty that had drawn her attention in a crowded room and forced her to change her perspective on everything she thought she knew about herself.

"This doesn't have to change who you are," Regan said. "We can still be friends. Just... friends who occasionally do this."

Hannah smiled. "I don't want that. I want to be people who do this and occasionally watch a football game together."

Regan laughed. "I think we could make that work."

"Yeah?"

"Mm-hmm." She brought her hand up and teased Hannah's nipples. "You have magnificent breasts. I didn't get to spend near as much time on them as I wanted."

"Next time," Hannah said.

Regan nodded. "Next time."

They settled against each other, neither of them suggesting sleep but both giving in to the urge. Hannah smiled as she drifted off, her leg still draped over Regan's waist. She had confirmed to herself that could definitely be with a woman, no question in her mind. In fact, the thought of going back to a male partner felt like a massive step backward. No finesse, no tenderness, just penetration and friction. Being with a woman was like dancing with a professional partner, someone who knew all the steps and didn't mind teaching a novice how to follow along. But with that settled, she was still intensely curious about what was in the bottom drawer of Regan's nightstand. She smiled as she drifted off. Maybe next time.

Then again... maybe not.

COMMON TONGUE

Alone in a foreign city where she didn't speak the language, that was adventure to her. That was throwing everything to the fates and seeing how she fared. It wasn't brave, because she had plenty of money to make up for any confusion. It wasn't daring because she could always just retreat back home. It was rebellion, jumping out of a plane and not knowing when exactly she would pull the chute. She would pull it. She had no death wish. It was just a question of how long she could bear the fall before fear took over.

Chloe's trip to Athens had been a spur of the moment decision. She did no preparation, made no itinerary, and somehow managed to find herself on a train to a country she'd only seen online and in movies with little more than what she was carrying. She had a bag with the essentials, of course, and enough money in the bank to support her no matter what happened. But the moment she left the station she couldn't shake the feeling she'd made a horrible mistake.

She forced herself to ignore all those misgivings and focus on the beauty all around her. She checked into a hotel, rented a scooter, and went wandering through the winding streets. She occasionally used her phone's map to guide her, but mostly she just allowed herself to get lost. The entire city was magnificent. She lost herself in the buildings and the ancient sites, even transfixed by the graffiti and rundown modern buildings. By the time she stopped for lunch she had forgotten her misgivings to focus on the magic, tropic paradise in which she found herself.

When she was hungry enough to stop for lunch, she found a small café which overlooked the sea. The water was as blue as it always appeared in fiction, an unreal color that put the sky to shame. She ordered an Apple of Discord tea based on its name and a toasted prosciutto sandwich to eat while watching the pedestrians. A black dog weaved through the crowds, pausing whenever someone showed the slightest bit of attention to him. He sniffed hands and only moved on after determining they didn't hold food. He moved toward the café with hope in his eyes and his mouth spread into a wide smile.

Chloe wondered about the proper etiquette. She was the closest to the street, so she would be the one faced with offering him a slice of ham or refusing him to keep him from hanging around all afternoon. The café management would probably prefer she refrain, but how could she refuse such a happy face? She looked past the dog in the hopes she would find an ally, and instead she spotted something infinitely better.

She was standing on a bench, rising above the crowd with her body canted forward like a figurehead on the bow of some ancient sailing ship. The bottom few buttons of her blouse were undone and the wind caught the two sides, whipping them up to reveal her tanned stomach above the waistband of her faded jeans. Her hair was thrown about by the same wind, a tempest of sun-kissed black-blonde that kept getting in her eyes. She turned slowly and scanned the crowd, and Chloe intuited that she was looking for the runaway pup that had just reached her table.

Chloe took a piece of ham to gain the animal's trust, fed it to him from her palm, and lifted her other hand in the air. "Aňoj!" she shouted, then whistled. The statue turned toward her, and Chloe pointed one finger down toward the dog. The woman held her hands out in a cheer, hopped down off the bench, and moved through the crowd toward them.

"*Me synhoríte... sygnómi...*" When she reached Chloe and the dog she exclaimed brightly and knelt down, cupping the dog's face. "*Pou ton vríke! Efcharistó!*"

Chloe said, "*Prosím, nemáte zač.*

The woman looked up. "Czech?"

"*Ano*," Chloe said. "*Mluvíš česky?*"

"*Milás Elliniká?*"

Chloe assumed they had both asked about their own language. She shook her head. "*Ne...* Um... English?"

"Mm-mm." The other woman patted the dog on the head. "Cisco."

"*Dobrý den,* Cisco." She smiled as the dog turned and licked her face, then put a hand on her own chest. "Chloe."

"Penelope," the other woman said.

"*Odyssey.*"

Penelope laughed in the way of someone who had heard the joke a million times. She pointed at the dog and, through a series of hand gestures, conveyed that the dog had run away and caused a bit of panic. She said something that contextually must have been a thank you, and Chloe tried to indicate she was happy to have helped. She gave Cisco another scratch on top of his head and stood up to take her leave of the goddess and her newly-retrieved pet.

"Radiation Canary?" Penelope said.

"Eh?"

Penelope gestured at Chloe's chest. Chloe looked down and saw that her blouse was unbuttoned enough to reveal a partial logo from the T-shirt underneath. It was indeed a T-shirt she'd purchased at a concert the American band had given in Athens in 2007. She'd chosen it as part of her wardrobe because of the Art deco Parthenon in the design; she figured it would be apt for her journey.

Penelope gestured again: were you there?

Chloe shook her head and gestured: no, bought online.

"Ah," Penelope said. She had been there, she indicated, then made an awestruck face. She patted a hand over her heart and swayed. "I'm not going to miss you when you're gone," she sang, "Baby, I'm going to carry on, carry on..."

Chloe smiled and clapped. "Brava, brava!"

Penelope laughed and rocked back and forth on her feet. Cisco kept moving around her feet so she bent down to show him some attention. Chloe straightened and gestured back at the café, lifting her hand in farewell as she started to retreat. Penelope stood.

'Wait, wait,' she seemed to be saying. 'Do you want to walk with us for a bit?' She was gesturing at the dog and then along the brick walkway that ran parallel to the water. She pointed at her eyes and then at the dog. 'Could use someone else to watch after this rascal.'

Chloe looked back at the café and her scooter. She could always come back for the scooter, and even if they didn't have a shared language, it would be nice to have someone to keep her company for a while. She nodded and moved closer again. She shrugged and waved her hands in front of her a bit.

'Sure, sounds like fun,' she hoped the gesture conveyed.

'Great!' She prompted Cisco to lead the way.

As they walked together, Chloe tried to figure out what they could possibly get out of hanging out together. Of course, she got to look at a perfectly tanned Greek goddess in painted-on jeans and a shirt that still occasionally lifted to show off her belly. But what did Penelope get out of the deal? Penelope stuck her hands in her pockets and made a sound of thinking before she finally spoke.

"Radiation Canary..."

"*Ano, ano,*" Chloe said. "Karen *a* Lana..."

Penelope crossed her arms over her chest and swooned. "Ah! *Tóso romantikó!*"

Chloe laughed. She had been so disappointed when Karen and Lana broke up. But they seemed happy in their new relationships, so she couldn't be too bitter about it. She took her iPod from her bag and unwound the headphone wire, scrolling through her music library to the Canaries. Penelope looked at the screen and made a sound of recognition as she pointed at the screen.

"*Rome Burning,*" she said.

"*Dobře.*" Chloe hit shuffle and offered one of the earbuds to Penelope. The first song that came up was 'Forgotten Lore,' and Penelope immediately began moving to the rhythm. Chloe watched Penelope instead of listening to the lyrics. She swayed her shoulders and altered her pace so that walking almost became a dance, biting her bottom lip as she moved her lips to the lyrics. At the chorus she turned sideways and rocked her shoulders, flipping her hair into her face as she mouthed Lana Kent's words.

Two songs into their private concert, Penelope patted Chloe on the arm and pointed off the street. They changed direction and arrived at a row of steps that led down to a narrow ribbon of sandy beach. Penelope swept away the sand with her shoe and made a gesture of presentation. Chloe chuckled, did a mock curtsey, and sat down next to her new friend. She put the iPod on the step between them. Penelope put her hands on the ground behind them and stretched her legs out. The position turned her body into one long line interrupted by distracting curves, and Chloe found herself staring. Penelope glanced over at her and Chloe smiled. She couldn't have apologized if she wanted to, so she just kept quiet and looked out over the water. Cisco darted out over the sand. Penelope called a command out to him as he bounded toward the water.

Chloe brought her feet up close and wrapped her arms around her knees. She thought it was crazy to be sitting here with someone she couldn't communicate with listening to a singer they also couldn't understand. She knew the translations of the songs, of course, and there was a Czech band who did covers on YouTube, but she loved hearing the original voices. And it helped that Lana Kent and Karen Everett were gorgeous and openly gay. They were her role models. To stand in front of a crowd and kiss the woman she loved...

She bit her lip and looked out over the water. It always came back to that. She left Hlinsko for its exact opposite, the frigid winter traded for a tropical shore, so she could escape the world she'd always known. She had spent so long in secret relationships. She was sick of telling people that the woman she loved was just a roommate or a close friend. But she was also terrified of being out of the closet. To have people know she was gay was to expose the most private part of her life. She looked at Penelope, who looked at her in anticipation.

"*Jsem homosexual*," she said.

Penelope smiled blankly. "Je... semho...?" Her voice trailed off.

Chloe waved the air between them as if erasing it. "*Nevadí, nevadí*."

"*Entáxei*."

Cisco had finished chasing birds and came back to hover around them. The music shifted to "Scene of the Crime," one of the sexiest songs the band had. Even without hearing the words, there was no mistaking the growl in Lana Kent's voice, the moan of the guitar, the whine of Karen's violin. The song sounded like a woman on the verge of orgasm, and Chloe hoped that she could blame any blushing of her cheeks on the sun.

It turned out she needn't have worried; when she looked at Penelope to see if she was staring, she saw the other woman's eyes were closed, her lips parted as she swayed to the music. Penelope had tilted her head slightly to offer her neck to an unseen lover, her hair sticking to the thin layer of sweat that had accumulated there. Everything in Chloe wanted to lean over and taste those tiny beads, to pull the hair away with her lips, to see what her new Greek friend tasted like. Instead she moved her hands to her lap and focused on the water.

"*Latrevó aftó to tragoúdi*," Penelope sighed as the song faded away.

Her voice was so sexual, so post-coital, that Chloe almost moaned in response. Instead she said, "*Ano.*"

Penelope turned and met Chloe's gaze. At that moment it didn't matter that they spoke different languages; she'd seen that look before. Her heart jumped and lodged into her throat, and she wet her lips. The next song started, but neither of them were paying attention to it. She twisted her torso to face Penelope more fully, to offer up body language that indicated she was aware of and fully accepted what was happening between them.

Cisco chose that moment to slam into Penelope from behind, forcing her to break eye contact and shatter the moment. Chloe almost hated the dog at that moment, but she only laughed awkwardly as Penelope wrangled the beast onto her lap. "*Thélei na páei sto spíti,*" she said, scratching him behind the ears. She looked at Chloe and revealed regret that whatever had passed between them had ended so abruptly.

Chloe gestured at her own eyes and then up and down the street, shrugging. 'Will I see you again?'

Penelope shrugged and nodded at the same time. 'I hope.' Her eyes flashed with a sudden idea and she held up a finger, picked up her bag, and took out a pen. After a bit more digging, she produced a piece of envelope. She examined it, found it to be disposable, and quickly wrote something on the back of it. When she was finished she tore off a piece and handed it to Chloe. It was a street address, a name she assumed was a club or restaurant, and a time: 7pm.

Chloe pointed down to indicate 'tonight?'

Penelope nodded.

"*Ano,*" Chloe said as she enthusiastically bobbed her head up and down.

"*Thavmásios!*" She said something nonsensical - Chloe assumed - to the dog and then got up. The earbud had fallen onto her shoulder when Cisco attacked them, and she handed it back. She said something that Chloe decoded from context: 'Thank you for sharing your music with me.'

Chloe said she was welcome and hoped the meaning was conveyed. She held up the note and stuck her thumb up. Penelope mimicked the gesture and chuckled under her breath as she patted her hip. Cisco fell into step beside her. Chloe watched them walk away for a long minute, then faced the sea again. She was floating on the afterglow of what she'd just experienced until it suddenly dawned on her that she had no idea what the dress code would be for that night. Even if it was casual, her wardrobe was extremely limited.

She got up, brushed the sand from her rear end, and went in search of the address so she could at least see what she certainly hadn't packed properly to attend.

It turned out to be an open-air diner with live music. She chose a baggy white blouse and black leggings with a sweater casually tied around her waist in the event it was more casual than she assumed. She arrived a few minutes before seven and chose a table where she could see the street. The band was already playing when she gave her drink order. The music was fantastic, far more than she would have expected from such a venue, and she found her foot tapping to the beat. Even though, once again, they were singing in Greek and she had no idea what the words were.

"*Edó eísai!* Penelope said, coming into the dining area. She wore a blood-red blouse that was open at the collar and a skirt so short it was almost eclipsed by the top. Her legs certainly justified such an outfit, and Chloe was already afraid of how hard it would be to keep from staring.

She stood up and they embraced briefly. Penelope smelled absolutely amazing. When Chloe stepped back, she made an exaggerated sniffing sound and then said, "Ah!"

"*Efcharistó,*" she said, then gestured at Chloe's outfit. "*Ómorfos!*"

They were still standing close to each other, Penelope's hand on Chloe's wrist. In a moment they would turn, take their seats, and then try to make it through dinner without the ability to converse with each other. Or Chloe could give in to the other urge that had been stewing since the band began playing. They weren't Radiation Canary, but there were two guitars and a piano player, and there was a clear area where the management obviously intended customers to use as a dance floor.

She slid her fingers into Penelope's palm and squeezed. 'Come on.'

'No, we shouldn't.'

'It'll be fun!'

Penelope laughed, unable to come up with an argument she could convey in gestures and facial expressions. Chloe stopped on the dance floor and began to move with the music. Penelope joined in a bit reluctantly, glancing over her shoulder at everyone else in the restaurant as she shifted from one foot to the other. Chloe was emboldened, no longer the shy or reserved person she would've been back home. There she would have been worried about someone she knew being in the crowd, seeing her, understanding what it meant.

That was when she realized she had put Penelope in the same uncomfortable situation. She might have friends or coworkers in the crowd. They might not know she was gay. She might have just created some horribly awkward social situations. She slowed her dance and gestured toward the table. Penelope shook her head and began dancing earnestly, whatever misgivings she had disappearing as she began to move her feet, swinging her hips as she had while listening to the iPod earlier. The difference now was that she was unencumbered by walking at the same time, so she gave her entire body over to the dance.

Her movements were hypnotic, perfectly fluid as she twisted her head to flip her hair. Chloe laughed and took the chance of sliding a hand around Penelope's hip to draw her closer. Penelope allowed it and draped one arm across Chloe's shoulders. She kept moving her body but steadied her head her bangs caught in her eyelashes. The moment that Cisco had so rudely interrupted suddenly returned ten times as strong, almost taking Chloe's breath away with its power. Penelope looked equally stricken, her eyes wide and unblinking.

Neither of them missed a step, but their bodies had closed in against each other. Chloe could feel Penelope's breath on her face and she knew that if she breathed she would see it blow through Penelope's hair. The thought made her shudder, and she moved her hand to Penelope's shoulder.

She tapped her finger against it slowly, up and down, as she nodded her head. "*Ano... ano.*" Tapping equaled yes, equaled keep going, equaled consent. Penelope nodded that she understood. She flattened her palm and brushed it over Penelope's shoulder in a glancing motion. Too soft to be a slap. She shook her head. "*Ne... ne...*"

"*Nai,*" Penelope said, tapping a finger against Chloe's hip while nodding her head. She shook her head and brushed her hand.

"Óchi."

Chloe swallowed and leaned in. Penelope began tapping Morse code on her hip with both hands, speed increasing until finally their lips met. Chloe moaned and put both arms around Penelope, as thrilled with the kiss as she was to be doing it in public, in full view of a crowd. Her hands splayed against Penelope's back, she used her tongue to part Penelope's lips and felt the rapid-fire tapping on her hip pick up in speed once more.

"Chloe," Penelope whispered when their lips parted. She had a fantastic accent, guttural and melodic, hitting the consonants while flowing across the vowels like waves over stone. *Chl-*, hard and nasal, *-oe* cooed, sighed, carried over the wind across her tongue.

Chloe shivered. "Penelope."

"*Filise me*, Chloe," Penelope said, tilting her head again, moving her hands to cup Chloe's face as their lips met again. They both moaned, for the first time speaking the same language. As they kissed, all twenty of their fingers fluttered in a series of frantic taps as if a flock of tiny birds were trying to carry them away. Chloe's hands went into Penelope's hair, and Penelope closed her fists in the material of Penelope's shirt. She could feel Penelope's body under the barely-there material and she wanted more, she needed to feel the heat of it against her palm.

"Chloe."

"Penelope."

Penelope's hands tightened. Her voice was a growl as she crowded against her. "*Chloe.*"

"*Ano*," Chloe said. They weren't going to have dinner anymore. They weren't going to fumble through another conversation. She tapped her fingers against Penelope's skin again to confirm she understood, kissed her lips once more, and then grabbed her hand. She didn't know where they were going; she was trusting that Penelope knew somewhere they could go that had a bed. If not, they could always go back to her hotel. She could care less about the details; all she needed to know was that when she looked back, Penelope's face had a delirious and hungry expression that matched her own.

They locked eyes and both of them laughed as they left the bright oasis of the restaurant for the dark streets that surrounded it.

Deep in the back of her mind, she knew there were risks. What if they went to Penelope's house and someone was there to abduct her, sell her into a sex slavery ring? What if they went back to the hotel and Penelope did have sex with her, but when she woke up all her stuff and a kidney was missing? She looked at the way the skirt moved against Penelope's ass when she walked and thought the second version might actually be worth it. Penelope topped and faced her when they reached the intersection. She pointed at herself and then stretched her arm out toward the north. She waved her hand, indicating far. Then she pointed at Chloe hopefully.

Chloe pointed at herself, then east, and held up two fingers. She was staying two blocks away. Penelope smiled, tightened her grip, and they continued east.

Theft and kidney it was, then. No problem. She hadn't packed many things that couldn't be replaced, and how often did she use both kidneys, anyway? She was willing to take the risk when the reward promised to be so damn sweet.

Only a handful of people were in the street. Chloe wanted to shout to all of them what was about to happen, why she and this gorgeous creature were fleeing through the streets of Athens. After hiding for so damn long, she wanted people to know. She wanted to tell everybody she knew. She closed the distance between them and wrapped her arms around Penelope from behind, kissing her neck as they entered the empty lobby of her hotel.

"*Káne ypomoní*," Penelope laughed, stroking Chloe's arms. She pulled Chloe to the stairs and spun to face her. Another kiss, fuel to get them up the stairs to the room.

Chloe held up two fingers. Second floor. Penelope nodded and led her up, then let Chloe take her to the right door. A card swiped, a green light, and then tumbling through into the dark room. Penelope put her hand on Chloe's shoulder and guided her to the wall. She muttered something under her breath just before their lips met again. Chloe tapped her fingers against Penelope's back again and melted against her.

"*Řekni něco*," she whispered against Penelope's lips. She didn't know how to make her desire known, but she wanted to hear Penelope talk. Even if it was nonsense, even if it was the sexiest dirty talk ever uttered, she just wanted to hear it. "*Mluvit*, speak, *milás, hablar...*"

"Ah, ah...," Penelope whispered, pecking Chloe's lips. "*Eíste tóso ypérocho. Tha ítheles ti stigmí pou se eída. Ta cheíli sas entyposiakí géfsi.*" Her hands slipped under Chloe's shirt. "*Thélo na skíso ta roúcha aftá ta makriá sas. Thélo na sas akoúso na ourliázoun.*"

Chloe whimpered. "Penelope..."

"Chloe."

They moved each other toward the bed, one pulling as the other pushed, and Chloe dropped hard onto the mattress. Penelope was on top of her in seconds, the delay explained when Chloe put a hand on Penelope's shoulder and felt bare skin. She gasped and brushed her fingers up to the slope of her neck, skipping over the bra strap before disappearing into her hair. Penelope whispered her name again and bowed down. She kissed Chloe's neck, moved to kiss her breasts through her blouse, her hands pushing up the outside of her legs.

"Penelope, *ano...*"

"Sh, sh." Penelope sat up and hooked her fingers under the waistband of Chloe's leggings. Chloe nodded, biting her bottom lip as the tights were peeled off. She kicked them away and put her feet down on either side of Penelope's body, lifting her hips in a not-so-subtle signal of what she wanted next. Penelope touched her legs for a moment and then reached for her shirt. Chloe helped her pull it off, then reached back to unhook her own bra. And then she was naked, lying underneath the gorgeous creature she'd first sighted on the Grecian shore, and she knew she had to be dreaming.

"Chloe," Penelope whispered, then said something else as she bent down and kissed one breast. Her tongue circled the nipple before moving to the other, moaning during the transition. Chloe rolled her eyes back and said Penelope's name, a desperate and short cry that ended when Penelope's hand moved to her inner thigh.

"*Prosím... Penelope...*"

Penelope stretched up Chloe's body, her hair dragging over sensitive parts of her anatomy in a very tantalizing manner. Penelope put her hand over Chloe's mouth and dipped the first two fingers inside. Chloe curled her tongue around them, sucking them to the second knuckle to make sure they were properly wet. She was shaking in anticipation. All she could feel was Penelope's body against hers. The room around her and the bed underneath her were just vague sensations compared to the full breasts flattening against hers as she sucked the fingers of her beautiful stranger.

When Penelope withdrew her hand, Chloe flicked her tongue out to give the tips one last taste. She spread her legs further apart, holding her breath as Penelope stretched out beside her. Chloe looked up at her face in the darkness and gasped when Penelope cupped her. She lifted her hand to tap her fingers against the curve of Penelope's breast.

"Chloe... Chloe..." Penelope put her free hand on the back of Chloe's neck while the wet fingers of her other hand stroked Chloe's folds. She whispered something in Greek and Chloe shut her eyes. It was like her hands were joined together by an electric current and their placement made that charge pass through her body. The tip of Penelope's forefinger pushed inside and then immediately retreated, just enough of a tease to make Chloe's heart skip. Before she could recover, the finger pushed in again, this time staying in place as her middle finger teased.

Chloe cursed in Czech, but Penelope seemed to understand the meaning well enough. She laughed and shushed her. She pulled Chloe's head up and found her lips. Her tongue darted and tease in a perfect mimicry of her fingers. Chloe ran her hands over Penelope's body, resting a hand on her hip and tapping just in case there was any doubt left about what she wanted. The tapping had stopped meaning 'yes' and now meant 'more' or 'harder.' It didn't matter how Penelope interpreted it as long as she responded.

Her breathing changed when she was about to come. She held her breath... and Penelope stopped doing what she was doing. Chloe gasped in frustration.

"Ah-ah," Penelope teased.

"Penelope..."

She ran her finger in a circle around Chloe's most sensitive spots, making her twist and jerk but getting her no closer to finishing. She closed her hand around Penelope's wrist and guided her back.

"Penelope... *prosím*..." She was almost sobbing. "*Prosím!*

"Ahh," Penelope said. She bowed and kissed Chloe again, and both fingers slid back inside. When the pad of her middle finger stroked Chloe's g-spot, Chloe cried out into her mouth, rising off the bed to press her body hard against Penelope's. One of her legs pushed between Penelope's and she felt wetness on her thigh, proof that she wasn't the only one who had been affected by this game, and she was desperate to know what she tasted like.

When she felt as if she could move without causing aftershocks, she used what strength she had left to roll Penelope onto her back. She posed on top of her, resting on all fours, thighs wet from her orgasm, and stared down at the lovely face surrounded by a wave of dark hair that spread out across the sheets. Penelope brought her hand to her mouth and held eye contact as she tasted one finger, then the other, dragging it along her bottom lip.

'Wonderful,' Penelope said, or probably something similar.

'Yes, you are,' Chloe said. They kissed before Chloe moved down her body. She kissed Penelope's breasts, sucking both nipples before she licked between them and sank lower. Penelope's stomach quaked under her mouth. Chloe eased off the mattress and crouched next to the bed, biting her lip as she arranged Penelope's long legs. She put them onto her shoulders and Penelope hooked her ankles together, pinning Chloe in place.

'Now,' Penelope was saying, 'now, now, Chloe, god...'

She had kept her skirt on, something Chloe approved of, and she lifted the cloth out of the way like a chef unveiling her masterpiece. The underwear was flimsy and black and left nothing to the imagination. Chloe understood that Penelope had chosen these panties to be seen, to be seen by her, and she smiled as she pressed a kiss to the crotch. There was no translation require for the noise Penelope made, somewhere between a groan and a cry as Chloe teased with her wet bottom lip.

Penelope reached down and, with a trembling finger, pushed the underwear aside. Chloe kissed the knuckles of Penelope's hand, dragging her tongue along them from nail to knuckle, then took the hint. She pressed the flat of her tongue against Penelope's sex, noting that she had a thick bush of dark hair protecting her labia, and she breathed deep to inhale the scent of the moisture caught in the curls before she pressed a kiss to what it was covering. Another cry that was universally understood as Penelope's other hand moved to the back of Chloe's head.

"*Den stamatoún...*"

She dragged her tongue over the puffy lips and kissed Penelope's clit, teasing it free and gently sucking based on how desperately Penelope grasped her head. She pushed inside with her thumb and her middle finger, smiling when Penelope released a long, keening cry. Her entire body twitched and jerked, and she stroked Chloe's hair before tightening her grip again.

'Yes, yes,' Chloe thought she was able to translate, along with, 'I'm close, don't stop.' But there was also a long string of words that could have been gibberish for all Chloe knew.

"Penelope," Chloe said.

She took the hint. "Ahh... Chloe. Chloe, Chloe, Chloe."

Chloe put a hand between her own legs and teased herself to a second orgasm seconds before Penelope came. She stroked with her tongue and finger before she lifted her head, kissed the patch of dark hair, and then kissed both of Penelope's thighs. Each kiss was rewarded with a twitch and a gasped, "Ah!" from Penelope, who sounded like she was moments from passing out. Chloe squirmed up her body and rested her head on Penelope's chest, holding her tight. Penelope kept her legs around Chloe's body and rocked against her, moaning softly.

"Chloe."

"Penelope."

"Say a Prayer," Chloe said, quoting part of a Radiation Canary title.

Penelope chuckled and completed it: "If you've got one."

Chloe closed her eyes and kissed the spot she could reach without moving her head. She listened for Penelope's breathing to slow before she allowed herself to drift off as well.

Chloe's first thought upon waking was that she still felt like she had two kidneys. She wasn't sure how that would feel, really, but at least she didn't feel as if something was missing. When she opened her eyes, the window was open to let in the sea breeze. The curtains were fat with it, blown into the room like the cape of a superhero. She stretched and rolled away from the idyllic view to find another one waiting for her: Penelope, early riser and opener of windows, sat cross-legged behind her. She was wearing only her blouse and the fancy underwear from the night before. Her hair was a mess and her face was puffy from sleep, but she looked even more beautiful than she had when Chloe first spotted her. Chloe wished she had a camera.

"Good morning, beautiful," Penelope said in Czech.

Chloe blinked at her, stunned, and Penelope laughed. She reached behind her and revealed the phone that she'd hidden. The screen was filled with an online translation tool.

"Good morning, beautiful," Penelope said again. "Eh... last night... was... superb."

Chloe took the phone and typed, then sounded out the words on-screen: "I'm... g-glad."

Penelope smiled brightly. She pointed at herself, then the bathroom, then did a sexy mime of showering. Then she took the phone and opened a new page.

"For you."

Chloe thought she knew thank-you: "*Efcharistó.*"

Penelope climbed off the bed, shedding her blouse as she walked into the bathroom. A few seconds later the water began running. Chloe looked at the phone and saw Penelope had opened a note. It was written in Czech, a sort of broken translation that had no doubt come from the internet. Chloe was able to fix the mistakes and read the letter as it was intended.

'Chloe. This is so odd. I've gotten used to not speaking to you. Or rather not being understood by you. It was so freeing! I hope you feel the same way. It gave me a chance to see who you really are instead of some pretense. Even without knowing a word you were saying to me, I could see you were running away from something. I hope you found it with me. You certainly seemed to be distracted last night! Our meeting came at the perfect time for me, as well. I was dumped, left all by myself without a hint of warning, and I felt unloved, undesired, and lonely. So lonely I borrowed my brother's dog just to have a bit of companionship. Cisco, as crazy as he is, led me to you. You took care of all my worries. The way you looked at me. The way we bonded without saying a word. The music! You made me feel like someone who might be desired, even before our dance last night.

'I don't know what happens next. The language difference is sure to become an issue if this goes on for much longer, but can we at least hope to carry it on as long as possible? If not I'll understand. But I want to keep this going as long as possible. I feel more comfortable not speaking with you than I've ever been with anyone else. And I suppose now that the ice has been broken, now that I've broken our game by communicating, we can use this for the trickier topics.

'I'm going to leave it up to you. You know what I want, but I'll go with whatever you decide. For now I'm going to stop writing and watch you sleep, because you look amazing when you sleep. Content. Peaceful. Thank you for coming into my life, Chloe, for however long you're in it. Penelope.'

Chloe wiped her eyes and put the phone down. She thought about how to respond, how to write a note that would be even halfway as powerful as what Penelope had written for her. Of course she wanted to continue as long as possible. What good did conversation do? What was that saying? Or maybe it was a song lyric... Words are the solutions for problems caused by words. She would never have been able to approach a beauty like Penelope with something as conventional as conversation. She would have been awkward or shy. The way they met was the only way they could have met, and it seemed like a tragedy to throw that away.

She put down her phone and retrieved her own, not trusting Penelope's to be decipherable, and did a quick search and headed into the bathroom. Penelope was standing in the shower, her back to the tile and her arms crossed over her breasts. She looked worried as Chloe pushed back the curtain, eyes full of unspoken concern.

Chloe smiled. "*Kalimera, ómorfi kyría.*"

Penelope's worry evaporated, and she held her arms out. Chloe stepped over the lip of the tub and joined her in the shower. They embraced under the spray, neither of them speaking as the water doused them.

Who needed language?

FAMOUS OLD PAINTERS

A WOMAN *seen in partial profile, one hand pinning her hair to the back of her neck. Her head blocks the sun, causing a golden glow to shine around her fingers as if the hand is made of gold. Her face is bathed in heavy shadow, but one can see that her eyes are downcast and her lips are parted. Even obscured her expression is one of intense weariness, something supported by the threadbare collar of her dress visible just along the bottom of the frame. A maid, perhaps, or a housekeeper taking a moment before continuing with her endless duties.*

- *The Heavy Halo*, Rembrandt, 1662, oil on canvas, 19.3 x 29.6 cm

Of course it wasn't Rembrandt. By that point in his life, he wasn't permitted to trade as a painter. It was an unspoken truth in the family, though no one came right out and admitted it was a fake out loud.

It hung in her grandfather's library for as long as Alice Carlisle could remember, nestled between two small lights with necks like swans, each shade turned toward the painting as if trying to counter the sunlight and reveal more of her features. Alice did her homework in the library and often found her attention stolen by the mystery woman. Her grandfather had a myriad of stories about where the painting came from. Found in the back of a Napoli bakery, believed to have been traded for a loaf of bread. Recovered from a Nazi stockpile. The only piece still hanging in an Austrian mansion scheduled for demolition.

Whatever its origins, the painting was bequeathed to Alice when her grandfather died. She was barely out of college, living in a loft apartment with three other former students trying to figure out what the rest of the world had to offer. Her roommate Jeffrey watched her install the anchors and carefully make sure the frame hung perfectly amid the milk crate bookshelves and the hamper overflowing with unwashed laundry.

"No way is that a Rembrandt," he said, leaning against the doorframe as he spooned another heap of Froot Loops to his mouth.

"Of course it is," she said. "Mike Rembrandt, from Queens. He was a butcher. He painted this with dyed oxblood."

"Sounds sanitary."

Alice smiled and crossed her arms over her chest.

"So who really painted it?"

"I don't know."

"You never tried looking it up?"

Alice had to admit the thought never occurred to her. It was always just a not-Rembrandt, from some anomalous place in mid-central-eastern Europe. She looked at the woman and decided to make it her personal mission to solve the age-old family mystery once and for all.

It filled her free nights and weekends, emails and phone calls with various family members to see which of her grandfather's stories had the most truth to it. She dug through books and chased provenance just in case there was any validity to the Rembrandt claims. Her quest was a dead end, but it inspired her to major in art history and eventually led to a job in a gallery. There, she forged relationships with people who knew more about the art world than could ever be written down. She eventually found an accurate trail leading from her grandfather's library to an Italian convent in the seventeenth century. So even if though it wasn't Rembrandt, it might still be worth some money.

"You should take it on that Antiques Roadshow thing." one of her triumphs suggested. The painting now hung in Alice's bedroom in a different loft, one she lived in alone save for her dog. It was hard to miss on mornings like these, when Alice was lounging naked under a sheet and the woman she'd brought home the night before was doing a scavenger hunt for her discarded clothes. This particular partner was named Lisa, and she held a blouse in front of her breasts. With the light coming in from the window, she was doing an effective recreation of the painting. "It could be worth a fortune."

"I suppose," Alice said.

Another year, another apartment, another woman. This one was named Lily, and she was close to twice Alice's age. She was married to the owner of Alice's gallery, scandalous, though she claimed they had an arrangement. Alice could have asked, confirmed before she slid her hand under Lily's skirt outside the show, but if it turned out to be a lie, then she would have been forced to go home alone. Lily had her face against the wall as Alice kissed her neck, easing down the zipper of her dress. Lily happened to look to the right and saw the painting.

"That's gorgeous. Is it a Baglione?"

Alice stopped with the zipper pull just above the dimples in the small of Lily's back. She'd started to think of the painting as just 'the Halo,' since calling it her Rembrandt was misleading and erroneous. "No... why would you think it's one of his?"

"The use of light," Lily said, shrugging out of the shoulder straps. "I saw something very similar to it once in Chicago. That was a Baglione."

"In a museum?"

"A professor's home... please, Alice, can we just...?"

"Right..."

She fucked her boss' wife and, in the morning, she got the information about where she'd seen the painting. She tracked down the professor and asked if she could see pictures of the Baglione. He was more than willing to share its history with her. It was a lost portrait, understand, discovered in the cellar of a French hotel. From what she could tell from the picture, it was definitely of a similar style to the Halo. It was from the same era and discovered in a similar part of the continent. She asked if he'd ever had the painting analyzed and he sheepishly admitted he hadn't.

She paid for the analysis and he forwarded the results to her. She compared them to the Halo and discovered they were both painted on similar canvas using almost identical materials. They were also close in age. There was no doubt in Alice's mind that the same person had painted both 'lost' pictures and it was neither Rembrandt nor Baglione. That was one mystery solved, or rather a theory confirmed. Now she had a whole new mystery to solve.

Who was responsible for the Halo and the painting that hung in the Professor's study? Why had the paintings been hidden and attributed to other artists? And, more importantly, where there any more waiting to be discovered?

A full-figured woman takes up the majority of the frame, reclining nude with a dark scarlet sheet winding around her body. Her right hand is next to her mouth. Her left hand is resting in her lap. The expression on her face is sheer exhilaration; joy and relief and happiness all revealed in the closed eyes and parted lips. An unseen light source causes her upper body to glow; it's as if the light is coming from within her.

- *The Rapture of Release*, Giovanni Baglione, 1600, oil on canvas, 20.5 x 29.6 cm

Alice examined both paintings in excruciating detail, scanning an image of each at the highest resolution so she could blow them up as large as she wanted. She spent every spare moment examining every square inch of both paintings. She ignored the wrong names assigned to each work and knew beyond a doubt that the same person had done both. There was just too much similarity in technique for it to be a coincidence. Her current girlfriend was an art major who helped her research Rembrandt and Baglione, trying to figure out why the forger chose those two.

"I think whoever it was just painted what they wanted, then assigned it to someone whose oeuvre matched. Portraits or landscapes or Biblical scenes."

Alice nodded and leaned closer to the computer screen. There seemed to be, in the tangle of threads of the Halo woman's collar, a pattern. Two threads were sticking up in a V, then a few more were vertical, and then one curled like a C. She zoomed in further to confirm the shape, then moved over to Release. She searched the corners, the curves of the sheet around the woman's body, and finally spotted it in the hairs sticking to the sweat on her neck. She took screen captures of both images and put them up side by side.

"He signed his work," Alice declared.

Her girlfriend moved closer to see, and Alice kissed her neck. She still didn't know what the signature said, and there was a chance she would never be able to decipher an actual name from it. But now she had something to look for. There was a thread, so to speak, that connected the paintings of this particular artist, and she could use that to find others.

A small cabin standing before a wall of evergreens, a mountain visible in the distance. On the porch, a singular figure leaning forward so that she's half in the sun and half in shadow. She's the smallest thing in the picture but the eye is nonetheless drawn to her: the lines of her body and the details of her clothing make her stand out against everything else. She has her arms outstretched as if she's just tossed something, but there is nothing visible if one should follow the logical arc of her hands. It's only after one has looked at the painting for a few seconds that the bird is noticed, near the top left-hand corner, its wings outstretched in freedom.

- *Flight*, Jan van Goyen, 1650, oil on panel, 17.7 x 27 cm

By the time Alice was thirty-six, she'd only found two other paintings by the mysterious VC. In the third, the woman releasing a bird from the porch, the signature was hidden in the tall grass near the trees. She got a scan of it from the Colorado museum where it was currently on display. The man she spoke to was very curt about answering her questions, and offended by the insinuation their van Goyen might not be authentic.

She spent her weekends researching online. She focused her search on lost pieces by the Dutch masters of the seventeenth century, since that seemed to be where the forger was drawing inspiration. She looked for evidence of the V.C. signature being discussed in forums or message boards. She asked docents if they'd ever heard of an unknown forger working in the mid-1600s, but none of them could help her.

The search would occasionally take a backseat to real life. Her actual work would get crazy, or she would be in a relationship where dates were more important than tracking down a Vermeer that wasn't really a Vermeer. Cassandra was the only girlfriend she ever had who shared her interest, but even she'd drifted away when there were no big discoveries. Three paintings uncovered in fifteen years. It wasn't exactly a thrilling hobby, but Alice could feel there was something worth digging for under the surface. She just had to keep looking.

On a trip to New York for her thirty-eighth birthday, she visited the Met so she could see a "discovered" Rubens in person. She couldn't get as close as she would have liked, but she took a picture with her phone and sat on a bench nearby so she could get a better look. She pinched and expanded the picture dozens of times in search of the hidden signature among the woodgrain or maybe in the curtains. She thought she could see something on the spine of a book in the corner of the frame, but the image was too pixelated for her to be certain.

"You know that's not a real Rubens, right?"

Alice looked up. The woman who spoke was standing a few feet away, turned to examine the painting Alice had photographed. Her hair was cut short around the sides but left long on top, making her look like she was wearing a shaggy blonde cap. Her eyes were obscured behind large glasses that may or may not have been affectation. She wore an off-white T-shirt under a blazer, jeans, and knee-high black leather boots. A brown leather bag was hanging off her shoulder, resting heavy on her hip like a gunslinger's holder.

"Art student?" Alice guessed.

"At NYU." She pointed dismissively at the Rubens. "But the point stands. The story says this was found in a Spanish convent. And they dated it and found it was from the right period. As far as I can tell, those are the only parts of the story that's true. Look at this woman... she's slender. Rubenesque is a term invented for the women in his works, and this poor woman is anemic by his standards."

Alice had never met anyone who was aware of the mystery. She was hesitant to reveal her own knowledge until she heard more. "So this is a forgery?"

"It was painted by an artist who spent her entire career unknown and unrecognized."

"Her?" Alice couldn't contain herself. "It was painted by a woman?"

"At the time," the woman said, "female artists were relatively uncommon. Those who did get recognized were either the daughters of famous artists or nuns. But if you were just a regular woman who wanted to paint, forget about recognition." She moved closer to the painting. "You can see her signature here on the book. Vittoria Caspi."

Alice nearly cried out. "Vittoria Caspi," she repeated, then hurried to write the name down.

"You probably shouldn't bother," the woman said. "You're not going to find her listed anywhere. Three hundred and fifty years later and people still don't know her name. No one even knows where to begin looking for her paintings."

"I do," Alice said. "I have one."

It was the other woman's turn to be shocked. Her eyes were wide behind her glasses, wide and green flecked with gold. "You own a Caspi?"

"It was attributed to Rembrandt," Alice said, "but I found out a long time ago that it wasn't his. I've been searching since I was twenty to find out more." She held out her hand. "Alice Carlisle."

"Maya Baxter." They shook hands. "I hope you don't think I'm being forward, but is there any chance I could see your painting?"

Alice's shoulders sagged. "I don't live in New York. I'm just visiting for my birthday. I do have pictures." She fumbled with her phone. "It's not the same thing, I know, but..."

"Please, anything would be wonderful." She waited patiently for Alice to find the pictures, then took the phone and brought the screen close to her face. The glasses were apparently prescription after all. She looked for a long moment and then sighed. "Caspi. There it is. I haven't seen this one before. It's absolutely gorgeous."

"I always thought so," Alice said. "I know of two other paintings. One is in Chicago..."

"The Baglione," Maya said.

"And a van Goyen at a museum in Colorado."

Maya said, "I hadn't found that one."

"But you've found others..."

"Yes."

Alice smiled and took her phone back. "Maya, could I buy you a cup of coffee?"

A woman's naked back, a shawl around her waist, her arms extended to open the blinds as morning light washes in. Through the heavenly sunshine, one can barely make out the roofs of nearby buildings. In the distance, rolling green hills that hint at the Italian countryside. The woman's hair is mussed as if she'd actually just risen from bed. Her back is a spectacular display of light and shadow that enhance her musculature. The piece is voyeuristic, even though only the hypothetical people outside her window are seeing any true nudity.

- Face the Dawn, Peter Paul Rubens, 1620, oil on panel, 120 x 64 cm

The coldness Maya had exhibited in the museum wore off as they walked to the nearest café. She'd gone from a smug know-it-all to an eager student, desperate to know more. Alice felt the same way. For years, the mystery forger had been her obsession. No one she knew cared as much about it and none of them could understand why it was such a big deal. And now here was someone who not only shared her excitement, she could fill in so many blanks.

Vittoria Caspi. She finally had a name. Her painting was a Caspi. She was looking for Caspi works. She laughed seemingly for no reason as they stepped out into the sunshine but, when she looked at Maya to explain, she saw a similar giddy expression on her face. She understood. Miracle of miracles, she actually understood the quest that had filled every spare moment of Alice's adult life. She laughed again and this time Maya joined her.

It didn't matter where they stopped as long as there was a place to sit and sustenance in the form of caffeine. They took a booth, ordered coffee, and stared at each other for a moment as they waited for the other to break the silence first.

Alice finally decided it would be her. "How did you discover her name?"

"That was actually where I started. I had a name and nothing else." She placed her bag on the table and dug through it until she found a notebook. Alice pulled her hands back to give Maya room to spread it out between them. "There was a grave marker in Tuscany marked with her name and the date 11 August. The inscription is... here."

She turned the book around so Alice could see the picture. She read the inscription aloud. "The last resting place of Vittoria Caspi, whose eye has seen the beauty of our world."

Maya said, "She was buried in a church basement, but her remains were taken away and destroyed. This was a memorial left by an anonymous mourner. If it wasn't for that, no one would ever have known who Vittoria was."

"And who was she?" Her heart was pounding. On other pages were transcriptions of genealogy reports, births and deaths records, and census results. It was an astounding amount of research.

"I had to go through the male members of her family to find that out. She was the daughter of a haberdasher, born in 1642, second daughter of five children. I'm assuming she worked in her father's store. The earliest Caspi paintings I've been able to date come from the sixties, when she would have been in her twenties. I dug up wedding records from that era and found that Vittoria's sister married a painter, which is where she would have acquired her supplies. She may even have apprenticed under him for a time.

"Women painters weren't unheard of back then, but they were rare. Without a famous name, she couldn't get anyone to pay attention to her. No one would buy her works, no matter how good they might be. Art is subjective, you know, so it was easy for potential buyers to ignore the obvious skill. There's also the chance her early work wasn't as good as what we've seen later on the... in her other paintings."

"The...?" Alice said. "You started to say something else."

Maya smiled, embarrassed, and brushed her hair back. She bumped the earpiece of her glasses and made them bounce on her nose.

"I call them the Possessed Collection. As if Vittoria reached through them and guided their hands. She matched their styles, their themes, but each work was distinctly her own. Your painting, for instance. Picture it in your mind. Do you think Rembrandt could have produced it?"

Alice immediately shook her head. "No. Not at all. And the woman who told me about the Baglione recognized it as the same artist."

"Vittoria's style was graceful. Her ability was almost photographic. It's easier to tell now, with the internet and a complete catalogue of every artists' work to compare, but at the time she was able to convince people it was the real thing."

"She sold them?"

Maya nodded. "A few. Enough to make a pretty good living for herself. And the patrons who were duped didn't want to admit they were fooled, so the paintings were hidden away or donated as anonymous gifts to churches. She may have ended up in basements or forgotten in storerooms, but for a time, Vittoria's work hung on the walls of the richest art collectors in the world. They might not have known her name, but she was granted a status alongside Rembrandt, Vermeer, Caravaggio..."

"I can't tell if that's inspirational or tragic."

"A little of both," Maya said.

Alice smiled as Maya returned the notebook to her bag. "I can't believe how fortunate this was. What are the odds of the two of us running into each other like this? Two people who happen to know about Vittoria, in the same place at the same time..."

"Well, the same time is a bit of a coincidence. But the odds were actually in our favor. I'm there a lot. I don't have access to any actual Vittoria paintings, so I go to that one when I can. It's sort of been my touchstone. It helps clear my head."

Alice said, "I really wish I lived in town so I could take you to see the Halo in person. That's what I call the one I own, the Rembrandt. Its full name is *The Heavy Halo*."

"Can I see it again, please?"

"Sure. I can email you the image if you want."

"That would be great."

She gave her email address and Alice sent it to her. "Huge coincidence or tiny one, I'm still glad we ran into each other. Knowing Vittoria's name is such a huge revelation. I can finally stop telling everyone I have a fake Rembrandt and just tell them who it really is. Thank you. You have to let me buy you dinner or something as a way of saying thank you."

"You showed me the Halo. That's more than enough.' She hesitated. "But I am a college student, so the idea of turning down a free meal is reprehensible to me. So I will accept."

Alice laughed. "It's my pleasure. Plus, it will be nicer than eating alone on my birthday."

"Happy birthday!"

"Thank you. And thank you again for the gift of Vittoria's name. I don't know if I ever would have found that on my own, so I really appreciate it."

Maya said, "I aim to serve. And honestly, you're the first person whose eyes haven't glazed over after I talked about it for two minutes. And you showed me the Halo! So meeting you was pretty great, too. Looks like it worked out for both of us."

"It certainly does."

They exchanged phone numbers and set a time for dinner, then parted ways. Alice found herself reluctant to leave the young woman behind, certain that if she lost sight of that floppy mop of blonde and the geek-chic glasses, Maya would cease to exist. She laughed quietly to herself and looked at the note on her phone. Vittoria Caspi. After searching almost half her life, the object of her obsession at long last had a name. Who knew how far that could take her?

The storm is depicted in a single color, blue, in a myriad of shades. The water is sharp and bright, while the sky is deep and violent. The ships are all center frame, cerulean sails filled with the storm's breath as they race toward safe harbor.

- *The Storm's Breath*, Ludolf Bakhuizen, 1662, oil on canvas, 92.4 x 127 cm

That night while she was getting ready, Alice found herself drawn to her computer so she could look up more about Vittoria Caspi. There was nothing, no articles or biographies, no list of found paintings or suspected works. When her friend Susan called to wish her a happy birthday, Alice explained everything she had discovered and what Maya had told her.

"You have a name!" Susan said. "That alone is huge."

"Right, but there's no literature whatsoever about this woman. It all exists in Maya's notebooks." A horrible thought occurred to her. "What if it's just a scam?"

Susan said, "What exactly would the purpose of that scam be? Did you give her any money?"

"No. I'm buying her dinner."

"Oh..."

"It's not like that. She's in her twenties."

Susan laughed. "How many thirty-seven-year old women said that about you?"

"I'm thirty-eight as of today, thank you." She was still clicking through images and leaned forward, trying to decide if the Bakhuizen was possibly Vittoria's work. "Okay, it's not a scam. It would be the strangest con ever if it was. But I'm looking now and there isn't a single website dedicated to this woman. There isn't even a footnote I can find that says some of these lost masterpieces might have been done by her. Do you realize how huge this might be? We could be famous."

"Maybe that's the scam."

"Maybe." Alice looked at the clock. "I have to finish getting ready. I'll text or email you later with any new details. I love you."

"Love you, too. Try not to get conned."

Alice laughed and hung up. If the stormy sea was a Vittoria, it was the first one she'd seen without any people. She clicked back and opened the folder where she kept images of all the pieces she'd uncovered so far. She lined them up and clicked through them, pausing between Halo and Dawn. There was only a hint of the face in Dawn, just a sliver, but she could compare the two easily enough. She was seventy-five to eighty percent certain it was the same person. She was breathing hard as she clicked onward to Release. The naked woman masturbating, facing the viewer fully this time, so it was impossible to know what her profile looked like. But her hairline. The shape of her mouth and the curve of her lips. With a shaking finger she advanced to Flight. This woman was miniscule, hardly detailed, but now that she knew what to look for, it was obvious.

"Holy shit," Alice whispered. "They're all the same person."

Icarus is seen from behind, wings spread out to either side as if to shade his body from the sun. His arms are curled defensively toward his body. Near his body the wings are perfect, each feather so perfectly detailed that they appear to have been placed on the painting and covered with a light coat of oil. Farther out the feathers begin to blur and become sloppy, each one blending into the next until they are little more than smears of color at the farthest edges of the canvas. Several droplets of wax run down the naked back of the flying man while others plummet through the air behind him as he begins his fatal plummet back to the ground.

- Escape, Joachim Wtewael, 1620, oil on canvas, 78.2 x 54 cm

She presented her theory to Maya as soon as they were seated at dinner. Maya examined the pictures on Alice's phone as she pointed out the details. After going through each picture and going back to look at some of them twice, Maya looked up with a look of abject shock on her face. Her glasses magnified her eyes to comical proportions, and her jaw hung open.

"Holy shit."

"That's what I said."

"It's the same person in all the paintings."

Alice laughed. "So who do you think it was?"

"Maybe a sister? Her mother... no, the masturbating picture is a bit too... uh..." She pushed her bangs up to scratch her forehead. "They could be self-portraits. We could have been looking at Vittoria all along. She couldn't get recognition through her name, but everyone who looked at these paintings would be seeing her. They would know her, even if they didn't know it."

"That doesn't feel right." She couldn't say if it didn't ring true or if she just wanted a better story, but she didn't want to believe the artist had used herself. She wanted this mystery muse to be a piece of the Vittoria Caspi puzzle. One more thread to follow. She looked at Maya and smiled. "I know I've said thank you about five hundred times, but I just want to say it once more. You've given me more information in one afternoon than I've uncovered in twenty years. I don't think one dinner could make up for that, but I want you to know how much it meant to me."

"You're extremely welcome. Thank you for showing me all of these works. I don't know how I would have uncovered them all on my own. And now the thing about the model... who knows where that will lead, right?"

Alice nodded, then bit her lip. "You know we... if this turns into something real, if we really have found an unknown female artist from the seventeenth century, that's going to be huge news."

"Right. Your Halo painting is going to be worth a fortune."

"Yeah. I just want you to know that if it does blow up, I'm not going to cut you out. You're the one who found her. I just gathered a few puzzle pieces when they fell into my lap."

Maya said, "Thank you. I appreciate that."

"If we keep thanking each other, we're never going to get anywhere."

Maya laughed. "Maybe we should just order.

"Yes."

They put aside their phones and picked up their menus. Alice always treated herself on her birthday, and she insisted on Maya doing the same. Afterward Maya ordered her ice cream profiteroles for Alice but refrained from telling the waitress what the occasion was. "I don't think this is the kind of place where they sing to you," Maya whispered, "but just in case, let's just pretend it's in honor of Vittoria."

"To Vittoria," Alice said, biting into one of the amazing puffs.

They left the restaurant and Alice gestured in the direction of her hotel. Maya began walking alongside her without comment. They talked about other rumors they'd heard, potential Vittoria paintings that were hanging in the Louvre or other far-flung museums neither of them could afford to visit. Online pictures and scans were fine, but for true detail, it was hard to be certain.

"Well, maybe together we can make some headway into discovering who she really was."

Maya nodded. "Absolutely. Combining our efforts has already done so much. I feel like a whole book just got opened."

"No, you were much farther along than I was. You gave me her name. That's huge."

When they reached the hotel, Alice invited Maya up to look at some more images on her laptop. It was a much larger screen than the phone, so it would allow for more detail.

In the elevator, Maya said, "The museum has a cafeteria. If you want to meet up again tomorrow, we could grab some sandwiches there and really examine the Rubens."

"Oh. I'm flying out in the morning. I have to get back to work."

"Oh. That's too bad."

"But I definitely want to keep in touch. I was going to wait until I had you trapped in my room so you couldn't run away before I started throwing my phone number and email address at you."

Maya laughed. "I wouldn't have run away." They walked to the door and Alice fumbled for her keycard. "So you had a nice dinner, the profiteroles, visited a museum... are there any other birthday traditions you have that we didn't cover?"

Alice grinned and bumped the door open with her hip. "You mean like a birthday spanking? Nah, I only do that when I'm dating someone." She turned on the lights. "You can put your bag down anywhere."

"So you are single?"

"Sadly, yeah." She opened her laptop on the bed and bent over to power it on. "But not too sadly. I wouldn't have splurged on this trip if I was seeing someone, and I didn't want to share the experience with someone who didn't really understand the obsession. So it worked out for the best that I'm alone."

Maya said, "So... do you usually have sex on your birthday?"

Alice's fingers paused on the keyboard. She took a moment to process Maya's words, then turned to look at her. She was standing by the door, looking as if she wanted to flee.

"Sometimes."

"And the times when you do..."

Alice smiled. "It's with women."

"Okay. Uh..."

"Maya." She sighed and straightened up. She toyed with her necklace to give her hands something to do. "You're..." Too young? "I'm... I'm..." Twice your age? How many women had said that to her when she was Maya's age? How many thirty-eight-year old lovers had taken a twenty-something Alice to their beds? She had always loved older women. But now that she was pushing forty, maybe it was time for her to start working the other side of the equation. Maybe she owed it to the hook-up gods who always sent her gorgeous women twice her age who were willing to sleep with a student.

She sighed again and walked to where Maya was standing. "You want to fuck me?"

"Yeah."

"You have to say it."

Maya's cheeks pinkened. "I want to fuck you, Alice."

She got the words out just before her mouth was covered. Her arms went around Alice's waist and she moaned to punctuate her statement, sagging forward. Alice took her weight and slipped her tongue into Maya's mouth, holding her tight enough to spin them both around and walk her toward the bed. She might have preferred older lovers, but she'd had her share of younger women. Maya might be on the low-end of the scale if she was forced to make a chart, but she was by no means fresh territory.

They stood by the bed and broke the kiss only to undress, lifting arms or sweeping hair away from eyes as each article of clothing fell to the floor. Maya took off her glasses and tossed them as carefully as possible toward the pillows. Maya was wearing what Alice called a 'laundry day bra,' with a tear on the cup, and she was a little touched that this wasn't a planned seduction. She bent down and kissed the rip as she hooked her thumbs in Maya's underwear and dragged them down.

Maya was still wearing her shoes. She sat on the edge of the bed and Alice, naked only from the waist up, crouched beside her and pulled off the sneakers and socks. Maya leaned back and Alice gazed at her body. She had a navel piercing and a small mantis tattoo on her hip. She brought her hand up and brushed her thumb over the lines of the insect.

"Maybe we should get Vittoria tattoos."

"Sounds good to me. Do you have any ink already?"

"Find out."

Maya grinned and leaned forward to kiss her. Alice crawled forward between Maya's legs and pushed her down. She stretched out on top of Maya, who took advantage of the new position to unbutton Alice's pants and inched them down her thighs. Once they were out of the way she kicked them away and sat up, settled on Maya's hip, and looked down at her. So beautiful and *young...* her hair had fallen back to expose more of her face than Alice had seen all day. Without her glasses on, she looked so much younger. It was startling to think they'd met less than twelve hours ago in front of a painting.

"To Vittoria," Alice said.

Maya smiled and cupped Alice's breasts before sliding her hands up to her neck. "How do you think she would feel about her paintings leading to this?"

Alice said, "Jealous. So very jealous."

Maya grinned. "But if I'm going to fuck you, shouldn't I be on to~"

"Sh," Maya put a finger over Maya's lips. Maya smiled and took the tip into her mouth. "You talk much too much, young lady. Let a master show you how it's done..."

"Yes, ma'am."

Alice slithered down Maya's body, kissing her everywhere that appealed, taking one pink nipple between her lips and using her fingers to tease the other. She moved her head to the inner curve of

Maya's cleavage and spoke without lifting her head.

"How many women have you been with, Maya?"

"Two..."

Alice whimpered. "Oh, you're just a baby. That's adorable." She kissed her way back up to Maya's neck, readjusting herself so one leg was pressed against Maya's crotch. "Hopefully I can teach you a few things." She put one hand between Maya's back and the mattress, the other on the back of her head, and held her as she rolled her hips forward. Maya craned her head up and parted her lips in search of another kiss. Alice teased her, allowing her a glancing touch before retreating. She brushed the tip of her tongue against Maya's top lip and cherished the way Maya groaned in frustration when it was withdrawn.

"Please..."

"What if I'm Vittoria?" Alice whispered. "Reincarnated, come back to find the woman who has been digging up my works?"

Maya whimpered again. Her bottom lip was trembling.

"What if you're my muse?" Alice was moving faster now, thrusting hard enough that the bed was starting to protest. "What if you once lived as the woman who occupies all my paintings? What if we've found each other at last?"

"Please, Alice... Vittoria... please..."

Alice kissed her. Maya clung to her, desperate and hungry, spreading her legs and planting both heels on the edge of the mattress. She lifted her body against Alice's thigh as they kissed, their hands exploring curves as they moved against each other. Alice whispered a command between kisses, her tongue brushing against Maya's as she spoke and obscuring the directive, but Maya understood. Her left hand dropped from Alice's side and moved between their bodies. She put the heel of her hand against her mound and used the middle two fingers on herself, her cries becoming more pointed as she thrust harder. Alice moved faster, lifting up to look down at Maya's flushed features. Her cheeks were bright red, her hair wild.

"I wish I really was Vittoria," Alice muttered. "God, look at you. I could paint you."

Maya laughed breathlessly. "I think of... I can think of other, other things you can do with your hands to me." She swallowed and threw her head back. "I mean, do to me with..."

"I know," Alice laughed. She moved her hand between them and covered Maya's fingers. "Like this...? Is this what you want me to do to you, Maya?"

"Yes..."

Alice put her lips on Maya's neck, teasing with her tongue as she guided Maya's hand. Maya turned her head and kissed Alice's ear.

"I want to taste you," Maya whispered.

"Yes..."

"I want to run my tongue all over your body."

Alice grunted and Maya echoed the sound. When Maya came, her free hand clutched Alice's arm hard enough to leave red marks. She bit off the sound trying to roar out of her throat before she finally clapped a hand over her mouth and let loose. Alice smiled at the sound and sat up to kiss Maya's fingers, nudging them out of the way with her chin and covering Maya's mouth with her own. Maya eagerly accepted the kiss and thrust her tongue into Alice's mouth before she began struggling.

"Roll over."

Alice obliged and put her hands above her head as Maya scrambled to get on top of her. They were both sweating, both gasping for breath, and Maya dragged her fingers down the center of Alice's chest.

"Fair warning," she said, "I'm not the world's best at..."

"I said I was going to teach you some things, sweetheart." She put her hand on the side of Maya's head and gently urged her down. "This is lesson one. Pay attention."

Maya grinned and settled between Alice's legs. "Should I take notes?"

"No, no. Your fingers are going to be much too busy for writing." She grinned and put her hand on top of Maya's head to get her started.

Tuscany, 1668

The kitchen had the best light in the mornings, the only time Vittoria could spend on her secret projects, so it became her studio. She kept a short prep table near the oven and there was a table in the corner where she could take her meals, but the rest of the space was occupied by easels and blank canvasses lined up along the wall under the windows. Vittoria was tall for a woman, made even taller by the wild tangle of black curls that she rarely tamed before midday. She wore battered old trousers with the cuffs rolled up past her bare feet, and a man's shirt that she didn't mind getting paint on. The collar hung open to reveal her throat and upper chest, scandalous should anyone wander by and peer in.

Light poured through windows, each one six panes of fogged glass. Her current work was on the easel: an empty body-shaped space in the center with the background filled in. A pair of wings expanded from what would be the central subject's back. She spent the morning on the feathers, leaning in close to make sure each vane and barb was perfectly detailed. The nearer feathers had to be perfect to ensure the degradation at the extremities was clear.

There was a soft knock at the door and she looked up to see Natalija Krestic hovering on the threshold. She looked wary, as if a wrong comment could blow her back out the door and down the dirt road. Her hair was braided in a halo around her head, a crown of sun-bleached brown that continued in a plait over her right shoulder. She smiled nervously, looked down at her hands, crossed one foot in front of the other, and then finally raised her eyes again.

"Hello," Vittoria said.

"Hello." She took a step into the room, which seemed monumental.

Vittoria put down her brush and grabbed the nearest rag, wiping smears of oil from her fingertips as she stepped around the frame so they could face each other fully. Natalija tensed but didn't flee.

"I wasn't sure you were coming."

"Nor was I," Natalija said. "But your painting wasn't finished. I couldn't leave you without a model."

Vittoria said, "I don't care about the painting, Lija. I was frightened because I would have missed you. I would have been sad I ruined our friendship."

Natalija blushed. "You ruined nothing, V. If I gave the impression what happened was unwelcome, then I am the one who must apologize."

They stood silently with the studio between them. Under the windows was a divan where Natalija usually posed, her body contorted in whatever position Vittoria needed for her current work. A few days before, Vittoria had requested her to take down her dress to expose her bare back. Natalija sat backwards on the cushion, her hands folded in front of her. Vittoria had stepped up behind her and asked her to extend her arms out. She had lightly rested her fingers under Natalija's biceps simply to help guide her to the right position, but they moved of their own volition. The guiding touch became a caress, and Vittoria had lowered her lips to

Natalija's neck.

She snapped out of the memory and looked apologetically at Natalija. She, too, had been looking at the divan. She swallowed hard and crossed her arms in front of herself, a defensive posture.

"I can't stop thinking about what happened. How you~" Her eyelid twitched. "How you touched me."

Vittoria could still feel Natalija sagging back against her, surrendering to the embrace. She could still feel the smooth skin of Natalija's stomach as she slid her hand over it, down to where her clothes were bunched around her waist.

"Nor can I."

Natalija finally met Vittoria's gaze without looking away. The silence grew between them until it was almost as revealing as a conversation, and then Natalija looked away. Vittoria's eyes tracked the other woman as she walked toward the finished canvasses. She lifted one and turned it around to see a depiction of her features on a woman who was surrounded by a halo.

"Is this how you see me?"

"Yes," Vittoria said.

Natalija said, "But you could paint these with any model... it's your skill, your hand..."

"I'm nothing without the light and my muse. The same light is coming through the window right now." She picked up a jug and held it out. She turned it a few times, then tossed it dismissively onto the divan. "The light doesn't discriminate. It falls evenly across the entire world. But when it rests on your face, it becomes... it becomes this..." She gestured at the haloed picture. "I only wish I could sell it so others can see your beauty."

"I'm glad you can't," Natalija said quietly. "I'm glad they are for you alone, Vittoria."

Vittoria stepped closer.

"Though I do wish you achieved the fame and fortune you so richly deserve, I cannot help but be grateful that you have these in your home. I think of you looking at them and thinking of me when I cannot be here, and I... I'm..."

"Lija," Vittoria whispered. She put her hand on the back of Natalija's neck, under her hair. Natalija turned her head and Vittoria leaned close. "I do not need fame or fortune. All I need is you, my love."

Natalija's lips parted in a silent gasp as she turned to face Vittoria fully. "Love?"

"My love," Vittoria repeated. She was shorter than Natalija so she was forced to stand on her toes. Natalija bent down to bridge the distance and they kissed, something far more scandalous than Vittoria's revealing outfit or her choice of vocation. It was a sin and a crime to touch in this manner, but neither could help themselves. Natalija clutched the front of Vittoria's baggy shirt and walked backward toward the divan.

"Will you touch me the way you did before?"

Vittoria lowered Natalija to the cushions and straddled her waist, crossing her arms to pull the shapeless shirt off. "Lija, my love, I may never stop."

Natalija cried out softly and pulled Vittoria down to her.

Present day

Light fell across Alice's face, waking her from a dream that was already mostly faded. She blinked at the curtains and looked over her shoulder. Maya's hair was a mess, her face slack in sleep, her bottom lip protruding slightly as if mid-pout. Alice rolled over carefully so she wouldn't rock the mattress. When she was facing Maya, she reached up and gently brushed the hair out of her face. She went strand by strand, hoping she wouldn't disturb her sleep, but after a few seconds her eyes opened. She blinked and stared as Alice dropped her hand.

"Hi. Morning. Sorry."

Maya said, "Alice. Hi. Sorry. I can't see very well..."

"Oh." Alice sat up and spotted the glasses on the nightstand. She retrieved them, unfolded the earpieces, and carefully slid them onto Maya's face. "Better?"

"Much." She slid one hand under the pillow as she dragged the other up Alice's hip. "I can't believe I'm in bed with you. You're so beautiful and smart and I just met you one day ago. And you know Vittoria!" She laughed. "I feel like I made you up."

Alice said, "That's the sweetest thing anyone's ever said to me the morning after." She leaned in and, wary of her morning breath, kissed the corners of Maya's mouth instead of giving her a full kiss. "I feel pretty darn lucky, too. A city the size of New York and I happened to sit on the right bench at the right time to have so many questions answered."

"What time do you have to leave for the airport?"

"Check-out time here is noon, so..."

"Right."

"But the flight isn't until four. We could check out early and get some dinner."

Maya's face brightened. "I'd really like that. But... we could also spend the morning taking advantage of this big bed."

Alice chuckled. "We definitely could do that."

They kissed for a while, Alice deciding she didn't care about being minty fresh now that she was aware of how limited their time together was. Eventually they stopped to catch their breath and Alice found herself thinking of wild possibilities.

"I know you're a student so funds are limited, but if you get some free time, maybe I could fly you out. You could see the Halo in person."

"That would be amazing. That would... yes. Yes, I would get over how generous that offer is to selfishly see a new Vittoria with my own eyes."

Alice said, "Hopefully you wouldn't just be coming to see Vittoria."

Maya kissed Alice's cheek. "You'd be a nice secondary perk."

Alice laughed. "I just want to be sure we keep in touch. I've been aching to share this project with someone since I was... well, since I was your age. It's going to make every discovery so much better knowing you'll be there to celebrate with me."

"I'm honored you want me along." She linked her fingers with Alice's. "What if we end up hating each other?"

"I can bear to be around someone I hate if she goes down on me as well as you do."

Maya blushed. "Well."

"Besides, this is a big thing. Vittoria is going to be huge news when we finally have enough to reveal what we know. Whenever that happens, I wouldn't get that far without you. I would never cut you out of that. Even if the only thing we have in common is Vittoria and we occasionally sleep together... hell, I'd kill for that kind of relationship."

"Me too, frankly."

Alice nodded. "Okay. So let's just take it as it goes. We'll keep in touch, we'll visit when we can, we'll go on quests to see what new Vittoria masterpieces we can uncover, and we'll go from there."

"That sounds amazing. Where do we start?"

"With a shower."

Maya arched an eyebrow and threw back the blankets. As she fled into the bathroom, Alice climbed off her side of the bed and went to the laptop. She opened it and hit a button to see the desktop background, a photograph she'd taken of the Halo when it still hung in her grandfather's study. She didn't know where the quest for more Vittoria works would take them. They might even be at the end of the road, no more paintings waiting to be uncovered and no further information on her life waiting to be pieced together.

"Water's warm," Maya called from the bathroom.

"I'll be right there."

She shut the laptop and went to join her. Even if they never found anything else, Alice had a feeling the quest she started so long ago had finally gotten her where she needed to be.

Even Money

Marlin Kensleigh put her foot on the ground next to her motorcycle and pulled out her phone. She was parked at the curb outside of the Storm Dance, a brick and glass LEGO that was too bland to be considered ugly. She tapped the phone's screen and used her fingertip to trace the geometric design which would unlock it. "Nico Mitchell, $500" was written on the top line next to a red "OVERDUE - IMMEDIATE ACTION" notification. She sighed and put the phone back into her pocket. She hated confrontations, but she also hated people who couldn't be bothered to pay their debts on time. She had money going out, too, and she despised going out of pocket.

She climbed off the bike and went inside. It was before business hours so the place was empty except for a bulky man sitting at a table near the jukebox. He had a notebook open by his right hand, a tablet by his left. The TV behind the bar was showing a muted episode of SportsCenter. The man at the table lifted his eyes without moving his head.

"We're closed until nine."

"Door was open."

"Doesn't mean you can just walk in here, sweetie."

She stopped a few feet in front of the table. "Do you own this place?"

He finally lifted his head. "What's it matter to you?"

"It matters to me because that would make you Nico Mitchell, which would mean you're the guy who put a five hundred dollar bet on the Vikings last month. That debt was due as soon as the game ended. Considering it's been three and a half weeks, you can understand why I'd be a little unwilling to wait for business hours."

Niko sat up straighter and stared at her for a long minute. She was five-two, very slight, and wearing Elvis Costello glasses. He had a full ten inches and probably a couple hundred points on her, and she could see him dismissing her as a threat. He pushed back from his table and unfolded himself from the chair, letting her see just how big he was.

"Look, sweetheart. Times are tough. I put that bet because someone told me it was easy cash. Vikings decided to make a liar out of him. I'll get you the cash, but it's going to take a little while."

She closed the distance between them. "You've had your little while. I was very polite waiting this long, but I'm afraid I can't wait anymore. I need the cash, Mr. Mitchell."

He turned to face her. "Yeah? Well, then why don't you send your boyfriend after me?"

Marlin didn't consider herself to be a fighter; what she did in confrontations was closer to dancing than a fight. She moved her body and arranged her opponent's body into a new position that encouraged them to agree with her. Nico had one hand on his hip, the other on the bar. He was leaning forward in an attempt to loom over her but really just threw his center of gravity to hell. She moved too quickly for him to react, stepping in close to grab his wrist and turn his arm around. Big guys thought they were invincible, but they were as vulnerable as anyone else to someone with the right skills. Everyone had wrists and ankles and joints as weak as a man who had never set foot in the gym.

She grabbed his arm and stepped around him, pulling his hand with her like it was the buckle of a seatbelt. The move ended with his arm between his shoulders, and she pushed his knee forward with a gentle nudge of her foot. He went down hard, sagging against the side of the bar with a shout of pain and surprise. Marlin turned his hand so the palm faced out, putting more strain on every joint in his arm.

"I shouldn't have to say this," she said calmly. "but you're also banned from making bets with me ever again. So if you just pay me the cash you owe, I'll be out of your hair and you'll never have to see me again."

He grunted. "Fine. Under the cash register. Lockbox."

She released him and walked around the bar. Nico propped himself against one of the stools and rubbed his sore shoulder. He watched her open the lockbox and carefully count out four hundreds and five twenties.

"I'm one of the nice ones," she said as she folded the money and put it in her back pocket. "I could've charged you a ton of interest, I could've sent my brother who makes you look like a freshman to break your windows or something. I came here and I asked nicely. Whoever you place your next bet with isn't going to be as reasonable, Nico. That's just a warning, not a threat." She put the box back under the bar. "Have a good night, my man. Sorry about your Vikings."

She left the bar and got back on her bike. She had Mace in one pocket and a pair of brass knuckles in the other in case Nico decided their interaction wasn't finished, but the door remained closed. She had done everything in her power to prepare for a fight - four years of jiu-jitsu as a teenager and what seemed like a lifetime of dance classes as a child meant she could bob, weave, and subdue pretty much any untrained opponent - but she knew there was a point where a full-grown man would have the advantage over her. The weapons helped balance the playing field.

Before starting the engine, she took out her phone and checked it again. She thought she had seen something on the list and wanted to be sure before she drove off. She scrolled and spotted it again: an address just two blocks north of the Storm Dance. The debtor owed two hundred dollars on a game from the past weekend. Not enough to justify a violent encounter but enough that she could swing by and make herself known. She put her helmet back on and kicked the bike to life.

The garage was set back from the road, its entrance almost hidden by shrubbery belonging to the restaurant next door. The bay doors were all standing open even though there didn't seem to be any customers at the moment. Marlin pulled into the parking lot and parked next to the first bay, next to the offices. She rested her helmet on the bike seat and adjusted her glasses as she walked inside. She listened for evidence that anyone was still at work and heard a distance clanking. She couldn't see the source, and the office seemed empty.

"Hello?"

"Down."

She looked down at the floor and saw that the bay was open, revealing a cramped space underneath the garage where a woman was looking up at her.

"Hi. Are you Sidney Gracen?"

"Yeah. I'll come right up."

She stepped out of sight. Marlin paced toward the office as she waited for Sidney to appear. The garage *was* closed, according to the hours posted on the door. Sidney appeared on the ground level, suddenly appearing out of the darkness without the sound of a door or footsteps on stairs to explain how she'd ascended. She was wearing forest-green overalls with the sleeves cut off and neatly hemmed so there wouldn't be a fringe of loose thread. The top half of the overalls had been left undone to reveal a scoop-necked tank top. Marlin was more interested in the vast mosaic covering the mechanic's arms, chest, and neck. Her hair was cut mostly short, save for one long shank that hung over the right side of her face. It was dyed the same shade of green as her overalls.

"I would have just yelled at you that we're closed," she explained, "but you looked more like a woman on a mission than someone who needed my help." She craned her head to the side and looked past Marlin at the bike. "Is that an Indian Chief Classic?"

Marlin couldn't help but smile. "Sure is. 2009."

"May I?"

"Go ahead."

Sidney pulled a rag from her pocket and wiped it across her palms as she approached the bike as one might close in on a wild animal. "I love these bikes. How does she handle?"

"In my experience, they handle as well as they're treated. So this one handles pretty damn well." Marlin moved closer, hands in her pockets. "So you're kind of person who calls bikes 'she', huh?"

"Force of habit." Sidney ran her hand gently along the curves of the fuel tank. "Anything that is beautiful and gives me a good ride, I tend to think of as feminine."

Marlin laughed and, to her surprise, blushed. Fortunately Sidney seemed too enraptured by the bike to notice.

"So what's wrong with her?"

"What?" Marlin panicked for just a second, startled at the idea something might be wrong with the bike, but then she realized it was a reasonable assumption. "Oh. There's nothing wrong with it. I'm not here as a customer. I'm Marlin Kensleigh. You placed a bet on the Seahawks…"

Sidney said, "Shit. Right. What was it, two hundred?"

"Yeah, that's right."

Sidney gave the bike one last pat before she stepped away and gestured toward the office. "I have it in here. I was going to put it in the bank and then use that to pay off my credit card and pay you with the card, but if you don't mind a cash payment…"

Marlin said, "Cash works. Cash spends."

Sidney unlocked the office and went inside. She didn't bother turning on the light as she stepped around the counter. Marlin remained by the door and scanned the room. There were no typical pin-up girls or thinly-veiled pornography shots hanging on the walls, but there was a photograph of a Seahawks cheerleader posed and smiling for a candid shot on the sidelines.

"I guess I shouldn't bother asking who your favorite player is."

"Doug Baldwin." She followed Marlin's gaze and smiled. "Oh, her. Rebecca. She's actually an ex of mine."

"You dated her? Wow…" She moved closer to get a better look. "I don't know what she did to make her an ex, but surely you could've compromised."

Sidney said, "How do you know she didn't dump me?"

"Because I looked at you." She hadn't meant to sound so forward, but she wasn't going to cheapen what she thought of as a damn good line by taking it back.

"Well, that's all surface shit. Once you get down deep, I'm a real bitch."

Marlin said, "Deep down, who isn't a bitch? The point is I think I'd have a lot of fun digging." God, who was this person standing here flirting like a champ?

Sidney had the lockbox open and counted out twenties. "What did you say your name was? Marilyn?"

"Actually, yes. I was born Marilyn, after Monroe, but as I got older I kind of slurred it together. I go by Marlin now."

"Like the baseball team?"

"Not especially."

Sidney handed over the money. "Do I owe you any interest?"

"No, not this early. I'm one of the nice bookies." She took the cash and counted it out. Sidney put the lockbox under the counter. "So you like bikes, huh?"

"Oh, love 'em. Never get a chance to work on them because everyone takes them to specialty shops. You've got a nice one there."

Marlin said, "Thanks." She started for the door but decided to press her luck. She hadn't gotten any irritated glares so far, so why not see how far she could go? "If you want to go for a ride sometime, let me know. I have a spare helmet."

Sidney looked up and tilted her head so she could look around the wing of hair. "Yeah? You serious?"

"Sure. I respect a lady who respects a good bike when she sees one."

"Well, it's a work of art."

Marlin gestured at the tattoos made visible by the strategically-cut overalls. "You would know about art."

Sidney chuckled and then said, "Oh. Actually... uh..."

She came around the counter and unzipped the front of the overalls. Marlin tensed but tried to hide it, standing with her back against the door frame as Sidney stopped right in front of her. Sidney was just a little taller but, at this proximity, Marlin still had to tilt her head up to maintain eye contact. There was a slight grin tugging at Sidney's features - not quite a smile but a sparkle in her eyes and a certain set to her cheeks - as she shrugged her shoulders out of the green overalls.

"What?" she asked. "I make you nervous?"

"Me? No."

Sidney did grin at that, and she lifted the hem of her shirt to reveal her stomach. She turned sideways, revealing her flank. Somehow Marlin found the strength to break eye contact and look down at what was being presented to her. The first thing she noticed was the white elastic above the black boy shorts peeking out from underneath the overalls. Then she saw the tattoo and her interest shifted. She leaned down to get a better look in the dim light.

"Wow, *The Great Escape* bike."

"1961 Triumph TR6 Trophy. My dad used to show all his old movies when my friends were over. They would swoon over Steve McQueen, I was drooling over the bike. Those movies taught me two things about myself."

Marlin brought her hand up and traced her finger over the curve of the bike, much as Sidney had done to the real one earlier. She only belatedly realized she was touching Sidney's hip, dangerously close to the underwear. Instead of pulling back, she extended her fingers and cupped the curve, letting her palm rest against the motorcycle as she stood up straight again. Sidney responded by putting her hand on Marlin's hip as well, pulling her closer.

"So you wanna ride with me?" Marlin asked quietly. She was trying to regain some of the casual coolness she'd affected earlier.

Sidney said, "Yeah. I think it would be quite an experience." She shifted her weight. Marlin suddenly found herself pressed against the wall. Sidney's body was a firm pressure against hers. Every curve was impossible to ignore. Sidney put her other hand on the back of Marlin's head and leaned in close, their lips almost touching. Marlin's glasses almost fogged over but she could still see. After a long, lingering moment in which they just stared at each other and shared breath, Marlin moved her hands to the gathered material of Sidney's overalls.

"Think you could tell a motorcycle engine just from the sound it makes?"

Sidney wrinkled her brow. "Maybe."

Marlin bent her knees and slid down Sidney's body. She couldn't believe she'd just used that line. She had fantasized about it, dreamed about doing this, but it seemed like a ridiculous fantasy. She never thought she would have the guts to actually use it on someone in real life. She wet her bottom lip with her tongue and tugged on the heavy material of the overalls. Sidney swung her hips from side to side like she was swaying to a beat, and suddenly her legs and shorts were exposed.

Now or never. Marlin leaned forward and pressed her bottom lip and the tip of her tongue against the soft cotton. She didn't think, she just began humming. Sidney gasped and jerked away from her at first, but then she rolled her hips forward. She put her hand on the back of Marlin's head and held her in place. Marlin closed her eyes and focused on making the right sound, working the muscles of her throat and using her tongue to vibrate her lips.

"Ducati V-twin," Sidney said.

Whoa, the chick does *know her shit*, Marlin thought. She withdrew her tongue, wet her lips again, and pressed her mouth harder against the fabric. Another engine, thrumming low and long.

"Hah-Honda... uh, Honda V4..."

Close enough. She was so turned on she could only thing of one other engine sound, and she extended her tongue a little more to gain the maximum effect.

Sidney grunted and said, "Ugh, no, don't make me come with a Harley..."

Marlin looked up at her. "You're about to come?"

"I could be persuaded," Sidney said, "but I'd prefer to put it off for at least a couple of minutes."

Marlin stood up and kissed her, thinking it was strange to kiss someone's underwear before kissing their mouth, but nothing about this encounter had been normal for her. She would normally let the other person be more aggressive, or at least set the tone, but she didn't want to risk missing out on things she really wanted to do.

"I want to lick your tattoos."

"Yeah? I got some that would be really fun to lick, I bet."

"Show me."

Sidney leaned back and pulled off her tank top, dropping it as Marlin reached back to unhook her bra. They were both breathing heavily when Marlin dropped her head and ran her tongue along the inner curve of Sidney's left breast, following the wing of a hawk that seemed to be rising out of her cleavage. Sidney kept her hands busy in Marlin's hair, teasing and tugging gently on it as Marlin moved her lips to a different tattoo: a cupped hand under a name written in cursive that she didn't bother trying to read.

Sidney was standing with her feet shoulder-width apart, her back bowed to give Marlin room to explore. It was a good position but it couldn't have been very comfortable, so Marlin moved her mouth up to the line of Sidney's throat to be within whispering distance of her ear.

"Take me somewhere I can lay you down."

Sidney growled and put her hands on either side of Marlin's head and kissed her. "Mm. A beautiful, sexually aggressive nerd girl with a bike... where have you *been* all my life? Do you keep the glasses on when you fuck?"

Marlin was still a little lightheaded from the kiss. "Well, sure. I've gotta see all these tattoos." She stepped back and, again acting out of character, reached down and swatted Sidney on the rear end. "Pull up your pants. I'm taking you home."

"Yes, ma'am," Sidney said.

Marlin left the office and walked out to her bike. She had no idea what she was doing. She had no idea who she was acting like, because that *definitely* hadn't been her back in the office. Sexually aggressive? Beautiful? No one had ever called her either of those things before. Nerd, yes, she'd gotten that before. But never quite in the same way Sidney had said it. Like it was a title, something to be bestowed on someone else.

She put on her helmet and started the bike, letting its engine rumble and echo off the surrounding buildings. The lights inside the garage went off and all but one of the garage doors rattled down. Then Sidney came out of the garage, hips swinging and dripping with swagger, and she realized why she'd had to up her game. There was no way she would've let this green-haired work of art get away. She had unconsciously decided to be bold so she wouldn't spend the rest of her life kicking herself.

"Do me a favor," Sidney said as she moved to climb onto the bike. "Unzip your pants."

"What?" It came out sharper than she intended, but she was taken aback by the request.

Sidney threw a leg over the bike and sank down onto the seat. Marlin had sat high up on the seat to give her room. Sidney's weight against her pushed the crotch of her jeans even harder against the swell of the fuel tank. She decided they were past the point of playing coy, and she was intrigued to see where Sidney was going with it, so she sat up straighter and tugged down the fly. She sat back down and Sidney put an arm around her, pulling her back. Her other hand brushed up and down Marlin's thigh before moving back up.

"You need me to hold on tight, yeah?"

"Yeah," Marlin said.

"Okay."

She put her hand against the crotch of Marlin's pants. Before Marlin even had a chance to gasp in surprise, the fingers squirmed inside and flattened against her underwear. She lifted up and Sidney extended her fingers, cupping her completely. Marlin squared her shoulders and flexed her fingers on the handlebars before she looked over her shoulder. Sidney's smug grin would've been infuriating on anyone else, but Marlin found herself smirking back. She faced forward and shifted her hips to press them more firmly against Sidney's warm palm.

"Okay... let's ride."

Marlin rolled forward and pulled through the parking lot in a wide arc, aiming for the exit back to the main road. Sidney's free hand snaked across her stomach for a better grip. The Indian's seat allowed Marlin to sit up straight instead of hunkering over the fuel tank so she felt the full length of Sidney's body pressed up against her. She was more focused on the way the engine's vibrations made each one of Sidney's long fingers tremble ever so slightly against her panties. She was already wet from what had happened in the office, but now she was on the verge of needing to pull over.

At the first stop light, she heard Sidney say, "Did you hear any of that?"

Marlin shook her head. Between the engine noise and the helmet, any sort of communication was impossible.

"Shame," Sidney said. "I was telling you all the things I wanted to do to you."

She was sure Sidney felt the shudder that washed over her. "Keep a list!" she said.

"Will do."

The light turned green and Marlin surged forward. Sidney sagged back and her hand pressed harder against Marlin's sex, and Marlin grunted in response. The sound was swallowed by her helmet but hopefully Sidney had felt something from it: a vibration in her body or the sharp exhale of breath afterward. She didn't want to come before they got back to her place, but she knew that even if she did, Sidney wouldn't consider her work done.

They definitely had a long night ahead of them. She resisted the urge to speed through the next intersection.

Sidney's hand didn't remain still; her fingers twitched and twisted and danced, applying pressure and then relaxing, stroking and then moving in wide ovals. At the next light Marlin heard "--come if you want to," and it was almost enough to push her over the edge. She shook her head no but flexed her fingers on the throttle, lifting her butt off the seat and dropping it back down. She was rubbing against Sidney's crotch like she was in heat, but she couldn't help it. Damned clothes...

A car pulled up beside them. The woman behind the wheel glanced over, her head jerking back in a classic double-take. Marlin was grateful for the helmet so the woman couldn't see her blush. Sidney didn't seem quite as shy; her free hand moved up to Marlin's breast and she pressed harder against her. She thrust her hips and applied steady pressure with two fingers, and Marlin couldn't help but roll her head back in pleasure. When she opened her eyes, she saw the other driver was facing forward with bright red cheeks and a nervous grin plastered on her face.

"Green!" Sidney said.

"Huh? Oh..."

Marlin and the other driver pulled forward at the same time. Marlin's underwear was wet, and it was all she could do not to shout at Sidney to just fucking put them inside, but she knew patience would be rewarded.

They were lined up with their voyeur again at the next light. This time she didn't even try to disguise her staring.

Sidney said, "We could invite her along..."

"Oh, God," Marlin groaned.

Sidney laughed. She held up her hand to the woman and made a clicking gesture. The woman laughed, the sound blocked by her window, but she lifted her phone. Sidney's hand disappeared from Marlin's hip and the woman laughed as she snapped a picture.

"What did you do?" Marlin asked.

"Universal symbol for eating pussy," Sidney said. "Two fingers up, flapping tongue. Don't worry. I'm much more artful when it's the real thing." She drove her point home by moving her middle finger in a circle and making Marlin's entire lower body clench. She bit down on her bottom lip under the mask and goosed the engine when the light turned green.

They lost their voyeur at the next corner, just one block away from Marlin's home. The rational part of her brain nudged her about the fact it may have been one of her neighbors, someone she would cross paths with again, who had watched her getting a hand job on her bike. The adventurous part, the part that seemed to have been awoken when she met Sidney, suggested maybe Sidney's comment about a threesome wasn't entirely impossible.

Somehow she managed to park the bike without coming. Sidney freed her hand and mercifully peeled herself off Marlin's back. Marlin took off her helmet, shook out her hair, and adjusted her glasses.

"So, this is your place?" Sidney asked.

Marlin reached for her hand. "Yep. Come on..."

Sidney laughed as she let herself be dragged toward the stairs.

Marlin's apartment was small, but it was perfect for her; she hated unnecessary space. The living room served as a bedroom and, in exchange for a lack of living area, she had an amazing view of the lake. She unlocked the door and pushed Sidney inside. Sidney stumbled and stepped to one side, flattening herself against the wall. Marlin followed, kicked the door shut, and covered Sidney's body with her own. Her whole body was buzzing, both from the bike and from Sidney's hand between her legs for the entire trip. She pressed her leg between Sidney's thighs and bent her knee, urging Sidney down as they kissed.

When they broke for air, Marlin reached for the front of Sidney's jumpsuit and pulled it open. "Ready for another ride, grease monkey?"

Sidney grinned and rocked her hips. "Hell yeah..."

Marlin kissed her again as Sidney shrugged out of the jumpsuit. This time she didn't stop at the waist, shoving the material down. Marlin withdrew her leg only long enough for the jumpsuit to be dealt with. The shorts went down as well so when she put her thigh back where it had been, she discovered just how eager Sidney was.

"Oh! Well... I guess you enjoyed that ride as much as I did," she said.

"Almost as much as the lady in the other car did."

Marlin laughed and kissed Sidney, then tugged her away from the wall. "I thought I told you I wanted to lay you down."

"Then take me somewhere. You're the one in charge here."

"Hell yes, I am."

She walked Sidney across the room, sidestepping the couch, and guided her down onto the mattress. Marlin sat up and began undoing the buttons on her shirt. "Take off your top," she demanded. "Show me all those tats."

Sidney pulled the tank top off, unhooked her bra, and scooted higher on the mattress. Her right arm was entirely covered with an intricate design - shapes and symbols and cursive lettering - while the left had smaller individual designs. She had a sparrow on her stomach just below her breast, and a compass rose decorated the hollow where her shoulder met her collarbone. Sidney put her hands under her head and arched her back, twisting one way and then the other to show off her tattoos.

"What do you think?" she asked.

Marlin tugged her arms out of the sleeves of her blouse and tossed it. She dropped her pants, the wallet with the money she'd gone out to collect weighing them down. She climbed onto the bed, straddled Sidney, and loomed over her.

"I think this is the first time I've liked the canvas better than the art."

"Good answer."

Marlin settled between Sidney's legs. Sidney grabbed Marlin's ass with both hands and craned her neck up to kiss her. Marlin pulled her head back, making Sidney work for it, and Sidney laugh-growled and bit her bottom lip once she got close enough. Marlin stuck her tongue out and Sidney met it with her own. Marlin smiled and dug her knees into the mattress. She moved a hand down and put her fingers to work. Sidney reached down as well with one hand, leaving the other on Marlin's ass to guide her thrusting. Their arms crossing between their stomachs and Marlin moaned in appreciation.

"Better angle," Sidney whispered.

"Mm-hmm," Marlin agreed.

They stopped talking for a while. Sidney squeezed Marlin's ass when she wanted her to move faster, Marlin tried to coordinate the movement of her tongue and fingers for maximum effect. She moved her head to the side and opened her eyes, momentarily distracted by the lines and planes of Sidney's face. Her nose was long and sloped, her eyebrows naturally arched. Her lips were parted and her eyelids were closed but fluttering. There was just a bit of sweat on her upper lip and Marlin kissed it away.

She burrowed her head against Sidney's shoulder as she came, every muscle in her body clenching before liquefying so that she melted onto the stone of Sidney's frame. Sidney held her, and Marlin somehow managed to keep her hand moving until Sidney grunted and then cried out with her own release. Marlin kept her head where it was; she had a prime necking position and took advantage of it once Sidney's hands began exploring.

"Feel free to place another bet any time, Miss Gracen."

Sidney laughed. "You charge a hell of a high interest rate. But I think I'm willing to pay it." She turned her head. "Lift up." Marlin lifted her head and Sidney kissed her. "Can I stay? I'd hate to surrender this position we've found ourselves in."

"Yeah..." She closed her eyes. "It's a pretty good position."

Sidney moved her hand up into Marlin's hair. "You don't sleep in your glasses, do you...?"

Marlin didn't know if she answered, or if Sidney took them off for her, because she slipped into an easy unconsciousness halfway through the question.

Sidney sat against the corner of the couch, her legs stretched out across the cushions with her feet crossed. Marlin was seated behind her at the table to monitor the website and keep track of her bets. She found herself distracted by the game more than usual, turning to watch Sidney watching the game. They'd been dating for a few weeks, long enough that Sidney didn't even have to ask if she could watch the game at Marlin's apartment. She had the big TV, she had the deluxe cable package, so it just made sense. And it made sense for Sidney to start keeping her game-day jerseys in Marlin's spare room.

They weren't moving too quickly because she wasn't moving in. She was just keeping some things there for convenience.

"Baby," Sidney said, "is it too late to place a bet on this game?"

"It's the third quarter. So yeah." She pushed back her chair and approached the couch from behind. "I might be willing to make an exception, though. What are you looking to risk?"

"Blindfold if I lose."

Marlin rested her arms on the back of the couch. "Blindfold and restraint."

Sidney hissed through her teeth, eyes still on the game. "You're harsh, but I think my guys will pull it out. You're on."

Marlin held her hand over the back of the couch. Sidney reached up and squeezed it, their bet made official.

"Pleasure doing business with you."

"Same," Sidney said.

Marlin went back to her computer. "I hope you're not offended I'm rooting against your guys."

"Hell, given the terms of our bet, I'm rooting against them a little bit now."

Marlin chuckled and went back to her spreadsheets. She had a lot of other games to watch, bigger bets to keep track of, but there was only one game she cared about now. And even if she lost, she knew she wouldn't mind paying out what she owed. Sidney cheered for another touchdown and Marlin laughed. It was her favorite kind of bet; no matter the outcome, she knew she was going to have a hell of a night.

EVERY SAVAGE CAN DANCE

I HAVE noticed and, on occasion, had it pointed out to me, that a familiar terrain often becomes unknown and treacherous at night. Once the sun flees and darkness descends, even those lawns with which we are most intimately aware become alien and strange. I experienced such a reversal seven months ago with my friend and confidante, the Lady Almira Stainton.

Mira was always a beauty. I would have to be blind not to notice the way her thick brows arched above almond-shaped eyes, or the way a soft brown curl rested upon her cheek. But I didn't notice the breadth of her smile or the kittenish way she batted her eyelashes when she was being coy. I paid no attention to the curve of her hip or the voluptuous spread of her upper body unless she wore certain gowns that made it impossible to avoid. My dear friend Mira was quite blessed in terms of her shape and I was often quite envious of the sidelong glances she received when we walked together.

Envious, or so I thought at the time. Perhaps the proper word is jealous. I hated that they could look, that they were allowed to openly covet her. Meanwhile I was closer to her than they could ever hope to be but I selfishly wanted more. Of course my feelings for her were strictly platonic at first. When we met I craved nothing but her friendship and she gave that to me freely.

The day my feelings changed was drowned in a downpour, the fourth day of such rains. The entire countryside was underwater or so it seemed from the window of her parlor. I was visiting her when the rain began so she invited me to make use of her spare bedroom until the storm passed. I expected to be on my way come morning but imagine my surprise when we woke to find the clouds still hovered overhead. Mira was not put out and suggested we spend the day indoors.

We became like the schoolgirls we'd been when we first met. We laughed. Gossiped and shared tales of mutual acquaintances. She gathered her correspondence and read me letters from her brother in the Arabian countries. We stayed up much too late into the evening and only retired when neither of us could keep our eyes open any longer. Her library was full of books, more than any person could read in a lifetime, and she made a stack of recommended titles for me to read.

"So many pages," I exclaimed when I saw them. "It must be impossible to carry them all!"

"That's why I have so many friends. To make them carry my books."

One evening saw us traipsing upstairs together, my head on the softness of her bosom and her hand tightly clutched to my waist. I think about that night often now, how I might have given myself away had I known how my feelings would change in a few scant hours. But at the time she was nothing but my dearest comrade, and when she pressed her lips to my cheek in farewell I felt only a warm admiration for a friend.

The rain continued, relentless. She had no permanent household staff, and no one was venturing out into this most peculiar of storms, so we were all to our lonesome until the sun deigned to shine again. We quickly grew weary of the company. Our eyes grew tired of reading. We paced the rooms of her suddenly claustrophobic manor, spent of activities and bored with the sight of one another. We began to irritate each other and ourselves. I snapped at her over breakfast and she scolded me for leaving a glass in the parlor. I longed for the comforts of my own home and my own clothing - I had taken to borrowing hers, and my shape was far less buxom than hers. The dresses were cinched and pinned but still managed to drape from my frame.

On the fateful fourth evening, we were startled by the sight of something white flashing by the parlor window. We both rose to see what it was, since there had been no rumble of thunder preceding it, and saw that one of her horses had gotten loose.

"I must not have secured the door this morning," Mira said with a resigned sigh. She had been running to and fro in order to feed the poor things. I had never seen her doing this, since every morning I awoke to the sound of rain meant I could go nowhere and do nothing anyway, so I remained in bed until truly scandalous hours. I watched out the window as she rushed off somewhere, and I kept an eye on the loose creature in case it left her property.

"Is he still out there?" Mira asked when she returned.

"Yes, near the~"

The words shriveled in my mouth when I turned and saw her. Gone was the dress, the tight corset, the proper attire with which I associated her. In its place was a man's shirt, loose at the collar to make up for her anatomy, and a pair of brown dungarees. The cuffs of the trousers were rolled up almost to the knee and her legs extended from them like two delicate branches. As I stood mouthing the air like a fish, she stepped past me to look out the window for herself. She brushed against me and I felt the queerest of tickles at the base of my stomach.

"Okay. Stay by the door, Helen. I'll shout when I'm on my way back inside."

"Right."

We moved to the kitchen and she went out through the servants' entrance. Once she was gone I pushed the door shut and moved to watch her through the window. She moved quickly across the grass. Every step threw up a spray of water from the flooded lawn. She spread her arms out to the side and seemed to dance with the horse. She was already completely soaked through by the time she got her hands on the magnificent beast and calmed it enough to start moving back to the stables. She had to move slowly so it wouldn't get spooked. By that point there was nothing she could do but resign herself to being completely drenched.

I watched until she reappeared, running pell-mell for the house. I opened the door for her and she gasped as she burst through the veil of rain shimmering down off the rooftop. I took a towel from the counter and wrapped her in it. She bent forward and began scrubbing hard with both hands. I made certain the door was securely latched before I faced her again. She had stood up straight and wore the towel loosely around her shoulders like a shawl.

"That was quite invigorating!" There was laughter in her voice, so I smiled, but to be honest I was too stricken to know what she had said.

With her hair slicked against her forehead, in a man's outfit, she looked like a man. But her collar hung open to reveal the decidedly unmasculine slope of her upper chest which glistened with water from the rain and I found I could not make myself look away. Her décolletage shone like the sun dancing on a lake's waves. The tip of my tongue pressed between my lips as if to lick away the moisture and eliminate the temptation to stare.

"Helen?" She moved closer and I could see the peaks of her nipples pressing against the cotton of her shirt. "Are you all right?"

"Simply worried for you, Almira," I choked out. "You'll catch your death in those sodden clothes."

"You're absolutely right. I must look like a drowned kitten!"

"You look…" I daren't finish my thought, for everything I could have said next would only betray the strange feelings swirling within me. My mouth was dry but my palms were sweating. Seeing her capture the horse, seeing the way the clothes clung to her natural curves, the stretches of skin so blatantly on display and temptingly wet from the rain… no, I couldn't compliment her with my mind in such a state!

Fortunately, she walked away from me then so she wouldn't have to see me stammer and grow red. She removed the sodden blouse as she ascended the stairs and I was treated to a glimpse of her bare back. A bead of rainwater traced her spine and I felt it like the finger of a ghost being dragged down my own. I tensed to suppress the shudder and hugged myself. Only minutes ago the sight of Mira's naked flesh would have affected me not at all.

That night I lay in my borrowed bed, in my borrowed clothes, surrounded by the scent of her, and I touched myself. I squeezed my eyes tightly shut and tried to imagine she was a man, but a man with the breadth of her shoulders and the shape of her body. A man with her voice and her gentle touch and her lips. I imagined she was a man but the illusion never held. I knew my Mira far too well to force her into a different shape. Looking back, I believe it's quite possible I simply didn't want to succeed. As my fingers moved between my thighs, I wanted it to be the Lady Almira Stainton giving me such pleasure. I rolled onto my stomach and pressed my face into the pillow so she wouldn't hear my cries.

The rain finally stopped the following day, a blessing that I wouldn't have to spend any more time alone with Almira and my newfound confounded feelings for her. All I could think about was the scent of her hair, the feel of her hand on top of mine, her perfume. Getting away from her home would help. I could remove her from my thoughts and things could return to normalcy.

Of course it wasn't to be. I thought of her constantly. When I bathed, I remembered the droplets of water on her chest. At night I dreamt of those long and lonely nights at her home with rain pounding on the roof above our heads and I wondered what would have happened if she'd suggested we share a bed during those long nights. Would I have turned her away? Of course not. We were friends. We had spent many an evening sharing a bed, in fact.

But now...

We spent a few days apart, ostensibly so we could miss one another but also because I was avoiding her. Our reunion was unplanned, on the street outside of a teashop we both frequented. Her eyes were cast downward and my thoughts were elsewhere so we very nearly collided as I came outside just as she was entering. We both cried out in surprise. Almira grabbed my arm to keep me from falling backward and my hand went to her waist, and we held together like dancers whose music had just stopped. I looked into her eyes as a smile spread across her face.

"Why, it's my Helen!" she said.

All of the improper thoughts I'd harbored for the past few days came rushing back to me. She called me hers. She looked so much more beautiful than I remembered, and beautiful in a way I still wasn't accustomed to. My heart swelled in my chest and my hand tightened on her waist and I remembered her smile wavering as she tried to read my face. She moved her hand to better support me, cupping my shoulder, and I was still leaning back so it felt as if she was dipping me.

Mira opened her mouth to ask if I was all right and I covered her lips with mine. She squeaked in surprise as I moved my hand to the back of her head. She pulled back until we were both upright and I leaned against her. I could feel the air being sucked out of the room as her tongue teased my bottom lip. Sparks shot from my heart to my brain: she wasn't pushing me away or ending what I was certain would be a horrible offense.

In the end it was I who ended the kiss, turning my head to break contact, gasping for air even as my hand curled on the nape of her neck. Mira laughed a delighted giggle and pressed her lips to my cheek. I kept my eyes closed so I wouldn't see everyone staring at us.

I was horrified and elated in equal measure. How could I have done such a thing? Where did I find the courage? How could I possibly face Mira again after such a faux pas?

"That was a lovely hello," Mira said softly so only I would hear. "We must make that standard."

"I... I-I..."

She pushed me back so I was forced to look into her eyes. "Now, Helen, don't lose your pluck now. Unless you didn't enjoy it... did you?"

I couldn't speak. I dipped my chin once in the affirmative.

"Splendid. Then we're agreed." Mira hooked a finger under my chin and lifted my head. Before I could wonder at that, her lips were upon mine again. The humming had gone down in my ears enough that I heard people around us hissing whispers. The gossip was likely already making its way to neighboring businesses, up and down the alleys and streets to the ears of everyone we knew: Almira Stainton and Helen Alves, wantonly kissing in public!

She ended the second kiss. She put her hand on my cheek and laughed. "Goodness, darling, you're blushing."

"I'm..."

"Sh, sh." Mira threaded her arm around mine and turned us both, guiding us out of the teashop and back onto the street. "I know we became thoroughly sick of one another during that ghastly storm, but I've missed you. I doubt either of us has gained new topics of conversation but that can be overlooked. Nothing marks the true depth of a friendship more clearly than one's comfort in an extended silence."

"Mira..."

"Yes, my Helen?"

I looked back and saw people watching us through the windows. "They'll talk..."

"Let them. Let their prurient minds run wild with what they just witnessed. Only you and I will know there was nothing lewd about what just happened."

My heart crashed. "There wasn't?"

"No. If it was anything, it was... overdue."

I looked at her and saw a hint of innocence under her carefree smile. She was putting on a brave face. She was acting confident. But I could feel the tremor in her hand as it clutched my arm. I put my hand over hers and hoped that together we could stop the shaking before anyone noticed it. Her lipstick was smudged on my mouth but I wanted to leave it there, if just for a bit, to remind myself that it had really happened. The whole thing was already beginning to feel like a particularly vivid daydream.

But if Almira was to be believed, I would have plenty of future kisses to remind me of its veracity.

People did talk. Oh, how they talked! "Scandalous," they said when they thought I wasn't listening. "Simply outrageous behavior by two alleged 'ladies.'" I was terrified to appear in public for fear they were only talking behind my back because they couldn't find me to say these things to my face. I was an utter coward and once again cloistered myself behind the safety of walls and shaded windows so I wouldn't have to face the controversy. Almira had no such qualms. She went about her business as if nothing had changed. She wrote me letters asking me to dinner or to shop with her. I couldn't bring myself to respond to them.

It was on a Saturday, a day when I normally would have been sequestered in my rooms anyway, when she finally tired of waiting for me. I answered a summons to find her standing on my doorstep. She seemed to be vacillating between anger and concern. I was so startled to see her that I stammered a greeting and finally looked down at her shoes. The toes poked out from beneath the hem of her dress.

"Mira. What a surprise. What are you doing here?"

"I'm here to rescue you."

My brow wrinkled in confusion. "I was not aware I required rescuing."

"But you must," she said. "For I have received no letters from you, no response to my repeated invitations to spend time with you, and no one has seen hide nor hair of you in days. If you are not in dire need of assistance I shall have to feel quite offended."

I blushed. "I apologize, Almira. I've... I-I've been under the weather..."

"You look fine to me. So I suppose that means you can't bear to be seen with me. This must be torture for you." She gathered her dress with one hand as she turned. "I'll leave you be..."

"Wait! Please." It had been so long since I'd seen her. I ached to hear the sound of her voice, her laugh, and I stepped outside to put my hand on her arm. "I most certainly want to see you, Mira. In fact, you may be the only person in this entire country I want to see at the moment. I've missed you so very much. Please come in."

Almira said, "No. If you wish to see me, then we must go out."

"Out..." I looked past her at the street.

"You cannot hide yourself away because of what a few silly goats might say. I've missed you, terribly, Helen. And just when our friendship had taken the most interesting of turns."

I'm certain I blushed. "Don't you see? That's the very reason I feel as if I cannot venture out into the world with you. The rumors..."

"Again rumors!" She rolled her eyes to the heavens. "Let them talk. Let them speculate and whisper behind their hands. They talk about our lives because theirs are so dull and uneventful. I refuse to allow their petty close-mindedness prevent me from enjoying my life and spending time with my friends." She took my hand. She squeezed it tightly. "I treasure you, Helen, whether we are friends or... whatever we are or become in the future. That is all I care about."

I put my free hand atop hers. "Then I feel the same. Give me a moment to change and we'll go wherever you wish."

"Change?" She looked me up and down. "You look fine to me."

"But~"

She pulled me close and reached out to shut the door behind me. "If their whispering bothers you, we shall simply have to laugh louder until we cannot hear them."

I smiled at her confidence and pressed tight to her side. "I believe that would be a valid defense. Where shall we go?"

"We'll figure it out. For now, we'll simply see where our feet take us."

I nodded and turned my face to the sun, warmed by it for the first time in days and just as boosted by the company of my very dear friend. I rested my head on Almira's shoulder and let her lead me.

In the days which followed, we became reacquainted with one another. Spending time together was much less daunting now that we had the option of escaping to our own homes once in a while. One afternoon she fell asleep with her head in my lap and I found myself too distracted to continue reading. I stared down at her, the slackness of her lips and the way her eyes darted beneath the lids. I had always been drawn to her. From the moment we met, she was like a flame and I was a helpless moth. And once again I found myself acting on impulse rather than any coherent thought. I lowered my head and pressed my mouth against hers.

Mira responded in sleep, turning her head so our kiss was more properly aligned. We were behind closed doors in the safety of her library. She had already made it abundantly clear that she appreciated my kisses. So this time I was able to enjoy the sensation without guilt or worry about what anyone would think. My hand strayed up the length of her arm. It traversed the slope of her shoulder and came to rest at the lacy collar of her gown. My tongue pushed against her teeth and she relaxed her jaw, not quite inviting me in but also no longer barring me from going further.

My fingers stroked her neck. I was aware that I wasn't breathing and I exhaled through my nose. It had the effect of relaxing my body and I adjusted my bottom lip against hers. Suddenly she returned the pressure and brought her hand up to the side of my head. I felt my cheeks reddening as she stroked my hair and teased my tongue with hers but I couldn't bring myself to stop. It felt like a first kiss, what with the freedom I now had to simply enjoy what was happening.

"Oh, Helen," she whispered against my mouth after untold seconds. "I've dreamt of kissing you. But I much prefer waking up to it."

"I'm sorry, Mira. It was presumptuous..."

"Hush." She sat up to face me. Her fingertip traced a line down my cheek. "We've wasted so much time on words, speaking them and reading them, when we could have been filling our time with kissing. Let's see how long it takes us to tire of that."

I couldn't stop myself from looking at her lips. "Fair warning, my dear..."

"I know. It may take me quite a while as well."

We kissed again. It was becoming as natural as a handshake or a hug. I was growing accustomed to the feel of her lips on mine. Never before had I understood the appeal of kissing but now... oh, now. I could kiss Mira forever. I moved closer to her on the divan. She responded by putting her hand on my thigh, the one farthest from her. I could almost feel the warmth of her through my clothes. I said, "Oh," into her mouth and she responded with something that may have been a moan, may have been a word, but I didn't care either way.

She pulled away and left me breathless. Our faces were still close, closer than propriety may have allowed. I could feel her breath on my mouth and it made me want more. She sighed and rested her forehead against mine. Our noses bumped against each other.

"I admitted I've dreamt of these kisses, Helen," she said. "Have you dreamt of me?"

"I've done more than dream."

Her eyes opened and locked onto mine. They were deep and dark, a brown almost black, and I was lost in them.

"Tell me," she said.

I shook my head. Kissing was one thing, but saying those words was quite another. "I can't," I whispered. "Don't make me."

"I won't make you do anything you don't want," she promised. "Perhaps I can guess. Did you lift your dress, Helen?"

I nodded the affirmative.

"Would you do it now?"

I wouldn't have thought it was possible to blush redder. but I believe I managed it when she asked me that. But scandalous as it might have been, I found my hands gathering the cloth and raising the hem of my dress above my knees to expose the tops of my stockings. She glanced down but then returned her eyes to mine. She brought her hand up and brushed two fingers over the tip of her tongue, wetting them. My fingers tightened in the material of my dress. Though my brain refused to admit what was about to happen, it still sent signals to my legs. My knees fell apart as she put her hand on my knee. I shifted on the couch cushion, turning more to face her.

Mira's hand felt so warm on my thigh. It was hidden by my dress now, the point of no return so far as I was concerned. I moved my hand to her wrist to prevent her from pulling it away in the event this was just some cruel joke. But no, I could feel the tremors in her hand.

"You must tell me what you did next," she whispered.

I guided her hand higher. "You know," I said.

"Tell me."

Gathering my pride as I had gathered my dress, I looked her in the eye. "I touched myself. Alone in my bed, with thoughts of you, I brought myself to climax over and over again."

"Was it lovely?"

"It was the sweetest thing," I said. "But I feel my next shall be even sweeter."

She bit her bottom lip and pushed her hand higher. It pressed to the crux of my legs and my breath stuttered in my throat. She tensed and leaned toward me, so I captured her lips with mine. As I said: it was becoming our natural state, to be kissing. But now there was the added element of her hand pressing against my sex and I never wanted that to stop, either. Her fingers moved in circles against my underclothes, rubbing it against my folds. My feet drummed against the floor in a quick drumming tempo before curling my toes to keep them still.

I moved my hand to her collar and thumbed one of the pearl buttons. I thought about asking permission but then I felt her tracing the lines of my labia and knew we'd moved beyond that. I wasn't sure I could form words at that moment, anyway. So I undid one button and gave her the opportunity to tell me no. When she said nothing, I undid the next one and then the next. Her breasts rose and fell with each rapid breath. I bent down and pressed my lips to one curve. I kissed down to the hem of her undershirt and, with a glance upward, pulled it out of the way to expose one pink nipple.

"Helen," she said, "please..."

My tongue found her nipple and drew it into my mouth. I matched the rhythm of her fingers, my other hand cupping her breast through her gown. I felt my orgasm approaching like a swell in my stomach, growing larger and larger until I could no longer hold back a cry of pleasure. I craned my neck to kiss hers, running my tongue up the length of it. She pulled back like a snake recoiling and, at first, I thought she was disgusted by my wetness on her hand. I looked up to apologize but she pressed her mouth over mine in a sloppy and unorchestrated kiss. Her tongue slipped wantonly across my mouth and I failed in my attempt to capture it, instead smacking her cheek.

"Helen," she said, echoing the sentiment thrice over before she removed her hand from my unmentionables. I moved my head to her shoulder and looked down. Her breast was still exposed, the erect nipple shining and wet from my tongue. My body tingled in a way I hadn't thought possible. I pressed a series of small kisses against the curvature of her neck.

"Please," I whispered, "please tell me we'll do that again."

"Again?" Almira said. She pushed me back and looked into my eyes, truly confused. "How can we do it again when we aren't even finished with this encounter?"

My eyes widened. "We're not...?"

"Oh, my love." She laughed and adjusted her clothes, then took my hand. "Let us take this somewhere more comfortable and

I'll show you everything that was in my dream..."

I blushed deeper than I ever have but, though I doubted my ability to walk properly, I stood and let her lead me to her bed.

We became inseparable. In the weeks that followed I rarely left Almira's home and, when I did, we were together. We cuddled together in the private darkness of a carriage and held hands as we walked through town. When we stopped to eat, we would lace our fingers together on the tabletop. Occasionally we sat together on the same side of a booth. At first I was ashamed of how people stared at us and the whispers I overheard, but Almira was only spurred to be more contrary. She kissed the corners of my mouth when we parted ways.

One fine Friday afternoon, we crossed paths with a pair of older women who eyed the way my arm looped around Almira's. They waited until they were well past us before one turned to her companion and said, "Sad that two girls so lovely have to resort to such demeaning behavior!"

I would have been fine with ignoring it, but not my Mira. She stopped cold and turned us both so we were facing the older women, our about-face so abrupt that the women seemed to sense it. They turned as well, eyes wide with surprise as if curious what could have prompted such attention. Almira smiled her beautiful smile.

"Lady Bristow and Mrs. Fallows! I couldn't help but overhear your critique and I must say it is quite a shame that Miss Alves and I were forced to find companionship with one another. I had resigned myself to settle for her humor, her beauty, her kindness, because I cannot for the life of me figure out how to be courted by a man." She raised her eyebrows as if an idea had just occurred to her. "Perhaps you can assist me, Mrs. Fallows! You're quite skilled at finding husbands. You must be on your third by now." She turned to Lady Bristow as Fallows' face seemed to collapse in on itself. "And you Lady Bristow... ah... well, I suppose if you had any expertise on the matter you wouldn't be spending your days in the company of a woman old enough to be your mother."

She touched the brim of her cap to those who would judge us.

"Until then, fair ladies, I shall try to make do with the one person who finds me worthy of her company. Good day to you both."

Almira turned her back on them and led me away. I waited until we were around the corner before I allowed myself to laugh, and even then I smothered it with my sleeve.

"Oh, Mira, I never knew you had such a split tongue!"

"Don't posture, Helen, you are quite familiar with the skills of my tongue."

I blushed, but not as much as I might have done a few weeks earlier. "Perhaps I require a reminder when we return home."

"Perhaps I may oblige."

She loaded me into our carriage and hollered to the driver, "Take us home at once, and don't spare the horses!"

In the privacy of the carriage, she gave me a hint of just what her tongue was capable of and she had told no lies.

It was a very, very talented tongue.

OPEN SESAME

IN A rough neighborhood in a rough city that was part of a rough country, Alison Barber strolled down a street even the bravest of police officers refused to patrol. She wasn't especially brave or foolish; it was simply the quickest route home. Over her shoulder hung a satchel filled with that day's haul of wood. She was a carver, and she sold her little animals and effigies at the town market. It was never going to make her rich but it put food on the table and kept her happy enough. The wood was heavy and weighed down on her shoulder. Taking the detour was risky, but going the long way added a full mile to her journey. If she did that, she would be too tired to carve and she wouldn't have money to buy food on the weekend.

Alison stopped at the corner and let the satchel fall to the ground. She rolled her shoulders and checked the area to make sure no one was lurking, then jumped up and pulled down the fire escape ladder. She needed to rest for a few minutes, but she wasn't going to do it in the open where anyone could see. She climbed up to the roof and concealed herself behind the brick outcropping. The sun had been beating down all day but now, at dusk, there was some relief. She stretched her legs out in front of her and rested her head on the concrete ledge behind her.

She lay on the roof, her feet out in front of her, arms resting on her belly, and enjoyed the pain in her muscles. The work had made her stronger and turned her rubbery little arms into steely muscle. She could now wrestle the neighbor boy Danny to a draw, when before his challenge would have led to a beating for sure. She smiled and curled her right arm, patting the little stone under the skin with her left hand.

A rumble came up from the canyon between buildings. Alison rolled onto her stomach and scooted closer to the ledge. She knew no one would be able to see her from the street, but it was best to be cautious. She peeked over the concrete lip of the wall and peered down as a fleet of motorcycles filled the street below. She counted thirty, maybe as many as forty, as the bikes pulled up in front of a closed garage door. The man in the lead dismounted and approached a small pad beside the door. The growling of their engines had quieted now that they were idling, and she could clearly hear his voice.

"Open sesame!" he intoned.

The garage door creaked and groaned as it rose. Alison's eyes widened at the sight. The leader stepped to one side and his gang rolled inside. Alison saw now that each bike was weighted down by heavy saddlebags. They had also enjoyed a productive day, it would seem. Once everyone was inside, the leader got back onto his bike and followed them in.

Alison remained where she was even after the door closed. She didn't dare get caught on the street when the bikers came back out. She was sweating now, a different sweat than before. The sun moved closer to the horizon as she waited. Shadows stretched wide across the rooftop, as if the heavens were drawing themselves shut to provide her better cover.

The door at last opened again. The bikers poured forth like bats swarming from a cave, some going east while others went west. The leader was the final one out, and he again climbed off his bike to approach the pad. "Close, sesame!" he intoned, and the door began a slow descent to the ground. He waited to make sure nothing slipped inside before getting back on his bike and heading off to the east. Alison listened to the roar of their engines until she could no longer hear them, even straining her hardest. Only then did she leave her hiding place.

When Alison was back on the ground, she walked furtively toward the garage door and its mysterious pad. She looked around to make sure the street was still deserted, then cupped her hands around her mouth.

"Open, says me."

Nothing.

"Open see me."

Nothing.

"Open sesame."

She jumped when she heard the mechanisms shudder back to life. Her heart pounded. Her breath refused to come at normal intervals. As soon as the opening was large enough, she dropped down and scuttled underneath into the darkness. She jumped up and moved to the pad on the inside.

"Close sesame!"

The door stopped, paused, and then began lowering. She didn't know if that would damage the door, but she figured the risk was smaller than having the door stand open. Once it had settled back in place with a solid "THUNK!", Alison took out her phone and used its light to see where she was. Her eyes widened as she turned in a slow circle and saw what she had discovered.

Morgan looked up at the sound of the door opening and smiled when she saw who it was. "Ali Bahbah," she said, her London accent curling around the Rs in Ali's name. She was sitting on the floor, one long leg spread out in front of her with the other tucked up under her. A basket of laundry to her left was turning into a tower of folded clothes to her right. Her workspace was in the basement, and very few people from the building ventured down the stairs without having a very good reason. "You are late, little girl. Did you finally take my advice and stop using that dangerous shortcut?"

"No, Morgan." She dumped the heavy satchel next to the door and stretched out her back. "Something happened."

"Come." Morgan pushed away the rest of the laundry and motioned for Alison to sit between her legs. Alison sat on the floor with her legs folded in front of herself. Morgan took a bottle from her pocket, poured some into her palm, and rubbed her hands together. She pushed aside the collar of Alison's shirt and gripped the tired muscles where shoulder met neck. "Tell me about what kept you so late."

"I took my shortcut, but this time there was a gang. Bikers."

Morgan gasped. "Did they hurt you?"

"No, no, they never even saw me, no." She closed her eyes as

Morgan massaged away the tightness in her muscles. "But I watched them go into their den. I heard the secret word that opened the gate. I... I tried it, Morgan, and it worked. The door opened for me. I went in."

Another gasp. "And you left immediately without touching anything?"

Alison hesitated and Morgan slapped the back of her neck. "Ow! That hurt!"

"Then I did it hard enough. Ali Bahbah," Morgan said, "but if the men had come back and found you there, you would have been hurt. You could have been killed!"

"I know." Alison turned and knelt in front of Morgan. "But I couldn't help myself. I saw what was inside and I thought about how hard you work and how many creatures I would have to carve to earn even a fraction of what was secreted away in that warehouse. And there was so much, Morgan. You could chop down the entire forest and I could carve every creature on the Ark and we wouldn't come close to such riches. And with such wealth, I knew they would never miss a small portion of it."

Morgan tensed. "Ali, what did you do?"

Alison took the pouch from her pocket. "It was so small to them, Morgan, but it would change everything for us."

Morgan took the pouch and opened it to look inside. She tried to stop herself from gasping; she failed. Alison hadn't counted exactly how much it was, but it had been in a stack of dozens more just like it. The riches within could pay rent and keep them fed through their slower months. Alison put her hands on top of Morgan's and leaned in closer to her.

"You can take fewer shifts. You can rest when you get sick."

"We take care of each other," Morgan said. "That's how this works, Ali Bahbah. But this risk... you have to take it back."

Alison shook her head. "They'll never notice it disappeared. I'll start taking a different route so they never see me again. We'll be smart with the money."

Morgan looked at the money again. "It is so much..."

"A pittance compared to what I left behind. I swear to you, even the most eagle-eyed would never spot its absence."

Morgan nodded once, slowly. "Okay."

Alison cupped Morgan's face and kissed her. Morgan put the pouch down and linked her fingers on the back of Alison's head. Alison moved forward and unfolded her legs, draping them over

Morgan's to sit in her lap. Morgan dropped her hands to pull Alison closer, their kiss becoming more passionate with each breath. Soon Alison was plucking at the buttons of Morgan's uniform blouse. Her own shirt was loose enough to be tugged over her head, and she lifted her arms when Morgan did just that. She tossed it toward the pile of clean clothes and guided Morgan's head to her breast.

Morgan's lips parted so her tongue could sweep across the brown flesh. She followed the curve up to Alison's collar and then kissed a broken trail back down to her nipple. Alison rolled her head back and played with the thick rings of Morgan's hair. She pushed her hips down against Morgan's, wishing they were skin to skin already, hissing through her teeth as Morgan gently sucked her nipple.

"You have always known my magic phrases, Morgan."

Morgan chuckled and buried her face between Alison's breasts as her shirt was pushed off her shoulders and left to fall. Alison brought her hands back in and traced circles over Morgan's back. She bowed her head, resting her cheek against her lover's shoulder as Morgan's long fingers explored her curves. When Morgan lifted her head, Alison captured her lips and pushed her down onto her back. She felt Morgan smile against her mouth as she began squirming and tugging at their remaining clothes, kicking her pants aside and finally, blissfully, settled naked against Morgan's hip.

Morgan moved her hands to Alison's buttocks, gripping tightly to guide the smooth rhythm of Alison's hips. Alison pressed down on the hard muscle of Morgan's thigh, sitting up so they could see one another properly. Her Morgan, the most beautiful thing she had ever seen, with her skin the color of wet sand, her eyes darker than a night, lashes so long they could almost double as wings, and lips so full and beautiful that became magnificent when parted with a gasp of pleasure as they were now. She had never felt drawn to any man, any woman, with the same pull she felt when she crossed paths with Morgan.

What Alison loved most about moments like these, being with Morgan, wasn't the orgasm. It was simply being naked with her. It was hearing the harmony of their breathing, each gasp and moan blending with the next into a rehearsed symphony. The smell of her skin mixing with Morgan's. She looked down and followed the track of a sweat droplet moving along Morgan's collarbone. When it was about to drop off to the floor, Alison bent down and pressed her lips to it.

"I will take you away from this place," she whispered without lifting her mouth from Morgan's warm skin. "I will take you away from the laundry and the kitchens and everything that keeps you kneeling."

"Well... not everything that I kneel for is bad, my love."

Alison grinned and nipped at Morgan's throat. "You are a caution."

Morgan laughed and rolled them both. She arched her back, hands spread over Alison's breasts. She began to move her body like a wave cresting on the beach, once again making Alison think of her sandy skin. She linked her hands on the back of Morgan's neck and hung from her. She lifted her ass off the floor and pressed her pussy hard against her lover's thigh, her own thigh wet from Morgan's arousal.

"Give this to me." Morgan's thumbs brushed across Alison's nipples. "Give me this, which you give to no other."

Alison's eyes rolled back, her teeth digging into her bottom lip as she climaxed. Before Morgan, she never would have shared this moment with anyone other than herself, only trusting the middle two fingers of her left hand for something so private and intimate. She opened her eyes and looked at Morgan, letting the air out of her lungs with a lengthy sigh as she sank back down to the floor.

Alison wiped her hand across her lips. "Did you finish?"

"Not yet." Morgan took Alison's hand, took the first two fingers into her mouth, and wet them with her tongue. Alison smiled and her hand to be placed between Morgan's legs. Morgan held her breath and then said, "Oh-h," as Alison cupped her mound. She stroked the outer lips with two fingers and watched the subtle tremors and waves wash over Morgan's body. Then she eased her middle finger inside and her grin threatened to split her face at how Morgan cried out and arched her back.

"Every time," Morgan whispered. "I am surprised by how good that feels... every... time..."

Alison said, "Me too, my love."

Morgan moved her hips forward and back. Alison put her other hand on Morgan's waist to guide her movements, stroking with her middle finger. Finally, Morgan closed her eyes.

"Now," she whispered, "now, it's now..."

Morgan put a hand over her mouth to stifle her cry and, when she moved it, her body collapsed as if she had released all its air.

Alison took Morgan in her arms, holding her tightly with both arms. They harmonized as they caught their breath. Alison turned her head and looked at the money pouch which held the answer to so many of their problems. She dragged her hand up Morgan's spine, which made her shiver.

"I will take you away from all of this, my love," Alison whispered. "I promise you that."

"I know you will," Morgan said. "You are my Ali Bahbah."

Alison smiled, closed her eyes, and buried her face in Morgan's hair. The money wouldn't solve everything, but it would go a long way in helping her keep her promise.

When morning came, Morgan kissed Alison's cheek and slipped away from her bed without waking her. Her job required her to be awake before anyone else in the building, gathering their laundry to be taken next door and washed. She would then spend her day cleaning while the residents were at work and, at night, she would retrieve their clothes, fold it, and return it to them the following morning. Today she had to wake a bit earlier than usual to finish the previous night's laundry. It was fine with her, however. She would take precious time with Alison over sleep or mundane chores any day of the week.

Morgan didn't particularly like working in the building, but it was one of the decent-paying jobs available to her. It paid for her medications and there was usually enough left over for their savings. She smiled at the thought of escape. It was still far enough away that it hardly seemed real, but Alison assured her she was serious about it. She wanted to take Morgan somewhere far, far away, somewhere safe, somewhere they didn't have to hide how much they loved one another. It was a nice fantasy, something wonderful to dream about, but she couldn't see it actually happening.

She put all the clean and folded clothes on her cart and hauled it up the stairs to begin her rounds. The clothes were left in baskets next to every threshold, and the next day's clothes were hanging from hooks next to the door. She left one parcel and took the other. She was still on the ground floor when she heard a commotion at the front of the building. She pushed her cart to the end of the hall and peeked around the corner to see what was happening.

A group of men in biking leathers were loitering near the bottom of the stairs. She could see more outside, flanking the door. One man moved further down the hall and examined the closed doors as if they held clues to whatever he was searching for. He knocked on one, then another, and finally at a third he received a response. He was very polite when he asked if a wood-carver happened to live in the building. The old man, Mr. Ben, said that she lived upstairs. The biker thanked him and walked back to the men waiting by the door. He lowered his voice but Morgan could still clearly hear most of what he said.

"...in the daylight. We'll come back tonight when the carver is likely to be home."

"How are we going to find this place again?" one of the thieves asked. "It looks like every other building on this street."

The leader pulled out his knife and crouched in the doorway to carve something on the frame. "We'll just look for that marking."

Morgan remained hidden until the bikers were gone, back against the wall as she chewed her bottom lip. The men had obviously discovered their stash was discovered. One of them must have seen the bag of wood Alison said she'd left on the street. Somehow they had followed her here. They had probably asked at every building on this street to see which one Alison had come home to, and Mr. Ben had unwittingly told them where she would be.

After the rumble of motorcycle engines faded, Morgan went to the door to investigate the mark that had been left. It was a small, wide X carved deep into the wood. She couldn't erase it or cover it up; any attempts to destroy the marking would be far too obvious. She looked up and down the street at the other buildings, tall shoeboxes with identical rows of windows. Some had children's toys littering the small scrap of dead grass in front of them, there were bicycles and barbecues and all sorts of vaguely identifying objects, but the thieves likely hadn't taken notice of them. The leader had gone to the trouble of leaving his mark and that was what he would be looking for.

Morgan took out her own knife and hurried to the next building. She crouched and carved an X into the doorframe. She made it as close to the original as she could, but she knew the leader wouldn't remember exactly what his X looked like. She went to the next building and marked it as well. She repeated the graffiti on every building until every doorframe in the neighborhood bore the thief's mark. When she finished she went back to their building and tried to think of other ways to keep Alison safe.

That night when Alison appeared in the basement, Morgan

had already rushed through the laundry cycles so she could leave immediately. She took Alison's hand, led her to the roof, and showed her the tent she'd set up earlier that afternoon. There was a hotplate, a pot, and a pan, along with cans of soup. As Alison cooked, Morgan explained what she had seen and how she had copied the bikers' mark on every door in the neighborhood.

"But if they come back, they might not need the mark. They may still find you."

"I should never have taken the money," Alison said.

Morgan stroked Alison's hair. "Your heart was in the right place, love."

In the tent, they ate a small dinner and discussed their day. Alison carved while they talked and Morgan held a candle to light her work. She loved watching Alison take her knife to a fresh piece of wood. The beauty of nature was slowly sliced away and left something new and glorious in its place. It was almost as if Alison was carving around something that already existed in the wood, her fingers working so quickly, so mechanically.

Near midnight, when Morgan was close to falling asleep, they heard movement on the street below. Alison was up first and signaled to Morgan to stay behind. Alison crawled to the edge of the roof and peered down. Morgan tried to stay by the tent, but her curiosity was too powerful. She crawled forward and peeked over the edge with Alison. Far below she could see the bikers clustered at the intersection, a handful of them shining lights on doorframes. They were whispering angrily among themselves. One pointed at the door nearest to him, and the man he was angry with pointed to a different one.

Alison rubbed Morgan's arm. "You fooled them, sweets."

Morgan smiled tightly, proud but also uncertain how this could end well for them. Their home was surrounded by thieves from whom they had stolen. She was terrified that it could only end bloody.

The thieves moved aimlessly for a bit. After what seemed like hours, one of them cursed and waved his arm toward the building in a wide, sweeping gesture. The thieves moved toward the buildings and pushed through the doors as one. Morgan and Alison backed away from the ledge and faced each other.

Alison grinned.

"Oh, no."

Alison crawled across the roof to their tent and grabbed the pot and pan they'd used for their dinner. Before Morgan could stop her, she banged them together to create a clanging echo that sounded like church bells. She stomped across the roof, then began whooping and hollering at the top of her voice. Morgan cringed and held her hands over her head as if she could physically stop the sounds.

"On the roof!" someone shouted from below.

"Quiet down up there!" someone else shouted through a window.

From inside the buildings, the ruckus grew louder. People had been pulled out of bed in response to the clamor and discovered a horde of biker thieves in their stairwells. Even in a neighborhood this bad, sirens began howling almost immediately. Based on the sounds of scuffling from within the buildings, some residents weren't waiting for the police. The bike engines roared as a few bikers tried to escape, but Morgan could tell they didn't make it far before their escapes were blocked.

Morgan heard someone in the stairwell of their building and ran to the door. She threw her weight against it just as it began swinging open. Alison joined her and, together, they dug their feet into the tar of the roof and managed to keep whoever was on the other side from pushing it open. The street was awash with blue and red flashes now, and she could hear chatter from police radios echoing between the buildings. Pushing against the door with all their strength, their shoes skidding across the ground, the two lovers looked at each other.

Alison smiled, the crazy smile that meant she was having a good time despite the danger.

And, even though it was foolhardy and dangerous, Morgan couldn't help smiling back at her.

The police ended up arresting all forty of the bikers. The street was closed down while they interrogated everyone who had been involved with the brawls, but Alison whispered to Morgan that they had to leave before they got swept up as well. The thieves were all going to prison, and soon the police would know about the stash. There was enough loot there to put all the thieves away for a very long time. But if she and Morgan were quick enough, maybe there was a chance they could make away with just a bit of the cash before it was labeled and filed away as evidence, never to be seen again.

They jumped to the next building, and from there to the next, and then one more just to put some distance between themselves and the road block. From there they ran to the warehouse, never stopping to rest or look back. Morgan didn't have to ask what they were doing; to ask would only introduce the question of whether or not it was wise.

When they reached the right street, Alison stopped to make sure none of the bikers had remained behind to stand guard. The building was empty. The windows were dark. She squeezed Morgan's hand as she approached the pad and bent close so it could hear her breathless voice.

"Open sesame!"

The garage door rumbled up. Morgan's hand tightened around hers as Alison led her inside. Morgan stopped at the threshold and stared in wonder at the riches that surrounded them.

"Hurry," Alison whispered. "We have to hurry."

They grabbed what they could carry and, when they were finished, found a bag that was large enough to hold everything. Alison slung the bag over her shoulder and ushered Morgan back outside. She bent down and said, "Close sesame." They waited until the door hit ground before they walked away, hand-in-hand. Neither of them spoke, neither of them acknowledged what they had just done or where they were going. Morgan released Alison's hand but wrapped her arm around Alison's arm like a snake on a tree branch, hanging off of her as they neared the boundaries of their town.

"We'll find somewhere," Alison said to Morgan's unasked question. "We'll settle down. We won't be extravagant. We'll keep working, but we'll work better jobs. Jobs we love, not because they pay the bills. We will thrive. The money will buy you doctors and medicines and you'll be yourself again in no time. And we'll live, Morgan, we will finally be able to just live."

Morgan smiled and rested her head on Alison's shoulder. "Well, if the great Ali Bahbah says it, then it must be true."

Alison turned her head and kissed Morgan's hair. "And so it is."

Thus Alison Barber and the woman she loved lived all their lives in wealth and joyance in a world that had once seen them as paupers.

KNOCKOUT STAGE

MOST NIGHTS Steph goes back to the field in Madrid. That moment lying on her back staring up at the stars, the thunderous roar rising up in the stadium that made it sound as if the AstroTurf underneath her was about to open up and swallow her. August in Spain, but not as bad as she'd been anticipating. In the moment she had closed her eyes and let the sound wash over her. An entire country was overjoyed because she failed; another country was devastated for the same reason. It all pivoted on her inability to jump that last hand-length to block a stupid ball from flying into that stupid net. Four years of practice, planning, and preparation came down to one moment in one game.

The moment ended when Chelsea Quinn came over and held a hand out to help her up. "C'mon, Dagger," she said. "On your feet."

Sometimes those words echoed through her head as she woke up. *On your feet.* But Quinn wasn't there to help her up. Her girlfriend Sophie wasn't there anymore, either. No, Sophie hadn't left her because she botched the most important game of her life. Not directly. But after a few months of moping and watching the game tape and bitching about what she could have done differently, Sophie had finally decided she had enough. Steph couldn't blame her. She would have left, too.

She went through the motions. Showered and dressed and went out for a jog. No one wanted to see an Olympic failure suddenly gain three hundred pounds and become an object of pity. She went back to her day job at the hardware supply store. Before the Games, there'd been a sign in the front window wishing her luck and announcing that an Olympian worked there. People had smiled knowingly at her as she helped them pick out bathroom fixtures. The sign was gone now. The customers avoided eye contact as much as possible.

Maggie at the bar still liked her. "What's one bad game compared to your whole career, eh?" she said whenever Steph was feeling maudlin.

"One game that the entire world watched," Steph reminded her.

But Maggie would give her free beers, was lax with the tab, and provided enough ego stroking that Steph kept going back. She always took the farthest stool where she could rest one arm on the bar, her back against the wall, and watch the big screen TVs hanging from the ceiling. One was tuned to sports, another to some entertainment news channel, and another to regular world news. She was old enough to remember a time when drunks went to bars to keep their heads down, never looking up from the glass of whatever painkiller they'd been poured. Or maybe she had only ever seen that on TV.

Steph wore a baseball cap pulled low over her eyes in a lame attempt at anonymity. Whenever someone came in with the team name on their clothes or asked for the TV to be switched over to soccer, she shrank into herself and fled as soon as she could without being obvious. The coach was letting her sit out until she was ready to come back. Translation, when she could look her teammates in the eye again. Those closest to Steph assured her that no one blamed her for the loss, but there had been very little eye contact in the hours after the game.

When the Closing Ceremonies were over, when the team boarded their plane home, the slow slog through the airport amid a crowd of well-meaning fans, Steph had never felt more isolated. She was a pariah, even if she was imagining the stigma. The feeling still lingered almost eight months later.

She was supposed to be the star. She was young and pretty and sexy, and every interview she did helped increase public awareness of soccer. She went on talk shows. She did commercials. Magazines asked her to do photoshoots and interviews. For a while it almost didn't matter if she was any good on the field, because she was bringing in new fans and filling up stadiums. She could lose a game here and there. She could have a bad showing and brush it off. But the Olympics... she cost her team and her country the chance to win gold.

The media hadn't been kind. She'd only seen one headline - "Dagger Goes Dull" - before she declared a blackout on the internet. Her Twitter account and Facebook were still up, but she never checked them. She didn't need to see what the world at large wanted to say to her. She didn't go out except for the bar. She jogged early enough that anyone she encountered were as unlikely to want a conversation as she was.

She didn't know what would happen next. What she was supposed to do now. The team would probably welcome her back with open arms. They were all good people. They liked her. Forget the past and focus on the next one. The next games, in four years. She would have to wait four years for a chance to redeem herself. That was if they even qualified, if they made it as far as they had last time. There was no guarantee she would ever see another Olympics. Especially not if she kept sulking on the sidelines.

For now, it was all she could do to wake up and put on the blue smock of her store uniform. It was close to how it felt to put on her game jersey, but at least the colors were different. If the store had forced her to wear green and black, she wouldn't even have applied. She needed distance from the team. To heal. To forget. To get past the worst five seconds of her entire life. She couldn't do that in green.

During one of her shifts, in a long stretch of slow foot traffic, Steph was working at the cash register near the doors when she noticed a woman standing just inside the sliding glass doors. She was dressed like a typical suburban minivan warrior - blue jeans, plaid shirt tucked in but unbuttoned to reveal a plain blue T-shirt underneath. Her hair was cut short and feathered across her forehead. Her arms were crossed over her chest as she ran her eyes slowly along the entire length of the store.

Steph put on her best false cheer. "Hi. You look like maybe you're a little lost. Is there something I can help you with?"

"Not lost," the woman said. "Overwhelmed, maybe. I have a lot to do, and I'm not exactly sure where to begin."

"What's the project?"

"I'm adding a room to my house."

Steph was impressed. "That's a big job for one person."

The woman smiled. "I have a couple of big strong musclemen helping me out. But I'm taking charge of supplies and general overlord of the job."

"Can I see your list?" The woman handed it over and Steph skimmed it. "Okay, well, we're right next to this section. So why don't we start there and just work our way north?"

"Sounds good to me. I'm Cindy."

Steph gestured at her name tag. "Stephanie."

Cindy followed her down the aisle. As always, Steph was braced for the recognition or the "Have I seen you somewhere before...?" comment, but it didn't come. She focused on spelling out the differences between brands, offering her own personal recommendations when she had them, and soon she was completely focused on the job at hand. To her relief, Cindy actually seemed to know what she was talking about. She had a plan, she knew her stuff when it came to construction, and Steph had no doubt she was capable of taking on the room addition. So many people, men and women both, came in expecting to be weekend warriors. "Just hammers and nails, right, how hard can it be?" She felt like she was the last line of defense between well-meaning imbeciles and an electrical fire or a roof collapse.

"Have you done any projects like this before?" Steph asked.

"Nothing this large. I put up a wall to create a second room, but that's about it."

"You've certainly done your homework."

Cindy smiled. "I don't like half-assing things."

"Whole-ass one thing."

"Ron Swanson," Cindy said. "The patron saint of anyone with callouses."

Steph smiled. "Ah, a woman after my own heart."

Cindy said, "I'm just glad I ran into you and not one of these macho jerks who usually work at places like this. 'Now, sweetheart, do you know what drywall is...?'"

"God. Yeah, we've got a couple of those here. But they're good guys, for the most part."

"The good guys are the worst! 'I just don't want you getting hurt.' I mean, guys. Come on. I know I look femme, but I'm butch where it counts, okay?"

Steph tried not to react, but she immediately reassessed

Cindy's looks. Maybe a little plain, but attractive nonetheless. Steph did like soft butches, the kind of woman who could strip off an evening gown and put on a pair of jeans to go hiking. If they'd met in a bar, she would have gone through her list of come-ons to get her into a bathroom stall or out in the backseat. Meeting her at work was a bit more awkward. She would have to ask her out on a date, they'd have to go through the motions of having dinner together or seeing a movie. It seemed like so much work just to get laid.

They wandered the length of the entire store, but Steph's expertise ensured they wouldn't have to backtrack more than a few times. When they'd crossed off the entire list, Steph recruited the help of their six-foot-two assistant manager to push the unwieldy carts back toward the front. Steph took up position at the cash register and began to scan the items. Cindy rested her arms on the counter and watched as each item was scanned.

"Do you get a commission on this stuff?" Cindy asked.

"I wish. I'd make a killing off you."

Cindy laughed. "Oh, well. I did my best."

"You sure did. Even if you do have help, there's a lot of work to be done. I hope you've got someone lined up to give you a massage when you're done with all of this."

"Why, are you volunteering? You'd be pretty good at it. Big strong hands."

Steph glanced over at her. Despite the confidence in her voice, there was a hint of apprehension in her eyes. She wasn't sure if she'd just gone over the line or not and refused to look back until Steph responded.

"No complaints yet," Steph said with a smile.

Cindy relaxed. "I thought. I mean, I hoped. You're exactly my type. But then I dropped that line about being butch and you didn't give me anything..."

"I'm trying to be professional here."

"My apologies."

Steph said, "I wasn't complaining." She smiled and finished ringing up the purchases. "So... the massage..."

"I'll be working on the room all weekend. Sunday night, I should have lots of knots to work out."

"I'm not working Sunday. Six o'clock? We can have a bite to eat first."

Cindy nodded. "Sounds good." She pulled one of the

advertisement flyers from the slot next to the cash register and scribbled information down in the margin. "This is my address. This is my cell. I'll see you Sunday at six."

"See you then. Oh. Wait, I'll have Burt help you take everything out to the car."

"Thanks. Looking forward to seeing you again, Stephanie."

"Steph."

"Ste... Steph." Her brow furrowed slightly and she tilted her head to one side. "Not the Dagger."

"Yeah. That's me."

Cindy's eyes lit up. "Wow. I didn't realize... the name suddenly clicked. Wow. Uh... is the date still on?"

"Why wouldn't it be?" Steph tried to hide her disappointment. So close to spending time with someone who didn't know who she was, who didn't know her shame. Of course she probably would have Googled and found out the truth by the time Steph arrived on Sunday, so there was no point in trying to hide it. "You're still going to need that massage, right?"

"Absolutely. So... I'll see you then."

Steph nodded. "Sure."

Cindy left and Steph took out her phone. She entered Cindy's number so she wouldn't forget it, then sent a text. "So you'll have my number, too. Just in case."

Cindy sent back: "Good thinking!"

Steph returned the phone to her pocket. It could've been a lot worse. It could've been someone who recognized her immediately, a huge soccer fan who knew every stat from every game. Steph had gone home with a few of those women and it never, ever ended well. At least in this case she got asked out as "Helpful Hardware Store Employee" rather than a celebrity. She could live with that.

She spent the rest of the day trying not to think of Cindy, the soft butch whose sore muscles would need a strong touch.

They started calling her "Dagger" in high school. She could go from standing upright to a horizontal dive in the blink of an eye, flying parallel to the ground like she'd been shot from a cannon. Her coach once measured her lengths and confirmed she could average eight yards, the full length of the goal. When she was eighteen, getting ready for the state championship, her coach had reached over to massage one of her thighs. It was an innocent move on the coach's part - she was straight and happily married - but

Steph never forgot the thrill of having a woman's hand touching her there. Every fumbling encounter with a boy was erased by that one casual and platonic grope.

She went to college on a scholarship, where she majored in history, but her main goal during those years was finding a way to duplicate that feeling. She did everything she could think of with boys before she decided the gender of the person touching her was more important than anything else. She went to a bar, got drunk enough to ask someone to dance, and she had her first orgasm on the dance floor when her anonymous partner slid a hand over the crotch of her jeans.

Steph remembered pressing her face into the thick black curls as the dance came to an end and whispering, "I'm so fucking done with boys."

"Excellent," her partner laughed. "Let's celebrate."

She'd never thought of herself as gay because she could go through the motions with a guy. She didn't mind lying back and letting them do their thing. But once she experienced sex with a woman, once she'd had *sex*, she knew without question that she was on the right side of the sexuality scale. She needed women, she wanted women, and she could live without whatever novelty men might hold.

She chose not to spend any of her career in the closet. She came out to her team early on and she never played the pronoun game when interviewers asked about who she was dating. "I'm keeping my options open," she once said, "just in case the lucky lady is still somewhere out there." Lesbian-centric websites interviewed her. Magazines offered her the cover when she was still a college player. When she became a member of the national team, everything exploded. She was suddenly a celebrity in a way she couldn't have ever expected.

And the women. She had no idea where the women came from, but suddenly they were always there. They slipped her hotel room numbers, phone numbers, email addresses. She received photos in the mail. She didn't always respond, but sometimes if she was in the right mood and feeling horny, she would choose someone at random. Sometimes a husband or boyfriend would be there. "He can just watch," the women would say, "unless you're okay with him joining in." Steph didn't see why not. She didn't mind a guy in bed, and it acted like a sex toy with a mind of its own.

There were a few instances where women tried to blackmail

her. There were pictures "leaked" online. Her phone was hacked. There was nothing to be ashamed of. Her lovers had all been consenting adults. She had a good body. She didn't care if people saw it, she didn't care if people knew she could be aggressive when pursuing a lover.

Of course, that had all been before. She wondered if there were still girls wearing her jersey. If there were women looking to fuck her brains out just for the honor of saying they'd been with the Dagger, she hadn't found any. The last time a woman had gasped, "I can't believe Steph fucking Thomas has her hand in my panties," between kisses was in the Olympic village. Her name had been Maria, and all of her English was deliciously tinted with enough of an accent to remind Steph of Salma Hayek. Now the women either didn't know who she was or pretended not to. She preferred that to pity, but she missed the acclaim.

She sat outside Cindy's house and stared at the lit window that overlooked the porch. She hadn't been on a date in a very long time. She wasn't positive she still knew the etiquette. And yes, they'd flirted and insinuated that tonight was only going to be about sex, but dinner changed that. Dinner meant conversation and spending time together that didn't involve kissing or undressing.

Steph flexed her fingers on the steering wheel and chided herself for being a coward. She got out of the car and walked up the front steps. The door opened as soon as she was in front of it and Cindy stepped out. She was wearing a concert T-shirt faded from a great many washings, and her jeans were ripped at the knee and just above. She smiled nervously and reached up to bundle her hair into a bun.

"Hey. I lost track of time. Give me a second to get ready...?"

"You look fine to me."

Cindy chuckled. "You're sweet."

"I'm serious. If you want to change, that's fine, but I think you look amazing."

"Then I'll stay like this." She gestured at the six-pack of beer Steph was carrying. "Should I put those in the fridge?"

Steph handed them over. "I wasn't sure what brand you liked, so I just... I got the kind that endorsed me."

"Can't fault that reasoning. Come on in."

Steph shut the door and followed Cindy into the kitchen. She'd worn what she still referred to as her "interview clothes": slacks and a matching blazer over a collarless blouse. She'd almost thrown on a windbreaker and some sweatpants (her press conference clothes) but she wanted to make a decent impression. Now she felt overdressed, although she honestly did prefer Cindy in her jeans. The back of the shirt had a row of cities listed down the spine, with the year 2006 in the center in bright bold.

"So where did you see them?"

"Hm?"

"Radiation Canary. The, uh, the shirt."

"Oh! Las Vegas. Have you ever seen them?"

Steph nodded. "Yeah, when they were in Greece. We were there for a game and Coach got us tickets. They were amazing."

"I heard that was when Lana and Karen... you know..."

"Yeah, I heard that, too."

Cindy sighed. "Dash Warren. I don't care who I'd have to share her with, I'd consider it worth the effort."

Steph chuckled. "Threesomes aren't really all they're cracked up to be. Parts are really fun. But then someone falls off the bed or the other two are more into each other or... you know."

Cindy smiled. "You've really analyzed them, huh?"

"I've been invited to a couple."

"I'll bet you have." She stepped closer and ran her fingers down the lapels of Steph's jacket. "So. I guess we've decided there aren't going to be any barriers tonight. We're just going to say what we think regardless of whether it's appropriate."

Steph was very aware that Cindy's hands were resting against her waist, just under her navel. She returned Cindy's gaze without blinking. "Sounds good to me."

Cindy nodded. "Good. So I'm going to kiss you. Get that out of the way so it's not all I'm thinking about during dinner."

"Smart."

Cindy smiled. She moved her hands back up and tugged Steph forward by the jacket. Steph put one hand on the back of Cindy's head and aimed for the smile. She wondered why every date didn't start with a kiss. Kissing could tell you so much more about a person than an hour of small talk ever could. Steph closed her eyes and pressed Cindy against the counter. Cindy moved without hesitation or resistance, revealing she was willing to play the passive role. But when Steph parted her lips, Cindy's tongue only flickered against her mouth once before retreating. So she could be a tease.

Steph smiled and moved her hand under the hem of Cindy's shirt. She pulled back from the kiss but stayed close. Cindy's eyes were closed, her lips parted in anticipation of the kiss resuming.

"We're going to have a nice dinner. A respectable date. Get to know each other."

"Mm-hmm," Cindy said.

"But first you're going to take off your pants and I'm going to go down on you. Is that okay?"

Cindy's hands were already moving to the button of her jeans. "Yes." She pushed the denim down and shimmied a little to let the pants fall. Steph kissed her once more, then sank to her knees. She ran her hand over the curve of Cindy's ass, the other hand trailing up the inside of her thigh to ease her legs a little further apart. Cindy leaned against the counter. She put her hands on Steph's shoulders as Steph pushed aside the thin obstacle of Cindy's plain white briefs and leaned in to kiss the soft hair underneath.

"Butch underwear..."

Cindy's chuckle was breathless. "You expected frilly panties?"

"Not even a little bit."

She moved her mouth lower and Cindy whimpered. Her hands tightened in Steph's jacket, bunching up the material as she bent her knees and rolled her hips forward.

"Oh... wow... you're pretty good at that..."

Steph pulled back and touched her tongue to the moisture on her bottom lip. "Lots of practice." She looked up. "Does it bother you that I've been with a lot of people?"

Cindy put a hand on the back of Steph's head and pushed her back to where she'd been. "Not when I'm re... reaping the benefits of the work. God... there. Yes." She moved her hand to the counter and held on tight, breathing heavier now, moving her hips. Steph moved her tongue to Cindy's clit and teased it, bringing up her hand to gently pinch the wet folds between her first and third knuckles. She bent the middle finger and pushed it up in a matching rhythm to what her tongue was doing.

"Steph..." Cindy grunted and the muscles in her legs tensed, her hand dropping back to Steph's shoulder as she came. Steph moved up Cindy's body, kissing her stomach and breasts through her T-shirt. She tilted her head to kiss Cindy's neck and Cindy, her whole body overly sensitive from the orgasm she'd just had, twitched and jerked as she chuckled self-consciously. She wrapped her arms around Steph and held her tight to keep her from backing away.

"Are you good?"

"I'm very fine." Cindy found Steph's neck with her lips and assaulted it for a moment. Steph squirmed in appreciation. "What about you? I'm not sure I can do everything I want to do to you before dinner is ready."

"That's okay. I was planning for delayed gratification. I just had to get into your pants." She pecked the corners of Cindy's mouth before giving her a nice, solid kiss. "You can pay me back later."

Cindy said, "I like the sound of that."

"Do you want me to put your pants back on?"

"Please."

Steph stepped back and crouched. She pulled the jeans back up and smoothed her hands over the material, a chance to grope Cindy one more time before she stood up. They both looked down and watched as Steph fastened the button and tugged the zipper back up.

"I never thought about someone dressing me being as erotic as undressing."

"Anything can be erotic if it's done right," Steph said.

Cindy smiled. "I should check on the food."

"Okay."

Steph remained where she was, pinning Cindy to the counter, staring into her eyes. Finally Cindy laughed and shoved Steph's shoulder.

"Move, stupid."

"Do I have to?"

"No. And you moving farther away isn't my first option, either, but we should be responsible adults." She looked at Steph's lips and then let her eyes drift lower. She exhaled sharply and looked away. "So move before I choose in favor of starving to death."

Steph chuckled and stepped out of the way. They moved to the stove together and Steph put a hand against the smell of Cindy's back.

"That was just playing. Flirting. If you really wanted me to move, I wouldn't have refused."

Cindy looked at her, confused. "I know."

"I know you know. It's just... I'm strong. Stronger than a lot of the women I've been with. I don't want any miscommunications."

Cindy turned around to face her. She crossed her arms at the wrist. "Grab them."

"I'm just covering~"

"Grab them."

Steph wrapped her hand around Cindy's wrists.

"Lift my arms above my head."

Steph had to adjust her grip to comply. The move forced Cindy to push out her chest. She kept her eyes locked on Steph's

"I like strong women. I like women with muscles who can lay on top of me and push me into the mattress. I like women who can do whatever they want with me. But the only thing that matters is that she also knows when to stop. So retreat. If I ever want you to stop playing around, I'll just say 'retreat.' Okay?"

"I can work with that."

"Retreat."

Steph relaxed her grip. She slid her hand down the length of Cindy's arms, pausing to caress her bicep before moving lower. She skimmed her fingers around to her back and pulled Cindy to her. Cindy angled her face against Steph's and accepted her kiss, lowering her arms so they looped around Steph's neck. Their tongues touched again and Steph knew they were getting close to forgetting all about dinner. She moved her hand down and swatted Cindy's ass.

"Ow!"

"You wanted food first. Behave."

"And if I don't?"

"I do it harder."

Cindy's eyes sparkled. "That's no punishment, Dagger. But I take your point." She untangled herself and pulled away from her. "You're turning out to be a pretty dangerous person, Steph."

"Because I'm dominant and I like to swat you when you're being bad?"

"Because you might have a hell of a time getting rid of me when you want to move on."

Steph surprised herself by saying, "Well. Maybe I won't try very hard."

Cindy chuckled and focused on the food. Steph busied herself with setting the table, which led to her discovery that one wall of the dining room was gone. The hole was covered by a sheet of semi-transparent plastic that ruffled slightly in the evening breeze. She put down the plates and silverware then went over to take a peek at the room in progress. She pushed aside one corner and looked at a simple, bare cube with two empty sockets where windows would go. Several buckets and abandoned tools were clustered in the center of the space.

"It's not much to look at," Cindy said from behind her, "but when it's finished, it'll be a beautiful little reading area."

"Are we still being uncomfortably blunt with each other?"

"I'd expect nothing else."

"I want to fuck you in that room."

Cindy said, "Well, the food would get cold..."

"I meant when it's finished. As soon as you declare it done, I want to come over here and christen it with you."

"Huh. I hadn't planned on doing anything like that, but mainly because I didn't have a partner. I'll be sure to give you a call."

"You'd better." She let the plastic fall back into place and joined Cindy at the table. "I like the blunt conversation. No games. No trying to figure out where we're at. It's comfortable."

"I agree." She settled in and looked across the table at Steph. "So I can ask something that might be otherwise taboo on a first date without asking if it's okay."

Steph shrugged. "You can ask. I might not answer."

Cindy said, "Fair enough. Why don't you play anymore?"

Steph considered the question before answering. "I don't technically 'not play.' I'm just not playing right now. I'm taking a break."

"Okay. So why? I watched some videos. You're really good. Hell, you're an Olympian."

Steph winced. She picked up her glass and took a sip, wet her lips, and put the glass down. "If you saw that, then you saw what happened in Madrid?"

Cindy nodded.

"That doesn't answer the question?"

A line appeared above Cindy's forehead. "I watched the highlight reels, but I didn't see anything that would send you running."

"It came down to two people. Me versus a player from France. I wasn't good enough to stop it, so the road to the Olympics ended."

Cindy said, "Doesn't that happen a lot? Pretty much every single game has one side going home without a win. This time it just happened to be you."

"But this was the Olympics. I've dreamed of playing in the Olympics my entire life, and I finally get the opportunity and I ruin it. I ruin it for the entire team, for our country. All because the Dagger went dull."

"I saw some of those bullshit articles," Cindy said. "I also saw the dive. It was no different from a dozen others I watched."

Steph gave a weak smile. "Dozens?"

"You have excellent form. And you look sexy in those shorts."

"I could run home and get them."

Cindy hesitated with the edge of her glass against her lip. "I think you're joking, but I'd actually be really, really into that."

"We'll see how well you behave tonight."

Cindy chuckled and took her sip. "So... you're sitting out because you lost the game? I mean, yes, it was a big game with a lot at stake, but I don't understand why that means you're turning your back on the whole thing."

"Because I can't stop thinking about it. Because when I go to sleep, I see myself lying on my back in that stadium with the crowd cheering for the other team because of me. I can't get past that block. I feel like if I went back out on the field, I'd freeze."

"I don't believe that would happen. I think you're stuck in the moment because you're not using it right. It's fuel. It's like if you had a big meal and then never metabolized it. It's a rock sitting in your belly. You need to set it on fire and let it loose. You need to use that as fuel. Go back out there and refuse to end up on your back again. Get back to the Olympics and this time you bring back that motherfucking gold medal that you deserve."

Steph blinked in surprise. "Wow. That might be the best pep talk I've ever gotten."

"You obviously needed a good one. You worked your whole life to get to that point. It would be wrong if you surrendered just because you didn't reach the summit the first time you went for it. Or maybe I'm just talking out of turn. I mean, we just met..."

"No, you're... you're not wrong. You've given me a lot to think about. Maybe it is time."

Cindy shrugged. "If it isn't going away on its own, then letting it fester won't help. You need to start actively kicking its ass. Put on your cleats and beat the shit out of that ball."

"Wait, is this whole pep talk a trick to get me into my uniform."

"Mm, you look so hot in it..."

Steph laughed. "I'm going to have to find a costume for you to wear."

"Oh. I've got costumes."

"Oh really."

Cindy arched an eyebrow. Steph, suddenly motivated, picked up her silverware and started eating. She didn't know what the plan was after dinner, but the look in Cindy's eye told her she didn't want to wait longer than absolutely necessary to find out.

ISTANBUL
Four years later

Steph "Dagger" Thomas lay on her back in the AstroTurf, staring up at the sky. She still hadn't caught her breath and the palms of her hands hadn't stopped stinging yet. It had come down to seconds, to one point, to the opposing team aiming one final missile in her direction to force extra time. She had launched herself and flew like Supergirl across the threshold of their goal, arms outstretched, hands flat, eyes locked onto the ball spinning impossibly fast toward her. She had prayed for an extra inch in height, just twelve more inches, because it looked like she was going to come up short. She swung her arm.

The ball flew back toward the other players. She hit the ground hard enough to rattle everything in her body, her lungs clenching like fists and pushing all the air out of her. She rolled onto her back. She was vibrating with adrenaline and her eyes were wide with confusion as Chelsea Quinn appeared over her again. But this time Chelsea was smiling, and she was followed by everyone else on the team. Chelsea helped her up and they were both instantly crushed by their teammates.

Someone was carrying their nation's flag. Steph grabbed it and wrapped the cloth around her fist as she escaped the huddle. The flag trailed behind her as she ran across the field. She saw flashbulbs exploding in her periphery and, as she expected, the internet was soon filled with shots of her victory lap. She ran to the sidelines and, amid the crowd, spotted Cindy in the front row. Steph smiled and ran for her wife. The woman who had pulled her out of a morose funk, who had put her back on the right path, who was in the midst of building their new home.

They embraced on the sidelines. Steph wrapped the flag around Cindy and cinched it at her throat like it was a cape. Cindy cupped Steph's face and kissed her hard, another picture that would flood Twitter and Facebook. She moved so that anyone would assume she had just put her head on Cindy's shoulder, but in reality she wanted to whisper in her ear. She kept her voice low despite the roaring crowd; Cindy could focus on her voice no matter how loud their surroundings were.

"So... the gold. Does that mean you're going to follow through on our bet?"

"A deal's a deal," Cindy whispered back. "But I get to pick the girl."

Steph tingled in anticipation. She thought the cape would cover up the fact she groped Cindy's ass before breaking the hug, but she didn't care if the whole world saw it. Let them know she appreciated the curve of her wife's rear end.

"I gotta get back to the girls."

"Go. I'll catch up with you later."

Steph kissed Cindy again, then turned and jogged back to her team. Her road back to the field hadn't been as rocky as she feared. The girls all welcomed her back with open arms, and she'd performed well at every practice and every game. Cindy's pep talk had been part of her recovery but it wasn't the most important part. Her true recovery came with realizing she didn't care about the gold anymore. She didn't care about winning the game. She only cared about looking good for Cindy, and Cindy didn't care if they won or lost.

Playing for Cindy's easily-won approval took away any stress she might've been carrying. She found her center and the Dagger came back at full strength. By the time qualifying rounds came up again, she had no doubt she would get her girls back to the Olympics. Now they had their medals, she'd redeemed herself in the eyes of anyone who still remembered the team's previous appearance on the world stage. It was nice. It felt great. But none of it mattered. She'd been focused on her humiliation in the eyes of the world but now she couldn't care less what the world thought. There were other prizes much worthier of her attention. Prizes like Cindy's attention, a medal she won every day of her life.

Everything else was just a game.

A PERFECT STRANGER

SOFIA KENNEDY remembered every detail of the encounter extremely well, despite the fact she was drunk and exhausted. She remembered with such clarity that sometimes she feared she imagined the entire thing. But no. There was enough corroborating evidence to convince her that the night really happened exactly the way it lived in her memories. It was a treasure that she allowed herself to revisit in times of need and want.

Her journalism professor was having a party at his house. Sofia spent the entire week dreading it, wondering if she should bring something and too nervous to come out and ask. She respected Professor Lawrence was equal parts impressive and terrifying. The idea of making a bad impression on him was keeping Sofia up nights. Finally she decided she would just bring a bottle of wine. Then began the panic of what kind to get. She didn't want to get something too expensive; it would be like she was showing off. But if she got the cheapest thing available, she would look disrespectful. In the end she just grabbed a bottle off the shelf and didn't worry about weighing it against any others.

The party was amazing. Enough of her friends showed up that she didn't have to worry about the night being an awkward affair filled with older academics, and she was surprised to discover she was having a good time. Professor Lawrence was a dynamo on the barbeque grill, but his wife was the true revelation. Lydia Scott-Lawrence was charming, funny, smart... she ran marathons, she was a published author, and she hiked Mount Rainier. Sofia found herself trying time and again to get into the older woman's orbit just to overhear what she was saying.

Her friend Angela Ellison was there, too. Bisexual and enthusiastically polyamorous Angela, with the tattoos skillfully hidden under her sweater in deference to the academic environment. Angela was a gamer, and Sofia knew enough about video games to have an interesting conversation with her by the pool. Angie had been a picture-perfect daughter all through high school, going to church on Sunday and getting straight As. Now that she was in college, she was (responsibly) letting it all hang out. Despite her antics, she was still keeping up with all her classes. She was majoring in Law, minoring in Psychology or, as she called them "Mickey Mouse classes."

In addition to bouncing between the two intriguing women, Sofia also made time to ensure Martha King was having a good time. Martha was from the Midwest - Iowa or Nebraska, Sofia could never remember - and being in a city like Seattle was terrifying to her. If left to her own devices, she would never have left the dorm, and Sofia made a point of taking her out whenever possible. There were cracks in her shell, hints that one day she might be comfortable in the big city, but Sofia wanted to be sure Martha knew she wasn't abandoned.

As the party wound down, Sofia became aware that she was a bit lightheaded and woozy. She'd lost count of how many glasses of wine she'd had, and that was before she started drinking beer with the barbeque. A few people started to head home and she considered asking them for a ride. She could always pick up her car in the morning. But she knew that if she just took a few minutes to lie down, it would clear her head enough that she could get across town. A cop would definitely disagree, and her mother would have impounded her car, but Sofia knew her tolerance levels. A few minutes lying down would get her back to near-sober enough to get back to the dorm.

She slipped away from the party and went down a dark hallway, only peeking into rooms with the doors left open. She didn't want to be accused of snooping, after all. Finally she found a bedroom with a pile of coats neatly stacked on the near side of the mattress. She went in and closed the door partway behind her. She left the lights off and sat on the foot of the bed, slipping her shoes off before she laid back. The sounds of the party drifted down the hall like white noise. She heard laughter and music, Professor Lawrence's strong voice booming in from the patio, and soon she realized she was drifting off to sleep.

She didn't know how long she had been lying there when she became aware someone else had come into the room. It could have been Lydia discovering a student had intruded into the house, or maybe Angela or Martha coming to retrieve their coats. Sofia remained where she was, not quite asleep but also not fully awake, either. Her hands were folded on her stomach, her feet still on the floor. She mentally formed her apology if it was Lydia, if she was asked to leave and rejoin the party. But at the moment the bed was just so comfortable that she didn't want to get up until it was absolutely necessary.

The newcomer sat down on the bed between Sofia and the coats. She didn't say a word, but she gently brushed the hair off Sofia's forehead.

"Are you awake?"

The question was whispered, so it wasn't possible for Sofia to identify the voice. Or maybe she was just too tired or drunk to remember exact details. Either way, the stranger put a hand on Sofia's shoulder and squeezed. She started to get up, but Sofia moved her hand to touch the other woman's wrist. She didn't know what she was doing. She just knew that lying on the bed with someone touching her so gently was not something she objected to.

She moved her fingers to the other woman's palm, stroking the soft flesh of it before linking their fingers together. The woman squeezed Sofia's hand.

"Don't go," Sofia said.

"I was just going to cover you up."

"Stay."

There was a long pause before the woman, her voice even softer now, said, "Okay."

She repositioned herself on the bed, scooting up higher so that her body was more aligned with Sofia's. They lay together for a long time, so long that Sofia almost drifted off again. She wasn't a virgin, but her grappling in the backseat with two high school boyfriends and the time she'd let Kim finger her on a late-night bus ride from a swim meet felt like kids' stuff. Being in the Professor's house, in one of his finely-appointed guest rooms, made the situation feel very grown-up. She was very aware of the person breathing beside her.

Sofia knew her visitor was staring at her. She didn't know how, but she knew. She could feel the examination and hoped whatever judgment was being made would be kind to her. She didn't want to risk opening her eyes. She didn't want to ruin the magic of not knowing who it was. They were still holding hands, she realized. The other woman's hand was soft and warm. Sofia guided it to her stomach, then moved it up as she untangled their fingers.

She heard the other woman take a sharp breath as she realized where Sofia was guiding her hand. But once it was in place, she spread the fingers out of her own accord. She massaged Sofia's breast through her blouse as her breathing became heavier and more ragged. Sofia moved her own hand down and put it on the other woman's hip. She arched her back into the touch, hoping to leave no doubt that she was definitely onboard with what was happening. She knew if she was in the reverse position, she would be worried about taking advantage or lacking consent.

"I want it," Sofia whispered.

"I—"

"Sh." She didn't want any further clues to the other woman's identity. Her heart was pounding. Voices were still coming down the hall but she tuned them out. She didn't want to hear anyone and rule them out. The woman lying next to her could conceivably be anyone, which meant she didn't have to worry about it being awkward the next day, which meant she could go as far as she wanted. She wet her lips and moved her hand over the other woman's thigh. The woman shifted so she was lying on her side facing Sofia and slid her hand away from Sofia's breast.

"No..." Sofia whimpered and arched her back.

"Sh."

The hand skimmed along her ribs, making her shiver. She moved her knees apart in anticipation of the touch, biting her bottom lip and swallowing the lump in her throat as the stranger's fingers lifted the hem of her blouse and stroked the skin just above the waistband of her skirt. Sofia put her other hand on the bedspread and gripped it in a tight fist, breathing hard. She desperately wanted this to happen, but she didn't want to rush it. The other woman repositioned herself again, and Sofia could sense her moving her head.

If her eyes were open, they would have been looking into each other's eyes. Sofia wet her lips, half afraid she would touch the other woman's mouth when she did so. The stranger closed the distance and kissed her. Sofia parted her lips and lifted her head to deepen the kiss, seeking her unknown lover's tongue. She could smell perfume now, but fortunately she couldn't tell where she had smelled it before. It could have been anyone. It was anyone.

It was Lydia, the Professor's wife, a woman who had put aside her urges for far too long. A woman who was eager to take what this girl was offering to scratch an itch she'd long ago learned to live with.

It was Angela, the wild girl, the rebel who had once said she "wanted to taste everyone in the world." A girl who was eager to take the opportunity to be with a girl she knew would back out of any experimentation under normal circumstances.

It was Martha, too shy to make a move with the lights on, but unable to resist the opportunity once it was dropped in her lap. The girl who may have still been a virgin, still figuring out her own sexuality, taking the chance to test drive lesbianism or bisexuality for a night.

Sofia reached down and gathered up her skirt. The hand on her stomach hesitated, then helped her move the cloth out of the way. The other woman broke the kiss. Her breathing became rougher. It seemed as if she realized just how far this would and could go. She stroked Sofia's stomach for a few more seconds and then she reached under the gathered material of her skirt to touch Sofia's thigh.

"Your mouth," Sofia whispered. Again, hesitation. "Please."

The weight lifted off the mattress next to her. For a second she panicked and thought she'd scared the stranger away, but instead of leaving the other woman pushed Sofia's legs apart.

"Oh, shit." Sofia covered her eyes with one hand. "Please. Please."

Her skirt was lifted and then there was someone underneath it, hands on her inner thighs, breath warm against the crotch of her panties. Sofia was worried about hyperventilating, struggling to stay calm even as her cheeks and ears burned hot. "Please, please, please," she said, her new mantra. Her toes curled. She was about to begin her chant once more when her underwear was pushed away and she felt the first brush of her partner's lips.

She swallowed the word and groaned, moved her hand from her eyes to cover her mouth. The door was still open. She heard Professor Lawrence laugh and knew that if she was too loud, everyone would hear her, too. She imagined everyone still at the party rushing down the hall to her aid and flinging open the door to see her getting eaten out by... by...

Lydia looked up and stared at her betrayed husband.

Angela looked up, licked her lips, and slyly asked if they would mind shutting the door when they left.

Martha kept her head hidden under the skirt, mortified by being discovered.

Sofia put her hands on top of the other woman's head, safely enshrouded by her skirt so she wouldn't be able to see hair color even if the lights were on, and finally opened her eyes. The room was brighter than she remembered, or her eyes had adjusted to the darkness while closed, and she could see the shape of a dresser and a closet door. She was slammed back into reality; this wasn't a fantasy or a dream, this was real. She had a woman between her legs and she didn't even know her name.

"Oh, God, what am I doing...?"

The lips stopped moving against her.

"No, no, no. Don't stop. Please don't stop." She laughed softly. "Oh, my God, keep going." She barely stopped herself from crying out as she was kissed again. Her folds were flicked by the tip of a tongue, her gathering moisture spread across her labia before being dragged up to her hooded clit. This was infinitely different than what the boys had done. This was even different than the bus with Kim, their laps covered by a coat. This was *sex*.

She didn't feel her orgasm coming. She was so surprised by the sudden climax that she almost forgot herself and shouted. Instead she put her hands on her lover's head and whispered, "I'm sorry, I'm sorry," as her entire body tensed as if it was trying to compress her into a fist with the stranger's head in the center. She gasped as her muscles relaxed and she fell back to the mattress.

There were tears in her eyes; she didn't know why. She wanted to laugh and she wasn't sure what was funny. The stranger lifted her head, smoothed down Sofia's skirt, and stretched out next to her again. Sofia kept her eyes closed though she was sure they were too teary for her to make out any details. She turned her head and was kissed, and she cupped the other woman's head so they could kiss again, and again, and once more, and deeper this time. She tasted herself on the other woman's tongue and moaned as her sex throbbed again.

"That was amazing. Thank you. Thank you."

She reached for the other woman's crotch, but her hand was intercepted. It was lifted and the knuckles were kissed, then the stranger brushed her cheek against the backs of her fingers. The message was clear; Sofia wasn't going to get a chance to reciprocate. She wanted to. She desperately wanted to make this woman - whoever she was - feel as good as she'd made her feel. But she knew it would be pointless to push the issue. She curled her fingers around the other woman's hand.

"Thank you. Can I have another kiss?"

"Mm." Soft lips met hers and lingered just long enough to make Sofia want more. Then they were pulled away, the weight lifted off the bed, and a hand on her hip urged Sofia to remain where she was. She did as instructed. She put her hands back on her stomach, but now they were quivering with the aftershocks of her orgasm. Her skin felt electrified, and she worried about her ability to walk back into the party without announcing what had just happened. She wiped the tears off her face, laughed at the fact they'd been there in the first place, and finally looked toward the door. It was open just a crack, just enough to let in the ambient light from down the hall. There was no sign of her mystery lover other than a lingering scent of perfume.

After a few minutes Sofia straightened her clothes and sat up. She saw that what she'd thought was a closet door really led to an en suite bathroom, so she went in to splash some water on her face. The memory of what happened was already fading. It seemed unbelievable even in the harsh bathroom light, but her skin was still sensitive to the touch. She was still euphoric from the orgasm. She looked at her face in the mirror and laughed, cupping her cheeks to feel how warm they were compared to her palms.

Finally she had no choice but to leave the bathroom and go back to the party before someone came looking for her. She stepped back into her shoes and went out. There were only about a dozen people still at the party, a few students gathered around Professor Lawrence's grill while two others had their feet in the pool. The rest were in the living room. A quick scan revealed that all three of her suspects were present and she felt relief at knowing nobody had been eliminated.

Lydia was in the kitchen, standing over the sink. She looked up as Sofia entered and she smiled. "Hello, sweetheart. Everything okay?"

"Yes. Why? Fine..."

Lydia looked at her for a beat longer than necessary. Looking for signs of regret? Or just noticing that Sofia seemed flushed and nervous? Lydia went back to what she had been doing... washing her hands? Why? Maybe she'd been putting away the barbeque and got sauce on her fingers. If she got close enough to smell Lydia's perfume it would help solve the mystery, so she took a step back.

"Do you need any help in here?"

"No, no," Lydia said. "You're here to enjoy yourself. Did you... enjoy yourself?"

Sofia's mind raced. Was there subtext in the question? "I did. It was amazing. Best night ever."

Lydia smiled. "Good. I'm very glad." She wiped her hands on a towel. "But I was serious. Tonight is supposed to be for unwinding and relaxing. No chores for you tonight."

"Okay. You'll let me know if you change your mind?"

"Of course."

Sofia turned to leave, then stopped. "It was really great meeting you, Lydia."

"It was wonderful meeting you, Sofia. We'll have to do this again sometime."

Now that... did that have some hidden meaning? "I'd like that a lot. If I don't see you before I go, thank you. For everything."

"You're welcome."

In the living room, Angela was sitting in the middle of the couch with her arms draped over the back. She was looking through the sliding glass door at the pool area. She looked over as Sofia approached and a cocky smile spread across her face. There was nothing to read into with that; Angela was always cocky for one reason or another.

"Hey, there she is. Where'd you get off to?"

"I went to sober up a little. I laid down in the guest room." She sat next to Angela. "What did I miss?"

"Not a lot. But sleeping at a party, Kennedy? That is next level lame."

Sofia grinned. "Maybe." Angela brought her hand up and teased Sofia's hair. Playful and friendly, or coyly intimate? "Ange?"

"Mm-hmm?"

She knew Angela would confess if she asked. "Nothing. I just... ah... n-nothing."

"You okay, kid?"

Genuine concern. From Angela. Maybe she was just tired.

Maybe the not knowing was going to drive Sofia crazy.

"I'm fine. I'm just a little out of it. Napping and waking up in a strange place."

"I hear ya. If you want a ride home, I'm planning to leave soon."

Sofia shook her head. "No, the whole point of lying down was so I could drive myself home. Thanks, though."

"Sure, Sofe."

A girl standing near the bookshelf caught Sofia's eye. She was looking toward the couch and smiled when she realized she'd been seen. She lifted her cup in greeting and Sofia nodded back to her. Who was to say the mystery woman was even someone she knew? It could actually be a stranger, like this girl. Or maybe this girl had seen or heard something and was letting Sofia know the secret was safe with her. Or... or maybe she just thought Sofia was cute. The possibilities were endless. And really, every woman at the party was potentially her mystery lover. She didn't know if the mystery would ever be cracked. She didn't know if she wanted it to be.

"I think I'm going to head out," she said.

Angela looked at her, suddenly serious. "Everything okay?"

"Yeah." She patted Angela's leg. Were her pants the right texture? Hadn't her mystery lover been wearing something with smoother material? She had to get out of the house before everything became a clue. "I'm just tired."

"Professor Lawrence will probably let you borrow a room if you want."

And what did *that* mean? She didn't want to speculate. "I'm sure he would. But I want to get home. Thanks."

"Sure."

She got up and sought out Professor Lawrence. She was able to be friendly and casual with him even knowing there was a thirty-three percent chance she'd just had sex with his wife. She thanked him for the party, said her goodbyes, and made a direct line for the door. She was nearly there when Martha showed up with Sofia's coat draped over her arm.

"Sofia. Hey. Angela told me you were leaving." She held up the coat. "I didn't want you to forget this."

"Oh. Thanks." She took the coat. "I... I forgot they were back there..."

She opened the door and stepped outside. Martha followed her. "Sofia, wait. Since we're alone, I-I just... I wanted... I wanted to say thank you. For... you know."

Sofia froze. This was it. The mystery was solved, and the meek little wallflower was her lover. "Thank me? F-for...?"

"For making me feel included. You came over and talked to me, and you included me in conversations. I was really nervous about coming here tonight, but I had a good time. So thank you for that. For always being there to make sure I don't disappear into the wallpaper."

"Sure." And the mystery was once again unclear, the truth murky. "Martha... next time, don't wait for me to bring you in. Okay? You're a great person. Just be confident and people will respond to that. You deserve to be seen and heard."

Martha smiled. "Thanks, Sofia. I'll see you Monday."

"Yeah."

Martha waved goodbye and went back into the Professor's house. Sofia waited until she was alone on the stoop before she put on her coat and buttoned up the front of it. The chill in the air helped sober her up even further, and the encounter seemed even further away and more surreal as she walked to her car. How would she feel in the morning, or on Monday? After she had a couple of nights worth of sleep, would she convince herself it had just been an extremely vivid fantasy? Was there a chance that was all it was?

When she arrived at her car, she had come to the conclusion that she didn't care. Whoever her partner had been, she would leave it up to them to come forward. If she never did, it could remain their secret. A taboo little tryst that no one ever had to know about. She was only certain about one thing: her unknown lover wasn't going to be the last woman she took to bed. And she was damn sure she would know who the next woman was.

SEXILED

ISABEL KEATON stopped at the end of the hall and stared at the whiteboard on her dorm room door. The illogical part of her brain hoped by staring at the message she could make it go away, but the bright purple message stubbornly remained. "12:15 - 1:30!" in Gabby's unmistakable handwriting, the cartoonish loops doing little to lessen Isabel's irritation. She thought about banging on the door and storming in anyway. She didn't care if Gabby and her boyfriend were currently engaged in sexual acts both acrobatic and creatively impressive. She was exhausted and all she wanted to do was sleep.

Maybe if she ran in, jammed her headphones on, and dove under the blankets she could avoid seeing anything she didn't want to see. It was just past twelve-thirty, so whatever was going on had to be well underway. Gabby could get... vocal... when things were going well and Isabel didn't think she had any music loud enough to drown out a full-blown performance. She would end up being awake until whenever Gabby finished no matter what, so she decided to spend it in the library. Peace and quiet would help shut down her brain so by the time she could return to her bed she would fall asleep without delay.

The library was epic at night; the lights were turned down to the bare minimum and silence seemed to grow out of the shadows.

The closing door echoed behind her. She walked past the abandoned circulation desk on her way to one of the tables farthest from the door, adjusting the strap of her bag so it wasn't cutting into her shoulder. It would be hard for anyone to see inside from the street, but she wasn't foolish enough to sit in front of a window by herself after midnight.

Isabel walked past an aisle, stopped, and peeked back to confirm what she thought she'd seen from the corner of her eye. A girl was sitting in front of the shelves, her legs folded in front of her with a book open on her lap. She was slumped forward and her hands had fallen limp onto the floor next to her. Isabel recognized the symptoms of "I just closed my eyes for a second" syndrome and went down the aisle.

"Hey. Hi there." She bent down and tilted her head to make sure the girl was breathing. She was torn between shaking her and just letting her be, but she didn't want to leave someone out in public along and so obviously vulnerable. After a moment she sat down across from the sleeper, dropped her bag with enough noise to hopefully rouse the other girl, and pulled out her eReader. She knew how precious sleep was, and she had no intention of cutting someone else's short. The least she could do was watch over her.

Isabel was halfway through the chapter when the other girl lifted her hands and rested them on the open book. She drew in a slow breath and straightened like the inhale had filled her with air. When she was fully upright she pushed her hair out of her face and blinked at the empty space in front of her. A second later she turned and looked at Isabel.

"Hi."

Isabel smiled. "Hi. Sorry. I didn't want to wake you up, but I also didn't want to leave you all by yourself. Might have been kind of scary."

"Thank you." She looked down at her book, then reached into her pocket to retrieve her phone. "Ugh. Damn. I'm going to be here all night."

Isabel smiled sympathetically. "Sorry about that. I'll leave you to it."

"No, stay. I mean, it's spooky here at night. I wouldn't mind if you want to sit with me for a while. We can make sure we both stay awake."

"Sure. I only have to kill an hour. My roommate is getting lucky."

The other girl rolled her eyes. "I know that song." She leaned forward and held out her hand. "Gina."

"Isabel." They shook hands. "So what are you studying that's so riveting?"

"Economics. That's one reason I'm sitting on the floor. I thought it would be just uncomfortable enough to keep me awake. Looks like that was a failure." She glanced down and focused on Isabel's sneakers. They were custom Chuck Taylors with a purple-pink-black harlequin pattern on the body and a pink tongue. "These shoes are awesome."

"Thanks. My mom was worried that wearing boots would make people think I was a militant lesbian or something, so this was my compromise."

"They're still pretty butch."

Isabel grinned. "Then my plan worked perfectly. I'll let you get back to your work."

Gina nodded and sighed heavily. She pushed her hair out of her face again, trying to pin it behind her ear. Isabel let her gaze linger for a few seconds longer than might be socially acceptable, but Gina was quite pretty. She had a sharp chin and high cheekbones, two features that could have overwhelmed the rest of her face to make her look harsh or severe. But her eyes were a soft green and her lips were full. The overall effect was of power and strength, and it was an incredibly attractive combination.

She tried to focus on her book, tapping her finger against the screen to turn the page. She stretched her legs out alongside Gina, the admired shoes crossed on the floor next to Gina's hips. Gina was wearing a knee-length skirt, her feet tucked underneath her so Isabel couldn't see her shoes. After a few minutes of silence, during which Isabel read two full pages without comprehension, Gina suddenly reached for her pocket.

"I don't think there's anyone here to shush us... how about some music?"

"Sure. What do you have?"

Gina gestured with the iPod she had taken out. "Come take a look."

Isabel got up just enough to shift across the aisle. Gina unfolded her legs and stretched her feet out in front of her so they could sit side-by-side. She held the device so Isabel could see the screen and began scrolling through the list of albums slowly enough that Isabel could read the artist names.

"I'm fine with anything, so whatever you see that looks good .."

"It all looks good. I think we have the same taste. In music, I mean."

Gina chuckled. "What else would you have meant?"

"Nothing. Ooh." She pointed at the screen. "Is that the new one?"

"Yeah." Gina opened the album and hit shuffle. "Have you heard it yet?"

Isabel shook her head.

"Get ready. It's her best yet."

"Cool." Isabel wasn't sure if she should get up and move back to where she had been sitting. Gina put the iPod on the floor between them and turned the volume low. If Gina asked, she would just claim she wanted to keep the music as low as possible. That was it. That was a totally plausible reason to remain close enough to smell Gina's perfume and feel the heat off her arm. Isabel looked down at her book and tried not to focus on those things. One of the reasons her roommate's late-night visitors bothered her so much was because Isabel hadn't had any of her own since the end of freshman year.

"What are you reading?"

Isabel gestured with the device. "Oh, just some stupid mystery thriller flavor-of-the-week thing."

"It's not *Twilight*, is it?"

"I know we've literally just met, but I hope you have a higher opinion of me than that."

Gina laughed and closed her Econ book. "I could use a little light entertainment. Read me some of it."

Isabel raised an eyebrow. "Read to you?"

"Sure. Why not?"

"Because... I don't know." She laughed anxiously. "I'm in the middle of a chapter. You don't know the story."

Gina grinned and shook her head. "Okay. Never mind."

Isabel only hesitated for a moment. "You know what?" She tapped the screen and searched for a collection of short stories. "I can find something short and start from the beginning."

"You don't have to."

"No, it'll be fun. And it might help pass the time." She scratched her chin as she looked at the table of contents. "Okay. This story is called 'Typing Lessons.'"

"Sounds riveting."

"Shut up, this was your idea."

Gina chuckled and folded her hands on top of her book. Isabel cleared her throat. "'The first thing I noticed about her were her hands. The long tapering fingers, the smooth pink nails perfectly trimmed and painted with a clear polish so that they glistened whenever she moved. Her shirt sleeves were short enough to reveal a jumble of bracelets hanging on her elegant wrist. The jewelry was loose enough so it wouldn't pinch the skin, but snug enough that they wouldn't clatter against each other.'" Isabel kept reading, but the subject matter of the story quickly became apparent. She stopped at the first mention of gender. "Oh. This story is about lesbians."

"So?"

"I just thought..."

"It's fine." Gina scooted closer. "Keep reading."

Isabel hesitated but then focused on the screen. "'I felt self-conscious holding her hands. My stubbier fingers with their chewed-on nails looked grotesque next to hers. Everything about Julie was long; her fingers and arms, her neck, her torso, her legs. It would help my self-esteem if she was lanky or awkward at all, but she carried her height like a horse-' Gee, that's flattering..."

"In the right circumstances, anything is romantic," Gina said. "Keep reading."

"'I fell in love with her hands first. I watched the way they would glide across the keyboard. She was a hunt-and-peck typist but she was fast. Her hands hovered above the computer and the tips of her fingers flew to the four corners of the keyboard to type out her papers. Later, after we got together, I learned the true limits of her abilities. Her fingers were deft and knowing, and when they touched me...' Oh. Okay..."

"What are you doing?"

"Uh..."

"We're both adults here." They'd both been speaking softly out of respect to the library, as if they were telling secrets they didn't want the books to hear, but now Gina's voice dropped even lower. It went from deferential whisper to intimate murmur. "Keep reading."

Isabel wet her lips and looked at Gina. She seemed impossibly close now, close enough to feel her breath and the warmth of where their arms were almost touching. After another moment's hesitation Isabel looked at the page again and picked up where she left off.

"'...and when they touched me, I learned where she was really skilled. I felt as if she was writing words on me, typing an entire essay on my breasts and thighs. When her fingers were insi-inside me...'" She cleared her throat and focused on the suddenly blurry words. "'I felt like she was transcribing an entire novel in some unknown language that only she knew and she was trying to teach me. And I ran my own hands over her body, my relatively thick and awkward fingers making a map out of her. I learned every bump and plane, every spot where her skin was pulled tight over muscle.'"

Gina shifted slightly and put her hand on her thigh so it spanned skirt and skin. She curled her fingers and pinched the hem of her skirt.

"Keep reading," Gina said.

Isabel looked and saw Gina's eyes were closed. She was still debating the action when she put down the eReader and covered Gina's hand with hers. Gina opened her eyes and found Isabel staring at her. They remained perfectly still for a few seconds. The quiet hum of the heating system was louder than their breathing as Isabel moved her hand higher. Gina twisted her wrist out of the way and lifted her skirt just enough for Isabel's hand to move underneath it.

"Any ideas how the story ends?" Gina asked.

"I can show you some theories."

Gina smiled and leaned forward. She didn't have far to go, but Isabel still met her halfway, kissing her as she stroked the warm skin hidden under the tartan material of her skirt. Gina arched her back at the touch, covering Isabel's hand with the skirt between them. They didn't even know each other's last names and, at the moment, Isabel didn't know if she considered that a pro or con. She turned her head and teased her tongue against Gina's lips. Gina shifted her weight and turned more toward Isabel, her legs falling apart and almost forcing Isabel to move her hand higher. She felt the soft brush of cotton against her fingers. She gasped and Gina's tongue flickered into her mouth.

"I don't... do this..."

Gina said, "You're doing it right now."

"Usually. I mean I don't... usually..."

"Maybe you should." Gina nipped at Isabel's bottom lip. "You seem to be awfully good at it."

Isabel laughed breathlessly and pressed two fingers against the crotch of Gina's underwear. Gina reached for her then, lifting her shirt and grasping blindly for the catch of her jeans. She said, "Okay?" against Isabel's lips. Isabel tried to say yes, tried to nod without breaking contact, but it came out as a muffled noise and a bizarre wobble of her head. She hoped that by continuing to kiss Gina she was giving her permission.

"What do you want me to do to you?" Gina asked, her lips moving against the corner of Isabel's mouth. She had gotten the button of her jeans open and was now working the zipper.

"I... don't..." She closed her eyes and rolled her head back. "Kiss my neck."

Gina made a hungry sound in the back of her throat as she tilted her head. She used her cheek to brush the collar of Isabel's shirt aside and dragged her lips from the curve of her shoulder up to just under her earlobe. Isabel shivered in response and twisted her fingers to push Gina's underwear out of her way. She bit her bottom lip and closed her eyes as she began to stroke. Gina's lips and tongue attacked her neck like some cheesy B-movie vampire.

"Keep talking," Gina said. "Your voice is sexy..."

The compliment distracted Isabel enough that she almost stopped moving her hand. No one had ever said that about her voice before, but she was willing to capitalize on it. She moved her lips closer to Gina's ear and tried to think of something to say.

"You're... so fucking hot..." She grimaced at herself. "Sorry. Let me start over..."

"There are no do-overs in dirty talk. Just power through." She lifted her head, kissed Isabel hard on the lips, and then began to suck on the other side of her neck.

Coherent thought was a struggle for Isabel. She'd always been turned on by being kissed on the neck, and Gina had a damned talented tongue. She swallowed the lump in her throat and decided to go with that. "I love your lips on my neck. It's turning me on so much. It's making me wet." She nipped at Gina's earlobe, breathing harder. "I can feel how wet you are."

"Now you're getting it." Gina was rubbing her underwear now. "Can you feel how wet I am?"

"Yeah. Yes. You're so wet for me..."

Gina chuckled and leaned back. Her eyes were dark, her dangerous cheekbones flushed red. She lifted her hips against Isabel's hand while her own fingers curled and rubbed between Isabel's legs.

"I want you to come for me," Isabel said, holding eye contact.

"I want to make you come."

Gina whimpered, her free hand clenching and relaxing on the carpet in an attempt to find something to grip. "Then keep doing that..."

"Yeah...?" Isabel moved her hips against Gina's hand. Somehow she had found her inner seductress. "What if I want you to make me come first?"

The muscles of Gina's arms flexed as she worked her hand inside the confines of Isabel's pants. Isabel curled her middle finger and lunged forward to capture Gina's mouth again. Their tongues met, their moans combining as Isabel lifted her ass off the floor and pressed against Gina's hand with all her weight. Isabel broke first, her moan turning into a gasp. She brought her hand up to stroke Gina's cheek as she closed her thighs, imprisoning Gina's hand between them as her orgasm crested. Waves of pleasure washed from her shoulders down to her feet and then coursed back up to swirl around her middle.

After the initial braindead response to coming, she redoubled her efforts on Gina. "Good girl," she said in a surprisingly weak voice. "Want your reward?"

"Yes..."

"Come for me, then." She grazed her lips against Gina's and then kissed her properly. She pushed two fingers into Gina and savored the moan of pleasure that rose at the back of her throat like a distant siren growing ever closer. Gina swung her arm up from the floor and grabbed a handful of Isabel's hair, moving wildly against her before finally her body went rigid. Her fingernails dug into the side of Isabel's head and she broke the kiss to exhale sharply, baring her teeth before taking in a shaky breath.

They both sank back to the floor as if they had been floating, pulling apart and stretching their legs out. Gina brought her hand to her face and lightly brushed the fingers over her lips. She covered the move by also tucking her hair behind her ears, but Isabel saw and blushed. She lifted her hips so she could tug her jeans back into place. She pressed her lips together and made sure her bag and eReader were where they were supposed to be.

"Wow. In the library. That's gotta be a bucket list item, huh?"

Isabel laughed nervously. "I've never done anything like that before."

"You should start."

Isabel laughed for real at that. She looked at her phone and saw by the time she walked back to her room, Gabby's visitor would be gone. "Oh. I can go to bed now."

"Oh."

"Do you want to walk me?"

Gina said, "I have so much... actually, you know what? Yeah... yeah. Hold on. Let me get all my shit together."

Isabel stood up and waited as Gina gathered her books and stuffed them into her bag. They walked out of the library together and hesitated on the front steps as they determined how far they could walk together before they had to split up. Isabel bundled herself up against the cold and led the way. Gina took a deep breath and then looked at Isabel before facing forward again.

"So what happened back there... one-time thrill or the start of something more?"

"I don't know. You?"

"I don't know, either. But I know one thing."

Isabel said, "Yeah?"

"I want a proper experience before I discount any of the possibilities."

Isabel ducked her chin and chuckled. She reached out and looped her arm around Gina's, pulling her close. She didn't know if it was going to be the start of a relationship or not. Whatever it was, the magic of the evening had yet to die. And she wasn't going to let it go until she'd drained the absolute final drop of it. She tightened her grip on Gina's arm, and Gina leaned heavily against her, and they walked together into the uncertain night.

STORM SIRENS

THE WAIL seemed almost natural at first. It slowly gained volume so it could be heard over the wind, its pitch flattening out into a piercing whistle. Olivia grew up in the Plains and knew ignoring that sound when she was out in the open was as good as suicide. She had been walking all morning, and the storm clouds ahead of her just got more and more ominous with every mile. Finally an ice cold blast of wind cut through the late-Spring heat and signaled the storms arrival. But still she walked, putting up her hood and securing her backpack to make sure it wouldn't leak.

She didn't mind getting a little wet, but the sirens were another thing entirely. She was on the very edge of a town she didn't know the name of, surrounded on all sides by fields and roads spider-webbed by cracked pavement. Her only possible refuge was a barn standing on the edge of someone's private property. The area was so empty it was hard to gauge distance, but it couldn't have been more than a mile away.

Olivia put her head down and ran through the icy darts, slowing down only when she reached the wooden fence. She put her hands on the top bar and vaulted onto the other side. The mud pulled at her sneakers but she tugged them free without losing either of them. Sprawling pools of water were impossible to avoid but she did her best to leap the deepest sections. By the time she reached the barn her jeans were soaked from mid-thigh down. She prayed the door would be unlocked and, for once, her prayers were answered. She slid the door along its track just enough to slip inside and pulled it shut behind her.

Barns weren't exactly the best place to ride out a tornadic storm, but it was better than being out in the open. She pushed her hood off her head and looked around as she caught her breath. No animals, which was good. The interior of the barn was almost pitch-black, with deep shadows in every direction. She could see a little bit in front of her face, and she could see the outline of tools neatly arranged on either side of the center aisle.

Her plan was to wait out the storm and slip out before the owners even knew she was there. She didn't know if there was a shelter in the barn, so she climbed up to the hayloft so she could stay out of sight if anyone came in. She took off her backpack and rested it against the wall. The storm became more aggressive as she settled in. Rain slapped against the side of the barn like waves lapping at the shore, and the old wood groaned under the constant assault of the wind. Despite that she didn't see or hear any leaks. The building seemed secure enough to protect her for the moment.

Olivia knelt in front of her backpack and made sure nothing was ruined from being out in the storm. She didn't have much, but it seemed like what she did have made it through unscathed. She had just returned everything to the pack when she heard a noise by the door. She pushed the bag against the wall and dropped onto her stomach, hands flat on the wood and hay tickling her stomach where her shirt had ridden up. If the owner of the house had seen her, she didn't want to present herself as a threat. People in these parts tended to shoot first and not bother with questions.

The door slid open on its track. "Get in... hurry..."

A second person yelped as she hurried inside out of the weather. Both were women so Olivia relaxed slightly. She slid forward on her belly until she could see over the edge of the loft. The taller woman pushed the door shut against the rain. She wore a dress that was probably pale yellow but had darkened to a deep brown in the rain. Her hair was similarly drenched and hung from her head like black seaweed. She was wearing knee-length rubber boots that were caked with mud.

It was the other woman who frightened Olivia, though. The one wearing the police uniform. The rain made the leather of her belt shine, and the butt of her gun seemed to sparkle even in the meager light from the lantern she was holding. She had been wearing one of those hats with the wide round rim, but she took it off and touched her dry blonde hair as she let it drip onto the floor. Olivia's heart thudded against her chest. How could the cops have gotten there so quickly? Could she possibly know who Olivia was? Could she actually have been following Olivia and—

Both women started laughing. The civilian leaned against the barn door, and the cop put down the lantern at their feet. When she straightened up she stepped forward to brush the hair out of the other woman's face. She rested her hands on the other woman's cheeks with her thumbs moving back and forth over the wet skin.

"Oh, Audrey," the cop said. "You look like a drowned rat."

Audrey's face was streaked with rain water, but her eyes were so full of love that it was obvious to Olivia even in the darkness.

"Ever the romantic, huh?"

"You want romance or you want honesty?" She brushed her thumb over Audrey's bottom lip. Audrey opened her mouth wider in an attempt to catch it without taking her eyes off the cop's face.

"Honesty."

"Okay. You look like a drowned rat. But you're still the most gorgeous woman I've ever seen in my life." She tilted Audrey's head up ever so slightly and kissed her lips.

Olivia pressed her hand against her mouth to stifle any sound that might have escaped. The rain was still pelting the barn, and the wind whistled around it on all sides, so she doubted they could have heard her gasp. She wasn't going to take any risks. The two women were standing in a halo of light from the cop's lantern, but the rest of the barn was so dark it might as well have not existed. She knew they weren't able to see her but making noise would give her away.

"Are you sure he won't come out here looking for you?"

Audrey shook her head. A wet strand of hair caught on her cheek and the cop brushed it away. "He's passed out. He won't wake up for another hour, and he probably won't realize I'm not in the house for another hour after that. We have time. Vanessa, kiss me." She cupped the back of the cop's head and moaned as their lips met again. Thunder rumbled close enough that it seemed like a physical force trundling along the countryside.

The cop, Vanessa, pressed Audrey against the door and moved her hands down, brushing the backs of her hands over her breasts before spreading her fingers on Audrey's hips. Their kiss became more passionate as Vanessa closed her hands and pulled the dress up. Olivia's eyes widened as she saw the pink lace of Audrey's underwear. Audrey took Vanessa's hand to guide it between her legs, shifting her weight from one foot to the other so her legs were spread further apart.

Everything seemed heightened by the storm. The air was electric and heavy with the not-unpleasant odor of ozone. All around them was the sound of splashing water and the occasional growl of thunder, but the world had shrunk to that small circle of light on the lower level of the barn. The women were whispering to each other now, their voices too quiet for Olivia to hear, but Audrey's words were punctuated by grunts of pleasure. Her hand was still wrapped around Vanessa's wrist, and Vanessa had started to rock her hips forward in rhythm to the movement of her arm.

Olivia lifted her hips from the floor of the loft, one hand still over her mouth as the other moved slowly down the length of her body. She was grateful she didn't have a belt, glad she didn't have to risk the buckle clinking when she undid it. She worked her fingers under the waistband of her jeans and cupped her mound. She parted her lips and sucked her middle finger as she watched the couple below her.

Audrey rolled her head back and put her hands on Vanessa's shoulders, parting her lips in silent or gasps too quiet for Olivia to hear. Her entire body moved against Vanessa's hand as she lifted onto her toes, her knees bent as if she was about to take flight. Vanessa dropped her head and began kissing, licking, or sucking Audrey's neck, and Audrey clapped a hand over her mouth to muffle herself.

When she sagged against the wall, trembling from completion, she put her hand on Vanessa's head and turned her until they could kiss again. Audrey pushed away from the door and turned them both in a quick ballet. As they turned Olivia got a good look at their lips, saw Audrey's tongue as a pink flicker moving between their mouths as she put the cop against the barn door.

Olivia pumped her finger in and out of her mouth as her other hand cupped her mound, massaging gently as Audrey took off Vanessa's belt and broke the kiss so she could look where she was putting it down. As she was dealing with that, Vanessa unfastened her pants and shoved them down. Her underwear was dark gray boxer briefs, but they quickly joined her uniform around her knees. Olivia had to bite down on her knuckle so she didn't make a noise at the sight of the cop's bush, the hair covering her sex darker than the hair on her head.

She left her uniform shirt on as Audrey kissed a path down her body. She kissed Vanessa's breasts and reached down to stroke her bare thighs as she knelt in front of her. Vanessa looked down at her lover and ran her fingers through hair the rain had turned curly, gripping it with both hands and smiling as Audrey looked up at her. Vanessa moved her legs apart, shackled by her pants, and began breathing hard as Audrey kissed her inner thigh and then lifted her head.

Olivia moved her hips against her hand, sucking hard on her finger as she watched the cop. Vanessa ran her hands through Audrey's hair, rocking her hips forward as her gasps became more desperate and eager. Olivia put two fingers inside herself, knowing that Audrey was probably doing the same under her dress.

There was another crack of thunder so loud it sounded like a gunshot, and all three of the women in the barn startled at it. Before flinching, Olivia saw Vanessa's hand drop to her waist to grab the gun now laying at her feet. She smiled nervously and put her hand back in Audrey's hair and looked down.

"Scared me," she said.

"Me too."

"Don't stop. I'm close."

Audrey moaned and leaned forward again. Olivia watched with wide-eyed fascination. She'd never actually been with anyone before, but she knew when she did she would choose a woman. But she had never actually seen it in real life. She'd never seen two real women making love. She dragged her finger out of her mouth and dragged its wet tip over her bottom lip, imagining it was the juices Audrey was tasting at that moment. She wished she could reposition herself but she couldn't risk making a noise. She kept her knees apart and her hips lifted. It was an awkward position that left her shoulders on the ground as she rubbed herself through her panties, but she would worry about that later.

"Audrey," Vanessa moaned, lifting one foot off the ground and stomping it as she grunted through her orgasm. "Oh, babe, yes..."

Audrey kissed Vanessa's body as she stood up, cupping her breasts as they found each other's mouths again. Vanessa gripped Vanessa's ass, the rain-heavy material of her dress molding to the shape so that she might as well have been bottomless. Audrey settled between Vanessa's legs and thrust her hips forward and they both moaned in concert, then laughed at each other as the kiss broke.

Olivia turned her head to rest her cheek on the floor of the loft, biting down hard on the inside of her cheek to keep from crying out as she came.

"That was fucking fantastic," Audrey said.

"It always is. I just wish..." She bit down on her bottom lip and looked away.

Audrey said, "Say it."

"No."

"It's fine."

"It's not fair to you."

Audrey stroked Vanessa's cheek. "You wish it was easier. No lies, no sneaking around. You deserve that."

"And I know you can't give it to me." She kissed Audrey's cheeks, cradling her face tenderly with both hands. If you left him, he would just make both our lives miserable. This isn't ideal and it's not what I would choose, but if five minutes huddling with you in a barn during a storm is all I can get then it's what I'll take."

They kissed once more, and Audrey helped Vanessa pull her pants back up. Olivia took advantage of their distraction to pull her hand free and reposition herself more comfortably. She was still on her stomach, head close to the edge so she could peek at them some more. They were whispering again, but the rain had died down enough that she could make out their words.

"~wake up? If he's in the kitchen when we get back in the house, or if he sees your squad car?"

"You'll tell him what we talked about. You thought you saw someone in the back field. You thought there was an intruder in the barn, and you called me to check it out. You know how he feels about trespassers. If he thinks I was personally patrolling his borders, he'll feel like a big man and everything will be fine."

Olivia smirked in the darkness. She wasn't sure if it counted as irony or not, but it certainly was amusing to her. She was also a bit concerned about squatting in the barn of someone who had strong feelings about trespassers.

"My hero."

"Always." She put her hat on Audrey's head and bent down to pick up the lantern. They did a final check on their clothes, kissed one more time, and then Audrey turned to push the door open. She checked outside just as lightning lit up the field. Vanessa put a hand on Audrey's back and they both made a break for it at the same time. Vanessa turned, slipping a little in the mud as she pushed the door closed.

Silence and darkness fell once more. Olivia remained where she was, frozen and silent, face to the floor, trying to hear the sound of their running footsteps as they fled back to the safety of the house. Finally she felt confident enough that she pushed herself up and scooted back to the wall where she'd left her backpack. She unbuttoned her pants and slipped her hand inside. She relaxed with her feet planted wide apart, closed her eyes, and proceeded to run her mind over what she'd just witnessed again so she could appreciate it properly.

Olivia didn't sleep that night. She listened to the storm as its intensity waxed and waned. Sometimes it was a deluge that sounded like Noah's flood coming back to finish the job, and other times it wasn't clear if she was hearing rain or just the water dripping off the roof. Thunder continued to rock the air, distant cannon fire and nearby explosions that made her jump every time. She used her pack as a pillow and kept her hands laced on her stomach as she stared at the ceiling in the darkness.

The storm was seemingly chased away by the rising sun. Olivia gathered her things and slipped her arms through the straps of her backpack. She had kept one thing out of the pack, and she put it into her front pocket as she descended the ladder. She walked past the spot where Audrey and Vanessa had made love the night before and stepped out into the humid heat of dawn.

Instead of heading toward the fence, she walked directly toward the house. She had her hood up to shadow her face as she approached the sliding back doors of the kitchen. She didn't have a plan. She didn't know what she would do if Audrey or god forbid Vanessa were inside. She only knew what she had to do.

There was a two-foot brick lip on the porch and she stepped over it. She could see into the kitchen now, and a man was standing at the counter making himself breakfast. He wore a suit and a sour expression, attacking the food as if it had personally wronged him. She'd heard of people who had punchable faces before, but this man had an entire body begging to be assaulted.

Olivia didn't even make it to the back door before he noticed her. His head snapped up and he fixed dark, animal eyes on her. "Hey!" he shouted. Olivia darted to one side as he stepped around the kitchen island. She jumped over the lip of the porch as the back door was yanked open behind her. "~king garbage people... hey!

This is private goddamn property, you little slut!"

Olivia darted around the corner of the house but, instead of continuing to flee, she pressed her back against the stucco wall. He appeared a half-second later, slipping on the mud, and Olivia lashed out with the item she'd removed from her bag. Blue light arced from the tines of the Taser, entering him through the neck and freezing every synapse he had. He went down to his knees, splattering his nice suit pants with mud.

She stepped behind him and locked an arm around his throat. She fitted his neck into the crook of her elbow, grabbed her wrist with her other hand, and pulled it tight.

There were men, she knew, who couldn't be dissuaded from what they thought of as their "true nature." There were animals in men suits who did whatever they wanted because they knew the right things to say, the right friends to make, and how to act in public. To people like this, women were property. Things that could be trained and cowed into submission. Women were their pets. Their sexual aids. She tightened her grip and the man made a sound of desperation low in his throat.

She met a man like that when she was fifteen. He decided that was old enough and he wasn't interested in waiting until she was older. The first time she told someone, they didn't believe "a man like him" was capable of such a thing. He feigned innocence and told her how hurt he was that she would make such a godawful accusation about him.

The next time he took her, he made it hurt. He warned her that if she ever tried to tell anyone, or if she ever tried to trap him, he would just get out of it and he would make her pay.

It took her some time to work out the plan, but eventually she was able to make him stop. She knew he would never stop until she was dead. And if somehow she did get free of him, there would just be another girl in his sights. So she made him stop forever.

There was no proof of what he'd done to her, no evidence to prove what she'd done was justified, which made her a killer. Pure and simple, she was a criminal and he was her innocent victim. Odd how things worked out like that. But she had expected as much, and she'd known she could never stay at home after what she did. Escape was part of her plan, and she was out the door before his body even hit the ground.

She had been running ever since. A fugitive. A non-entity. A ghost. And as such, she was the only one free to do what needed to be done. The man in her arms went limp, but she held on a bit longer just to make sure he wasn't playing possum. He give a final violent tremble and then his weight sagged against her. She let him drop, falling face-first into the mud, and she stepped back to look down at his body, then bent down and emptied his pockets.

His phone and credit cards would end up a hundred miles away. His car would end up abandoned in the middle of nowhere. Hopefully it would be enough to keep the police from looking at Audrey as the killer. She was sure Vanessa would do everything in her power to make sure the investigation didn't focus on her.

Olivia was confident the cops wouldn't find her but, if they did, she would go down without a fight. The world was better off without the people she'd taken out of it. If her reward was spending the rest of her life in prison, then the tradeoff was worth it.

She walked to the garage and, after making sure the coast was clear, got into the dead man's car. It was a pristine Lexus Infiniti, something he obviously cherished and took great care of. She dumped her rain-soaked bag in the passenger seat and smeared the mud from her shoes on the floor mats. She backed out of the garage and followed the long, winding driveway back to the main road.

She hated the idea that Audrey would find the body, but hopefully she would get over the trauma given enough time and TLC from Officer Vanessa would get her through it.

Olivia smiled and revved the engine. She could still see thick black clouds on the southern horizon and decided she would see if she could catch up with it. It wouldn't be so bad, being caught in the rain. She pressed down on the pedal, gripped the wheel with both hands, and went chasing after the storm.

THOSE WHO CONSORT WITH BEASTS

Beverly, Mass
Early 1692. Winter.

"PLEASE LET her remember me like this," Sarah Putnam whispered in the silence as she waited for her daughter. She always felt closer to the spirits between forms, in the woods with her skin still tingling from its transition.

She crouched with her bare back against the rough bark of a dead tree. Her breath crystallized the air in front of her face and the sweat was drying on her skin as she searched the trees for her daughter. Sarah was crouched with one knee on the frozen ground. She was naked, covered with sweat that was turning to ice with each passing second. Her hair was a wild tangle of brown that curtained her eyes. She flexed the tightness from her fingers as she listened for sounds of pursuit.

A moment later a bush began to tremble with the passage of the younger Putnam woman. Phoebe entered the clearing in a burst of broken twigs and falling leaves. She ran on all fours, her body covered with a beautiful pale gray fur. She was breathing hard, not yet used to this kind of running, but she turned smiling eyes toward Sarah and yelped excitedly.

"Shh, little wolf," Sarah said with a smile. She reached out and smoothed a palm over the sloped skull of her daughter. She'd spent twelve years imagining what her daughter's *canidae* form would look like. She was absolutely gorgeous. She had her father's coloring but Sarah's eyes. Phoebe bounced side-to-side on her forelegs and vibrated from energy she had yet to expel.

"Listen to me." Sarah held the wolf's head with both hands, forcing eye contact. "I've shown you how to run. When you get older, you can run by yourself. But not until I have taught you how to be safe. Do you understand me?"

The wolf who was her daughter nodded her head up and down. She pulled away from her mother's grip and trotted back to the edge of the woods. She looked back over her shoulder and whined. Sarah chuckled.

"You'll be exhausted."

Phoebe reared up on her hind legs and pawed at the iced-over grass with her front paws.

"Okay, okay..."

Sarah stood up and Phoebe turned to watch what happened next. Sarah had never hidden her dual nature, knowing full well her daughter would one day keep the same secret. She wanted the wolf to be a normal part of their lives. She wanted her daughter to be comfortable with the nudity that came with transforming from one shape to the other, so she had no hesitation standing to full height even though she was nude.

Sarah rolled her shoulders and planted one foot slightly in front of the other. She flexed her toes and spread out her fingers before tightening her hands into fists. The wolf was inside of her, just as it had been since birth. She felt it pressing against the confines of her body and surrendered to its dominance. Fur spread across her chest, down her arms, and all the way down her legs. It was black down the length of her spine and faded to mahogany on her flanks and legs. Her chest had a flare of white shaped like a diamond. She dropped onto all fours and arched her back, reveling in her new shape.

Phoebe bounded forward and then came back, urging her mother forward. Sarah nipped at Phoebe's hind leg, a warning to calm herself down. There were hunters in these woods, as there were hunters in all woods, and it wouldn't do to announce their presence. She nudged Phoebe forward and watched the pup tear off into the underbrush again. She couldn't help but huff and shake her head.

Safety was paramount, of course, but there was something to

be said about exuberance.

She wanted her daughter to remember these days, not the frightened days that were certain to come. She wanted Phoebe to know the fun of being a wolf. The wonder of every smell the forests had to offer even in the aptly named dead of winter. To hear the scurry of animals and know they were running from her because she was a predator. That was truly what she wanted most. She wanted her daughter to know she could be powerful when the world rose up and insisted she was nothing but prey.

Phoebe Putnam was a woman and a *canidae*. There would be no shortage of men telling her to sit down and be quiet. Sarah wanted to teach her how loudly she could bark in response.

They descended the hill back toward civilization. Phoebe slowed down before she could be seen from the road. She hunkered down with her snout close to the ground, paws out in front of her, and waited. Sarah proudly nuzzled the girl-pup's head before continuing past her at a cautious crawl. Only a few homes stood between them and safety, but all they needed was for Uriah Whitney to be heading out for a midnight constitutional when they passed through his backyard.

She heard: the water lapping at the shore in Beverly Cove; birds overhead rustling leaves and feathers as they shifted position in slumber; the breathing of her daughter but no one else. She smelled smoke and ash from a fire long since extinguished. No human sounds. No human smells.

Sarah motioned Phoebe forward with a flick of her head and they moved from the protection of the woods. Together they ran down the middle of the road so they could duck to either the left or right if anyone happened to appear. Sarah reached their home first and rounded the corner to the backyard. She mentally thanked the wolf for its speed and intelligence as well as its heightened senses, then politely asked for control of her body back.

The wolf faded, her bones popping back into place with a familiar ache. She was sore as she stood on the back porch and pushed the door open. Phoebe brushed against her thighs as she ran inside, the fur cold and beaded with moisture from their run. Sarah smiled and looked out once more to make sure no one had witnessed their homecoming. Content they'd gone unseen, she closed the door and moved to light the lantern sitting on the dining room table. She heard the thump of a small body hitting the floor in the living room.

"You should lie down." Her voice was rough, her throat dry. She touched the hollow of her neck where the collarbones met and coughed lightly. The wolf always left her hoarse. "Until you're accustomed to how much it can hurt, you shouldn't~"

The girl slammed into her from behind, startling her so much that she thought it was an attack. She smiled when she realized it was merely a joyous hug. She patted Phoebe's arms where they crossed her stomach and twisted to look down at the mop of pale blonde hair.

"Thank you, mother," the girl said.

"You are very welcome, my dear."

"When can I go out on my own?"

"You are a very long way from that, my love."

Phoebe said, "But one day?"

"Yes, Phoebe. One day. Go get dressed. I'll make you something to eat."

"Okay, mother."

She watched Phoebe scurry into the other room and chuckled. The girl was bound to have a dangerous life, but her excitement was a very good sign. For now, she needed protein. Being the wolf was hungry work.

Sarah stayed up to read after putting Phoebe to bed. Being a wolf meant many nights losing sleep, giving it up in exchange for letting the wolf run wild. Sarah was used to only getting two or three hours a night, but Phoebe was still young. She was still on the verge of falling asleep when she heard furtive movement on the porch. Her eyes snapped open and she sat up straighter in her rocking chair. She held her breath so as not to cover any further noises, every muscle tensed in anticipation of leaping up to attack.

Fingernails scratched at the window in a familiar rhythm. The tension faded from her body as she rose and moved silently to the door on the balls of her feet. She undid the latch and pulled it open. The cold night air swept in with an audible breath, raising the gooseflesh on her bare arms and legs. A moment later the hunched shape of Delia Ewer entered so quickly it was as if she had been carried in on the gusts.

Sarah closed the door behind her friend. Delia rose to her full height and tugged at the cloak covering her naked body.

"What on earth are you doing out here so late?" Sarah demanded in a whisper. "And on such an evening."

Delia matched her volume. "I hope the circumstances of my arrival will prove to you my news is dire. Is Phoebe asleep?"

"She is."

Sarah retrieved a thick blanket from the linen closet. Delia traded her wet cloak for it and wrapped the heavy cloth tightly around her body. Sarah draped the coat over a chair so it could drip dry. With that done, she turned a concerned face to Delia.

"What circumstances?"

"Constance Morse has been arrested."

Sarah's eyes widened. "Connie? What could they possibly~"

"Consorting with the beast."

"Oh, good heavens." Sarah felt faint so she moved closer to the table. She sank into one of the chairs and put a hand to her forehead as she processed the information.

Constance and Delia lived in Salem Village, the next town over. They were part of the same pack, a group of female *canidae* who occasionally joined together for runs. Constance joined them a few months ago and Sarah struck up a quick friendship with the newcomer. Connie was a transplant from a small town in England called Faringdon and she welcomed the kindness. Soon she was a frequent guest at the Putnam house, for dinner and conversation, and quite a few nights had been spent in wolf form running along the shoreline.

Their relationship became sexual on one of those runs. They were both in human form, but the animal instincts took over before either could come to their senses. Sarah remembered kissing and being kissed though she didn't know who instigated the clinch. Wolves were extremely fluid with their sexuality and intimacy like this was not unheard of, but both Sarah and Connie knew there was something more in the encounter.

Only a handful of people knew the true nature of their relationship. Delia was one of them.

Delia moved closer and sat down in the chair to Sarah's right. "The Gardner girl claimed she and her friends saw Connie in the woods. She was naked and writhing in all sorts of unnatural contortions."

"Transforming."

"I have to assume, yes."

Sarah closed her eyes. "Damnation. Where is she now?"

"She's being held in the basement of the church. They were going to put her in the jail, but no one wanted her escaping. They figured it was best to let God watch over her until tomorrow when she could be put on trial."

"I suppose that's something. It will be much easier to free her from the church than it would the town jail."

Delia said, "And if we get caught, we'll be locked up alongside her."

"That's a risk I'm willing to take. For Constance."

"I was afraid you'd say that. What about your little girl? What happens to her if the town decides you're a witch, too?"

Sarah looked toward the dark bedroom. "I can't simply abandon her..."

"Are you talking about Constance or Phoebe?"

Sarah didn't rightly know. Both, probably. "When will they put her on trial?"

"Tomorrow."

"So soon?" Sarah exclaimed, only remembering to lower her tone halfway through the second word. She put a hand over her mouth and looked toward the bedroom. They waited to hear if Phoebe would awaken, but there were no sounds. "What is the rush?"

"The girl was obviously traumatized. Constance had no reasonable explanation for what she had been doing or what the girl had seen. The best case scenario is an illicit romantic encounter, but she would still have consequences being guilty of that."

Sarah swore softly under her breath. "We cannot simply let her be put to death. What does the rest of the pack have to say?" She watched Delia's expression shift in the dim light and understood the answer. "They have decided to do nothing in order to protect themselves. The cowards."

"They are doing what is prudent."

"Obviously you don't agree with them, or else you wouldn't be here."

Delia said, "I'm here because you deserve to know what is happening. I know you and Constance are... closer... than some might know."

Sarah's cheeks flushed red. "And it is for that reason I cannot stand idle as she is put to death for a crime for which I, too, am guilty."

"You cannot place your own neck on the chopping block because of some misguided ideals."

"I don't intend to. I merely intend to save a person I've come to care for very much."

Delia made a derisive noise. "Fine. I'll let you believe that."

Sarah went to her friend and pressed a kiss to her cheek. "Will you remain here with Phoebe until I've returned? If I haven't returned by afternoon, assume the worst and take her somewhere safe."

"You have my word. But Sarah, promise me you'll be safe."

"On that you have *my* word. But if I was in Connie's position, I would want to know someone was coming for me. I cannot let her face this hell alone."

Delia nodded that she understood.

Sarah went to the door and stepped out into the night. Her clothes were left in a pile on the corner of the porch and, by the time her feet hit snow, she had partially transformed into the wolf. She was fully changed by the time she reached the edge of the forest. Salem Village wasn't far on foot, and the distance was even shorter for the wolf. She was guided by muscle memory and scent, the moonlight too dim to push back the many shadows of night.

She followed the edge of the Bass River north until she reached farmland. She paused to make sure there were no insomniac people wandering or animals milling about. The wolf could occasionally be distracted by slow, dumb animals. A lethargic horse or a dumb cow could lead her to be distracted from her true goal.

Once she determined the coast was clear, she started running again. Out of the woods and in the clear, the moon offered a bit more illumination.

When she reached Salem, she stuck to the back alleys and side streets where she was less likely to encounter anyone. A feral cat crossed her path and nearly distracted her, but their brawl never escalated beyond hisses and growls.

The church was impossible to miss. She heard the singing from a block away and, when she changed course to investigate, saw the building was still shining with the light of two dozen candles. A small group of women stood in front of the church singing hymns. Sarah moved through the underbrush until she could see the back door. Three men armed with rifles stood watch, none showing sign of falling asleep any time soon.

It would seem breaking Constance out wasn't an option. Sarah lowered herself to the frozen ground and stared at the building. She wished there was some way to let Connie know she was there, but she couldn't risk alerting the guards as well. She assumed the Magistrate would want to hear "evidence" as early as possible. Sunrise was in a few hours. Sarah only prayed it was enough time to come up with a plan of action.

Obed Swain was the first to see her. He was one of the few men in Salem she recognized on sight, a drunk with a mean streak according to his wife. Sarah and Constance sometimes had drinks with her before going out on a run. He had been standing guard all night and didn't seem to realize she was real at first. He blinked, steadied himself on his feet, and swung his rifle around to aim it in her general vicinity.

Sarah wore a heavy wool cloak she'd borrowed from Eliza Friend, another wolf from their pack. She pushed back the hood so he could see her face. The other guards raised their weapons as well, all three turning to stand between her and the door. She could see empty beer bottles standing in the tall grass next to the steps.

"Don't you worry, miss," one of the men she didn't recognize said. His voice was slightly slurred but not enough that she could hope for him to be blind drunk. He held his weapon dead-level. "If you're one of 'em, we'll get to you eventually. No need to come find us."

She stopped a few steps away from him. "My name is Sarah Putnam. I reside in Beverly with my daughter. The women behind you are Judith Myrick, Eliza Friend, and Valina Joy."

Two of the men turned to see three women had approached while they weren't watching. She had gone to them during the night to enlist their help. Once they heard Connie was imprisoned to await trail, they eagerly abandoned their warm beds to begin plotting her release. Valina came up with the speech but it was decided Sarah would be the one to give it. She was tall and seemed strong, and they all believed she would be able to stand her ground against the armed men. At the moment, Sarah wasn't sure if she believed in herself, but the die had been cast. She could only play it out now.

Obed adjusted his grip on the weapon. He turned sideways so he could see both Sarah and the three women behind him. "Now hold on, ladies. We don't want to hurt none of you..."

"Oh, that's not true." Sarah stepped closer. "You want very much to hurt women. You accuse us of being witches who wield unearthly powers. You claim you are protecting yourselves and your neighbors, your sweet and innocent children, from the horror of a powerful woman. You fear that thought so much that you're willing to hang us, to drown us, to crush us with stones. You burn us alive at the mere suggestion we might have power. But we are not the powerful ones.

"The true power is wielded by the young women who accuse us. Because of the Gardner girl, you have locked up a woman with no evidence. You will try her and find her guilty, and then you will put her to death at the word of a child. Just as you believed the word of Betty Parris and Abigail Williams. You honorable men marched to the home of Sarah Good and became her murderers based on the testimony of a child! You murdered again with Sarah Osbourne, who died in jail awaiting your judgment. And then you stand in church and count yourselves among the holy."

Obed's weapon was shaking when she grabbed the barrel and pulled it away from him.

"These children are the true powerful women you should be wary of. Question their lies, validate their stories. Don't simply react out of fear. If you truly want to keep women in our place, start with the children. Now Constance Morse has done nothing wrong. My friends and I are going to march into this church and free her. We'll take her home and we'll put this madness behind us once and for all."

Obed started to say something, but one of the other guards cut him off. "Let her go in."

"Alex~"

"Let them go in, Obed."

The men lowered their weapons. Sarah nodded to the one who had granted her passage and stepped around Obed Swain. The rest of her group followed her up the stairs and into the dark church.

The back door led into a small pantry, walls on either side lined with shelves crowed by sacks of flour, cartons of eggs, and other sundry food items. Sarah led the way up a ramp into a slightly elevated room. A man was sitting on a wooden chair next to a door with a bright, shining padlock hanging from it. He jumped when he saw Sarah and scrambled to his feet when he saw the women behind her. He brought up a flintlock pistol but Sarah held out her hands in a peaceable gesture.

"We're here to retrieve our friend."

"The hell you are!"

Alex, the guard, had followed them inside. "Unlock the door,

Cotton."

Cotton sputtered, furrowed his brow, but lowered his gun. "Alexander, I don't—"

"I know you're simple, but just do it!"

He grimaced, growling low under his breath as he fished the key out of his pocket with the hand not holding his gun. He shoved the door open and stepped aside. Sarah smiled at him as she passed, but he only glared at her. She stepped into the cramped, windowless room and found Constance immediately. She was huddled on the floor, her hands shackled together in her lap, head bowed.

"Connie?"

She looked up, eyes widening when she saw who had arrived. Sweat had pulled her hair into knots that hung like weeds over her face. She narrowed her eyes in disbelief. "Sarah?"

Sarah smiled and sank to her knees. She cupped her lover's face, wishing they were alone so they could greet each other properly. She remembered the first time they had ever touched intimately, naked and breathing hard from a run through the woods. Her senses had still been in overdrive so she felt every touch like fire, smelled everything so distinctly that it was like seeing colors. The blue of Connie's breath, the green-yellow of her sweat, the brown of her skin. She remembered everything at that moment but couldn't betray her emotions.

The chains rattled against each other as she brought her hands up to Sarah's shoulders. "I've been thinking about you all night," she whispered.

"Are you unharmed?"

"For the time being. But how did you convince them to let you in?"

Alex said, "Well, that was simple."

Sarah twisted to look up at him. He was blocking the doorway now. Judith and Eliza were in the hallway between him and Cotton, while Valina had come into the makeshift cell with Sarah. He smiled down at her, arms crossed over his chest.

"We just thought," he said, "what kind of women would come to help an accused witch? We have to assume they're witches as well. Consorting with the devil in unholy orgies in the forest. Sickening. We let you in to save ourselves the trouble of hunting you all down for your own trials later."

Cotton raised his gun again and aimed it at Eliza. Alex's gun centered on Sarah's head.

"There are some more shackles over in the corner, Miss Putnam. Whyn't you put them on yourself 'fore I decide to save the Magistrate the trouble."

Sarah slowly rose to her full height. "I was so hoping it wouldn't come to this. There's still time to save yourself, Alexander."

"I'm going to count to three."

"How long have we been inside, Eliza?"

Eliza, who had been counting in her head, reported, "One hundred seconds."

Sarah sighed. "Plenty of time to retrieve our friend and walk outside with her. If you hadn't interrupted us. If you weren't trying to imprison us. We could have just taken her outside and none of this would have to happen."

Alex twisted his lips to ask what she was talking about, but he was stopped by a sudden scream from outside. The scream was as horrible as how quickly it was cut off. When Alex faced Sarah again to demand an explanation, he saw her drop the cloak to reveal her naked body. He instinctively looked away from the brazen display.

"What in the blue blazes!" he shouted.

Sarah couldn't have responded even if she wanted to. By that point, she and Valina had begun transforming. Eliza had thrown herself at Cotton, taking a bullet in the shoulder, and wrestled the weapon toward the ceiling as Judith transformed into a wolf. Alex looked toward the flash of gunpowder and was frozen by what he saw: a creature halfway between human and wolf, its jaws closed around Cotton's arm. He still held his gun but there were too many targets for him to choose one. He looked at Sarah just in time to see her jaws flash as she pounced on him. It was the last thing his eyes would ever behold.

The men who had been guarding Salem's church would never be found. Their bodies were moved out through the now-undefended back door and buried in the woods. The church ladies singing hymns on the front steps were persuaded to go elsewhere. Eliza stopped just short of threatening them when she hinted they might not want to be anywhere near the church for the next hour or so.

Constance helped remove the bodies. If they had still been intact, most of the men would have been too heavy for the women to move. As it was, even Judith, the weakest of the women, could find a piece they were able to carry to the unmarked graves. Valina dug the pits herself, her blouse heavy with sweat by the time she'd gotten it deep enough. Sarah, meanwhile, cleaned blood from the floorboards inside the church. There wasn't much to be done for the gore left outside other than hope it would snow and cover up the evidence of what had happened.

Once their crime was concealed as well as it could be, the women joined Valina in the woods to fill in the graves. Delia arrived with Sarah's daughter, who was told what had happened on their trek between towns. Phoebe hugged her mother, made sure that she was unharmed, and bent to join the other women filling in the hole.

"You shouldn't have risked your lives to save mine," Constance said. "I am immensely grateful, of course, but now we are all in danger."

Eliza sniffed and brushed a hand under her nose. It left a smear of dirt across her cheek. "We were all in danger regardless of what we did today. If we said nothing and let them hang you, we'd be as guilty as they are."

Judith said, "And when they came for us, whether it was tomorrow or a week from now, we'd have lost the right to ask for help."

"And they will come," Sarah said. "As long as they fear our power, they will come."

Valina said, "So what can we do? Kill all of them? That's their battle plan."

"You are correct, Valina, and we cannot reduce ourselves to their monstrous plans. But neither can we huddle in our homes and pray they ignore us for someone else." She tossed down the spade she'd been using to dig and looked at the woman gathered around her. Her pack. Her daughter's pack. "These men fear our power even as they underestimate us. So while they hunt us down and put us on trial, while they build gallows and erect pyres for us to burn upon, we will make it our duty to protect as many as we can. Wolves. Witches. Innocent women whose only power is the strength of her mind or her curiosity. We will find these women and we will protect them."

Judith said, "And the men who try to stop us?"

Sarah looked toward the town of Salem. She put an arm around Phoebe's shoulders and drew her close. She held out her other arm to find Constance and their linked their fingers together.

"Then those men shall become our prey, and they will become neighbors to the men we have just buried."

The church bells began ringing. Eliza said, "They've most likely discovered Constance is gone. They'll be coming."

"Let them come," Valina said.

The women stripped off their cloaks and blouses. Skirts were wrapped around shirts and the ends were tied together, slung over shoulders, or hooked around neck to hang down like capes. They transformed, dropping to all fours on the overturned dirt, pausing only briefly before running into the woods.

Sarah watched Phoebe, her young pup, join the older women before she turned to face Constance. They shared a smile before Constance stepped closer and pressed her lips to Sarah's. They held each other tightly knowing that their days of long runs together in the woods were numbered. With the law and the church hunting them down, it was unlikely they would ever again have another lazy afternoon by the ocean or spent an evening running together in the woods. They kissed to remember those joyous times and to mourn them, to remind each other that even in hardship they would at least have their love.

Constance broke the kiss and touched Sarah's bottom lip with her thumb. "Show me your wolf, my love."

Sarah smiled and stepped back. She transformed and shook her fur loose, then watched as Constance joined her. They took a moment to groom each other, Sarah licking down the fur on Constance's face as Sarah nuzzled her neck. A cry went up in Salem, a call to arms, and both wolves turned their heads toward the sound. Soon they would come. The men with guns, the religious leaders certain they were on a holy mission, the frightened people who didn't know better.

Sarah looked at Constance and gestured for her to lead the way. Constance ran, cutting through the underbrush with a graceful leap. Sarah would miss the community of Beverly, the neighbors and the shop owners she had come to know and love. The baker who always gave Phoebe misshapen muffins because they made her smile. The seamstress who mended their clothes without commenting on the occasional odd tear or claw mark in exchange for Sarah reading to her on Sunday nights. She prayed it wouldn't be long before sanity prevailed and they could return home, but she couldn't think about that.

For now, she had to think about protecting her daughter and the woman she loved, and she could sacrifice the comforts of town in order to do that.

For now, she had her pack.

Unscripted

When the sex was over, Caroline took a long shower before making the drive home to start dinner for her wife. Penelope was always running late. Left to her own devices she would feed herself a Hot Pocket or a convenience store hot dog and call it a meal. When she got home she changed into her comfy nighttime clothes - pajama pants and a tank top - and alternated between texting Poppy and checking Gordon Ramsey's instructions on the internet.

Penelope arrived when she was starting step seven. Their kitchen and living room were combined at the end of a squat hallway that led to the front door. Penelope took off her shoes and immediately headed to the stairs. "I'm home, Carodise," she called. "I'm going to wash up before dinner."

"Plenty of time," Caroline said. She stepped around the kitchen island and looked up as Penelope appeared at the railing. Her face automatically fell into a smile at the sight of her wife for the first time that day. "Darling. Long day?"

Penelope grunted and pushed her curly blonde hair out of her face. "Tedious. But at least I got to work with Nicola again."

Caroline's eyes flashed. "Ooh, Nicola. She's amazing. I want details."

"Always. I'll just be a few minutes."

"No hurry."

Caroline went back to the stove. She could hear the water humming in the pipes as Penelope started the shower. As she stirred, she thought about Nicola Andreas. Greek, Amazonian in stature, long black hair like Caroline's but with a squarer jaw and bright green eyes. She'd been to their house for dinner a few weeks earlier in a sexy red dress cut high to show her leg, dipping low in the back. Her thoughts wandered. By the time Penelope came downstairs in her pajamas - a T-shirt and baggy shorts - Caroline's face was dotted with sweat that had nothing to do with cooking.

Penelope stood behind Caroline and gathered handfuls of her thick, ink-black hair in her hands. She idly began to braid it as her wife put the finishing touches on their meal.

"How was your day today?"

"Not as good as yours. I worked with Tommy."

Penelope groaned and made a face that Caroline could sense even if she couldn't see it. She was bisexual so she didn't mind performing with men, but Penelope was strictly anti-hetero. Penelope didn't care if Caroline did scenes with men, but she didn't like hearing the details. The food was ready at the same time Penelope finished with her hair. They plated their meal together and went to sit at the table next to a window that overlooked a steep hill so they could see a nice stretch of the city at night. Nearby there were residential homes lit up from within, closed up in grids sketched out by street- and traffic lights. Beyond that, invisible in the darkness, was the ocean.

"Tell me about today," Caroline said as they settled in. 'You and Nicola."

"Seems like you've been filling in the blanks yourself." She reached across the table and cupped Caroline's cheek. Her palm was cold but quickly warmed up. "You're all flush."

Caroline turned her head to kiss the inside of Penelope's wrist. They'd met six years earlier on a movie set. Both of them had been in the industry for a few years at that point so the idea of being intimate with a stranger wasn't new. But Penelope seemed so nervous during their rehearsal that Caroline finally had to ask her if everything was okay. There was still a chance the director could replace one of them if there was an issue. Penelope sheepishly admitted she was star struck.

"I've seen some of your movies." She looked away and her hair - it had been straight then - fell across her face. "A lot of them, actually."

Caroline had reached out to tuck the hair behind her ear. "That's so flattering. But would you be more comfortable with someone else in the scene?"

"No!" Penelope had snapped her head back up, eyes wide. "No. I've... I've kind of been waiting for this for years. I'm just nervous."

Caroline grinned. "I'll take care of you."

And she had. Their scene together had gone overtime and completely off-script. When the director finally managed to pull them off each other, Caroline asked Penelope out for dinner. Dinner turned into drinks and dancing and then making out in the car. They'd spent an hour together just that afternoon, naked and kissing and thrusting against each other, but none of it affected the strength of the kiss. The sex had just been about going through the motions. They'd both actually had orgasms, but it was just part of the job. Here, in the dark, Caroline clutching the lapel of Penelope's jacket while Penelope buried her hands in Caroline's hair, the kiss was the intimacy that mattered. The kiss was when they fell in love with each other.

"~so we start kissing, and she's wearing one of those long slinky black dresses..."

"Wait, sorry. Sorry, I was drifting." She took a sip of her water. "I wasn't paying attention."

"What were you thinking about."

"How we met."

Penelope twisted her lips. "I'm telling you about fucking a gorgeous-ass woman that you've had a crush on for as long as I've known you, and you're thinking about us?"

"Yeah."

"You're so dull."

Caroline stood and leaned across the table to kiss Penelope. "I know. I promise I'll pay attention this time. Please, tell me how she ravished you."

"Why do you assume she did the ravishing?"

"You almost always play the submissive. Besides, Nicola is older than you. You're working with Fem First Films, right? They like older women seducing younger women scenes."

Penelope said, "Usually. Not this time."

Caroline felt a twinge of arousal. She sat up straighter. "You topped Nicola?"

Penelope grinned like a feral cat. "Nicola played my professor.

The scene started with me coming to see her at home to dispute my grade on some paper I'd done about human sexuality."

As she described the scene, she casually ran her fingertip along the edge of her plate. Caroline stared and listened to the hypnotic rhythm of her wife's voice. The details, though juicy, didn't matter so much as how Penelope shared them. It was like she was telling a horribly inappropriate bedtime story and Caroline was devouring all of it. Penelope lowered her voice and leaned forward as if someone might overhear - "...she was in this black skirt, and I put my hand on her knee and started stroking higher... higher..." - what she was saying. Her voice had a "dirty talk" purr to it now.

Caroline shifted in her seat, knees together, hands resting on the edge of the table as she pictured her wife straddling Nicola Andreas' lap. She could almost see those long slender fingers pushing underneath Penelope's top, cupping her breasts as their kiss became hungrier and more wanton. Caroline's toes curled and her fingers slipped around the lip of the table. She scooted closer to the edge of her seat and her knees fell away from each other.

Penelope's eyes were locked onto her now. She was marking every tremble of Caroline's bottom lip, the tempo of her breathing, the barely-noticeable narrowing of her eyes. Penelope knew every signal the way scientists could detect minute changes in the bedrock before an earthquake. She played up to her wife's desire, focusing on the parts she knew would get the biggest reaction. "...between her legs. She was still mostly dressed at this point, but she started to unbutton her blouse as I kissed my way up..."

"Tell me what you were wearing." Caroline's voice was barely more than a whisper. She didn't trust herself to speak louder.

"Little baby blue panties and a matching bra."

Caroline took a deep, slow breath and suppressed a shudder. "Go on."

"Where was I?"

"Kissing your way up her thigh. Was she wearing stockings?"

"Of course."

Caroline nodded. She closed her eyes as she pictured the scene. She would eventually watch it, cuddled together with Penelope in bed, touching herself as she watched another woman fuck her wife. Penelope watched her scenes, too. The movies were for the public, the world at large, but sitting alone in their house and reliving it together was just for them. It was like hearing Penelope recount a wet dream only with the added benefit of being real.

"After that," Penelope said, "I curled up on top of her. She stroked my hair, kissed my neck..." She trailed her fingers down the throat, following the trail, "and that was that."

Caroline took a slow breath in through her nose and let it out through her lips. "Very nice."

"And how was your day, my love?"

"It was a boy-girl scene. You know. Blow job, bang bang bang, come shot."

Penelope said, "Did~"

"Mouthwash and brushed my teeth. I used the scrubby tongue thing you got me, too."

"Thank you, baby."

Caroline winked. Her body was buzzing with untapped arousal, but now that the story was over, they could focus on their food. She let the warm settle throughout her body as she picked up her fork and began eating. Penelope didn't mind the fact that Caroline did straight scenes, but she also didn't like what she called "overlap." Caroline was happy to do it. Most of it was stuff she did post-scene anyway, but she didn't mind going the extra mile if it made Penelope more comfortable.

When Caroline first moved to California from Indiana seventeen years earlier, she'd been married to a man who thought he shared her interest in having an open marriage. She was a voyeur and an exhibitionist, and she thought it was a natural segue into swinging. Everyone got to have fun and no one went home with hurt feelings. No one except her husband, of course. He very quickly got tired of sharing his wife with anyone who caught her eye. He finally gave her an ultimatum. She didn't feel the need to spend much time pondering it.

Newly single, she saw porn as a way to meet new and exciting strangers without worrying if they were clean or if they would murder her in a cheap hotel room. Everyone was tested at the studios she had contracts with. Everyone was clean and the sex was always safe. It was the best of both worlds, plus being filmed professionally meant she had the best sex tapes she'd ever seen. She knew there were people in the industry who weren't there by choice, who were damaged or had been abused, but she was truly there by choice.

The same was true for Penelope. She'd revealed her life story on their third date. Innocent kid from Nebraska, stealing her brother's *Playboys* and watching Cinemax after everyone else went to bed. She told herself she wasn't watching for the women, but the truth was she couldn't take her eyes off them. When she was eighteen, she became an exotic dancer. A trip to Las Vegas with one of the other dancers led to an invitation to dance at a local club, where she met someone who claimed to be a producer, and the phone number on his card turned out to be real.

"He asked if I would consider doing girl-girl scenes. It was the first time it ever felt like saying yes would be okay."

The rest was history. They both worked under stage names, since Caroline Rudolph and Penelope McGinnis wouldn't exactly pop on the cover of COUGARS AND PREY VOL 4. Caroline had chosen the name Wanda Lust on a whim but stuck with it for the rest of her career. It served her well. Penelope, on the other hand, liked to switch things up. Whenever she moved to a new studio or signed a new contract, she considered changing her name. So far she had been Cupid, Lilly Liddell, Cammy, and Peach. Her latest moniker was Evie Archer, which also happened to be Caroline's favorite of the bunch.

When they finished dinner, Penelope washed up. Caroline took her laptop to her corner of the couch and answered emails with the television providing white noise. One of her favorite directors wanted to know if she was available for two weeks in July. Her schedule revealed yes, she was, so she sent him a confirmation. When the news came on, Penelope turned off the TV and put on some music. Caroline vetoed her first choice and they settled on Larkin Poe as a compromise.

They went up to bed together, Penelope lingering behind Caroline to check locks and turn out lights. The bedroom took up the majority of the second floor, the largest bathroom tucked away behind the truly massive closet that was the main selling point of the house as far as Penelope was concerned. Penelope got into bed and kicked the blankets out of the way, sitting forward to rearrange the blankets as Caroline undressed next to the bed.

By the time she crawled onto the mattress, the only light in the house was provided by the bedside lamp. They left the curtains open so the entire valley served as a nightlight for them. Caroline moved slowly forward on her hands and knees, running her eyes over her wife's body. She knew every inch by part. Hell, a good portion of America was familiar with Penelope's measurements. Caroline bent down and pressed a kiss to the top of Penelope's foot.

In the scenes they'd done together, they'd explored all manner of kinks that never made it to the bedroom. It was a safe place to explore, another benefit to their shared profession. They didn't have to buy any gear, the wardrobe was provided by the studio, and even the sets were an easy way to facilitate fantasies. They'd been a teacher and student, old friends, and, in one particularly kinky scene, stepmother and stepdaughter. Bondage and threesomes. Caroline being more dominant than she ever would've been in reality.

She wondered how their fans pictured their private lives. They were open about the fact they were married, and she was sure the people who regularly watched porn had all kinds of ideas about what the stars did in the privacy of their homes. Drug-fueled orgies, debauchery at every turn, masquerade parties like from that Nicole Kidman movie. She imagined they saw her lounging around in lingerie and high heels waiting for someone naked to wander into her vicinity.

But the truth was that they were extremely vanilla. In bed by eleven, laundry on Saturday, cooking dinner or ordering takeout, just like everyone else in the world. And just because they happened to have sex with other people on camera didn't mean their personal lives were anything similar to what ended up on film. Caroline hooked her fingers in the waistband of Penelope's shorts and dragged them down her legs. Penelope lifted one leg and then the other, putting her feet on Caroline's hips.

"What was your favorite scene we did together?" Caroline whispered as she pulled Penelope's legs around her.

Penelope closed her eyes. "I'm not counting the first one, because that was… magic."

"So special," Caroline agreed.

"So second favorite… the gender, gender-flip or gender swap thing. When you wore the suit and a strap-on. I called you sir." There was a tremor in her voice that matched the shuddering that had been going on inside Caroline over dinner. Caroline wet two fingers and rested the heel of her hand against Penelope's mound, her fingers aimed down to rest against Penelope's folds. There was a hitch in Penelope's voice when she spoke again. "Y-you ha-ad a little thin mustache on your upper lip. You looked so m-masculine. But still you. It was so fucking hot."

"Really?" She bowed her head and kissed Penelope's stomach. Her tongue stroked the flat spot just above her navel as she massaged with her fingers. "The woman who refuses to go hetero?'

"It wasn't hetero, it was you. You with a cock. You with binding on your tits and... a-and that sleeveless white T-shirt. Your arms..." She passed her tongue across her lips and a moan escaped. "Your hair all slicked back. Caroline..."

Caroline moved her hand. She kissed the thin strip of pubic hair above Penelope's sex. That was one thing she didn't like about their jobs; it required so much grooming to "look good on camera." She preferred a more natural look. She ran her tongue along her bottom lip and used her fingers to open Penelope's sex, sliding the back of her fingers over the folds before exploring with the tip of her tongue. Penelope arched her back and gripped the sheets on either side of her waist.

"Keep going," Caroline prompted, keeping her mouth against Penelope to let her voice and breath wash over her.

"I can't..."

"Poppy." She brushed her cheek against Penelope's thigh. "Please."

Penelope groaned, writhed, and put a hand over her eyes. "You were so strong, Carodise. When I w-walked in and saw you in the suit, the tie, the hat over your eyes, I almost forgot we were being filmed. I wanted you so bad..." She cried out as Caroline's lips and tongue played against her, teasing her, drawing back when she got too close to orgasm. Penelope cried out but knew enough not to protest; she knew Caroline wouldn't tease her just to be mean.

Caroline crawled up Penelope's body, kissing the curve of her hip and easing her onto her side. She kept one hand on Penelope's stomach and slipped the other between Penelope's body and the mattress as she assumed the big spoon position. She pulled Penelope tight against her and pressed her lips against the shell of her ear.

"Do you want to know my favorite scene?"

"Please..."

It was unclear if it was a response to the question or a request to keep going, so Caroline did both. She felt the tremors cascading from Penelope's shoulders down to her tailbone as she began stroking again. Her middle finger slipped inside, shortly followed by her ring finger. Penelope tensed, then folded in on herself, then released a quiet gasp as she reached back to grip Caroline's hip. Her fingers dug into the skin, almost hard enough to leave bruises, but Caroline didn't mind.

"The party scene, at the mansion in the Hills. The way we met was so unusual that sometimes I wish we had a more conventional story. You were in that gorgeous white dress with the lace bodice. You looked like a Disney princess on her wedding day. Your hair up in curls. Opera gloves. High heels laced up almost to your knees. You were a–"

"Hngh, God, don't stop..."

"There?"

"Mm-hmm."

Caroline kissed her shoulder and continued. "You were a goddess. The moment I walked into the room, it was like the room was full of cardboard cutouts. You were alive, vibrant, glowing. My eyes were drawn to you and I couldn't look away. You were supposed to fuck Dana in the first scene, but I told the director no. I told him that I had to be with you right then and there. All the years we've been married and I was still begging to have sex with you."

Penelope pressed back against her. "Caro... Caro..."

Caroline kissed Penelope's neck as she came. Holding her tightly as her lower body jerked with tremors and spasms. Her thighs closed tight around Caroline's hand; she'd once sprained Caroline's thumb when she caught it in an awkward position. They were both more careful now. She held Penelope tight through her orgasm, feeling the throb of her pulse against her lips and tongue. When the tension finally went out of her body, she twisted in Caroline's arms so they were face to face. She put her hand against Caroline's lips, and Caroline took the fingers into her mouth and wet them with her tongue.

"I was so confused when you came over to me." Her voice was meek now, like it was when she first woke up in the mornings. She brushed her wet fingers down the center of Caroline's chest, over her stomach. "I didn't know the director had changed the script. When you kissed me, it felt like we were breaking the rules. Like... I'm married to you, but it felt like I was cheating. On you, with you."

Caroline closed her eyes and spoke in a rushed whisper. "It was how I'd want us to have met, if we had to meet in the real world. Eyes meeting across the room. Yes, Poppy. There."

"There?"

Caroline cried out and braced her hand on Penelope's hip. She arched her back, rolling her hips forward to give Penelope a better angle.

"You took me into the bedroom," Penelope recalled, "and I forgot the cameras were there. Sometimes I watch that scene when you're on location. It's the most like us... the real us... no characters and no scripts, just you and me. That's how you make love to me when we're alone." She nipped at Caroline's bottom lip, but she was too carried away to return the kiss properly. "That's your favorite scene?"

"Yes." Caroline spoke as if hypnotized, Penelope's fingers in her, the warm curve of her palm against her clit.

"Do you want me to make you come, Caro?"

"Mm-hmm..."

Penelope moved her hand and scooted forward. Caroline moved in concert with her. Penelope, more petite than Caroline, shifted so that she was on top when their legs crossed. She bent her knee against the mattress and Caroline repositioned herself onto her thigh. She lifted her own leg until she felt Penelope's sex against it, warm and wet from earlier, and put her hands in the small of Penelope's back. She opened her eyes and saw Penelope gazing at her. She nodded and bent down to kiss Caroline's neck.

Caroline pulled Penelope toward her. Penelope placed one hand against the headboard, shoulders hunched, and moved to the rhythm Caroline had set. She moved her lips from Caroline's neck to her ear.

"I know you want to come for me, Caro. I want you to. I want to make you come."

Caroline shuddered and pressed her hands harder against Penelope's back. She could smell the sweat on her, could feel the beads of it under her fingers threatening to ruin her grip. Penelope was moving faster now, still whispering dirty talk against Caroline's ear as they thrust against each other. Caroline couldn't remember if she'd been as vocal in bed before porn, could barely remember when sex had only been a private bedroom activity and not her livelihood, but she couldn't imagine having sex with someone who remained quiet the entire time.

They both loved dirty talk. The tone depended on mood. One night it was "my beautiful goddess, I'm going to worship you until dawn," and the next night it could be "get on your knees like the filthy whore you are." They didn't prefer one to the other and they both knew that no matter how raw the talk got, there was always love and passion at its root.

"I'm going to come, Poppy," she whispered.

"Good girl," Penelope said. "Come for me, baby. Good girl..."

Caroline shuddered and slid her hands up, gripping Penelope's shoulders from behind. The fires Penelope had been stoking since dinner finally erupted, and her legs shot out straight underneath them, her lower body rising off the bed, her fingers digging into the soft tissues.

"Bruise me," Penelope said, "bruise me with your orgasm, Caro."

Caroline held tighter and rolled her head back, trembling as she came, clinging to Penelope with both her arms and legs. She felt like if she concentrated she could lift into the air anchored only by the small blonde woman wrapped around her. As she came, she was aware of Penelope's breath against her face. She knew Penelope was coming again and tried to focus enough to move her leg, to rub her thigh against her pussy, but her body wasn't complying with her attempts to control it.

Slowly, slowly, she came back to herself. Her muscles relaxed, her sweat began to dry, and she caught her breath. Penelope settled on top of her, dead weight that occasionally twitched or whimpered as a sign she was still alive. Caroline put her hands in the beautiful blonde curls and tugged gently at them, straightening each one before letting it collapse back in a spiral. Penelope McGinnis, Cupid and Lilly Liddell and Cammy and Peach and Evie Archer, her sister's friend, her coworker, her boss' wife, a stranger at a party, her student, her stepdaughter. A million women in one body and they were all hers. All she had to give in return was everything she had, and that was a price she was willing to pay.

The next day was Thursday, an off day. While they were lying in bed planning their day, Penelope suggested a beach trip. If they went after nine o'clock, people would be at work or school and they wouldn't have to deal with crowds. The idea excited Caroline enough to get her up. She showered while Penelope put together a bag. When she got out of the shower, Penelope jumped in and Caroline checked to make sure everything was packed. Books, snacks, towels, sunblock, extra sunglasses. She put on a T-shirt and shorts over her swimsuit. When Penelope joined her for a quick breakfast, Caroline could see the bright yellow of her bikini under the thin material of her blouse.

Before they left the house, they both donned sunglasses.

Penelope put on a hat, and Caroline braided her hair in pigtails since she never wore that style in movies. Neither of them were wearing makeup, which made it even less likely they would be recognized. They didn't wear as much as some in their profession; so many of them seemed to have a completely different face painted onto their heads, which Caroline understood but why not just wear a mask? Still, they wore enough that their plain faces might not warrant a second glance.

The twenty-mile trip to the beach took nearly an hour. When they arrived, Caroline set up their area and started to read while Penelope went out to swim for a bit. She came back dripping, her hair plastered back against her skull, out of breath and sore. It had been too long since she'd been out in the water and her muscles forgot how to fight the tide. Caroline spread her legs in a wide V and let Penelope collapse between them. She massaged the knots out of her arms and shoulders and soon Penelope was sagging against her like a rag doll.

"Do we need a bucket to make a sand castle?"

Caroline said, "Probably. For a good one."

"Maybe I want to make a shitty one."

"Then no, I think you can just mash some sand together."

"I might do that when I can move again."

Caroline squeezed. "No rush on my account."

She looked out at the ocean and watched the waves crash against the rocks. A few yards away, a group of college-age kids were getting ready to play volleyball. Years ago she'd come to California with someone she thought she could share everything with. She'd been wrong about the partner but right about everything else. She couldn't imagine doing anything else. She couldn't imagine a better partner to do it with. She brushed her hands down Penelope's arms and then up into her hair. The sun had started to dry it and the curls were exploding into potential tangles. She would have to comb it out later.

"I should get up," Penelope murmured. "I don't want to fall asleep on you."

"Worse things have happened." She kissed Penelope's temple. "If you want to nap, nap."

Penelope relaxed against her. Soon her breathing steadied and Caroline knew she was asleep. If she was still sleeping in twenty minutes, Caroline would wake her so she didn't burn. Until then she was content to be a pillow. In a couple of hours, they would pack up and go home. They would take a nap together and then maybe watch a movie or go out to dinner.

In the morning, Caroline had a seven o'clock call time for a new shoot. She was going to be in a scene with Rita Lamour. Rita was great fun; she was an old friend who always made their scenes together fun. When she came home she would share what happened with Penelope and spare no details. It was the least she could do in exchange for the story she'd gotten the night before. And she knew that tomorrow Penelope was probably scheduled to do a scene, too. Maybe someday soon they could arrange to work together again. That was always extremely nice.

Until then, they would have their private, unscripted moments. Caroline wouldn't trade those for anything in the world.

WITHOUT HIM

IT BEGAN with a man, and for a man, a request made and a willingness to go along with something which seemed simple enough. Titillation and amusement, games, taboo and forbidden. I know I was drunk, and I remember the taste of beer on her lips and tongue, so she probably was as well. We were smiling when our lips met. We had been laughing as we turned toward each other to silently gauge each other's reaction to the question. "I'm game if you are," is what I sent to her, and it's what I received in response.

So I smoothed my hand over my dress and leaned toward her. She leaned in as well and our lips touched. She adjusted her position on the seat to face me more fully and my hand went to her cheek. It was what I did when kissing men, so it seemed natural enough. But her cheek was smooth and her tongue was a gentle touch against my top lip, and we were enveloped in a cloud of perfume, and I found it difficult to take a breath. Her hand was in my hair and I found mine had dropped to her shoulder. I toyed with her collar as her tongue teased just inside my mouth.

Her laughter didn't make a sound but I could feel it. In her lips and the slight tremble of her body as she leaned into me. It was all for him, so she put on a show; she pulled back and traced my lips with her tongue, her eyes to one side so she could watch his reaction. I was trying to catch my breath and laugh at the same time.

There was something so erotic about that slight touch of her tongue on my mouth. I knew it was probably something she'd seen in porn, but at the moment I didn't care.

It began with a joke, from Ruby, stretched out catlike across the divan beside me. Her shoes were off and I remember at some point during the night I'd started massaging her feet. She was gorgeous, with flame red hair and dangerously arched eyebrows that reminded me of Michelle Pfeiffer in that Batman movie. I would say I'd never thought of a woman sexually before that night, but that's a lie. I've decided to stop lying about anything, even to myself.

Ruby, named for the color of her hair, had smiled at the way Leo and I flirted and teased each other all night. Though she played it off as a joke, as simple and innocent jealousy, but I could see that there was true longing in her eyes. She was lonely and it hurt her to see us being a couple. Leo was sitting behind me, his hands constantly somewhere on my body. He would stroke my arm, hold my hand, tease my hair with his fingers.

I didn't want to torture poor Ruby. I didn't want her to leave. And I didn't want her to think I was pitying her, either. Finally I was woozy-headed enough to come up with the perfect option. I lifted away from Leo and, eyes locked on Ruby, said, "I'm being selfish, hogging all this attention for myself. Ruby, do you want Leo to play with you for a while?"

Leo laughed; it was a rumbling sound. Ruby's laughter was more melodic. "Well, Janet, if we're going to share, I'd rather play with *you*."

"Now *that* sounds like a nice compromise," Leo said.

Ruby and I locked eyes. We had our silent conversation.

We kissed.

I honestly don't remember much else, the details of what exactly when or who did what to whom. I remember Ruby reaching for me more than I expected, and the look in her eyes when she was being pleasured. I don't even remember if it was me or Leo pleasuring her when our eyes met and her lips curled into that blissful smile. Ruby was what I remembered most from the flashes of memory I retain through the alcohol haze. I'd been with Leo before but Ruby...

Seeing her naked, discovering the way she kissed and the sighs she made when coming, the way her weight felt on top of me... it all burned itself into my brain. I remembered her fingers inside of me and her mouth on my breast. She didn't go down on me, my only regret from the night, but I vaguely remembered having my head on her thigh and an unusual taste on my tongue.

In the sober light of day, Leo got up first to make us coffee. I woke up alone in the bed with Ruby, her face veiled by her hair. My hand trembled as I pushed it out of the way so I could watch her sleep. I didn't know how we'd gotten from the couch to bed, but I remembered enough of the night before to know it wasn't a dream. That didn't make it any less strange to see her in our bed, naked, knowing what we'd done to each other. I wanted her again. I wasn't the sort of person to want sex constantly, especially not the morning after, but it was all I could do to keep my hands to myself.

The smell of coffee woke her. She blinked me into focus and, after a second of wide-eyed surprise, she smiled warily.

"Hi."

"Hi," I whispered back to her.

She glanced down and moved her arm, shifting her legs under the blanket. "Uh. So... uh..."

"Yeah. You okay?"

"I think so. Are you okay?"

I nodded. "I'm very okay."

"Would it be weird if I kissed you?"

I answered the question by kissing her. I didn't know the rules of what had just happened. Leo was in the kitchen, but surely this couldn't count as a betrayal. Not after what they'd done together while I watched. I didn't want to think about what kissing her meant, or why I couldn't seem to get enough of it. None of the men I'd ever kissed made me feel this way. None of them made me want to kiss them and never stop, not even at the beginning of the relationship.

"Are we starting again?" she asked.

"No," I said, a little embarrassed. I put my hand on her shoulder and realized how close my palm is to her breast. "No, I just... I just didn't want you to think I regretted anything. Except maybe the amount of wine I drank."

She kissed my forehead. "I have a sure-fire hangover cure. Come on."

She threw back the blankets, grabbed a shirt off the hamper (one of Leo's) and pulled it on as she left the bedroom. I took the time to find one of my own shirts and buttoned it as I followed her out into the main room of the apartment. Leo was at the stove cooking us breakfast while Ruby was searching the fridge for elements of whatever her hangover cure might be. I wasn't sure if there would be a repeat of the night before, or if it would be just a one-time fantasy fulfillment, but at that moment I knew our friendship would survive. That was all that mattered.

Life went on. Ruby and I continued catching lunches together when we could. Leo and I continued on the natural path of our relationship. Sometimes when we got tipsy, I would meet Ruby's eye and we'd both laugh. One night we shared an Uber home from work and she put her head down on my shoulder. The weight was comfortable, familiar, and I closed my eyes to see if I could remember other things about our night together.

The main change was that I started seeking out lesbian porn. I don't think I watch more porn than anyone else, or that I'd never seen a girl-on-girl scene before. But after that night, if Leo worked late and I wanted to enjoy a bubble bath, I would be very specific about what I wanted: redheads, who looked a little like Michelle Pfeiffer, who performed with women. I didn't use any of my phallic toys during those moments. It was fingers only, to remind me of Ruby.

Leo and I continued to have sex. Nothing changed. Our relationship progressed, plateaued, evolved. We fought and then we made up. We fought and made up. We fought... we made up. We fought... It was the typical roller coaster of a relationship that we'd both been through before. Fights that were dropped instead of being resolved. Soon enough we both accepted it was over and started the waiting game to see which of us would pull the trigger first.

It ended up being him. I was only annoyed that I had to be the dumpee, not the dumper, and I wished him well. It hurt, but it wasn't the end of the world. Leo was a great guy. He wasn't *the* guy.

A few days went by before Ruby emailed me. "Heard what happened. Email if he's a jerk, text if he's just doing what's best. Either way, meet me for coffee!"

I laughed and sent her a text. We met up at a café near my apartment and, after I assured her I wasn't in need of a posse to go kick his ass, we started talking about normal things. Work, the classes she was taking at night, the stray cat she was taking care of outside her building. It was exactly what I needed: a reminder that just because my world suddenly looked different, everything else carried on. The rest of the world was still turning even though I was on a new page. I'd catch up in my own time.

When we were getting ready to go, she said, "I'm sure you'll recover from this little hiccup in no time. Leo wasn't exactly... well... I always imagined you with someone more handsome."

I laughed. "So shallow! But you thought Leo was good-looking."

"Not really."

"Liar. You wanted... I mean, that..." I glanced around to make sure no one was eavesdropping. I leaned in and lowered my voice. "That night, you jumped at the chance to be with him."

She looked at me in the oddest way, then smiled and shook her head. "Honey, I jumped at the chance to be with *you*."

I'm pretty sure I blushed. I'm positive I didn't say anything right away, because I had no idea what to say. She finally put a hand on top of mine and squeezed.

"I didn't mean to... do whatever this is."

"No, no. I'm flattered. And surprised. I didn't know you were bisexual."

She shrugged. "I don't bring it up a lot. There have only been two women, and you're the only one I've actually... The others stopped at kissing. I didn't mind that Leo was there that night. But I also wouldn't have noticed much if he wasn't."

We said our goodbyes and made plans to do it again as soon as we could. The whole walk home, I tried not to think about what she'd said. If Leo hadn't been there, would we have still kissed? Would I have undressed her and taken her to bed? I thought about it while I cooked dinner. I thought about it while I pretended to read, while I worked out. I didn't think about it in the shower, where I was wet and naked and vulnerable to potentially wandering thoughts and hands. But lying in bed, in the dark, my mind went back to it.

Would I have kissed her if I hadn't been trying to turn Leo on?

Probably not.

Would the sex have been as good without Leo there? I tried to think of anything spectacular he added to the experience, but he was a known quantity. I'd fucked him before. I'd fucked men before. But being with Ruby was amazing and unique. And she was damn good. Even working with the alcohol fog, I remembered being utterly and completely satisfied with the outcome. So, would the sex have been as good without Leo?

I'm sure it would have been. Maybe even better.

Did I want it to happen again...?

I refused to answer on the grounds I might incriminate myself. Or even worse, hear myself saying the answer and know I couldn't take it back.

I thought about it over the next couple of days. I thought about it more than I want to admit, even now. Ruby wanted to be with me. She wanted to *be with* me. And I enjoyed being with her. Sometimes she crept into my dreams and I enjoyed those, too. I enjoyed those a lot. She would call or email and I'd find myself wondering about her. Messages during the day, of course, were sent from work. But at night, was she lounging in bare feet on the couch? Settled into a bubble bath? Was she curled up in bed wearing her nicest lingerie, with me on her mind?

One night thoughts of her so distracted me that I had to go for a walk to clear my head. I found myself in her neighborhood but swore I wasn't going to see her. I went into the lobby of her building only because there was a bench and I wanted to rest my feet. I took the stairs to the third floor because I... well, I didn't have a good excuse for that one. I rang her doorbell and wondered what I would say when she answered.

The door opened before I was ready. She was wearing pajama pants and a T-shirt so old that the collar was stretched out in a wide oval. Her hair was clipped back and she was wearing huge glasses that I'd never seen before. She pulled them off in what I'm sure she thought was a slick move and hid them behind her hip.

"Janet? Hi. Was I expecting you?"

"No. I wasn't expecting me. I didn't know I was coming here until I was here."

Concern crept into her face. "Is everything okay?"

"I want to go to bed with you."

"What?"

I looked down the hall. "I want to~"

"Come inside," she said, pulling me into her apartment. She pushed the door shut and turned to face me, arms across her chest. "What do you mean you want to go to bed with me?"

"You said you wanted to sleep with me first."

"Sure... but I... I'm not..." She chuckled and looked away from me. "Janet, I'm not sure it would be smart."

I stepped closer. "So you haven't been thinking about me? Dreaming about... you know, what happened?"

"Of course I have," she whispered. "I'm worried that if we do anything else, I may not be able to stop thinking about it, and then I'd have to stop being your friend."

"Or—"

She shook her head. "Don't say or."

"Why not?"

"Because this isn't some lark, okay? This isn't kissing you when we're drunk to turn on your boyfriend, this isn't something we laugh about over breakfast. If we do anything else, it's going to mean something."

I swallowed. "Can I say something?"

She nodded, still not looking at me. I stepped forward and took the glasses out of her hands. I unfolded the earpieces and gently placed them on her face. She finally looked at me and I let my fingertips rest lightly on her cheeks.

"You look better with the glasses."

"Jan..."

"Ruby."

She leaned in and kissed me again. I decided to count this as our first kiss, since it was just for us. No one was watching, we weren't performing or hamming it up for an audience. I felt the tension in her and realized just how nervous she was. Nervous about... me? My anxiety level dropped with the knowledge that she felt the same way I did and I pressed against her. She put her hands in my hair and I put my arms around her waist.

During the kiss was when I knew that all my anxiety and uncertainty came from the fact she was a woman. If I'd been this obsessed with a man, I never would have waited so long to act on it. I wasn't the sort to pine helplessly over someone I liked. Ruby became more aggressive, more like the woman I knew, and I tried to match her intensity. When I pulled back, she put a hand on the back of my head to continue the kiss for a few extra seconds.

I nipped at her bottom lip when she finally relaxed her hand, but I didn't pull away. Our foreheads were touching and my hips were pressed against hers.

"Technically we've already had sex."

"Mm-hmm," she said, eyes locked on my mouth.

I said, "So we're not... not really... m-moving too fast if we.. if you take me into the bedroom?"

Ruby said, "Do you want me to take you in there?"

"Yeah..."

She put her hands on my hips and walked me away from the

door. Her eyes never left mine, and the lenses of her glasses made the blues look huge.

"You like someone who takes control?"

"Maybe," I said. "Your voice has this... husky thing right now."

She smiled. "You like that?"

"I do."

"That's the voice I use with people I'm about to fuck."

I couldn't help it. I gulped. She opened the bedroom door and kicked it out of the way. I let her guide me blindly into the bedroom. I'd never been there, so I trusted her not to let me fall.

"If you need something familiar, I have some things I can use."

"Oh. Uh. Maybe... next time. This time I th-think it should just be you."

She nodded. "I think that would be best."

"Yeah."

"Janet?"

"Yeah."

"I think you should take off your clothes."

My eyes widened. All the thoughts that had been running through my head, all the fantasies, now it was real. I could see a moment of doubt in her eyes as she misread my hesitation. I took her hand in mine.

"Don't worry. I like it. Being told what to do in the bedroom. I like someone being in charge. It's... it's hot." I brushed two fingers over the back of her hand. "Wh-what do you like?"

"Dirty talk," she said without hesitation.

"Okay. Uh... I w-want you to~"

Ruby interrupted. "No. I like to talk."

"Oh. Sorry."

She brushed my cheek. "It's okay. May I?"

I said, "Yes."

She leaned in, lips next to my ear. "When you rang my bell, I was thinking about you. How you felt on top of me. How you tasted. I may have been drunk, but I remember how you taste, Janet." She lowered her voice even further. "You tasted so fucking amazing. I'm so excited I get to taste you again. Just the thought is making me wet." Her lips grazed my ear. "Janet."

"Mm-hmm?" My eyes were closed, my voice trembling.

"I thought I told you to take your fucking clothes off."

I may have whimpered. But my hands went to the buttons of my blouse and, amid tremors that probably registered on the

Richter scale, started to unfasten them.

"Next time I want you to wear something I can tear off of you."

I turned my head and kissed her neck. "God, no wonder you love dirty talk. You're fucking amazing at it."

She giggled and let her hands roam over my body. "I'm getting impatient, Janet..."

"Sorry... ma'am...?"

"Yes."

"Ma'am."

Oh, god, what was *this*? What was that twinge I felt when I called her ma'am? Why did my heart skip when she pushed me down onto the bed? Before I could change positions she was on top of me. My hands automatically went to her hips, holding her in place as she bowed down and kissed me again. I stuck my hands under her shirt and felt her hips. The longer we spent in contact, the more I remembered about our first night together, and the harder it was for me to understand how I waited so long for an encore.

"I love feeling your hands on me," she whispered as she moved her lips to my neck. "I kept looking for people like you... looked like you, sounded like you, had the same hobbies. I can't believe I'm with the real thing."

I was sure I was blushing. I turned and kissed her hair. "I'm all yours, baby."

She took off my clothes. I took off hers. We held each other for a long time, kissing whatever we could, touching everything we could reach. Her hand was on my thigh and I tensed, then reached down and guided it higher. She looked into my eyes and teased me with her fingers. My whole body jerked and my hand tightened around hers.

"Sorry..."

"No, it was just... it's fine. Don't stop."

"Are you s~"

"Don't stop," I said.

She waited a moment before she started massaging me again. I closed my eyes and brought my feet up onto the mattress, arching my back, squirming, trying to press against every inch of her while also putting all my weight against her miraculous fingers. I ran my hands over her body and pressed the back of my head into the blankets.

"Janet..."

"Ruby…"

"No, Janet." I opened my eyes and focused on her. "You can touch me, too."

I stifled a curse. "Right. Sorry."

"It's okay."

I worked my hand between our bodies and cupped her. I watched her face, the way her eyes closed and her lips parted. I watched her tongue, a pink dart, flicker against the corner of her mouth as she bucked up against me. She whispered something I didn't catch and then put her head on my shoulder. Something told me we were past figuring each other out and pushing the boundaries and this was just about getting off. I closed my eyes and kissed her neck, focusing on the texture of her skin and the taste of her. I licked the shell of her ear and put two fingers inside of her.

She trembled when she came, and her voice was a hoarse gasp next to my ear. I cupped the back of her head and smiled, amazed at what had just happened. When she sat up, I kissed her. She shifted her weight and began to move.

"Where are you going?"

"Nowhere," she said. "You didn't come."

"No…"

"Right." She tucked her hair behind her ear and slid down my body. She kissed the skin between my breasts, licked my stomach, and eased my legs apart so she could kneel between them. I held my breath. The only time anyone had ever gone down on me without a specific request (okay, begging) it was her, with Leo. And now she was going back, and…

I made a crude noise. I never wanted her to be doing anything but this. I didn't want sex to ever be anything but what she was doing to me right now. I tried to stop myself from coming, but it was no use. There was no hope of maintaining control under such a dedicated assault. I whimpered helplessly as she kissed my thighs and then climbed up my body. She kissed my hips and stomach so tenderly, she nuzzled my breasts, and found a comfortable position on top of me and lay down, and I put my shaking hands on her back.

"We can rest and then we can do it again," she said.

I laughed. "I don't know if I can take it again…"

"Can we at least try…"

"Yes. Oh, yes, we can definitely try."

She lifted her head and I kissed her. "Go to sleep, pretty girl.

I'll be here when you wake up."

I closed my eyes and listened to her breathe. I was drifting off when I heard her exhale sharply, which became a chuckle and grew into a quiet laugh. She lightly touched my cheek and I heard her whisper, "Wow. Oh my god. Thank you." It took everything I had not to respond, but my heart soared. I'd never heard someone sound so sincerely happy, and it was because of me. It was because I was with her. I shifted my weight and put my arm across her hip. She nuzzled against me and chuckled again.

When I woke up, she was rising from the bed. I peeked at her with one eye as she hurried out of the room still naked, then came back with her phone. She turned it on, poked at the screen, and then placed it on the nightstand as Chely Wright started singing. She climbed back into bed and curled against me before she noticed my eye was open.

"Oh. Hi. Good morning."

"Morning." I waited and then smiled. "You don't kiss the people you wake up naked next to?"

She laughed. "No, I do, I just~" She kissed me once, twice, and then a lingering third time. Neither of us had brushed; neither of us cared too much. She finger-combed my hair out of my face. "I just wasn't sure if you would feel the same way now as you did last night. I don't know what prompted you to come over here and say those things and... do those things. I wanted to give you a chance to back off gracefully. Save the friendship."

I found her hand so I could link our fingers together. "This is the friendship, Rube. This is what our friendship evolved into. I'm not going backward to just meeting for drinks. Just like I wouldn't go backward to just being acquaintances, and I'd never want to go back to not having you in my life." I brought her hand up to my lips and kissed the fingers. I realized for the very first time, I could have everything I wanted and needed with the same person. "This was just our do-over of the first time. Addition by subtraction, you know?"

She nodded. "Yeah."

"Do you have anywhere to be this morning?"

"In about two hours, yeah."

I snuggled up to her. "Long enough. For now."

She put her arms around me and kissed the top of my head. "Yeah. For now."

We settled against each other and I let the music push me back into the moment between awake and sleeping. We didn't have to worry about the future or what this meant. All we had to worry about was how we felt in that moment. I know I felt pretty damn good and, judging from the way she was purring against my shoulder, I assumed Ruby felt the same way. That was enough for now.

Everything else would work itself out when the time came.

ABOUT THE AUTHOR

Geonn Cannon lives in Oklahoma. He is the author of several novels, including the Riley Parra series which is now a webseries for Tello Films, and an official Stargate SG-1 tie-in novel. Information about his other novels and an archive of free stories can be found online at geonncannon.com.

"Riley Parra is a strong, badass heroine for those that like their coffee and their cop fiction bitter." - P Industry

No Man's Land isn't the kind of place you go after dark, even if you have a badge. But Detective Riley Parra was born there, and she refuses to surrender it to the drug dealers, killers and criminals who have made it there home. The case of a body stuffed into a drainage pipe leads her to discover that there is far more at stake than she ever imagined.

~ Riley Parra, Season One.

"A good novel to while away a few hours in front of the fire." - Kitty Kat Reviews

Three years ago, Sofia Kennedy reported the tragic death of her girlfriend live-on air. Still in the closet even with her closest friends, she was forced to suffer her loss in silence. In the years since she's become isolated and sticks strictly to a routine that prevents her from encountering painful memories of the woman she lost.

Marion Vogt runs a small but well-respected catering service that feeds the elite of Seattle. When Sofia's consumer reporting segment does a story on Marion's company, the two women immediately butt heads. An unintended insult results in a scathing report that nearly shuts down the business. Marion's attempt to defend herself results in a deepening of their conflict until both women are ready to destroy one another.

They quickly find out Seattle can be a very small town when trying to avoid someone. As much as they want to avoid each other, fate keeps forcing Sofia and Marion to cross paths. Before long they realize they'll have to decide if they're going to hold on to bad feelings or risk forgiveness to discover just what they have to offer each other.

~ Breaking Anchor

www.ingramcontent.com/pod-product-compliance
Lightning Source LLC
Chambersburg PA
CBHW070925190726
48292CB00004B/1111